Nonna's Book of Mysteries

MARY OSBORNE

Lake Street Press
4064 North Lincoln Avenue, #402
Chicago, IL 60618
www.lakestreetpress.com
lsp@lakestreetpress.com

Cover photo by Mary Buczek; Cover design by DM Cunningham
Book design by Erin Howarth; map illustrated by Rachael McHan

This is a work of fiction. The characters and events are inventions of the author. Actual personages are true to time but have imagined personalities and interactions.

Cataloging-in-Publication Data (prepared by Cassidy Cataloguing)

Osborne, Mary A.

Nonna's book of mysteries / Mary Osborne. — 1st ed. —Chicago, IL : Lake Street Press, c2010.

p. ; cm.

(Alchemy series)

ISBN: 978-1-936181-16-2

Summary: In Renaissance Florence, fourteen-year-old Emilia Serafini dreams of becoming a painter. Her quest is guided by her grandmother's legacy, a book of alchemy.

Audience: Young adults.

Includes bibliographical references.

1.Painters—Italy—Florence—1421-1737—Fiction.2. Alchemy—Italy—Florence—1421-1737—Fiction. 3. Magic—Italy—Florence—1421-1737—Fiction. 4. Renaissance—Italy—Florence—Fiction. 5. Young adult fiction. 6. Historical fiction. I. Title. II. Series: Alchemy series (Chicago, Ill.)

PS3615.S274 N66 2010	2010920158
813/.6--dc22	1006

Printed in the United States of America
Printed on 30% PCW recycled paper

Acclaim for *Nonna's Book of Mysteries*

*"**Nonna's Book of Mysteries** is an exciting journey into the long-lost world of art, mystery, and magic. Filled with twists, turns, and surprises throughout, it will keep you riveted to your seat with every page. A marvelous read and one that will stay with you long after it is over."*

— Sonia Choquette, Ph.D, author of *The Answer Is Simple...
Love Yourself, Live Your Spirit and Your Heart's Desire*

*"**Nonna's Book of Mysteries** is a young adult novel that will appeal to readers of all ages in its celebration of icon writing, fresco painting, alchemical wisdom, and Renaissance Florence. 'Spunky' doesn't do justice to Emilia, the young heroine, whose fierce determination to make her own way in a man's world grows out of her deep rooted vocation as a painter."*

— Robert Hellenga, author of *The Fall of a Sparrow* and
The Italian Lover, recipient of a National endowment for
the Arts Fellowship and a PEN syndicated fiction award

*"**Nonna's Book of Mysteries** is the tale of a charming character who struggles against the strictures women faced in the fifteenth century. Emilia's journey is one rich with historical and artistic and alchemical details. Mary Osborne's thorough research beautifully informs this novel. I'm so glad there will be more in her alchemy series!"*

—Louise Marley, author of *Mozart's Blood*

In memory of Loretta Bloom Bohaty, who painted.

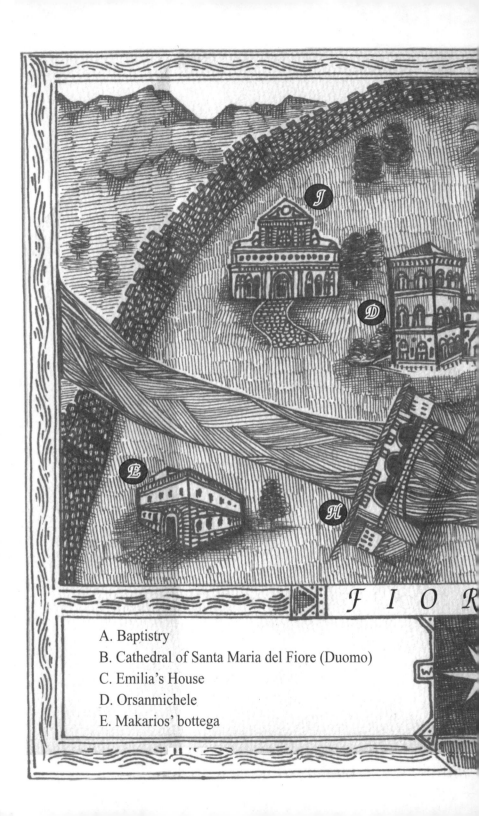

A. Baptistry
B. Cathedral of Santa Maria del Fiore (Duomo)
C. Emilia's House
D. Orsanmichele
E. Makarios' bottega

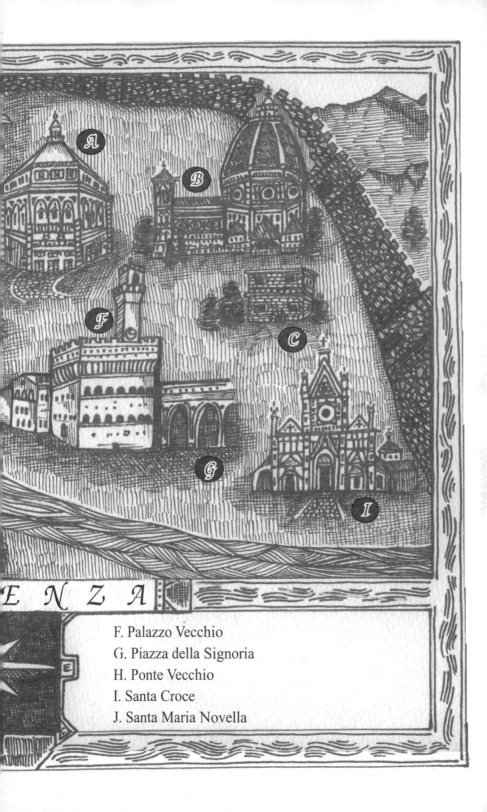

E N Z A

F. Palazzo Vecchio
G. Piazza della Signoria
H. Ponte Vecchio
I. Santa Croce
J. Santa Maria Novella

Acknowledgments

I am deeply grateful for the wise guidance of Jillian Maas Backman during the entire creation of this book. Sincere thanks to Joseph Malham, Mildred Kemp, and Silvia Foti for their astute readings; to Hazel Dawkins for her fine editing, attention to craft, and generous nurturing of this project; to Hannelore Hahn for founding the International Women's Writing Guild; to Theresa Gross-Diaz at Loyola University Chicago for help with Italian terms of address; to my Chicago *amici* for believing; and to Matthew Osborne for his acceptance of a mother who writes.

Contents

Prologue

During the golden age of Florence, the city's great ruler, Cosimo de' Medici, commanded his agents to search the monasteries of Europe for the lost manuscripts of the ancients. In the year 1460, a monk by the name of Leonardo of Pistoia returned to his patron with a Greek manuscript containing the mystical writings of Hermes Trismegistus, an Egyptian sage who was thought to be even older than Plato and Moses.

Astounded by the discovery, Cosimo instructed his young scholar, Marsilio Ficino, to suspend work on his translation of the Platonic dialogues and turn at once to the newly discovered *Corpus Hermeticum*, for this book by Hermes was thought to be of even greater significance than the work of Plato.

The teachings of the great sage as translated by Ficino promised attainment of the highest wisdom, though the codex was never made widely known. Instead, the ways of Hermes were passed quietly from teacher to student over the centuries.

Unless you are prepared to learn the secrets of the ancient mysteries herewith contained, gentle reader, proceed no further.

Benozzo

Emilia Serafini barely dared breathe as she waited for the master's reproach, although she had done absolutely nothing wrong at all. Inside Lorenzo Jacovelli's *bottega*, his famous workshop, beads of sweat trickled down her neck from beneath the brimmed cap she wore low on her head to hide hair that was too long, too glorious to cut. Everyone in Florence knew that painters' apprenticeships were not for girls, so Emilia was disguised as a boy. Wearing a shapeless brown tunic over a coarse linen shirt, she denied her true self.

"The workshop is no place for childish bickering. Go on, both of you. Scrub the courtyard." The enormous man whose panels and frescoes delighted the likes of the Medici and Rucellai was shooing her out the back door, all because of what Luigi had done. Emilia was fuming over the injustice of it all when Jacovelli's emerald ring caught on her cap. It slid over one ear and out tumbled her hair.

Quickly Emilia tugged the cap straight, stuffing her hair back inside, hoping that Jacovelli had been looking anywhere else but the back of her head. Sadly, she was wrong, for in a matter of seconds she felt his grip on her shoulder.

Jacovelli turned Emilia around to face him. Without warning, he removed her cap. Emilia's hair spilled out like golden wheat rippling in the wind. Her heart fluttered in her chest as he stood there quietly, taking a long, close look at his fourteen-year-old apprentice. She braced herself for another reprimand, but clearly he was more surprised than angry. After a thoughtful silence, his lips curved into a smile. "Something tells me your name is not really Alessandro," he said.

"Please, Signor Jacovelli. Don't send me away. I'm a hard worker. I'll do anything you ask."

The towering, gray-haired man shook his head. "You know well enough it is impossible. Even if I wanted to, the guild would never allow it. There are rules about such things."

She looked up at him, tears welling in her eyes. Jacovelli merely shook his head.

"Be a spinner, why don't you? That's a fine craft for a lady."

"I don't want to spin!" she exclaimed as Lorenzo Jacovelli walked away from her. "I want to be a painter!"

Dismissed by the master of the *bottega*, Emilia felt she had lost everything she'd ever hoped for. Finding another apprenticeship would be impossible. Her father would have every reason to marry off a daughter who cost too much to keep.

Disappointed and angry with all of Florence, Emilia broke into a run at the Street of the Painters, flying past the butchers' stalls in the Square of the Old Market, making her way to the Via del Corso, not slowing down until she could glimpse the tall, stone tower of the Palazzo della Signoria to her right and after another block the red-tiled Duomo to her left. From the Street of the

Proconsul she turned at the Bargello Palace onto Via Ghibellina and there she stopped running and stood, breathing hard, thinking about what had happened. It was a catastrophe. Luigi had ruined everything—*stupido*! The apprenticeship that would have given Emilia a profession of her own, *her freedom*, was lost.

It began to sink in that Giacomo—the young painter whose dedication and seriousness she admired—had betrayed her as well. It hurt to think that he failed to believe her, especially when she had always been quick to do as he said, unlike Luigi who often had to be asked twice to do something. Giacomo should have known it was not in her character to lie, but then he was always too preoccupied with his painting to notice anything much about her. She felt disappointed in him more than anyone.

The day had started out like any other at the workshop of Lorenzo Jacovelli on Via Tavolini. It was the summer of 1459. Overhead the Tuscan sun seeped into the red brick streets, bathing the surrounding hills and olive groves with warm, amber light. Inside the *bottega*, Emilia sat on her stool at the rough, plank table completing her task. In careful, even strokes, she applied the liquid gesso to the wooden board that would serve as the surface for her master's painting of the Virgin and Child with Saints Peter and Paul. She did not allow her thoughts to wander from her task because the gesso had to be flawless, laid down in even layers that would later be sanded to a smooth, white polish. Though she had been a mere apprentice, Emilia understood that each step of creating a panel required great care, patience, and exactitude, for these were creations that reflected the holy perfection of the Heavens and the glory of the Republic of Florence.

There was little breeze that morning, but she had willed herself to ignore the heat and to concentrate instead on the task at hand. She told herself suffering was only temporary while Jacovelli's painting would endure for years to come.

Across the room at another table, Giacomo was applying the undercoat to a panel. He worked silently, following along the pattern that their master had already etched into the gesso with a sharp stylus. As usual, Giacomo paid little attention to Emilia. From time to time she had glanced in his direction, eyed the sheen of his wavy, copper-colored hair, the graceful movements of his hands as he worked, though she was careful to conceal her notice. She supposed that even if she had revealed herself as the young woman she truly was, Giacomo would have kept on painting without skipping a beat.

Emilia used to look forward eagerly to the day when more would have been asked of her, when she would have been allowed to paint like Giacomo, or like Bruno and Enrico, who were off working in fresco at the cloister of the Church of Santissima Annunziata. For now she would be happy just to grind pigments and gesso the panels if Jacovelli would take her back. After all, each painting was created with the combined efforts of many hands. In precise, organized steps, Lorenzo Jacovelli's craftsmen worked together to create the magnificent works that adorned the great churches of their city.

At the end of Emilia's table, old Leonardo, with his characteristic half scowl, had been sanding a large board before the accident occurred. Next to Leonardo, Luigi was grinding pigments with a mortar and pestle. The usual, quiet hum of the workshop was interrupted when Luigi started singing, *"If a man will not be quick. The span of life is short. A man must not put off his duty."*

Before long, Giacomo spoke up. "Quiet, Luigi. You know he doesn't like singing in the workshop."

"He's not even here," the boy retorted, grinding with gusto.

"But the rest of us are," Leonardo muttered.

The words were barely spoken when an ear-splitting noise

filled the room! It was the sound of heavy marble hitting the hard, stone floor with a terrible crash. Emilia had glanced up from her work in time to see the horrified look on Luigi's face. She knew it matched the look on her own. Instinctively she rose to help, for when she saw the costly, red powder scattered everywhere like dust, she knew Jacovelli would be enraged. If only she had stayed put on her stool and steered clear of Luigi, she thought miserably.

But no, she had gone at once to pick up a scrap of paper to salvage the precious mineral from Spain that was used to make vermillion red. "Perhaps some of it can be saved."

Emilia recalled that Giacomo had come hurrying over and stood looking down at the quantity of scattered dust. He shook his head. "The master will be furious about losing so much cinnabar."

"He doesn't have to know about it," Luigi retorted.

"We keep nothing from Jacovelli," Giacomo rebuked him. "Try to save what you can of it."

Emilia and Luigi were down on their knees attempting to salvage the pigment when the front door opened to admit the imposing form of Lorenzo Jacovelli. He was returned from the Donati family chapel, which he had been inspecting for a new series of frescoes.

"What's the commotion about?" he barked, taking immediate notice of the two young apprentices who, bent low, were scurrying around like mice on the floor. Alarmed, Emilia had looked up but said nothing.

Giacomo was the first to speak. "I'm sorry, sir. Luigi dropped the mortar."

Then Jacovelli had come to inspect the powder of cinnabar sprayed every which way across the floor. "Such foolishness, Luigi," he admonished. "You had far too much pigment in the mortar."

Luigi flushed scarlet and blurted, "Alessandro bumped into me!" He turned accusingly to Emilia with the boldfaced lie.

She ought to have defended herself but was afraid to speak up. She had not wanted to make an enemy of Luigi, she preferred to remain as inconspicuous in the workshop as possible lest too many questions be asked of her.

"He wasn't looking where he was going," Luigi contended.

"I came over here to help you after you dropped the mortar, Luigi," she said. "Tell him, Giacomo."

The mild-mannered painter, apparently unsure of whom to believe, had looked from Emilia to Luigi in bewilderment. "I honestly can't say. I didn't see how it happened."

"Luigi's been too busy talking and singing this morning to pay attention to his work, if you ask me," Leonardo said without a pause in his sanding.

"It was Alessandro's fault," Luigi had insisted.

"But I was just sitting here preparing the panel," Emilia protested, the color rising in her face. "I was nowhere near Luigi. Tell him, Giacomo."

Jacovelli had raised his hand to silence her. "Time and money have been wasted and now Leonardo will have to make another trip to the apothecary. Your fathers will hear of this."

Taking firm hold of both Emilia and Luigi, he ushered them to the back door. That was when his ring caught in her cap and her disguise was discovered.

It was a disaster. Furthermore, Jacovelli might hold her and Luigi accountable for the cost of the lost cinnabar. Her father would be unforgiving when he got wind of the situation. It had been almost impossible to convince Francesco Serafini to pay Jacovelli four florins a year for the privilege of his teaching, as was the custom. Now he would blame her for spoiling the opportunity she had been granted and wasting his money as well.

Devastated by the day's events, Emilia came at last to her little two-story frame house on Via Ghibellina. Trudging slowly to the front door, Emilia dreaded admitting defeat to her father, though her mother would lend a sympathetic ear. Her mother would understand her despair because it was her mother, Violante Serafini, who had understood Emilia's dream well enough to suggest the outrageous charade in the first place.

"If we don't let her try, then she'll never know if she can do it," Violante had said, determined to persuade Emilia's father.

"You indulge her too much. She needs to understand the way things are in the world," Francesco Serafini insisted. "The sooner she accepts the fact the guild won't have her, the better."

"They'll accept her if they think she's a boy."

"You would have our daughter disguised as a boy, Violante?"

"Do you mean it, Mama?" Emilia said, poking her head in the room.

Appalled, Francesco looked at his wife. "Dio Mio! You are serious, aren't you?"

Now that her hard-won apprenticeship was lost, her father would surely decide the time was right to move forward with the marriage contract he was always holding over her head. He would have her betrothed to Benozzo Balducci—ten years her senior, oily-skinned, humorless, and exacting with numbers. Her father did not care that the thought of living with Benozzo made Emilia cringe. What mattered was that he could be trusted to keep the books and manage the small saddle shop Francesco owned.

While she suffered this horrible fate, Luigi, who caused her predicament, would be sitting at *her* worktable as though nothing had happened. She was a far better apprentice than he was and Jacovelli knew it.

Her mother would understand. Emilia hoped Violante would be back from the tavern, where she delivered the meat pies and *tortas*, or cakes, prepared in the family kitchen for her father's customers. When Emilia walked into the kitchen, she was relieved to find her mother shelling peas from the garden.

"Tell me what happened," Violante said as soon as she saw her daughter's long face. Though she was near forty, Violante was often mistaken for a much younger woman. She wore a simple but flattering rose-colored work dress, and her honey-colored hair was gathered in a heavy knot at the nape of her neck.

"Jacovelli discovered I'm not a boy. All because I tried to help Luigi when he dropped the mortar," Emilia said, flopping down on the wooden bench across the table from her mother. Breaking into tears, she related everything that happened at the workshop. "Luigi is despicable! How could he have done such a wicked thing?"

Violante stroked her daughter's cheek. "There, there, *cara*. It's not over yet. There's always another way."

"How? Every other workshop in Florence will know of me now. No one will have me. Everything is ruined!"

Violante looked out the window, far off into the hills, the way she did when she was dreaming up a plan. Her large green eyes grew mysterious. Then she turned to her daughter and said, "Don't suppose that because you tried once, you have done all you can. Your will is simply being tested."

"It's impossible. If no one will teach me, how can I learn?"

"I don't know the answer to that, Emilia. I do know that when you believe something is possible and you want it more than anything, then God is on your side."

"What will you tell Father?" Emilia knew he would have little patience for another of her and Mother's schemes. No doubt, he would try to put an end to her fanciful notions once and for all. Always there were too many bills and not enough customers but the bills had to be paid. And Emilia was the only one, her father liked to remind her, who failed to contribute to the family's income.

Violante thought for a moment. "We don't have to say anything right away, Emilia. There's no sense in worrying your father until you've found the solution."

"But Signor Jacovelli will demand payment for the cinnabar."

"I have a little money for such emergencies," Violante said slowly. "I will take care of Signor Jacovelli."

Emilia nodded, wanting to believe her mother, but not quite knowing if she could. Violante sliced an orange, sprinkled the wedges with cardamom and sugar, and arranged them like a flower on a green ceramic plate. Emilia ate the sweet fruit quietly before slipping upstairs to her room to read from the book that had been in the family for years and years. Mother said she should read *A Manual to the Science of Alchemy* when she was lost and could not find her way.

Emilia kept the alchemical text in a painted chest, beneath her wool undersocks and embroidered purse. Just a little longer than the palm of her hand, the book had a reddish-brown leather cover. It was hand-tooled with a geometric pattern of intertwining roses and gold lettering. Long ago, the book had belonged to Emilia's great-great-great grandmother, *Nonna* Santina, who was said to have been a midwife, skilled in the uses of remedies and herbs. Passed down through the generations, Violante had given it to Emilia on the recent occasion of her fourteenth birthday.

"I've used the book all my life, Emilia," Violante had said. "I suspect you will use it as well. Right now you

might not understand how, but the manual will guide you. When you find yourself at a loss, as we all do at times, I want you to remember this book. You will hear my voice within the pages, and your Nonna Chiara's voice, and your great-grandmother Elena's voice, and your great-great-grandfather Pietro's voice, and your great-great-great-grandmother Santina's voice. Whatever you do, you must never let the book out of your possession. Never. You must promise."

When she first received the manual, Emilia glanced at the intricate illustrations with fleeting curiosity, skimming through the strange passages. The first page attributed much of the work to a man known as Isaac the Jew, priest, adept in the Cabala, and master of the elixir of life and the philosopher's stone. The book contained numerous excerpts from ancient texts, passages from Plato and Hermes Trismegistus—the philosopher from Egypt—and recipes for the precipitation of metallic gold. Emilia considered the book a curious relic from the past, a family heirloom. It was sacred to her mainly for the reason that it had traveled back and forth from Spain and been passed down through the generations. Yet as she sat in her room on the day she lost her apprenticeship, she remembered her mother's words and wished it were true that the manual held an answer. *When you find yourself at a loss, I want you to remember this book.*

Emilia spoke aloud. "So now I am at a loss, *Nonna* Santina. What can your book tell me? What can I possibly tell my father so that he doesn't insist that I marry Benozzo?"

She closed her eyes as a warm breeze blew through her open bedroom window, turning the pages with an invisible hand. The spirits of her grandmothers and her grandfather Pietro were always present, Violante liked to say. Could her mother be speaking the truth about alchemy? Opening her eyes, Emilia stared curiously at the page chosen by the wind and read a passage written more than a century before.

Know this: thou art not born to suffer an unalterable fate and wicked destiny. Rather, thou art born to dominate the world and create! Yet this God-given right is oft forgotten. Children who come to this earth believing in the promise of life grow up to limit their imaginations and accept defeat. Corrupted to see themselves as weak and powerless, hopelessness, fear, and poverty prevail.

Yet this is not what God, in His infinite wisdom, has ordained. Rather, achieving the desires of the heart and mastering of the physical world by persistent efforts are the noblest of endeavors....

For sufficient reason, the methods employed by the masters have been shrouded in secrecy.

Looking up from the strange writing, Emilia gazed into the cloudless, Tuscan sky. *Nonna's* ancient manual would have her believe that everything was not in ruins simply because Luigi had spoiled her opportunity with Jacovelli. Yet now, as she sat in her little upstairs room, it was hard to see how she could ever become a painter without an apprenticeship.

Violante was always telling her she could do anything if she tried hard enough. When she was a little child, desperately wanting to make lovely pictures like the ones she saw on the walls at church, she struggled to make the lines of a limb, a hand, or foot look as they were supposed to. Though she sometimes felt like giving up entirely, her mother would encourage her to continue.

You cannot try once or twice or even a hundred times and say it's no use, Emilia. God will help you if your desire is genuine. But do not wait for Him to make you a great artist. This is your task, Emilia. Be an artist if you will. If you must. This is something for you to decide.

The words of her mother and her grandmothers would not allow her to sit there sadly, wallowing in self-pity. They were challenging her to take hold of herself, but she could not see a way out of the darkness. A future with Benozzo Balducci, who was nothing more than an asset to her father's business, loomed directly in front of her like a bad dream.

Makarios

D
ay after day that August, while Violante allowed Francesco to go on believing Emilia was still apprenticed to Lorenzo Jacovelli, Emilia set off alone to study the great works of art in her city. She went to her own church, Santa Croce, to study the effect of light in Taddeo Gaddi's *Annunciation of the Shepherds,* painted for the Franciscans. Inside the Humiliati's Church of Ognissanti she saw Giotto's high altar, the monumental Madonna. At the imposing Dominican Church of Santa Maria Novella in the western party of the city, she marveled at Orcagna's high altarpiece of the Enthroned Christ with gilded spiral columns and cusped arches.

Within these houses of God, she would search out the quiet corners, settle herself on the little stool she carried with her and take out her paper and charcoal. Then she would begin to draw and try not to think about Benozzo Balducci, the uncertainty of her future, the spiteful thing Luigi had done to her and the way Giacomo, whom she had admired, said nothing at all to defend her.

Hours later, after filling every corner of her precious drawing paper with charcoal copies of the masters, she would return home. *Fantastico,* her mother would say when Emilia showed her the sketches. When she was a child, her father had praised her talent for drawing, too. Now, the days when she could expect encouragement from Francesco were long gone.

It was an early morning in September when she journeyed south across the River Arno to the Church of Santa Maria del Carmine to study Masaccio's famed *Expulsion of Adam and Eve from Eden.* She could almost feel Eve's anguish as she copied the tormented face and at least for a time, her lost apprenticeship was forgotten. Though she still had no idea where her future lay, Emilia immersed herself in studying the images on the wall, the rich colors, and the life-like expressions on the figures. Here in the Brancacci Chapel she began to understand, for the first time, the effects of light and shade, the art of *colore* and *disegno*, color and design.

As she started drawing St. Peter, Emilia began to feel as though she knew him. Surrounded by the silence of the cool chapel walls, she could feel his compassion for those he touched; he was no longer a stranger. Rubbing away with her worn charcoal, light and shade emerged from the blank page. Soon St. Peter was coming directly towards her, looking out at her with deep, seeing eyes, while the searching cripples remained behind his magic shadow that had the power to heal.

She was so absorbed in her work that she did not hear the sound of approaching footsteps. A soft but deep voice spoke out—a foreign voice—startling her out of her reverie. *"Buon giorno."* Turning, Emilia saw a gray-bearded man of average height, round about the middle, a good many years older than her father, standing directly behind her.

The stranger bore an air of quiet dignity, his dark eyes smiled in amusement. He wore a simple brown tunic that showed a degree of wear. Suspended from a leather cord around his neck, he wore a curious miniature image of Jesus, carved into wood. Emilia saw that the man was staring not at her but at her drawing. Taken aback by the stranger's sudden proximity, Emilia eyed him warily but said nothing.

"You study Masaccio," he commented in heavily accented Italian.

"I like to draw," she said, feeling self-conscious as he stared at her work.

"You don't make drawings like this just to pass the time," the man said. "May I see?"

She handed him the paper. Though she had no idea who this man was, she needed little encouragement to share her sketches with someone who, for whatever reason, appeared to appreciate her efforts.

He took a long, close look at her rendition of *St. Peter Healing with His Shadow* and a grin spread across his tanned face. "A fine drawing." Then he looked from the drawing to Emilia's face. "Such a young girl. With a strange and wonderful talent," he said, handing the sketch back to her.

"Are you an artist?" she asked, now curious to know more about the stranger.

"I am Makarios Levantes of Constantinople," he said, bowing. "Painter."

She could not help but reply, "My dream is to be a painter."

"You wish to be a painter?" he said in a way that did not suggest she was ridiculous.

"I was an apprentice at Lorenzo Jacovelli's workshop for a time," she began. Since she did not know how to finish her story without sounding foolish, she said nothing more.

But Makarios Levantes seemed interested in her tale. "A female apprentice? How unusual," he prompted.

"Well, Jacovelli didn't know I was a girl when he took me on," she said, cautiously.

When Makarios chuckled easily, Emilia felt more at ease. "I should think that he sees this, no?" he said.

"The truth is that I deceived him—I dressed like a boy. I wanted the position so badly."

Makarios nodded and took a seat on the choir stall. "What is your name, young lady?"

"Emilia Serafini."

"And your mother and father—do they approve of your ambition, Monna Emilia?"

"Yes, very much. Well, not my father. But my mother thinks I can do it. She believes anything can be accomplished with God's assistance."

"Your mother, she is a wise woman." After a brief silence he began to speak again. "I left my country over five years ago—and went to Venice. Finally I moved to Florence." He paused. "Things are difficult in Constantinople now."

She nodded, having heard vaguely of the violence there, of priests slaughtered by the conquering Turks.

He continued, "I have a workshop not far from here. Just up the road from the convent."

"You do?" Emilia said, sitting up a little straighter on her stool.

Makarios observed her thoughtfully before asking, "Do you still hope for another apprenticeship?"

"Oh, more than anything, Messer!" she replied.

"It's not so easy to find someone who wants to work with me. I only have a woodworker who comes in once in a while. I have not been long in Tuscany." The old man pointed to indicate her drawing. "Anyone who draws like this has a talent given by God. It would be a shame to waste such talent. Have your father come to see me."

After he explained where she could find his workshop—a two-story, wood building with a red door, at the end of the road west of Santa Maria del Carmine—the old man inched closer to the frescoes. "It is a fortunate life that creates things of such beauty. The artists—they are the ones who remind us why we live."

Wondering how she would ever convince her father to visit the workshop of this old foreigner, Emilia studied the painter studying Masaccio. There was something different about Makarios Levantes, something that went beyond his foreign roots. He was kind, willing to give her a chance, and he was a man who had suffered unknown torments. He was unlike any of the other painters in Florence she had met. To Emilia he seemed something of a misfit, like herself.

When Emilia arrived home, hopeful and breathless, she bounded through the front door, calling out, "*Madre! Madre!* Where are you?" She could hardly wait to tell Violante about the mysterious appearance of Makarios Levantes at the Carmine.

Failing to find Violante in the house, Emilia searched the courtyard but saw only Veronica, the young girl who came to help with the laundry, wash dishes, and work of that sort. "Have you seen my mother, Veronica?" she called.

"Gone to market," Veronica replied, hanging clothes on the line.

Running upstairs to her room, Emilia looked out the window,

through the leafy, old chestnut tree, toward the hills. Mother said that the hills—so green and sparkling with light—were enchanted and that great artists were drawn to Tuscany by this mystical power that dwelt in their land. Thinking she had found a bit of magic at the Carmine, Emilia pulled out the *Manual to the Science of Alchemy* and began to read.

The ancient Egyptians, as the alchemists, sought immortal man. An Arab, known as Mohammed ibn Umail, who lived at the start of the tenth century, sought the secrets held years earlier by the Egyptians. Mohammed, known as Senior, broke into the inner chambers of the pyramids in search of their ancient knowledge.

Within one particular tomb, Senior found a statue of a wise man holding a tablet engraved with two birds; a winged bird lying over a wingless bird, as though the winged bird wanted to carry away the wingless bird, but was held back. The lower bird prevented it from flying away.

Herein lay the battle between spirit and matter: the struggle of the earthbound body (what we call the sulfur of the philosophers) to reunite with the pure soul (what we call liquid mercury). It is the task of every adept who strives to become a master alchemist.

Emilia studied the colored drawing of the birds and a red-orange sun and silver moon before turning to the next page. At the margin was a handwritten note in what she imagined was *Nonna* Santina's small, exact script.

There are times when a woman must become more like a man, and also when a man must be more like a woman. The king marries the queen; we complete ourselves in this way. Yet, alchemy is more than this. The divine spirit, which the alchemist seeks to marry to his mortal soul, resides hidden in the heart and can be released only after the successful completion of many trials. Be grateful then, my son, for the many trials God grants you along the path of wisdom, for these are signs of His love for you.

Emilia stared at the writing, considering the trials awaiting her that would be a sign of God's love. The old text was filled with mystery, or perhaps fancy. She thought of the winged and wingless birds that wanted to fly together, away from the Arab's tablet, and she could feel a part of herself that ached to be released as well. She dared to imagine there was something divine within her small, human self and that this part of her might create splendid wonders, if only her father would allow her the chance.

She was still reading when there was a knock on the door. Emilia looked up to see her father.

"Come downstairs, Emilia," he commanded. "Benozzo is joining us for dinner."

She wanted to protest, to say she was not well, or to disappear under the bed. "Why?" she asked, well aware she would provoke Francesco.

"He's leaving for Siena in a few days and he'll be gone for a while. We're opening a new shop," he explained brusquely. "I expect you to show him courtesy."

At least that was good news; it meant she would not have to see Benozzo for a time. "*Si*, Father," she said. "I'll be down in a minute."

Standing near the hearth, her suitor—grim-faced, his long nose shining—smiled weakly to reveal yellowed teeth when Emilia entered the room. Benozzo wore fashionable hose and a handsome blue doublet with silver buttons, but somehow he still resembled an emaciated crow.

"*Buon giorno*, Benozzo," she said, straining to be polite.

He reached for her hand, but then stared as though repulsed at her fingers. "What are the stains, Emilia?"

Withdrawing her hand, Emilia saw she had not scrubbed all the charcoal from her nails. "I like to draw figures," she said, unabashed.

"A strange pastime for a girl," he replied, unimpressed.

She knew there was no point in telling him anything about her admiration for Masaccio, her dream of painting, her love for art. The scrawny man who added and subtracted numbers with perfection would never understand her desire to paint. She looked across the room at her father and hated him.

The Bottega

"**O**f course we cannot allow our daughter to work with that old man!" Francesco Serafini bellowed loudly to his wife in no uncertain terms. Emilia was eavesdropping from her hiding place in the stairwell. "This *straniero*, foreigner—what do we know of him?"

Violante had explained to Francesco that Emilia was offered an unusual apprenticeship that would cost considerably less than Lorenzo Jacovelli's. Francesco had met Makarios only after much cajoling by Violante, but he was far from allowing Emilia to accept the position.

"It's true, he is a foreigner; but I think he's a good man," Violante offered. "You saw his workshop. He's a fine artist."

"He has no wife."

"Yes, he said she died some years ago."

"It's impossible. He has no servants to speak of. How would it look? She'd be all alone with him."

"I see your point. However, he does live like a monk. A very pious old man. Emilia would be quite safe," Violante replied.

21

"He wants to work her to death and have me pay him for the privilege!"

"Indeed, Francesco. Yet he would accept quite a bit less than what Jacovelli takes. And Emilia wouldn't have to disguise herself," Violante continued.

"He has no reputation. He's not even a member of the guild! Sandro says he never heard of the man."

"Is that true?" Violante mused. "Of course, Sandro is a carpenter. I imagine he doesn't know all the painters in Florence. Makarios is very good, didn't you say, Francesco? He would be a fine teacher."

"I agreed to allow her one year with Jacovelli—that was all. She cannot be allowed to continue on with this absurd notion. She's not a little girl any more. She must marry. You know that, Violante."

"She's still young, of course. And Benozzo is in Siena for a time."

"He will be good to her."

Emilia cringed every time she heard the name. She would have them send her to the convent rather than let Benozzo touch her, though she was little inclined to be a nun, even if the prioress did allow her to paint.

"Perhaps she would forget her misery after a while," Violante said quietly.

"It's only her best interest I have at heart. She must know that."

"Of course, Francesco," Violante agreed. "It's just that Emilia will not easily be dissuaded from her wish to be a painter. As you said, her passion is only for drawing right now."

"So she learns to paint—then what? Who would give her work? This has gone on far too long. It was a mistake to allow it in the first place."

Emilia listened to these discussions for a period of several days. Her father insisted that this was just another of Emilia's misguided attempts to enter an unsuitable profession and put off the wedding while her mother tried to persuade him otherwise with words, roasted chickens, and hazelnut tarts. As her father maintained hold over her future, Emilia alternately prayed, paced the floor of her room, or tried to busy herself with the spinning and weaving.

Then one day Violante put forth that she had received news from across the river. Quite casually, she said to her husband, "I don't know if it would make a difference, Francesco, as I know you have decided that Emilia should remain with Jacovelli for now, but Makarios sent word that he wishes to pay you three florins a year for Emilia."

"Pay for the privilege of teaching her? That's unheard of!"

Surely it was not what Francesco had expected. Such highly favorable terms could not easily be rejected, Emilia imagined. She was right, for the following day, softened by the prospect of the additional three florins, Francesco presented Makarios with a contract he wrote himself.

"One year," her father said when he returned from his meeting with the painter. "Next October you will put this aside once and for all. Benozzo will have things settled in Siena by then. You cannot keep him waiting forever, Emilia."

"Yes, *Messer Padre*."

One year? Emilia thanked her father and praised his skills as a man of business while wondering what she could accomplish in a single year. It was not nearly enough time to learn the craft. She would take what was offered and try not to think about Benozzo for the time being.

It was her father who accompanied Emilia across the river to the studio of the old painter from Constantinople. By horse they traveled along the main roads, Via del Corso and Via de' Tornabuoni, then across the bridge—Ponte Santa Trinita—and past the church, Santa Maria del Carmine. They continued down a narrow street of modest, wood multistory homes until they came to the building with the red door at the end of the road. On the door was a small but beautifully decorated sign with a repeating, geometric border, bearing the words, *Makarios Levantes, Painter*.

Bidding Francesco a strained goodbye, Emilia tried to conceal her nervousness as she walked ahead to touch her future. The wooden door was wide open, admitting the crisp September air and offering out freely the secrets of the art to all who would enter. As she stepped inside to the familiar scent of paint and charcoal, she thought that the workshop of Makarios Levantes was not unlike that of Lorenzo Jacovelli, though she wondered how patrons ever found Makarios in this remote corner of the city.

The workspace was roomy enough. She noted the familiar tools hanging from hooks, the plank table set up on horses, shelves holding jars of pigments, pens, and brushes, stacks of cartoons—the drawings used as guidelines for frescoes—against the wall, and panels of wood in various stages of preparation. Although it was a place of work and quite untidy, Emilia sensed an unusual quiet, an air of serenity she sometimes felt in the wide, open meadows beyond the wall.

"Come in, come in," her new master said enthusiastically from his desk, waving Emilia inside when he saw her still standing at the door.

"My mother sends you this," Emilia said shyly, taking the hazelnut tart, still warm and wrapped in cloth, from the lunch basket Violante had packed for Emilia.

Shuffling across the floor, Makarios moved forward to accept the gift. He opened the cloth with a flourish, inspected the cake and pronounced with glee, "A *torta*! *Grazie!*"

Not quite sure how to respond to his lightheartedness, Emilia remained solemn. "I want you to know I intend to work every bit as hard as a boy. I expect no preferential treatment."

Makarios chuckled and motioned for her to sit down on the bench. "No need to worry about that. You'll work hard enough. It's not so easy to find an apprentice who wants to come work for me. I have plenty enough for you to do."

"What would you like me to help you with today?" she asked, eager to get to work and prove her ability to her new mentor. "At Jacovelli's, I mostly mixed pigments and applied the gesso. Leonardo prepared the wood and painted the varnish, but he showed me how it's done. Giacomo used to trace the patterns, but I know I'm ready to use the stylus as well. And I'm very eager to learn to gild."

But Makarios seemed in no hurry to discuss Emilia's work assignment. Instead, he showed her to the back of the workshop, which served as his kitchen; there was a little table, a stone sink, a kneading trough, some bread bins and copper and iron utensils. Picking up a knife to cut the tart, he began to tell her where she could go in the morning to buy bread that was not too coarse, how she might prepare a simple soup for their meals, how he liked his wine watered down at lunch. Then he indicated the little nook behind the kitchen. Emilia peeked and saw a narrow straw bed and some blankets. Here she could take her *riposa*, her rest at midday. Emilia followed Makarios back to the workroom where he went about cutting two generous pieces of the *torta*.

"Your mama—she is a fine cook. Makes your father a happy man, no doubt," he said wistfully.

Emilia knew very little about cooking herself, Maddalena helped her mother with this at home. She felt unsure about making the soup he seemed to be expecting for his lunch. She was also wondering about Makarios' family and whether he had any living relatives, but she was afraid to ask him. It occurred to her that they might have been left behind in Constantinople or, worse, that they might have been killed by the Turks.

"Today you clean," he was telling her. "Wash the floor and the tables. I'm afraid I haven't kept the place up very well."

"Is that all?" she asked, not thinking to hide her disappointment.

He laughed good-naturedly and told her not to worry as he handed her a bucket, then showed her outside to the well. "You will learn everything in time. Be patient, Emilia. It takes more than a day to become a painter."

She went about the studio cleaning as efficiently as she could, swept up piles of sawdust, scraped away globs of paint and gesso with a spatula, and scrubbed the floor until her arms ached. It was clear enough to Emilia that she would be earning her keep at the *bottega*. She only hoped that coming to work for Makarios was not a mistake.

On the second day of her apprenticeship, she was clearing shelves and dusting off jars of pigments and brushes when she came across a panel such as she had never seen before. It was an image of three angelic figures painted in a manner completely foreign to her.

Emilia stared at the three beautiful, youthful figures seated before an altar table. The figure at the left wore a robe so luminous the fabric appeared to be spun from pink light. The central figure, wearing a tunic with a broad stripe running down it, pointed a hand, as though in blessing, toward the chalice in the center of the table. The figure at the right wore a mantle of shimmering green.

Something about the picture quieted her, almost as though she were listening to a prayer. She was so lost in contemplation of the panel that she did not hear Makarios approaching.

"So you have discovered the Holy Trinity," she heard him saying.

Startled, she looked up to see Makarios standing beside her.

"It's one piece I managed to keep with me from home," he added.

"It's a beautiful painting," she said.

"We do not call it a painting, Emilia, it is an icon."

"An icon?"

"A sacred image. This is what we do back home," he explained.

She returned her gaze to the panel. *A sacred image* Makarios had said. What did he mean that the painting was not a painting? She could clearly see that the style of painting in the icon was different from that of the work being done in the workshops of Florence. The figures were not fleshy, human, and alive with motion, as were the figures of Masaccio. Instead, there was a stillness about the figures, a mysterious, ethereal quality, but there was something else as well. The icon was ineffable, painted in a language different from the one she knew, a language without words.

It was a language she wanted to understand. "What makes it an icon and not a painting?" she asked Makarios. "I can see that it's different. But how is it made? And why don't you make them any more?"

"So many questions," he laughed. "The fact is, no one wants to buy an icon in Florence."

"But it's so beautiful," she said, looking at the Holy Trinity once more. "I wish I could learn to paint this way."

"What would you do with them?" Makarios asked.

"Oh, I don't know," she replied. "Just to make them would be enough. Will you teach me, Signor Levantes?"

"A young Florentine girl wants to make windows to heaven," he considered, smiling at her in a way that suggested this was not within her realm of knowing. "Perhaps one day. The Trinity is a mystery that takes time to understand, Emilia."

Throughout that afternoon she wondered how it was possible to paint the invisible. How did Makarios capture the mystery of the Trinity on wood and make a window to heaven?

If the icon could allow her to peek through to the world beyond this one, she wondered what she would see on the other side. This was impossible, of course. For all its beauty, the icon was essentially paint placed skillfully by human hands on wood. It was not real. Or was it? Either way, she was not sure if Makarios Levantes would ever teach her to paint anything. Her master had made it clear to her that she was not ready to hold the brush, much less approach a subject as sacred as the Holy Trinity.

When the church bells rang out at *sext* that day, a slightly hunched but sure-footed old man with a tanned, creased face sprang through the front door without bothering to announce himself.

"Who are you?" the old man asked, eyeing Emilia suspiciously.

"I'm the new apprentice," she said, wondering if he had wandered in by mistake.

"Apprentice? What is this, Makarios?" he demanded. "Why do you have a girl in the *bottega*?"

Makarios, unmoved by the visitor's obvious chagrin, made his way towards the front of the room. "Tedaldo is a very fine woodworker, Emilia. He has kindly come to help me with a delivery," he said, indicating a piece of furniture, almost as tall as she was, concealed beneath an old blanket in the corner of the workshop.

Ignoring Tedaldo's impolite stare, Emilia followed Makarios as he went to unveil the mysterious object, a silver cupboard he said. Makarios stepped aside so she could see the Last Supper painted upon the cupboard door.

"It's beautiful," Emilia murmured.

"A girl, Makarios? Why do you need an apprentice anyway? You're not so busy," Tedaldo interrupted.

"Maybe I'll have more work, Tedaldo. Besides, I'm getting old and lazy," Makarios replied. To Emilia, he said, "For the friary at Santa Croce."

"Santa Croce?" she repeated, wondering how he had managed to acquire a commission from her own church. She imagined her father would be quite impressed to know that the brothers of Santa Croce would be gazing at her master's work each day. It was a stunning painting, with brilliant effects of light, rich color, and masterful realism. To her young eyes, his work was nothing less than that of Masaccio.

"I have learned to paint what is popular," Makarios said, as though considering his piece nothing out of the ordinary. "The world changes. Cities change. I, too, must change the way I do things. One must look inside to find the eternal."

She thought she saw a wave of sadness pass over his face as he spoke, and she wanted to ask him more about the old style of painting from his country. But Makarios Levantes and Tedaldo were wrapping leather straps around the cupboard and when that was done, they carried it out the front door.

After the men departed and the *bottega* went silent but for the sound of the weavers upstairs, Emilia found herself wishing she was back home in her own familiar kitchen with Violante. She wandered into the little back nook and sat down to eat the bread, boiled eggs, and soft cheese that Violante had packed for her. She wondered how she would manage to clean and make soup and do all the things required of her every day. She wondered, as well, about strange and faraway Constantinople where Makarios once lived. There were hidden mysteries in the world of her master. Emilia felt as though the door to this world was locked and she would never find her way in.

The Apothecary

For several more weeks Emilia endured the uneventful routine at Makarios' studio, doing nothing more than cleaning, grinding pigments, and preparing panels as she had for Jacovelli. She could not see that she was learning much of anything from the old man, but she was not about to admit this to her father. Besides, grinding pigments was still preferable to an afternoon spent with Benozzo Balducci.

Emilia was glad one day in October when Makarios thought to send her on an errand across the river to the apothecary. She found the portly and balding Amerigo, dressed in a finely cut tunic with blue and orange stripes at the cuffs and hem, looking half asleep as he stocked his shelves with glass vials of green liquid. His expression turned from boredom to mild curiosity when she approached the counter to tell him she needed Spanish cinnabar, white lead, and some saffron threads for the St. John the Baptist her master was painting.

As Amerigo picked the small cubes wrapped in paper from trays stored high on the shelves, Emilia stood at the counter studying his wares, the variety of glass jars sealed with wax that contained colored tinctures and potions. When the shop door opened to admit a cool gust of air, Emilia turned to see a young man walk into the store.

"Giacomo!" she blurted without thinking.

"Yes," he replied slowly, staring blankly, trying to place her.

She almost started to tell him that she was Alessandro, from Jacovelli's workshop, but the subject of her disguise was too humiliating. Besides, she was still angry with Giacomo for having failed to stick up for her when Luigi lied to Jacovelli about the spilled pigment.

She pretended to turn her attention to the apothecary, handing him the coins to pay for her purchase. Trying to avoid Giacomo's curious but not unfriendly stare, Emilia gathered up the packages wrapped in white paper, wishing she could disappear. Suddenly, Giacomo came bounding over to her.

"Is it you, Alessandro?" he asked.

The color rose in her face as she met his gaze, trying her best to appear sure of herself. "My name is Emilia," she replied, her chin held high. "Emilia Serafini."

He remained expressionless for a moment, as though unsure how to respond to her change of identity. At last his serious demeanor changed and he broke into high-pitched laughter while a befuddled Amerigo looked on.

Emilia, mortified, walked briskly towards the door.

"*Aspetta!* Wait!" Giacomo called after her, trying to catch up.

She was on the street, pushing her way past a crowded outdoor food stand to make her way towards the river, when he was at her side once again.

"I meant no offense. It's just that I wasn't expecting to see you. Jacovelli told me what happened," he said. "You look quite different, of course. Your hair," he said, reaching to touch it.

She pulled back, warning him with her eyes not to come too close.

"I didn't mean to offend you," he said, stepping back. "It's just—you look like Angelico's Madonna."

Softening toward him, she asked, "Is everything well at Jacovelli's?"

"Yes, yes. He's working me ragged as usual—we've started a new series of frescoes for San Lorenzo. Your help is missed, of course. Luigi is considerably less dependable."

"If you hadn't doubted my word, I might still be there," she retorted.

"I didn't mean to doubt you," he replied. "Anyway, the workshop is hardly a place for a lady like you."

She replied curtly, "As it happens, I found myself a new apprenticeship. With a very fine painter."

At this, Giacomo broke into laughter again. "Don't tell me you're still disguising yourself!"

When it dawned on her that he would no doubt find her apprenticeship with an old foreigner completely ridiculous, she ignored him and started towards the river. "I have to hurry, I'm running late. Give my regards to Jacovelli and Leonardo."

"Where *is* this workshop?" Giacomo called after her.

Emilia waved to him, pretending not to hear. "*Arrivederci.* Good-bye."

"I will send greetings to Jacovelli from Madonna Emilia," he shouted.

She was painfully aware that once again she had managed to make a fool of herself in the company of Jacovelli's most talented painter.

In the weeks that followed, Emilia did not bump into Giacomo again, nor did her master assign her a task that she found the least bit challenging. She waited for Makarios to teach her something she did not know, but for the most part he asked her to tidy up after him, bring him his watered-down wine, fetch his tools, sand the panels, or grind pigments, just as she had done since the beginning.

She could not complain that he lacked kindness. Makarios smiled and laughed readily and thanked her for the bland soup she cooked for his noon meal. In his fatherly way, he made sure she took some exercise each day and often inquired as to the welfare of her family.

She was not sure what to make of it. Emilia wondered if the fact that she was a girl was working against her. Or perhaps Makarios Levantes did not think as much of her ability as he had led her to believe the day she met him at the Carmine. She was not about to admit defeat to her father. Benozzo might still be in Siena, but her father would have no qualms about putting an early end to her apprenticeship.

When she was home on the eve of All Saint's Day, Emilia turned to the alchemical text, half-heartedly searching for answers to her predicament at the *bottega*. Beneath an illustration of a skeleton standing atop the sun, she discovered another handwritten note—a list of herbs and spices, including saffron, lavender, and lemon balm, said to be beneficial for the condition of melancholia. On the next page was a cautionary warning from Isaac the Jew, author of the text.

> *The first stage of the alchemical process is known as the nigredo, the phase of utter darkness.*
>
> *To those who may be tempted to forgo the nigredo and advance directly to the white phase, or the albedo, take heed. For those who do not enter the abyss of Hell during life must enter after death.*

To deny the existence of the nigredo is to prolong its existence. Rather, the alchemist must bravely endure his great torment, bearing full responsibility for his suffering until the whitening is obtained.

Setting down the manual, Emilia considered her own *great torment*. Was it her fault that she was born female and no one in Florence thought her worthy of an apprenticeship, except for Makarios, who wanted her to cook and clean instead of paint? Despite her skepticism, she read on.

Upon accepting the foolishness and wickedness of his ways and the great sin he has brought upon himself, it is then possible for him to be changed. Truly, through the process of alchemy, many miracles shall be wrought.

On the next page was an illustration of the alchemist's cylindrical furnace. A strange recipe that included yellow sulfur, a sharp vinegar, and mercury was written on the opposite page. Underneath the picture, she read: *The material is melted down for a long, long time. It turns black, blacker than black. The alchemist must work hard and alone.*

Perhaps because of the advice in *Nonna's* book, or perhaps because Violante had admonished her when she complained bitterly about Makarios, Emilia departed for the workshop the next morning with a change of heart. She loaded the mule with flour, eggs, olive oil, lard, nuts, some jellied meat, bread, and spices. If Makarios Levantes wanted her to cook and clean, then she would cook and clean as well as she could. Along with the stores of food, Emilia also brought a soft, wool blanket for her bed, her *nonna's* book to read at lunchtime, her mother's favorite cookbook, and a supply of candles.

At the *bottega* she went about her work, cooking, carrying

water, and sweeping up the sawdust from the carving Makarios was making. Later that morning she consulted her mother's cookbook and read how to make a cheese pie with herbs.

> *Take some soft cheese and cream it well. Now take parsley and marjoram, and some chard, which must exceed the quantity of the other herbs, and clean them and chop them very well, and mix them together with the cheese. Add five or six eggs and enough pepper and a little saffron, ginger, and good lard. Put this filling into a pan with a bottom crust. Cover everything with more dough and bake it at the top and bottom. Then add some more lard and serve.*

The pie was perhaps not as good as Violante's, but for her first attempt Emilia thought it acceptable enough. After cleaning up the kitchen, she sat at the worktable and practiced drawing from the pattern book. She drew sheep with their heads up and sheep with their heads down, borders and trees and angels' wings, pictures of scrolls, and wise men. Makarios seemed lost in a world of his own.

Over the following days she developed a routine of moving back and forth between the workroom and the kitchen. While she grew more comfortable with her apprenticeship, she could not forget there were less than eleven months before she was supposed to wed. It was hardly enough time to become a painter.

One afternoon, as though sensing Emilia's worries, Makarios said, "Why don't you take a walk? Go and sit at Santa Maria Novella. Look at Masaccio's Trinity, Emilia. Look at the perspective. And the Last Judgement—Nardo di Cione's. It will be good for you to study. Take your paper and charcoal."

Eager for the opportunity, Emilia made her way through the cold and across the bridge to Santa Maria Novella. Inside the church, as she approached the third bay, she did not notice the brilliant composition and the magnificent illusion of the decorative architecture, she only noticed a man with a head of wavy, copper-colored hair. Lost in his own world, the man moved his pencil rapidly over his page as though trying to capture the image before it escaped him. She did not have to see his face to know it was Giacomo Massarino. She started to turn and leave before he could see her and question her about her apprenticeship again. Emilia did not need another man telling her she should give up painting. She remained frozen in the north aisle, wondering what to do.

The Magi

In the silence of the empty chapel, Emilia stood staring at Giacomo, wondering if she dare speak or quietly leave without saying a word. Before she did anything, the painter raised his head from his drawing and caught sight of her. At first he appeared startled by her presence, as though roused from a dream, but then his face lit up in glad recognition.

"Is it truly Emilia Serafini?" he asked, rising from his stool to greet her.

"What brings you here, Giacomo?" she said, determined to appear in full possession of herself in his presence for once. After glimpsing his charcoal studies, she already knew that he had come to study the masters.

"I'll be leaving for Pisa next week—along with Bruno and Enrico," he replied. "We have a commission for the confraternity for Santa Caterina."

She felt a pang of jealousy even while she told herself she had no reason to feel that way. "I'm glad for you, Giacomo. And for the Dominicans' patronage," she said with as much enthusiasm as she could garner. "You are blessed to put your talents to such use. Jacovelli has great confidence in you."

"That my pay would be as great as his confidence." There was, she thought, some bitterness in his voice as he went on to say, "Jacovelli has no desire to leave Florence. He'll come to Pisa once or twice, just to put his brush to the wall so it will bear his name. Then he will leave. But tell me about you. And this workshop you've found. Does your new master have work?"

"*Si.* He manages quite well. He just finished a Last Supper for Santa Croce," she replied, though she failed to mention it was not a fresco but a painted silver cupboard.

Truth be told, Makarios had only a small fraction of the business enjoyed by Jacovelli. Her new master, however, seemed in no hurry to find his next commission.

She went to take a seat and Giacomo moved beside her. Emilia found herself wishing that Makarios had an important patron she could boast about to Giacomo. To conceal her lack of confidence in her new *bottega*, she said, as though slightly put off, "Are you asking about my apprenticeship because you don't believe I've found one?"

He looked at her closely, as though trying to discern the truth. At last he answered, "I believe you, Emilia," he said. "But I am curious to know who took you on."

They sat quietly before the altar for a while, beneath the massive, robed figure of Christ who was seated but without apparent means of physical support. Finally, Emilia spoke the truth about Makarios Levantes and his small workshop near the Carmine.

"My new master will not be sending me to Pisa any time soon. He is old and he is content to work just enough to buy food and pay the rent." Hoping Giacomo did not think less of her, she studied his reaction.

He smiled, saying, "It is a wonder that you managed to find an apprenticeship at all, Emilia. You should be pleased."

At least he did not pity her. "Will you be gone for long?"

"It may take close to a year," he said with a hint of sadness.

"But you are no doubt pleased that Jacovelli is sending you."

"Jacovelli has a wife and five children. He is happy to send me in his place. The rest of us do not have the luxury of deciding where or when we work. Or of having a family, for that matter."

"Surely a painter is allowed to have a family," she said, thinking the Jacovelli she knew would not begrudge his painters the right to marry.

"Not the sort of painter Jacovelli demands," Giacomo insisted. "Perhaps one day, if I had a workshop of my own. But that is not so easily had."

"I wish this for you one day," she said, understanding that Giacomo had frustrations of his own to deal with.

"*Grazie*, Emilia. I wish you success, too. You want it badly enough—I can see that. Somehow, I think you might find it."

She felt warmed by the confidence he showed in her. It meant a great deal that he seemed to take her ambition seriously at last.

"Emilia," he began as he rose to gather up his sketches. "May I write to you from Pisa?"

Surprised by this request, she replied, "If you wish."

When Giacomo Massarino kissed her goodbye, Emilia was not sure what to make of his show of friendship. She reminded herself that Jacovelli's best painter had no time to give much thought to women.

Staying still as stone, Emilia watched Makarios closely as he painstakingly dropped tiny sheets of gold leaf onto the Virgin's halo and then tapped them into place with a square brush. The gold he used had been pounded into small squares, thinner than paper, and even a careless breath would send it flying through the air to land in a folded, ruined heap. It was a skill that required patience and steadiness of hand. No doubt tiring from the work, Makarios paused to set down his tools and shake out his hands. When he noticed Emilia sitting on a stool beside him, he smiled in surprise.

"How long have you been here, Emilia?"

"A few minutes."

"I mean since you first came to work with me."

"Nearly five months now," she answered. And only seven months till her contract expired and Benozzo would be waiting on the steps at Santa Croce, she thought. Her father had just sent another shipment of saddles and harnesses to the new shop Benozzo was managing in Siena. Her suitor was thoroughly occupied with matters of business for now, but it was only a matter of time until he returned to Florence.

"That long?" Makarios said, stroking his beard. "Why don't you work with the paints a bit?" he suggested, absentmindedly. "Take one of the small boards. See if you can start to get the feel for it."

So Emilia began to paint when she could steal an hour or so. She used the more common pigments, never touching Makarios' expensive purple of porphyry marble or saffron gold or blue of lapis lazuli. Over and over again, she used the same board, coating it with more gesso once she was ready to make another attempt. She was never satisfied with her work although Makarios always encouraged her.

"You have a fine eye for it, Emilia. Very fine. You're making progress."

But Emilia imagined her Madonna's position awkward, her expression troubled and her hands misshapen. Was Makarios only humoring her? Sometimes she was afraid that after all the difficulty of finding an apprenticeship, she would discover she had no talent after all.

Early in March, when the weather was still cold and wet, a letter addressed to Emilia at the workshop of Makarios Levantes arrived from Pisa. After dusting off her yellow, pigment-covered hands over the bowl of pulverized fish gallbladder so as not to waste even a speck of dyestuff, Emilia ripped open the seal and began to read the letter that she knew was from Giacomo Massarino.

Dear Emilia,

I promised this letter to you long ago and though I have thought of you often, my days in Pisa are long with work on the scaffold at Santa Caterina. The winter wears on and my time is all spent upon these walls, painting scenes from the life of the Virgin and Christ, but still I remember my friends in Florence with particular fondness.

The fresco will not dry this week. There is too much rain and dampness in the air, and Bruno made the plaster bad. At this rate, these walls will not be done for many months. Pray for clear skies above Pisa.

Please forgive me, but when I think of the disguise you succeeded in wearing for so long at Jacovelli's, it makes me laugh. I hope you will take no offense, for your determination deserves only the highest admiration.

Please remember your friend well until the time when I return to our beloved city.

Ever Yours,
Giacomo

Emilia felt glad to hear from him, though she was puzzled that he thought of her at all. Giacomo was familiar with her as the boy, Alessandro. He had known her just a little while as Emilia. Tucking the letter in her apron pocket and returning to work, she found herself wondering when Giacomo would return to Florence.

Though drawing with the charcoal stick came easily to Emilia, she found that modeling figures from the four basic colors she used—blue, red, brown, and green—was more challenging. Her figures seemed crude and her use of pigments too harsh or too soft. She wondered at the way Makarios could control his palette so well, how he balanced one color with another to achieve stunning effects.

She was mystified, too, how Makarios, not belonging to any guild, had managed to find his new patron, a French nobleman—a knight on a diplomatic mission for the Duke of Burgundy. The commission, a heavily gilded Adoration of the Magi for the knight's family chapel, was to be completed during his embassy in Rome.

"How did Messer Bertrand find you, if it's not a secret?" she dared to ask.

"It's no secret, Emilia," he replied. "A painter, a good friend of mine in Venice, has one of my old panels. When Bertrand admired the piece, my friend told him where he could find me here in Florence."

Emilia wondered at her master's wide circle of friends and acquaintances that he had acquired through his travels. She found it remarkable that he could work steadily, albeit slowly, without the benefit of the guild to recommend him. Makarios was teaching her after all, but she needed years with him, not mere months.

In spring, when the white oleander was in bloom, letters from Giacomo arrived more often. He seemed to be in high spirits now that the weather was warm and the plaster was drying. As their correspondence became something of a routine, Emilia expressed herself more freely, sending him words of encouragement, news from Florence, and trivial stories of her day. Miles away in Pisa, Giacomo had become her friend.

She shared details about the panel Makarios was making for the knight. Her master perfected Bertrand's likeness on the face of one Magi, according to his patron's wishes. At last he added the final touches, the subtle highlights. When Bertrand of Beaune passed through Florence upon his return from Rome, a purse full of coins was given in exchange for the small masterpiece. Emilia overheard a discussion between Messer Bertrand and her master and was given to think the payment was not exactly what Makarios had expected. But no argument ensued and the knight departed in good humor. Giacomo wrote back, saying he looked forward to meeting this foreign master who worried so little about money.

Around this time, Makarios began working on a new commission for the south aisle at Santa Croce. Emilia marveled that Friar Giuseppe had once again convinced his fellow brothers to hire his friend, Makarios. A prominent family by the name of Martini was funding the project, and apparently Donna Martini, a Sienese beauty, admired Friar Giuseppe and did not care one bit that Makarios Levantes was an obscure foreigner. No doubt, the Franciscan brothers had been sufficiently impressed by the Last Supper that Makarios had painted upon the silver cupboard.

When Makarios completed the preliminary sketches for the new panel—the Virgin and Christ with Angels—he surprised Emilia by asking her to paint the undercoat and draperies. Pleased that Makarios was putting more faith in her, she set to work with diligence and the hope that he would perhaps ask her to do more, to begin painting backgrounds, and then progress to figures before her year was through.

Although it was her opinion that Makarios had changed toward her, she became aware as well of a subtle shift in her own mind, a quieting of the worrisome thoughts that once plagued her. She was acquiring self-discipline, the ability to focus on her work.

While Makarios was taking his usual afternoon stroll that day, she took a few minutes to read from *Nonna's* book about the land of Egypt, the great god, Thoth, and the mysteries of alchemy hidden there. An Egyptian sage named Hermes Trismegistus, who the ancients associated with the god Thoth, wrote of eternity, the cycles of the cosmos, and the soul of man.

Strange and wonderful passages were attributed to the legendary Hermes. This portion of the manual was especially difficult to comprehend, and Emilia was fascinated by the image of the bird-headed figure of Thoth, the moon god, the inventor of hieroglyphics.

She read of the seven chambers through which the soul must pass after death. It was not unlike the process Plato discussed in the *Phaedo*. Emilia read the words that Isaac the Jew had attributed to the great philosopher. Plato warned against neglecting the soul and advised giving it loving care, for after death it was not possible to dispose of wickedness as one disposed of the body. Death, he said, was not a benefit to the evil ones….

She did not hear the workshop door open, though she became aware of a deep voice. Looking up to the bright light streaming in through the doorway, she saw the outline of a tall, well-proportioned man standing in a manner that resembled the pose of some heroic statue in a piazza.

When the man moved forward, she could see that he was

handsome. He had jet-black hair, quick darting eyes, rugged features, and his complexion suggested southern roots. He was dressed in the fine clothes of a gentleman—an embroidered tunic and hanging, scalloped sleeves lined with green silk, a plumed hat, and fashionable, pointed, red leather shoes, all suggestive of considerable wealth. She could not help but stare at him as he made his way into the room, not so much for his good looks but for the aura of confidence about him. She supposed he might be a nobleman or perhaps even some relation of the Medicis.

"The master is not in," she managed to say, taking in the sheer splendor of his appearance.

"The master from Constantinople is not here?" he said, gliding across the length of the workshop in just a few long, powerful strides. "I am Franco Villani," he said with bold assurance as he bowed politely before her.

"He will return soon," she told him, noting that his gaze had fixed upon her precious book, which lay open to the passage of *Phaedo* and an exotic, hand-colored picture depicting the anointing of the mummy, Osiris, with Isis in attendance.

"A most unusual text," he remarked, his eyes glued to the image.

"Oh, yes, it is rather curious," she said, closing the book while he stood glancing at the book over her shoulder. "Something bought from a bookseller for a trifling, I imagine." Emilia placed a charcoal sketch over the text, but still the man's attention would not waver from the manual.

"But I should say it looks extremely rare. And rather old. Is it yours?" the gentleman persisted.

"Yes, it is a very old book," she began, not knowing how to reply. Emilia could not very well tell this stranger that generations ago her great-great-great grandmother had acquired the text from a friar, who had spent years trying to translate the book and a lifetime trying to understand its contents and precipitate metallic gold.

"I confess its scope is beyond me. Only my mother says I must read something to practice my Latin," she said.

Much to her relief the door of the workshop opened and her master returned. She snatched up her book from beneath the drawing and stood to greet him. "Signor Franco Villani has just now arrived to see you, Makarios."

"Ah, the great master from Constantinople. It is an honor," Franco Villani proclaimed.

"You will find only Makarios Levantes here," he replied, bowing his head. "And his young apprentice, Madonna Emilia Serafini."

"Yes, we have met," he said, turning to stare at her. "A very lovely apprentice."

Ignoring his remark, Emilia went to tuck her book in the shelf alongside the pattern books.

Franco Villani came closer to inspect the drawing she had left on the table. "An unusual arrangement with just the two of you, is it not?"

"Indeed," Makarios admitted. "Yet an arrangement born of mutual necessity. But I only wonder how a gentleman such as you finds his way to my little shop."

Franco Villani laughed, revealing fine, straight teeth. "No need for false modesty. Bertrand of Burgundy sends me here."

"Ah, you are acquainted with the good knight."

"From my days in Genoa—he used to visit my shop quite often. He has an insatiable appetite for food flavored with cinnamon and ginger," Signor Villani replied. "A fine piece you made for him."

Makarios nodded his head in modest recognition. "You would consider a panel as well?" he asked.

"I have come to see you about a fresco," he said. "Bertrand assures me of your talent. And your fair price."

When Makarios did not reply immediately, Franco Villani added, "Don't worry. I can pay you well enough for your time."

For whatever reason, Makarios displayed little enthusiasm for this prospective patron. "Where would you have me paint this fresco, Signor Villani?" he asked at length.

"I have a villa—up in the hills, in Fiesole, just a few miles outside the gates. It's a pleasant respite from the city. I venture to say you might welcome the change of surroundings."

As Makarios stroked his beard and thought quietly for a while, Emilia could sense his reluctance. "I have much work right now, Signor Villani. You are kind to consider me, but I am an old man and very slow. It would be some time—"

"I have plenty of time. My fortune and I are returned to my beloved Tuscany, and I will not be leaving again," Villani said with confidence.

"Well, perhaps you can tell me a little more of your idea."

Emilia disappeared into the kitchen and tried to listen to the conversation as she poured wine for the visitor. Makarios, she imagined, could ill afford to turn down a wealthy patron. She imagined the visitor lived in a grand villa with fine silver, rich tapestries, and numerous servants. Emilia made a silent wish that her master would accept the commission so that she could accompany him to Fiesole and learn to fresco. She would write Giacomo in Pisa and tell him all about it as soon as the matter was settled.

The night after she met Franco Villani, Emilia could not sleep. Her mind was unsettled, filled with thoughts of Signor Villani's villa in Fiesole. He was only a prospective patron who perhaps thought too much of himself, but painting at his villa would be an opportunity of a lifetime.

She fell asleep reading about Hermes, the messenger god—the god of travelers and thieves, the guide of souls to the underworld. In *Nonna's* book he wore a broad-brimmed hat with little wings, sandals with wings as well, and he carried a caduceus. Hermes smiled slyly out at her from the page, as though sharing her secret. He was motioning her toward him, deeper into her dream.

Hermes led her to the island of Crete where she became lost in a labyrinth beneath a palace. In the distance, Emilia heard the roar of the Minotaur, the monster who lived in the labyrinth. Horrified, she saw the monster was Benozzo Balducci.

She awoke in a panic, her hair matted with sweat. Her apprenticeship with Makarios was half over; there were only six months left.

Tedaldo

Half expecting to see Benozzo Balducci hiding somewhere in her room, Emilia awoke with a start at the first light of dawn. But she was alone when she sat up in bed and reached for the alchemy manual, which still lay open to the picture of the messenger god. Beneath the image was a passage she had not read the night before.

Hermes, or Mercury to the Romans, is the guide of souls on their journeys. He is quicksilver, a mysterious union of opposites: metallic while also liquid. He is able to move at will between the worlds of spirit and matter.

The alchemist travels as Hermes, moving freely between realms. To become an adept of the Great Work, he must be willing to leave the safety of the laboratory and enter into places hitherto unknown.

Emilia closed the book, feeling as though she had discovered a secret that she did not fully comprehend. Like Hermes who traveled the uncharted skies of the alchemist, Emilia somehow believed she would travel to unknown worlds as well. For now she would keep this secret to herself.

When she arrived at the workshop, she found Makarios' painting of the Virgin and Christ with angels lying on the worktable. With gilding as bright as the heavens, the panel for Santa Croce was completed and Makarios could start the new commission, she thought.

Yet later that morning Makarios picked up his specially cut punch to create an intricate pattern in the gilded halos of the angels. After this was done, he would surely begin the fresco for Signor Villani. Studying his work the next day, however, Makarios decided the Virgin's complexion was a shade too dark to suit the taste of the Florentines, so he set about reworking her face.

Emilia began to think they would never begin the fresco for the splendid, countryside villa of Franco Villani. Several times she started to write Giacomo to tell him about the commission, as though writing about it would make it happen. Then, knowing her words untrue, she tossed them away. At one point she gathered the courage to ask Makarios when they would start, but his response was vague. *We will see, Emilia. We must finish one thing at a time.*

When the day finally arrived and her master declared the panel for Santa Croce finished, he left with Tedaldo to make the delivery. Emilia concluded her master would have no choice but to begin the fresco now. After all, they had to eat.

After Makarios returned from the friary, he surveyed his *bottega,* turning in all directions as though looking for something. He said, "It is not fitting that the workshop of Makarios Levantes has no ornament to bless these walls. I think it is time. Yes, it is time to do something about this."

"What do you mean?" Emilia asked, setting Makarios' cloak, which she was mending, to the side.

"I haven't written one in years. Too many years. So now you will see what we do in my country, Emilia."

"What are you talking about, Makarios?"

"The painting of my people," he replied. "I will write an icon and I will show you how it is done." He rose from the bench to gather paper and charcoal.

Emilia was taken aback by this announcement. She could not help but wonder what Makarios intended to do about the commission for Franco Villani. On the other hand she felt a sense of childish delight, knowing that she would finally see what she had wanted to see.

"What of the fresco?" she asked Makarios. "Surely you don't wish to lose the commission." With less than five months until her contract expired, she was afraid she would never have the opportunity to learn the technique.

"I have not forgotten Signor Villani. He will have his fresco in due time," Makarios said, unconcerned. "I put off something important for long enough. We will have an icon for these walls. The *Pantocrator*."

"The *Pantocrator*?" she echoed.

"Christ, the Ruler of All," he replied. "Tomorrow we will ask Tedaldo to cut the panel."

Emilia was too stunned to answer. Makarios was setting aside the request of a wealthy patron so that he might make a painting for himself. As much as she yearned to learn about her master's icons, his decision seemed highly imprudent and made her wonder if he was becoming feebleminded in his advancing years.

Emilia and Makarios ventured across the river to Tedaldo's house, in the western part of the city, to request a specially cut wood panel upon which the *Pantocrator* would be written. The old woodworker, who was feeding his flock of chickens when they arrived, refused to believe the panel was for no particular patron at all.

First he looked disbelievingly at Makarios, but then he nodded in complicity, as though finally understanding the real meaning. "So you do not wish to speak. You are keeping a secret," he said quietly. "Why don't you have your girl go inside the house with my wife?"

"Yes, it is a secret in a way. But this is for my own workshop. This will be a very special piece," Makarios replied.

Tedaldo spoke in a low, conspiratorial voice, trying to keep Emilia from hearing. "I suppose you have to worry about the guilds. You do a little work, they don't notice, but maybe now you have to be more careful. Artists are jealous men. Don't worry, Makarios. You're an old man, like me. We have to do what we can to survive. I will tell *no one* about your patron."

There was little point in trying to correct him. He promised to deliver the panel in two weeks time. Wordlessly, Tedaldo handed Emilia a basket of eggs as she departed with Makarios.

The poplar panel, which was being made according to Makarios' exact specifications, did not arrive two weeks later as promised. While Emilia grew impatient, her master appeared removed from all worldly concerns. He sat at his worktable perfecting his charcoal cartoon, the template for the panel.

Though she was eager to begin the icon, she wondered what

excuse, if any, her master had given Franco Villani for delaying the start of his fresco. Emilia wanted to ask if the commission would still be his or if Makarios thought the work would go to another workshop. But she remained silent on the matter as Makarios retreated to his private world of iconography.

Her apprenticeship was atypical, but then she had known as much from the beginning. She reminded herself that Makarios was teaching her well, even though he did not run his *bottega* like Lorenzo Jacovelli. Emilia only wondered how to reply to Giacomo's most recent letter; she found it difficult to explain Makarios' latest undertaking. For the time being, she decided to write instead that she had exchanged greetings with the well known Uccello when she visited Amerigo's apothecary several days earlier.

After another week passed, the panel had still not been delivered. Emilia busied herself in the kitchen preparing a thick, noodle soup. As she rolled out the dough for the pasta, she wondered how making an icon would differ from making a painting. Recalling the Holy Trinity that she had discovered months ago, she imagined Makarios would create something equally beautiful and mysterious. Her master was different from the Florentine artists of the day. He was a foreigner in their city, a man from a different world.

When Tedaldo finally arrived at the workshop with the panel, he did not scowl at Emilia as he had the first day they met. Instead, he handed her a muslin sack containing a plump, dead chicken and advised her how she should prepare it with fresh pork fat and a bit of onion and then when it was half-cooked she should add some almond milk, cinnamon, and pine nuts.

For the moment, Emilia set the chicken aside. Makarios could not begin to paint until she glued fine white linen to the board and applied the gesso. Not wanting to delay work a moment longer, she went about cutting the linen to size and soaking it in fish glue. The linen was necessary when making large pieces, Makarios had explained, and would keep the picture whole if the wood should ever split. This would be no ordinary panel and Makarios, she knew, expected perfection.

After the linen was soaked through, she began the careful work of applying it to the board. At the same time Makarios Levantes, working without pay, seemed in high spirits as he sat at his table and added the final touches to the drawing that would be transferred to the board. The parchment had been cut to the exact size of the panel and bore the half-length figure of Christ.

When the second layer of gesso was drying, Emilia studied the image he had drawn. Large and powerful, this awe-inspiring Christ was like nothing she had ever seen before. Imagining how the completed panel might look, Emilia felt compelled to tell Giacomo about iconography and the mysterious art of Constantinople. Despite the closeness she felt to Giacomo, she was not sure he would understand this latest undertaking. If he knew she was helping her master make a painting to adorn their own workshop, he might think Makarios had gone mad.

At the end of the day, as she walked towards the door, Makarios—dressed in his best tunic and familiar, wide-brimmed hat—followed directly behind her. She supposed he would be joining the goldsmith, Matteo, for a game of cards, or perhaps one of his friends from Santa Croce.

Taking the long route through the piazza, Emilia wove her way from Santa Maria del Carmine towards Santo Spirito. She was in no hurry to return home, where she would spend another dull evening with her parents and her brother. The sun was still burning bright in the sky, and the city was alive with young people in love on every corner. The sight of romance reminded her of the unpleasant fact of her upcoming betrothal. Blinking hard, she tried to force the thought of Benozzo from her mind; she wanted to think only of painting.

There was no denying that she felt lonely at times. Her dear friend, Tina, and many of the girls Emilia grew up with were already married. But to marry without love would mean defeat. Her freedom would be lost forever. It would be the end of Emilia. She remembered what she had read in her grandmother's book.

The alchemist is endowed with the ability to imagine and bring to life his unique dream....With God's divine assistance, the source of his power, he is charged with the responsibility of writing the story of his life.

Her present story was one she would never have written, Emilia thought as she came to the Piazza della Signoria—the busy, open square where the lofty bell tower of the palace, the Palazzo Vecchio, loomed overhead. The sound of a lute and viol floated sweetly towards her. On the steps of the Loggia della Signoria, two musicians were playing for anyone who would listen. A few children formed a ring and danced without care.

The rhythm and life of her city surrounded her. In that moment Emilia Serafini wondered if it was true that anything could happen. As she stood listening to the music, watching the children play, she noticed a figure in the distance. She thought she recognized the black hair, the imposing stature. He was not a man who could be easily mistaken for another. She was quite sure of it; the man was Franco Villani.

Franco

Emilia stood quietly in the Piazza della Signoria, wondering if Franco Villani would remember her. If he did remember her, she was not sure he would bother to take notice of her. Keeping her eyes focused ahead, she started across the square, wishing she had the courage to speak. She might be less timid if she had something to say to Signor Villani other than the fact that her master was occupied with work of a personal nature and had no time for his commission.

Emilia had reached the other side of the piazza and was almost to the Church of Orsanmichele when she heard footsteps behind her. Someone was approaching her, moving closer and closer. She walked faster, trying to keep a distance between herself and the stranger. She was about to break into a run when she heard a man's voice. Her heart jumped.

"The young apprentice, is it not?"

She turned to see Franco Villani. Standing tall and straight before her, the man appeared thoroughly pleased to have found her. "You are kind to remember me, Messer," she said, still slightly shaken after being followed.

"Such an apprentice is not easily forgotten."

"Nor is your kind patronage of Makarios Levantes."

"Ah, yes, the matter of Makarios Levantes. The old master from Constantinople is sought as though he was Giotto, it would appear."

"You mustn't think such a thing," she said quickly. "It's only that he's getting old and a little slow. Everything takes him so long."

"And he has only you there to help him," Franco noted. "Perhaps he might find another apprentice if he finds himself unable to keep up."

She could not very well tell him that Makarios had no other commissions at present. There was nothing she could say to explain her master's indifference. "I am very sorry," she tried. "I only hope you will give Makarios another chance."

Emilia was taken off guard when Franco Villani took hold of her hands. "Yes, to have the work of these lovely hands upon my walls, I will perhaps wait," he said, studying the pigment-stained fingers which had offended Benozzo.

Her cheeks flooded pink, thinking he was mocking her; it was of course her master's talent that Franco Villani sought, not hers. She tried to bid him good night, believing he would continue on his way, but Franco Villani walked by her side, regaling her with tales of the East Indian spice trade, shipwrecks off the Cape of Good Hope, and attacks near Java.

Emilia was at turns fascinated and unnerved by Signor Villani's attention. She could not help but wonder what Makarios would think if he saw her strolling through Florence with his prospective patron. She also wondered why Franco Villani had agreed to wait for Makarios. After all, there were a great number of painters in Florence and Makarios Levantes, though highly gifted, was new to the city, a foreigner and unknown. Perhaps Franco Villani was intent on finding a good bargain. Whatever the reason, she was glad if the commission was not lost.

As she neared her home on Via Ghibellina that summer night, Signor Villani still walked with her. It occurred to Emilia that her master's patron was displaying an interest in her that was not merely professional in nature. The idea was ridiculous, of course, but there he stood before her, a bemused expression on his face.

When he still gave no indication of moving on, Emilia finally asked, "What is it that detains you at this hour, Messer? Do you not wish to return home?"

He chuckled before asking, "Who is your father, Monna Emilia?"

"My father is Francesco Serafini. He owns the tavern nearest Santa Croce. And a saddle shop as well," she said matter-of-factly. "Why do you ask?"

He looked at her with keen interest, as though searching for some sort of explanation. "I cannot help but wonder how a young lady would come to paint with an old foreigner. The arrangement might have appeared as one of desperation."

At this affront, Emilia exhaled deeply and declared, "I consider myself most fortunate to work with Makarios Levantes. Such apprenticeships are not easily had. It was hardly an arrangement born of desperation, Signor Villani. He is a very kind man—a prominent painter from his country—and he was good to give me the chance. I want to paint more than anything."

Ceremoniously, the spice merchant lifted her hand to his lips, kissing her fingers. Emilia was not sure if she should curtsy politely in parting or run to her mother at once.

"I did not mean to offend you in any way. I apologize for my insatiable curiosity," he said evenly, holding her where she stood with his eyes.

After a moment, Emilia gathered the courage to say, "You are not the only one who is curious. I wonder where you were before you returned to Florence, Signor Villani. And what it was that brought you back."

He paused almost imperceptibly before replying, "My father sent me to live with his sister in Genoa when I was a boy—after my mother died," he said. "My uncle dealt in spices, quite successfully. He brought me up to learn the trade. When he died, it all fell to me. I kept delaying my return home, because I was rewarded so well, I suppose. Sometimes, one must pay a price for success. No doubt everyone has a price that he would sacrifice everything for."

Emilia imagined that Signor Villani's uncle—a wealthy, Genoese seaman merchant who exported precious cargos from the Orient—had been able to provide his nephew with a life of exceptional comfort. She could not agree that she would sacrifice everything for such comforts.

She replied to him with honesty. "I can only speak for myself, Signor Villani. For me, it would be impossible to sacrifice painting. Not for love, not for money."

He studied her, as though to ascertain if she believed what she said. Then he declared with certainty, "You will see, Emilia. In time you will see it's not so easy to hold fast to your lofty ideas. This world does not allow it."

"Perhaps the world does allow it, Signor Villani. Perhaps God allows it. The ancients believed that such freedoms might be found in this life," she said, wanting to hold onto hope that she could become a successful painter despite her father's plans.

Eyebrows arched in surprise, he replied, "A most bold and unusual thought for a young woman. Do you find such ideas in your book of Egypt?"

"My book of Egypt?" she said, surprised that he recalled her *nonna's* text and that he thought to mention it. She knew well enough not to speak openly of the book with anyone; Violante had warned her there were many who believed that the ideas put forth in the manual were dangerous.

"The book you were reading," he persisted. "That day I came to the workshop."

"Ah, yes, that old book. I remember little of it—the words were difficult to follow. I suppose I'm only repeating what my mother says. I'm afraid I share her fault of being far too outspoken. You must forgive me."

Franco did not appear convinced; it was as though he sensed she was withholding something. A dark and brooding figure, he walked off in the direction they had come from. Emilia was left to wonder what it was inside him that made him hold so little hope. She felt as though he had suffered a great loss of some kind. For all his fortune, Franco Villani was not a happy man.

When she entered her house, Emilia called out in greeting, "*Buona sera!*"

"Where have you been, Emilia?" Francesco demanded. "You are late tonight."

She was still thinking up an excuse when she saw Benozzo seated beside her mother in the salon. Violante gave her an understanding smile.

"Why aren't you in Siena?" Emilia said without thinking.

Francesco's face darkened but he controlled his anger, and said, "Benozzo has returned for a few days, Emilia. I know you must be surprised and happy to see him." As though determined that this would be so, Francesco ushered Violante out of the room to leave Emilia alone with her guest.

She kept her eyes on her shoes as Benozzo inquired as to her health. She could do nothing but listen as he spoke about the market for embellished, red leather saddles, the shop's modest success, which he attributed to his tireless dedication to detail, and the unseemly flamboyance of the Sienese.

"You will remain there for some time, then Benozzo?" she asked expectantly.

"Until our new man has proven trustworthy."

She could not help but hope the new man would prove to be a cheat so she could be left to her painting in peace. Benozzo knew little of her passion; her father had made it clear that she should not draw attention to this unseemly aspect of her life. She wondered if Benozzo would want to marry her if he knew how she spent her days across the river.

The Pantocrator

When she arrived at the *bottega* the following day, Emilia wondered what she ought to tell Makarios of her unexpected encounter with Franco Villani. Her master sat reading at his desk—sun streamed in through the square, open window so that it appeared as though he was lit from within. He looked up from his book to smile kindly at her.

"*Buon giorno,* Emilia."

She set down the basket of deep purple plums she had carried from home and blurted out, "It was not my plan, but by chance I ran into Signor Villani at the piazza last night."

"The mysterious coincidences of life," Makarios nodded.

"He still hopes you will do the fresco," she told him. "It would be a fine commission."

"Yes, the fresco. I suppose Signor Villani is not one who easily forgets once his heart is set on something."

Detecting a touch of sadness in his voice, Emilia stopped to wonder if her mention of Franco Villani conveyed a lack of gratitude for the lessons in iconography that her master wanted to impart to her. It was a bit careless of her to speak enthusiastically of the fresco now that Makarios was admitting her to the sacred place where his beloved art of Constantinople could be found.

"There will be plenty of time for commissions later," she added quickly, wanting to soften what she had said. "After you paint the icon."

"*Write* the icon," he corrected her. "It is the word of God we put upon the wood, Emilia. It is more than the mere act of painting."

"Of course, Makarios. I am so happy to *write* the icon with you."

"You indulge a foolish old man."

"No," she contradicted. "Signor Villani can wait."

"Perhaps he will," he replied, returning to his book. He looked up once again to add, "Be careful not to distract yourself, Emilia. You must be quiet inside when you write an icon."

She nodded in agreement, wondering if he could sense her thoughts of Franco Villani and his villa. Elysian visions of painting in a grand palace room with views of lush gardens came to mind, but she was not about to fail her master. If she wanted to learn the art of iconography, she had best pay close attention.

She offered Makarios a plum from her basket before taking one herself. As she bit into the juicy, sweet flesh, she saw a small, brown beetle nearly hidden against the dark skin of another plum in the basket. The insect crawled slowly across the terrain of fruit and Emila remembered the image of the *scarabaeus,* the Egyptian scarab, from her grandmother's book.

The Egyptian Scarab, the one horned beetle, is both male and female, a creature born of itself. Every morning, according to legend, the beetle pushes the disc of the sun over the horizon, causing it to rise in the sky and create a new day over and over again. In a papyrus text it is written: "The sun-beetle, the winged ruler, standing at heaven's meridian, was beheaded and dismembered."

Like Osiris, the beetle was divided into pieces and then resurrected. The scarab, in its various forms, is known to appear to the alchemist as he enters into a true commitment with the Great Work.

Emilia scooped up the beetle and cupped it in her hands before freeing him out the window. The mystery of her *nonna's* alchemy was everywhere.

In Makarios' icon, the fingers of Christ's right hand were bent like a priest's in blessing. His left hand held a closed book. Depicted more subtly were contrasting sides of Christ's face—a calm side and fierce side. Each detail revealing the hidden language of the iconographer, Makarios told her.

Emilia mixed a shade of blue for the dark mantle that Christ wore over his robe. The dark colors were applied first and then layers and layers of progressively lighter shades were applied with short, quick strokes. Makarios would apply twenty or thirty layers of paint before an area of one color was complete.

When the paint was prepared and poured into a small ceramic jar, Emilia carried it over to Makarios. Studying his progress, she asked, "Is He holding the Bible?"

"The Book of Judgment. *Then I saw a great white throne and Him that sat on it, from whose face the earth and the heaven fled away,*" Makarios said.

"*Whose face the earth and heaven fled away,*" she echoed, thinking over his words.

"Revelation. If you are to paint scripture, Emilia, you must know what you write."

Every time she thought she was coming close to understanding Makarios' work, he reminded her of how much she had yet to learn. "Sometimes I wonder if I'll ever become a painter. Much less an iconographer," she mumbled as she cleaned the brushes.

Catching her words, Makarios laughed. "Good. Very good, Emilia. At last a little doubt. When you live with doubt, so much more comes into view. It is a good thing."

Emilia shook her head in disbelief. She was not sure how her inadequacies could be interpreted as anything other than a detriment to her progress.

On Sunday, as was her usual habit after Mass, Emilia walked with her family from Santa Croce to their house on Via Ghibellina.

"Mama," she said, as her father and brother walked ahead, "the painting Makarios is working on now is not a commission. It is only for *himself*. He is painting in the style of his country—an icon."

"A painting for himself?"

"Yes, to hang in the workshop."

Violante paused before asking, "What does it look like?"

"It's a large panel of Christ. A half-length figure, about five *palmi* by three. He has only just begun, but it's different from what we make here," she said, trying to think how to describe what it was her master was doing. "Not so human. The image is very still. I don't know how to explain it, Mother. Something about it makes you feel as though the panel is almost holy."

"I would like to see this icon when it is finished," Violante decided.

"There's something else," Emilia said as they walked inside the house.

"Well, then?"

Emilia whispered her words to her mother, even though Andrea and her father had disappeared to the cellar to bring up the wine. "A gentleman came to the workshop a few weeks ago. A merchant—a very wealthy merchant I think—who moved here recently from Genoa."

Emilia told Violante about the possible commission in Fiesole. She also confessed her chance meeting with Signor Villani at the piazza, though she omitted to mention that the gentleman had walked her home. Violante listened attentively while salting the roast.

"It would be lovely to learn fresco at his villa," Emilia said. "Do you think we'll go? Do you think Makarios will accept?"

Violante, mixing chopped garlic with thyme and rosemary, replied, "Be careful, Emilia."

"Be careful of what?"

"Men like Signor Villani like to have their way."

"He is nothing to me," Emilia replied, knowing there was something about Franco Villani that had captured her attention.

The following day Makarios allowed Emilia to lay a layer of red paint on Christ's robe and to apply another coat of blue to the mantle. He watched her as she began to work and nodded in approval when she looked up at him.

After Makarios disappeared out the front door—for an early walk she presumed—Emilia worked carefully and cautiously, keeping her hand steady and her brush strokes smooth. As she continued, she grew calmer and less afraid of making an error. Focusing on the movement of her brush over the panel, the chatter in her mind was coaxed into silence. Finally she was aware of nothing but the expanse of blue on Christ's robe. She did not even notice when Makarios returned more than an hour later.

"*Bene,* Emilia," he said, looking over her shoulder. "You've found your rhythm."

"You think so?" she said, pausing to examine the work she had done.

"You have to be still in order to write. When you are quiet, you can look through the window and see to paradise."

Emilia smiled at the idea, wondering to herself what it would mean to glimpse paradise. Perhaps if she were to paint something truly sublime, then she would find this faraway place. Makarios Levantes, gazing at the panel, spoke like a poet and seemed to believe his own words. She was glad, anyway, that he was showing her glimpses of Constantinople.

"Why did you decide to teach me about icons, Makarios?" she asked him. "When I asked you before, you said no one wanted paintings like this anymore."

"I teach you how to write icons because I am old man with nothing better to do, Emilia," he jested. Then, more seriously, he added, "I suppose we all want to pass on what we have learned. Otherwise it dies with us."

Later that night when she was home in bed, she closed her eyes and saw an enormous image of her master's *Pantocrator* before her. He was not the kind, gentle Savior she had imagined when she was a child, the one her mother had taught her to pray to every night. This Christ was strong, mighty, severe, able to see her every small thought and deed, her every selfish desire, and yet His judgment would be entirely just. She fell asleep wondering if her sins already numbered too many.

The layers of paint applied to the icon grew progressively lighter as the days went on that summer. Emilia, mixing the pigments for her master, added tiny amounts of powdered ivory to the red cinnabar that she mixed with egg yolk and vinegar. She loved to watch the swirl of colors, the changing of shades, the artist's alchemy within the mixing cup.

Makarios taught her how to test what she had prepared by applying some of the color to a spare gessoed panel. The paint dried very quickly, requiring her brushwork to be precise and well thought out before it was applied. Emilia was allowed to lay several more undercoats to the red robe and to the flesh tones as well, while the precious lapis lazuli for the brilliant blue mantle was reserved only for the experienced hand of her master.

She tried to keep her mind focused completely on painting and forget about Franco Villani and his countryside villa. She held her concentration as long as there was a paintbrush in her hand, but when less was required of her, when she was cleaning brushes, cooking, or bringing in water or wood, thoughts of Signor Villani would come to mind.

Makarios, despite remaining thoroughly engaged in the creation of his *Pantocrator*, apparently sensed Emilia's wavering attention. As she swept the floor one afternoon, hoping that such menial duties would not be required of her at Signor Villani's villa in Fiesole, she realized Makarios was keeping his eye on her. She felt caught in some kind of act but told herself that her master, though highly perceptive, could not read her thoughts.

"The image of the unseen God," he said, looking to the panel. She was not sure what he meant. "Your icon, Makarios?"

"The letters of St. Paul—to the Colossians," he answered. "We cannot see God; we can only worship God. But Christ tells us in the gospel of John, *Whoever sees me sees the Father*. The icon is not Christ, it's not something to worship. It is a place to find Him—a bridge between Him and us. This is what we are making. What more could we ask of this life?"

Holding the broom in her hands, Emilia listened to her master's words. Makarios Levantes, it seemed, did not reside in the same hungry world as those around her. Others wanted expensive clothes, fine food, gold, and jewels and vied for power along with the Medicis, whereas her master seemed interested in nothing but his art and his faith. She admired him greatly for this, and in the deepest part of her heart Emilia wished to be like him.

At the same time, she knew she would never be like him. There were parts of her that wanted the small, shining trinkets of this life. There were parts of her that wanted to live in a palace, dine in a great hall, and sleep on a bed covered in soft furs. She felt ashamed of her desires, for they seemed greedy in comparison to the ambitions of her teacher.

"Makarios," she began. "I think I am not worthy of your art. I'm guilty of too many sins."

"We have all sinned. Thankfully Christ's love is not only for those who are perfect. This is why we have to approach the icon in a state of humility and prayer. It is more than talent that allows us to write the icon. It is also by the grace of God."

Even so, Emilia was acutely aware of her own human weakness. She cleaned the workshop with zeal that afternoon, as though removing the dirt from the floor and the tables would remove the stain of her sins. She vowed to go to confession the next day and to strive only for the ambition to serve God.

Emilia perceived that there were two paths in this life: the quietly persistent faith of her master, which sought no earthly reward, and the faith of those who were ambitious for the goods of this world and sought glorification of the self. While she wanted to follow the path of her master, it was not easy for her to deny the finer things in life such as a countryside villa in Fiesole. Few would not be tempted by the luxuries Franco Villani could offer, and Emilia was not at all sure if she was one of them.

Venus

Twenty layers of paint were laid on, then thirty or more when Emilia lost count. Shade upon shade, the colors grew gradually lighter as thin washes of egg tempera added tones like transparent veils of colored silk. With each passing day, the image began to take on a luminosity that was not easily explained.

As the divine image came to life, Emilia could almost imagine its light spreading out to touch her, transforming the dark, hidden places in her soul. The panel was her master's work, of course, and yet her hands had helped create it as well. Staring into this image of Christ, she felt as though something within her was shifting. It was as if light were being cast on her imperfect ways, cleansing her like the washing, the *albedo*, that Emilia had read about in *Nonna's* book.

This was the white phase, said to take place after the *nigredo*, the darkening, when the substance contained within the alchemical vessel was washed again and again. The blackness would turn white and then black, white and then black. It took many washings, twenty, thirty, or more, before the whiteness would stick.

As it is carried out with the metals, the prima materia, so it is accomplished within the alchemist's soul; this too must be distilled, cleansed of anything impure before the washing is complete. It may take several days, or several weeks, or even years. Thoughts that have been buried deep, locked away, will be unlocked, and the substance in the vessel will grow dark again.

The alchemist is tempted to give up or fall into a state of discouragement, and yet the darkening is only a sign that the soul is being purged of waste. He must persist through the very end of this phase lest he erringly progress with unknown impurities to the rubedo where the desired results would not be forthcoming.

Like *Nonna's* alchemy, perhaps the process of writing an icon could lead to the philosopher's stone. It was the stone that had the power to bring about change, to turn lead into gold, to transform the novice's very soul. Sensing the peace emanating from Makarios as he worked steadily on the icon day after day, she imagined there was nothing impure within him. His *Pantocrator* glistened with a light that seemed to come from the heavens.

"It's beautiful," she said, studying the panel.

"Yes, the rich silence of the icon," Makarios agreed.

He selected a very fine brush, only a few hairs in thickness, and dipped it into light pink egg tempera. He painted thin, parallel strokes, while in some areas he used a cross-hatching pattern to create spaces of deeper color. Using a straight edge as a guide, his big, bear-like hand was able to create delicate lines.

The next day, near-white highlights were added to create

creases around the eyes, the mouth, and the joints of the fingers. Shades of light brown and black were threaded through the hair, and the dark lines painted over the mantle made it appear like shimmering silk. When Emilia thought the image had reached an unsurpassable perfection, she asked, "Is it finished?"

"Nearly," he said. "Tomorrow, we will write the inscription."

The icon was not just a painting, as he had once explained to her. It was an image of the invisible. Emilia felt privileged that Makarios had conferred to her the secrets of his art. She was not sure what she would do with this knowledge or where the two of them would go from here. Part of her wanted to go on making icons though, as Makarios said, there was no one in Florence to buy them.

It was sheer foolishness to imagine one might work without patrons. Franco Villani, on the other hand, would pay them well. While she still looked forward to the commission, it occurred to Emilia that something very rare had occurred in Makarios' studio, something that would never occur again.

In July, after the icon was completed, Makarios invited his friend, Friar Giuseppe, to the midday meal at the workshop. Tedaldo, who was very curious to see what was painted on the poplar panel he had cut for Makarios, was also invited, along with his stout little wife. Violante, eager to view the work that Emilia had described to her, joined them as well.

Tedaldo and his wife were polite but subdued in their praise, though Friar Giuseppe and Violante were genuinely impressed.

Viewing the piece, Violante said to Emilia, "I see what you mean, *cara*. Makarios works with the angels when he paints."

Tedaldo, rubbing his chin as he studied the panel, looked as though he was trying to make sense of the enormous image of Jesus that had been made for no patron at all. Makarios, for his part, seemed unaffected by Tedaldo's indifference.

After the woodworker left, Emilia criticized his cool reaction to the piece, saying, "I don't know why he bothered coming if he had nothing pleasant to say."

"It is impossible to say what a piece of art should mean to someone else," Makarios told her. "With our *Pantocrator*, it is the friendship that develops between the image and the viewer; sometimes it takes more than a day."

With that said, Makarios sent word to Franco Villani at his townhouse on the Via de' Bardi: the master of the *bottega* was now at his disposal. Surprisingly, the wealthy merchant responded promptly to this announcement, despite having been put off for a number of months.

Several days later Franco Villani sat at their worktable looking over pattern books and mulling over possible motifs for his fresco. Their patron, for some reason or another, did not seem particularly receptive to suggestions offered by the master of the workshop, nor did he bring his priest with him to help in the selection of the subject matter.

"The fresco is not for Santa Croce after all," Franco Villani said after Makarios had offered a number of ideas.

Makarios then spoke of various sylvan settings beneath a trompe l'oeil arcade of arches bearing Franco's family crest. When Franco was not captivated, Makarios then suggested a peacock room, with a decorative motif of vegetation and birds.

"I want something no one in Florence has seen before," Signor Villani replied.

Sighing, Makarios said, "Perhaps you would like something with a mythological motif."

At this suggestion, the patron perked up his ears and began to speak of the ideals of the ancients.

"The stories of the classical gods contain the greatest of Christian virtues and truths, do they not?" Looking at Emilia, Franco said, "Boccaccio wrote of it in his translations. Have you read his *Defense of Poetry*?"

Emilia, embarrassed by his attention, looked the other way, pretending not to hear. Makarios spoke up, surprising her with a suggestion of a depiction of Bacchus.

"You're not serious, Makarios?" Emilia said before Signor Villani could comment. Perhaps Makarios was only joking about painting a subject matter so pagan, though he looked entirely serious.

"Our patron does not wish his great hall to resemble a church, after all," he said.

The black-haired merchant continued to peruse the well-worn pages, making no effort to conceal his glances at Emilia. His boldness unnerved her, and she was not quite sure how to respond. She tried to busy herself with bundling up a loose stack of drawings, pretending not to notice his attention. As he held his gaze for longer and longer periods of time, it was very hard for her to act unawares.

"Perhaps Monna Emilia brings to mind the image of a goddess. Like the birth of Venus," Makarios said pointedly.

Though Franco smiled, acknowledging that he had been observed, he did not appear abashed in any way. Then he said with sudden enthusiasm, "The birth of Venus! The goddess as she is emerging from the water."

"A glorious image," Makarios agreed.

The patron stood and dropped a purse full of coins on the table so that supplies could be purchased. With a nod to Makarios, he departed in good humor.

Emilia was left to wonder how Makarios had agreed to paint such a pagan subject matter. It was, to say the least, a significant departure from the *Pantocrator.*

That night when she slept, she dreamt again of the labyrinth beneath the castle where Hermes had guided her before. She was walking through the serpentine passageways, trying to find her way out, aware that Benozzo lurked somewhere in the distance.

The next moment she was at the sea, watching Venus, the goddess of love, floating in a blue-green mist. Her golden hair glistened with silver droplets of water and her skin was smooth and white as pearls. Emilia, seeing Venus was completely naked, offered a cloak of silk.

"It all falls away after death," Venus told her, refusing the cloak. "Clothes, wealth, titles."

The goddess submerged herself in the waves before reappearing playfully once more. Emilia stood watching, wondering how she herself would look when she died.

Awakening before dawn, Emilia's first thought was that she would soon be traveling beyond the walls of Florence. The idea of living away from home for the first time made her uneasy. She was also worried that her year with Makarios was going by all too quickly. When she could not fall back to sleep again, Emilia crept downstairs into the kitchen. There she nibbled on toasted almonds in near darkness until she heard her father's heavy footsteps. Not wanting to speak to Francesco, she slipped quietly out of the house.

When Emilia arrived at the workshop, Makarios was already working at his desk. He called out a greeting. The *Pantocrator* drew her gaze. In her mind she heard the words from the book of Revelation uttered in her master's voice, telling her, *The dead were judged out of those things that were written in the books, according to their works.*

Emilia felt as though she needed to confess something to Father Bartolo, but she was not sure what it was. She had done nothing wrong, though she had once thought too much about the fresco for Franco Villani rather than accepting the order of things as Makarios saw fit. She vowed to trust him more in the future. Of course, her days with Makarios were numbered if her father had his way; October was only three months away.

A great deal of work had to be done before they were ready to make the trip to Fiesole. The compositional sketches had to be completed. A model would be needed. Lime and sand for the plaster and all the pigments had to be purchased, and the final drawings had to be presented to Franco Villani for his approval before the cartoon could be prepared. These were the practical matters to be considered; she only wished she would not be so easily distracted by her patron's eccentric behavior.

She was a painter, like Giacomo Massarino, she reminded herself. She would focus on her work, just as her friend did in Pisa. Gathering a pen and paper, Emilia composed an overdue letter.

My dear Amico Giacomo,

I pray you will forgive me for the long delay in responding to your last letter. Makarios has kept me thoroughly occupied and we are now getting ready to depart for the villa of Franco Villani in Fiesole.

Signor Villani has commissioned a fresco of Venus for his great hall and Makarios is now preparing the drawings for this lovely, if pagan, subject chosen by our illustrious patron. I dare say it will be a change from our last commission.

We will be away for several months, I suspect. Though
I have not written, I think of you often. I wish I could see
what you are painting in Pisa, though I know the frescoes
will be splendid....

It was easier for her to write again, now that she could speak
of commissions, real patrons and frescoes. People understood
work that served a purpose and was paid for in florins. Emilia
could freely share what she was doing once more, though a part of
her wished she might confide in her friend about the mysteries of
her master's *Pantocrator*. She felt compelled to keep this, as well
as the eccentricities she had observed in her patron, to herself.

Primavera

Franco Villani sent his carriage to convey Emilia and Makarios across the river, through the district of San Giovanni, north through the gates of Florence and up into the hills of Fiesole. The driver veered off the main road and continued along a path lined with towering pines that formed a great canopy of green over the passengers. It was not long before their destination came into view.

Perched upon the summit of the hill was an imposing palace of cream-colored stone with two rows of arched windows flanked by olive green shutters and four elegant towers rising from the steep, pitched roof. To the young apprentice, the owner of such a home seemed more prince than merchant. This impression was reinforced by the impressive coat of arms—two red bands and one white on a field of gold—decorating the cornice. Gleaming in the morning sun, the estate was lush with flowering shrubs and trees and surrounded by expansive gardens and meadows.

A short, dark-haired man whose legs were as thick as tree trunks appeared as Emilia disembarked from the carriage. Erect posture, his chin held high, his manner could have been mistaken for the lord of the manor.

"Welcome to Villa *Primavera*, Springtime," he said with the authority of one who might hold proprietorship in the place. He bowed, adding, "I am Tomasso, at your service."

Standing beside Makarios, Emilia watched the manservant order two stablemen to carry the boxes of supplies, scaffolding, and heavy bags of sand and lime into the house.

"Only the supplies, Neri," he said as one of the men went to lift Emilia's painted chest, her *cassone*. The manservant's haughty tone was not missed by Emilia. "Leave the rest to me."

Tomasso led Emilia and Makarios across the front entrance, an imposing *portico* adorned on either side with two carved columns, and through the massive oak doorway. Once inside, Emilia's eyes followed the walls of carved stone up a series of arches to the high, vaulted ceiling overhead. The morning light fell obliquely through the windows, illuminating decorative carvings and gleaming marble floors. Emilia was still taking in the splendor of the surroundings when Tomasso proceeded to lead them up a flight of stairs. Pushing through an enormous door to the great hall, Tomasso announced their arrival to Franco Villani. Quill in hand, the master of the house sat at his capacious desk beside the intricately carved marble fireplace.

"I trust your short journey was pleasant," he said with a voice that reverberated around the walls of stone as he stepped forward to greet them.

"Yes, yes. What can compare to the beauty of your Tuscan countryside?" Makarios replied. He turned to an exquisite bronze sculpture of David that was perched on a marble pedestal. "Could it be Donatello?"

"Not quite as large as Cosimo's David, but rather nice nonetheless," Franco nodded, evidently pleased that Makarios had noticed.

"This is the room we will fresco?" Makarios inquired.

"Right here," Franco said, indicating the wall adjacent to the mantle.

"A prominent position," her master observed as the servants arrived with the first load of supplies.

"We will discuss the work later—after you've settled in. You must be comfortable if you are to do your best work, after all."

Dismissed from Franco's company, Emilia and Makarios followed the ever-present manservant up the wide, stone staircase to the third floor. Makarios was given a pleasant room with a sweeping view of the orange tiled rooftops of Florence. Emilia, expecting a modest space in the servants' quarters, was stunned when Tomasso showed her to another grand room down the hall. The sumptuous, curtained bed was made up with a red silk quilt and an array of soft pillows. Beside the porcelain washbasin an enormous bouquet of red roses and other seasonal flowers filled the room with their sweetness.

"The best room for you, Madonna," Tomasso said with a queer smile.

She was about to ask why, but he slipped away quickly, closing the door and leaving her unanswered question behind him. Drifting over to the flowers, Emilia inhaled the scent of roses. A gift from her patron? She supposed not as she went to look out the tall, open window. There below was a garden that might have been built by a rich Sultan for a lovely Persian princess.

Enclosed by rows of cypress and aromatic orange and lemon trees was an open pavilion paved with jewel-like mosaic tiles. In the center of the pavilion, a shallow, rectangular pool was lined with tiles of turquoise blue. Floating at one end of the pool, opposite a small fountain, Emilia saw an intimate gazebo, connected to the pavilion by a narrow walkway. Geometric flower beds were repeated on either side of the pavilion, and winding paths led from the garden to unknown, hidden places. Emilia imagined lovers would meet here in secret, midnight trysts.

Drawn to this oasis like a moth to light, Emilia bounded down the stairs. In her rush towards the door, she collided with a timid young maidservant who was polishing a sculpture of St. George slaying the dragon.

"*Scusa!*" Emilia said. "Forgive me. I was careless."

The girl would not look Emilia in the eye, though she mumbled an apology as well before solemnly continuing her cleaning. Emilia was tempted to strike up a conversation with the sad little thing, but she behaved as though she wished to be left alone.

Flinging open the great front door with only a passing thought that she might have used the servants' back door, Emilia Serafini stepped into the sun feeling fortunate. Her stay in Fiesole would be everything she had imagined it would be. She recalled what she had read months ago in the manual: *Achieving the desires of the heart and mastering of the physical world by persistent efforts are the noblest of endeavors.* Maybe it was true that her life could become the story she intended to write. Surrounded by the beauty of Fiesole, it seemed possible that she could be a painter. It seemed possible that she would never have to marry Benozzo Balducci.

Emilia followed the sound of bubbling water and singing birds and made her way to the back of the villa where she crossed the walkway to the gazebo of colored tiles; it sparkled like sapphires on the water. A place of enchantment, it was lush with silver and green foliage and infused with the heady scent of honeysuckle and roses. Sitting on the curved bench inside the gazebo, Emilia took in the serene beauty of the place. It almost slipped her mind that she had come to the villa for the purpose of painting. She felt more like an honored guest as she basked in the intoxicating beauty of the place. Whoever became lady of such a home would live like a queen.

She was curious to know why Franco Villani had not yet married. He was not old, but neither was he a young man. She guessed him well beyond thirty. Perhaps he had been too preoccupied with his work in Genoa to think about finding a wife. For a brief moment Emilia allowed herself to imagine that the handsome merchant might hold her in particular esteem. He had given her the best room, she told herself.

"The young apprentice has found my garden."

Feeling exposed, as though her thoughts had been overheard, Emilia jumped at the sound of his voice. "I'm sorry," she said, standing up. "I saw the garden from my room. It was so lovely—I had to come look."

"No need to apologize," Franco said, guiding her back to her seat and sitting beside her.

When he smiled, she felt more at ease. "You are a generous patron, Signor Villani. Your guests must never want to leave *Primavera*."

"I've had few guests—I've only just purchased the estate," he admitted. "I suppose I've grown accustomed to being alone."

"But to have such a place—you must want to share it."

"Yes," he said, reaching for her hand. "That's why I'm so glad you've come to paint."

The touch of his skin, warm and dark against hers, took her by surprise, though it was not unwelcome. She thought perhaps he was merely lonely, seeking some form of human companionship in this vast estate where he lived without a wife or children.

Abruptly, he stood, motioning her to follow him. He led her across the pleasure garden to a serpentine path that wound between two thick rows of cypress trees and eventually another garden came into view. Looking around, Emilia saw it took the form of an eight-pointed star, with each section planted a different color of the spectrum. The sound of falling water from a three-tiered cascading fountain surrounded her and the scents of lavender, rose, and mint wafted through the air.

"It's wonderful." Inhaling the sweet aromas, she darted from point to point along with the butterflies that flitted through the air.

He laughed, apparently gratified by her enthusiasm. Still standing at the entrance, Franco said, "You are a beautiful addition to my garden, Monna Emilia."

She felt sure he was admiring her, though it was not just her aspiring talent that aroused his interest. He was admiring her in the way a man admires a woman, the way he had when he walked her home from the piazza. She had no idea how to respond to this attention. She was a guest in his home, an apprentice who had come to serve.

"I confess I am overwhelmed by your kindness, Signor Villani," Emilia said, pretending his thoughtfulness was merely that of a polite host.

"It pleases me to have you here."

Emilia sensed the need for caution and prudence, though the more reckless side of her was not displeased by his flirtation. Before she could deliberate Signor Villani's feelings for her any further, he was walking ahead at a brisk pace. He left her to make her way alone down the winding path of cypress. Perhaps she was mistaken.

To welcome his guests, Signor Villani served dinner in the meadow under a row of arching lindens. The table was set with blue linen, silver dishes, and an enormous bouquet of plump, pink roses. Platters of smoked boar with apples, hare in wine sauce, and pasta with butter, cheese, and spices were served along with generous quantities of bread and chilled wines. Overwhelmed by these lavish indulgences, Emilia could not quite believe her good fortune.

The two men spoke of politics and art, the brilliance of Brunelleschi's magnificent cathedral dome, the second pair of baptistery doors which were currently under production by Ghiberti, and the architect Michelozzo's plan for Pitti Palace. Franco seemed to know everything that was happening in Florence and the details of every artist's commission, whether his reputation great or small. Her patron then remarked upon the great works being carried out at St. Marco's and on Cosimo de' Medici's fondness for the Dominicans. From this conversation it was easy to gather the impression that Franco himself was a member of Cosimo's inner circle.

"You have come to know your city's ruler," Makarios remarked.

Franco shrugged. "He is a most munificent man. Everyone in Florence seeks an audience with him, I suppose."

"You have been to his palace, then?" Emilia asked, quite impressed.

As Franco helped himself to some more of the soft, ripe cheese, he replied, as though without a care, "I am still quite new to Florence. Cosimo de' Medici has little time for a mere Genoese merchant, I can assure you."

She wondered if she detected a note of bitterness in his response, despite his attempt at lightheartedness.

"His interests are quite broad, I should think. He is said to be generous with his time," Makarios commented.

"Indeed. He is a thorough humanist," Franco agreed. "Cosimo's fascinations span the world and the centuries. His monks are off searching for the forgotten writings of the ancients. The only thing he cannot be bothered with is the ordinary. Indeed, why should he bother with the ordinary when he can be surrounded by the sublime?"

Emilia wondered if there was something about Florence's great leader that vexed her host. Franco was jealous, perhaps, of Cosimo's far greater wealth and lordship over the city, but surely Franco should be satisfied with all he had acquired. She turned her gaze from Franco to Makarios, who was watching his patron closely as well.

"Our days are, in fact, filled with the ordinary, Signor Villani," Makarios observed. "Most of our time is spent on the very routine tasks of life. There is honor in the work and routine of daily existence."

"You need not remind me," Franco was quick to say. "I have spent most of my life working like a fiend. I know well enough the routines of existence. But a man tires of them."

Emilia, tasting the sweet figs steeped in wine with cream, did not ponder at great length over Franco's words. She was content to sit at the long table in the meadow, surrounded by beauty. In the back of her mind, she could not understand why a man of such means would feel dissatisfied. If she lived in a place like this, Benozzo Balducci could never find her.

Filippa

I f Emilia was under the illusion that she had been invited to Primavera as a guest, Makarios was quick to remind her otherwise. The day after her arrival in Fiesole, the work of the *buon fresco*, the painting on fresh plaster, began. Two of the stablemen helped carry and mix the heavy bags of river sand and powdered lime in large buckets according to Makarios' most specific instructions. To this mixture, small quantities of water were beaten in to achieve the proper, butter-like consistency, so that the mortar would not form cracks on the walls. Wearing gloves to protect her hands from the burning lime, Emilia held a square board in one hand and in the other, a trowel to apply the plaster.

The art of fresco was messy work and she was dressed accordingly. Her hair was covered by a plain, white wimple and she had a stained apron over her old, brown work dress—Franco Villani would not look twice at her now, she thought. She only hoped her patron would not catch sight of her dressed like a common worker, splashed with plaster.

Emilia and Makarios spent hours laying down the *arriccio*,

the rough coat layer that would provide the barrier between the wall and the painting. Though the labor was tiring, Emilia was concerned not so much for herself but for Makarios. He did not complain, but Emilia could tell that the kneeling and long stretches of time on his feet took a toll on Makarios. She made an effort to cover as much surface with her trowel as she could in order to lessen the old man's burden.

When she was standing on the scaffold, preparing the highest part of the wall, Emilia heard Franco's voice.

"You waste no time, Levantes," he said.

Emilia turned to see her patron. He was dressed magnificently in a plum-colored tunic, elaborately embroidered in silver with stars and compasses at the neck and hem, a large, puffed hat on his head. Emerging from a leather scabbard at his side was the elegant handle of a gentleman's dagger. His princely clothing made Emilia feel all the more ridiculous in her worn work clothes.

Makarios, who had been filling in an area near the bottom of the wall, rose slowly to his feet to greet his patron genially. "There won't be much to see for a while. In a few more days we will start to paint."

"Take all the time you need," Franco said, clearly enjoying the sight of Emilia on the scaffold. "It is unusual to see a young lady carrying out such work."

"Perhaps it is unusual, Messer, but given the opportunity, women prove quite capable," she said, before realizing she had spoken out of turn.

Franco smiled up at her before turning to Makarios. "I must leave *Primavera* for a time. I have business in Prato, but I hope to return before long."

Emilia averted her gaze to hide her disappointment. Signor

Villani was leaving. He did not know when he would be back. It had been foolish of her to think that her presence at *Primavera* mattered to a man like him.

"Rest assured we will work diligently during your absence."

"I am in no hurry for you to finish," Franco assured him. "Take as long as you need."

When Emilia caught Franco looking up at her again, she grasped that this remark was meant for her. She was heartened by his words, but still the villa would seem large and empty without him. Emilia watched as the tall, colorful figure disappeared down the hall and the sound of Franco's red leather shoes on the tile floor receded into the distance.

The following day, when Makarios was snapping lines of chalk-coated string against the wall to mark his guidelines for the fresco, Emilia noticed he was scratching his hands. His skin was an angry shade of red, obviously irritated by the lime powder.

"You made sure I wore my gloves, Makarios, but you didn't protect your own hands."

"It's just a slight burn, Emilia."

"I have some of my mother's ointment. Let me get it for you," she offered.

Hurrying up the backstairs to her room, Emilia swung open the door to find the young servant who had been polishing the statue on the day of their arrival.

The wide-eyed maidservant jumped, dropping Emilia's silk handkerchief to the floor. Clearly the girl had been looking through Emilia's things.

"*Spiacente, spiacente,*" the terrified girl cried over and over.

"I'm sorry. I only meant to clean. I was admiring the painting on the chest, such lovely flowers and birds."

Emilia was not convinced. "You were not just admiring my *cassone*. But I haven't much worth stealing in there anyway. I should think Signor Villani pays you well enough that you don't have to steal from his guests," she said harshly.

"Yes, he does. Of course he does."

"Then why would you do such a thing? Tell me your name."

"Filippa."

"You must know Signor Villani would send you away in a moment if he discovered you stealing, Filippa."

Near tears, the girl said, "If you tell him you discovered me, Signor Villani will throw me out, no doubt."

Emilia returned her silk handkerchief to the chest, along with *Nonna's* book and a hair ornament, saying, "I will keep silent about this, Filippa. You must promise me never to do this again."

Emilia was taken aback that such a timid girl would take to thieving. Perhaps desperation had driven her. There did not seem to be anything cunning or malicious about the frightened little thing.

Emilia retrieved the jar of rich white calendula cream as Filippa fled down the hall. Taking care to lock her little chest before leaving her room this time, Emilia could not help but wonder what troubles had driven Filippa to try to steal from her master's guests.

In Franco's absence, *Primavera* grew still, frozen in time, as if under some enchantment. Makarios, completely absorbed in the work, showed Emilia how to apply the *intonaca*, the second and finer layer of plaster to the wall. They laid down the fresh mortar in the morning so that the surface would remain wet throughout the day, and they applied just the amount they could paint in a single afternoon.

Only a *giornata,* Makarios told her as she smoothed down the plaster with the trowel. No more, no less. Little areas would be added each day until eventually the whole wall was covered. After the coat layer was set, Emilia learned to move the square float in a circular motion to make the surface plane and equal. After that was done, she would once again smooth the surface with a trowel. Then she would hold up the cartoon while Makarios pounded the lines of the figures onto the fresh plaster with an ivory stick. As soon as he signaled for her to take away the cartoon, Makarios had to work very quickly, so that the paint was applied before the plaster dried.

It was a very different method from the painstaking, contemplative way he painted panels in his workshop. Emilia was surprised to see that her master could render an image so quickly on plaster. He seemed completely at ease with the art of fresco, humming in his low, quiet voice as his brush flew across the plastered wall.

When he had completed the lovely face of Venus, which was set against a patch of blue sky, Makarios set down his brush. "I must walk. *Domani,* tomorrow, we paint again."

Her master disappeared into the surrounding hillside and Emilia cleaned up behind him, gathering the buckets, pigments, and brushes. When this was done, she made her way to the gazebo with paper and charcoal, thinking she would make a few quick sketches. Violante would enjoy seeing pictures of Signor Villani's villa and garden.

Seated on the bench she had shared with Franco on the day of her arrival, Emilia imagined herself as the lady of the house. She was presiding over a group of gently bred guests while musicians played in the background. It was mere fantasy, of course, but there was no harm in dreaming. Was it a sin to enjoy the blessings of this world? Of course, earthly riches did not compare to the treasures awaiting the righteous in heaven; but there were men of great wealth who did worthy deeds and gave generously to those in need. It was the largesse of men like Cosimo de' Medici that allowed the artists to create works fit to glorify God in their city.

Later that evening, she sank back into plump, soft pillows on her curtained bed and read the words of Hermes Trismegistus, the ancient Egyptian sage, and passages concerning the phases of alchemy while the sweet scent of honeysuckle floated up through her open window.

> *As I have said, the purification, the albedo, cannot proceed until after one has completed the nigredo and emerged from utter darkness, when the raven has been achieved.*

> *Truly, if one does not go there during life, one must enter upon death. The choice is to continue on the road of the familiar, with its appearing and disappearing fortunes, or instead to embark upon the path of Egypt. The path of the eternal.*

> *The alchemist, choosing the latter, willingly releases his worldly existence. For the path of the eternal is the path of the inner world, where the external world has no value. Coming to reside in the real world of spirit, he begins his journey along the mystical path where he will experience the inexplicable wonders of his soul.*

Emilia closed the manual and replaced it in the painted chest, wondering if the text was telling her she must forsake, like a nun, all the physical pleasures of this world in order to secure her treasure in heaven. She was the daughter of a tavern owner, not wealthy by any means, but she had been raised with modest comforts.

Through the window, she saw the rich lands of Tuscany and considered the extravagant wealth of the Bardi, Pitti, Strozzi, Medici, as well as that of Franco Villani. Perhaps it was true that their imposing villas would turn to dust one day. Yet she did not believe the rich were condemned to the blackness of hell merely for their love for finery and the pleasures of this world.

This book of her *nonna's* was very old; it was not of Emilia's time. The manual contained strange passages, translations of writings that were said to come from the first century. If it held secrets of antiquity, that was well and good, but this figure looking out at her from the page, this Hermes Trismegistus with his birdlike, beaked head appeared the creation of someone's imagination. He was not real now, if he ever was, and he could not judge the people of her time.

Hermes Trismegistus could not know what it was to be a fifteen-year-old woman in Florence in the year 1460. Yet Emilia's mother had instructed her to refer to the manual in times of trouble and to hold the book close to her always. The text had been passed down from Santina through the generations, for over one hundred years.

She recalled the friar, *Nonna's* friend, who had traveled throughout Italy and finally to Spain in an attempt to find someone to translate the original text. He was said to have devoted his life to this book. Surely, Friar Calandrino could never have imagined that his cherished text would end up in the hands of a young woman in Florence, a painter's apprentice.

Emilia wondered if the friar would be amused or dismayed to know she was the new keeper of his book. Though she might not understand or accept everything written within the pages, she nonetheless treasured this ancient text.

With the manual at her side, she drifted toward sleep, still thinking of the friar and her great-great-great grandmother, who was said to have been a midwife, a maker of brews and medicinals. Emilia could almost see her little, gray-haired *nonna. Keep it close to you, Emilia. The manual is not for everyone to read. One cannot cast pearls before swine.*

Nearly asleep, Emilia wondered if anyone had ever made any gold and if the recipes were real. If they were real, then there should be gold somewhere. Piles and piles of gold. If alchemy was real, perhaps she could marry Franco Villani instead of Benozzo Balducci.

Tomasso

Though the fresco was little more than a solitary figure surrounded by an expanse of white wall, Emilia could see that the Venus would be extraordinary. She found it surprising that Makarios could move so easily from the solemn painting of Christ, the *Pantocrator*, to the pagan, though splendid depiction of a beautiful goddess wearing little but her long, flowing hair. If she had expected disdain on the part of Makarios for his non-Christian theme, Emilia was mistaken; he painted his Venus with the reverence she thought he might have reserved for the Blessed Virgin. There was a devotion to the piece that Emilia had not expected.

When she questioned his fondness for his subject matter, Makarios winked, saying, "I think our Venus will be a fine Christian when we are through with her."

"What do you mean?" Emilia asked, presenting him with a shade of cool, blue-green for the waters of the sea.

"Venus is born of heaven. She is a creature of great nobility—

she is divine love and charity," Makarios said. "She is dignity and generosity. Truth and splendor. An exquisite beauty, Emilia. These are honored and respected qualities."

She was amused to hear Makarios speaking like a true Florentine, enamored by the ancients. His version of Venus would not only be a noble soul, but a thoroughly Christianized deity. In her splendor upon the sea, Venus would embody the characteristics every Florentine patrician aspired to possess.

She tried to reconcile in her mind the pagan goddess with the regal Virgins of Orcagna and Lorenzetti. Perhaps her master was correct in suggesting that the two were not entirely unrelated. They could both inspire one to the path of the eternal, the path of Egypt she read about in *Nonna's* book.

Regardless of her opinion, Venus would preside over Franco Villani's lavish banquets, looking out knowingly at tables bountifully laid with rich delicacies and ever-flowing wine as servants hurried to and from the kitchen. The goddess would be the newly crowned queen in this home of exquisite luxuries.

Emilia smiled, imagining herself amongst the fine ladies in the great hall. As though caught by her grandmother, words from the text popped into her mind. *Eventually, everything held in one's hand turns to dust.* Not for some time, Emilia countered. Not for many, many years from now.

"Can one possess every luxury, Makarios," she asked, turning to her master, "and still be a true Christian?"

Eyes fixed upon the patch of blue he was painting around the curved hip of Venus, Makarios replied, "I do not know. I am fortunate, I suppose, for God has never tested me in this way. He was wise, no doubt, to keep me from such temptation. Not many are like your St. Francis, willing to give up everything." He looked out from his work for a moment. "Maybe it is easier for our poor souls to find heaven before we are encumbered by the weight of too much gold."

Emilia reasoned for herself that the quality of a rich man's soul depended upon how he used his wealth. He could give graciously, in a manner benefiting his city, to the poor, the sick, the orphans, as the merchant-prince Francesco Datini had done. Or he could bring inspired works of art to the citizens of Florence and promote the artists, such as those who had benefited from the largesse of Cosimo Medici.

Emilia's father believed the lord of their city was a good man, a keeper of peace and stability. No doubt Cosimo was a source of inspiration to many, including her patron, Franco Villani.

Late in the evening, not long after she had fallen asleep, Emilia awoke to strange sounds in the night—a man's surly voice, like one of the drunks at her father's tavern. Emilia feared an intruder at first. Or could it be one of the servants? Barely awake, she opened her bedroom door, straining to hear. She thought she heard Tomasso's voice. There was a woman's voice, barely audible, as well. Emilia crept down the dark hall, moving closer to the voices. She started down the stairs, stopped halfway to listen.

"*Idiota.* You make a disaster of everything," the man slurred.

Emilia was sure it was Tomasso, having drunk too much of the master's wine. Footsteps pounded across the floor below, in the direction of the staircase. Afraid of being discovered, Emilia flattened her back against the cold stone wall.

"It's not so easy as you think. I tried my best. Please, don't be angry with me," the woman begged. She was clearly upset and trying to respond to the man's angry rebukes. Emilia wished it was not Filippa, but she believed it was. The woman was pleading, very much afraid of something or someone.

Tomasso's angry voice trailed off in another direction. The front door banged shut, silencing the voices. Poor Filippa, Emilia thought, returning to her room. The girl seemed to have a way of inviting trouble of one kind or another.

When Emilia awoke the next morning, she recalled the disturbing conversation she had overheard in the night. After washing and dressing, she made her way towards the kitchen and noticed, from the corner of her eye, a figure in the loggia. Turning to look, she saw it was Tomasso, sprawled out in the master's wide, upholstered chair, which looked out to the reflecting pool and the sculpture garden below. She thought it presumptuous of the manservant to assume this favored place during Signor Villani's absence. However, the matter was none of her business and she passed on without a word.

Sitting down to her morning bread at the kitchen table, Emilia ventured to ask the cook if she had noticed anything out of the ordinary.

"I make the meals, Emilia. Whatever else goes on around here is none of my business," Bettina, the round, rosy-cheeked woman replied cheerfully as she put a pot of water over the fire. She lowered her voice, adding, "Just between you and me, I think people ought to stay in their own bedrooms at night. Nothing good can come of the servants getting too cozy with one another. The master won't have it."

"So you think it was a lover's spat, then?"

"I didn't say that," Bettina said, placing a generous plate of sausage cut in thick rounds before Emilia. "I told you, I don't know anything except what goes on in this kitchen."

Emilia did not accept the explanation that it was a lover's

quarrel as the cook suggested. She went about her work that day keeping her eyes and ears open for signs of the servant girl. Filippa, the brunt of Tomasso's anger, remained unseen.

Meanwhile, Makarios' Venus was emerging majestically from the sea and floating on a cushion of silvery blue foam. Her perfect, alabaster skin glistened like pearls in the sun and her golden hair, flecked with light, swept around her elegant form, covering her to a degree of appropriate modesty. On her head she wore a jeweled crown, the indisputable mark of royal heritage.

Makarios painted on steadily, gradually bringing the white wall to life, though Emilia sensed his fatigue toward the end of the day.

When he finally set his brushes aside and moved back to view the day's work, she asked him, "Did you hear the servants arguing last night?"

He shook his head. "What arguing?"

She spoke quietly, lest their conversation echo through the house. "It was Tomasso. And Filippa. I don't know what it was about. Filippa was sorry about something she'd done. Tomasso wasn't pleased with her, not at all."

Makarios nodded, thinking over the scene she had described to him. "There are unsettled matters here at *Primavera*. Filippa is an unhappy girl, I have noticed. I'm not at all sure she's being treated fairly."

Emilia recalled the day she found Filippa searching through her belongings; she had assumed the girl was stealing on her own behalf. The thought now occurred to Emilia that Tomasso might have, for some unknown reason, coerced the girl to action.

"Last week I caught her trying to steal from me. She was in my room, looking through my belongings," she whispered. "I wonder—do you think it's possible that Tomasso had something to do with it?"

"I don't know," he replied. "Filippa doesn't strike me as a thief, though."

"I thought as much the first day I saw her. When I caught her in my room she was so ashamed," Emilia said. "I don't want to tell Signor Villani, I'm afraid he'd judge her harshly. I'm not sure he'd believe Tomasso is capable of any wrongdoing."

"Yes, that is the risk, Emilia. Perhaps it is best in this case to say nothing. We don't wish to cause the girl more trouble."

Emilia felt uneasy about the matter as she washed out the brushes. Tomasso was altogether too sure of himself, and she feared he would continue to harass Filippa while Franco was away. She began to feel more and more certain that Tomasso was to blame, though she could do nothing to prove it.

Somehow, she needed to find out exactly what Tomasso had done while at the same time protect Filippa. If Signor Villani knew what was going on under his own roof, he would never allow it. He might even thank Emilia for her keen observation.

The maidservant was down on her knees in the vegetable garden when Emilia caught sight of her through the kitchen window the following morning. Setting aside her sugared roll, Emilia hurried outside to speak to the girl, who appeared flustered by the mere sight of Emilia.

"Are you all right, Filippa?"

Without looking up from the potatoes she was pulling, the maid stammered nervously, "*Si, si.* I'm well, thank you."

Emilia knelt down beside Filippa. "Don't be afraid. I heard Tomasso the other night. I heard your voice too, Filippa."

"I'm very sorry you were awakened," Filippa said, her face drained of color.

"I suspect Tomasso has been unfair to you," Emilia said, trying to encourage her.

"Please, if you wish to help me, don't mention what you heard."

"But Signor Villani should know how you're being treated."

"The master and Tomasso—they have an understanding."

Emilia nodded, well aware of the unmerited confidence Franco placed in his manservant. "I must tell you, Filippa, I have a suspicion that Tomasso was behind what I found you doing in my room." She looked deeply into Filippa's eyes, trying to see the truth hidden there.

Filippa would not return Emilia's gaze. Instead the girl looked to the ground and whispered, "I'm sorry, but it was my own fault. You can blame no one but me."

Emilia gave Filippa's hand a quick squeeze before standing up. The girl's reluctance to speak only reinforced Emilia's opinion that Filippa had not been acting of her own accord when she was thieving. She was not sure what Tomasso was holding over the maidservant's head, but somehow he was forcing her to do his bidding.

The following week Emilia tried to steer clear of Tomasso, but it was impossible to avoid him completely. She was returning to her bedroom one evening when the manservant came swaggering down the hall as though he were the Duke of Milan. He greeted Emilia with a show of gladness.

"*Buena sera,*" she replied curtly. The thought crossed Emilia's mind to tell him then and there that she knew exactly what he was about. But she respected Filippa's request for silence and had no wish to make matters worse for the girl.

"The fresco is coming along nicely. The master will be pleased."

"You, more than anyone, would know what would or would not please Signor Villani," she said coolly.

Apparently puzzled by her response, Tomasso finally replied, "It is my job to serve the master and to provide for your comfort as well, Madonna."

"I'm only an apprentice, Tomasso. You speak as though I'm an invited guest."

He nodded and smiled as though in complicity. "If that's the way you choose to look at it, Madonna. But Signor Villani has taken great care to ensure your comfort in particular."

Emilia decided he was trying to flatter her. She had made him uneasy and given him cause to think she did not trust him completely. Emilia reasoned that this was for the best; Tomasso should not be allowed to think his behavior during Franco's absence went unnoticed. Back in her room, she wrote to Giacomo and confided in him.

...Of course the fresco is my main concern, and Makarios' work is beyond compare. It is an unfortunate matter, this disharmony among the servants. Primavera is a lovely villa with the most enchanting gardens. Truly, it is like living in paradise. It would surely distress Signor Villani to know of the events I have witnessed, and I am loath to tell him of the cruel disloyalty I have discovered.

Makarios seems inclined to say nothing. He fears the girl will suffer if Franco comes to learn what has passed. But I wonder if I should not tell him the truth about Tomasso...

Sharing her thoughts with her friend afforded Emilia a measure of comfort. Though he was far off in Pisa, Giacomo provided a sympathetic, listening ear. She could tell him almost anything, except her deepest thoughts of Franco Villani. The flirtation between her and her patron was something she was not prepared to admit to anyone.

Phaedo

Catching sight of glorious Venus in the rosy light of dawn, the West Wind nearly lost his breath. Taking hold of himself, he puffed softly, sending the goddess across gentle waves to the island of Cythera. At the shore of the island, the three Graces stood by, ready to welcome her and dress her in a garment of the finest silk woven with diamonds.

When Makarios began to paint the famed myth, Emilia had a vague idea of how the finished fresco would look. As she took in the nearly completed scene that was painted on Franco Villani's wall a month later, she saw how small her imagination had been.

"I didn't know it would be so beautiful," she admitted.

"This is our job—to make beautiful paintings. How can we do less?"

With a small brush, Makarios was adding details over the dried fresco—painting in *secco*. In another day or two he would be finished.

"Maybe you are glad for Signor Villani's commission after all," she said.

"I must work, like everyone else," he said. "I wanted you to have a chance to write an icon first."

"We could have done that afterwards."

"Perhaps, Emilia. But after working here, maybe work at our *bottega* might seem small to you."

She found it hard to believe that Makarios had delayed Franco Villani's commission for her sake. "Do you think I take my craft so lightly?"

"No, it's not that. It is easy to develop a taste for certain things. Sometimes we find ourselves going in directions we did not plan."

"My plan is to be a painter, Makarios," she insisted. If she would be kept from painting, this would be her father's doing. After all, there could be no temptation by luxuries which had not been offered. "As you know, I am expected to marry soon."

He stood in quiet sympathy for a moment before saying, "Your father believes he is doing what is best for you, Emilia. Only God knows your destiny. This is greater than any plan someone else can make for you."

"Do you think it's my destiny to be a painter?"

"This is for you to discover, no?" he smiled. "Who knows? Maybe October will come and your father will think it is not so bad that Makarios is still teaching you."

For the first time, Emilia realized that Makarios did not want her to leave the workshop any more than she wanted to leave him. When she was alone in the quiet of her bedroom that night, she wondered why Makarios had said, *It is easy to develop a taste for certain things.* It was almost as though he could read her thoughts about Franco, as though he knew she was tempted by their patron's way of life. Of course she had no choice in the matter, for Franco would never consider her a suitable match.

Later that day, she picked up *Nonna's* book and read a curious passage from Plato's *Phaedo*. The ancient philosopher spoke of the fate of the soul after death and the danger of paying too much attention to the physical being while alive. Such a soul, heavily intertwined with the body, grows burdened by its weight after death, it was said. Continually drawn back to the world of the visible, it wanders through the graves, unable to return to life, unable to reach the land of eternal bliss.

Emilia read, as well, of what the author called the threefold division, the trinity of man, the human soul, and Spirit.

> *The soul is the means through which the body of man connects to Spirit. The soul is free to abide by the wishes of the flesh, or it may relinquish the body and seek communion with the Spirit. One is free to choose. And yet, after death, our clothing, our flesh falls away. As the outer coverings vanish, the true form is revealed. Nothing remains hidden.*

It was well to read of the soul, Emilia thought, setting the book aside. But she was a young woman, not yet close to death. It would be a long time before her deeds were judged. There would be ample opportunity to seek communion with Spirit.

The following day Emilia discovered that Franco was returned home. As though he had never departed, the master of *Primavera* was lounging on the sun-drenched loggia, his long legs outstretched in the same chair Tomasso had claimed days earlier.

"You're home," she said in surprise.

"Are you disappointed?" He smiled at her but did not move from the chair.

"Of course not, Signor Villani," she said. "Have you seen the fresco?"

He motioned for her to approach him. She complied and he

reached for her hand and held it very tenderly. "Your fresco has exceeded even my greatest expectations. It is a painting of supreme beauty."

"It is the work of Makarios," Emilia said, looking toward the reflecting pool to avoid the weight of his gaze.

"And yours as well."

"You mock me."

"I only mean to tell you how delighted I am," he said, finally releasing her hand. "I want the world to see your Venus."

"Then the world is obliged to visit your great hall."

"I believe you are right, Emilia. There must be a celebration for Venus. A feast in her honor. You will come, won't you?"

She was not sure if he was serious. A bemused smile remained on his lips, making it difficult for Emilia to divine his true intent, as was often the case with Franco Villani. She suspected his attention toward her was more of his meaningless flirtation. In the end, she merely smiled and thanked him before continuing on her way to the kitchen.

She had barely sat down at the table when the cook surprised her with news regarding Filippa.

"Gone. Right after she finished hanging out the laundry," Bettina whispered to Emilia.

"Why?"

"Thrown out. Just like that," she said, snapping her fingers. "Tomasso sent her packing right after he had a talk with the master. She'll have gone home to her mother's, of course. It's a big family she comes from. A lot of mouths to feed. It's a shame, really. She's a sweet thing, despite the trouble she had with Tomasso."

"Whatever Tomasso told Signor Villani, it must have been lies," Emilia said. "Filippa did nothing wrong."

"I don't know if she did, and I don't know if she didn't. It's none of my business. I don't concern myself with gossip," Bettina said, slicing a bird hot from the oven, aromatic with spices. "She got on the wrong side of Tomasso, that's for sure. I hope she'll find work somewhere."

Bettina turned her attention to Makarios as he entered the room. "I've got a nice, roasted guinea hen for you today, Makarios," she said, setting a heaping plate before him. "*Mangiate bene.* Eat well."

"Indeed I will."

As she ate beside Makarios, it was not easy for Emilia to dismiss the unfortunate fate of Filippa. There appeared to be little she could do to remedy the situation now that the girl had left. Emilia's stay at Primavera was nearly over, and it would be difficult to delicately broach the subject of Filippa's treatment with her host.

That afternoon, as Makarios completed his finishing touches on the fresco, Emilia felt unsettled, perhaps as much about leaving the villa as the matter of Filippa. When she brought her master another jar of paint, Emilia brought up the subject of the servant girl.

"She was sent away this morning. It doesn't seem fair," she told him.

"A cruel act apparently, but I suppose we may never know the truth."

"Perhaps you should speak to Signor Villani. He should at least know how Tomasso treated her."

Makarios was not convinced. "We must be cautious, Emilia. Signor Villani manages his household as he sees fit. He is not likely to appreciate our interference."

She said nothing as she mixed powdered bone with egg to make the white paint her master needed for the sparkle he would add to the sea. Though she remained silent, Emilia did not agree to remove herself from Franco Villani's affairs. She was sure that if her patron knew the truth of his manservant's behavior, he would see that Filippa had been treated unjustly. When the opportunity arose, Emilia resolved that she would tell Franco Villani exactly what she thought of the wildly arrogant Tomasso.

Although Emilia had every intention of speaking to Franco Villani on behalf of the mistreated maidservant, her patron was nowhere to be seen the following day.

"Our business is finished here," Makarios told Tomasso when their brushes, tools, paints, and buckets were gathered up and their personal belongings packed.

The manservant brought forth a bulging velvet sack of coins from his purse. "I trust the amount is correct."

Makarios accepted the coins without bothering to count. "Please thank Franco Villani for his hospitality. His cook has been especially kind." Then he added, "I hope all who come to *Primavera* will enjoy the Venus for years to come."

"Of course. Your work will forever remain one of our villa's great treasures."

Excusing himself to summon the stable boys, Tomasso walked away, his head held as high as a nobleman. Emilia watched the short, too well-dressed servant overseeing the loading of Franco's carriage and grew more and more indignant over what he had managed to conceal. Reasoning that she might never see Tomasso again, she seized upon the opportunity to confront him.

Nervous but determined to speak, Emilia marched up beside Tomasso. "I know why Filippa was sent away."

As though nonplussed by her comment, the man slowly replied, "You mean you are aware of the girl's lack of skill, honesty, and loyalty to her master?"

"If she was dishonest, it was because you forced her to do what she knew was wrong. You might hide it from Signor Villani, but you cannot hide it from me," Emilia said firmly, despite the uneasiness she felt.

Tomasso maintained an expression of utter bewilderment. "I can't imagine what would make you say such a thing to me, Monna Emilia. Filippa is, unfortunately, a lazy little liar. That is why she is no longer with us," he said calmly. "I only hope the paint fumes have not made you ill. Perhaps the work has been too much for you."

Emilia shook her head in frustration. "There is nothing at all the matter with me, Tomasso. I know you treated the girl unjustly. The matter is on your conscience," she said and walked away from him.

Tomasso stood firmly on the front steps as she followed Makarios into the carriage. He was a despicable little man, but Franco Villani was too preoccupied with matters of commerce and his costly imports from the Orient to know what was going on in his own home.

Venus would be left to preside over the troubles at *Primavera*. Emilia had lived in grandeur for a short time, and she had helped her master create a most memorable fresco. The commission had earned Makarios sufficient money to carry him through many months to come, and it had afforded her the opportunity to learn what she wanted to learn. What more could she ask for?

She would not admit it to herself, much less to her master, but there was something else she had hoped to take home from *Primavera*. The romance she dreamed of, the unlikely love affair that might have saved her from Benozzo, had not been. As the carriage returned her to the city, she began to imagine there must be a way to foil her father's attempts to marry her off, other than retreating to a nunnery. She needed a miracle of some sort, because October was less than two months away.

The Banquet

Once she had returned to the *bottega* south of the river, Emilia drifted into daydreams of Franco Villani and the pleasure garden at Primavera. The arrival of a young messenger at the door brought her back to her everyday life as an apprentice in Florence. When her name was announced, she held the fleeting hope that her patron had sent a note of thanks, or perhaps even an invitation. Signor Villani had said there would be a celebration—a celebration in honor of their fresco. As soon as Emilia saw the strong, precise script on the letter, she knew it was not from Franco Villani, but from her friend in Pisa. At least Giacomo had not forgotten her, she thought, tearing open the wax seal.

Cara Emilia,

I am thoroughly intrigued with the depiction of the goddess Venus that you have described. This fresco promises to be a work of stunning brilliance, and I admit feeling envious of your commission. While I have been blessed with sufficient work, it is another matter to find a private patron such as Signor Villani who will allow a painter such excellent freedoms.

I am sorry the disloyalty of your patron's manservant distresses you, dear Emilia. While the thought of upsetting your patron must no doubt torment your good heart, I agree that matters of his own household should not be withheld from him.

Here in Pisa, we are nearly finished with our frescoes of St. Thomas. I look forward to returning home. I miss my family and friends greatly. Perhaps this letter will find you back at the workshop, where I send my warmest regards to Levantes.

Ever yours,
Giacomo

Emilia tucked the letter into the pocket of her apron. She glanced over at Makarios, who was already engrossed in a new project—a Madonna, sculpted of wood, which would be a gift to the sisters of Santa Trinità. Working without pay once again, he hummed quietly to himself.

Back at Primavera her master had advised her to say nothing to Signor Villani about her suspicions regarding Tomasso. Now that Giacomo agreed with her, she wished she had gone ahead and confessed her observations. Regardless, Signor Villani would, she hoped, learn the truth about his manservant in time. She was looking out the window, remembering the comfort of her opulent bedroom at the villa and the mystery of Franco Villani, when Makarios suggested she pick up a paintbrush.

"Start a panel, why don't you?" he suggested. "You could write your first icon."

He presented her with the manual he had carried with him from Constantinople. The weighty book listed the rules for painting, the positions of the hands, the colors of a saint's robes, and all the particulars a craftsman would need to know in order to paint any number of subjects. Then Makarios passed over the pattern book. It contained his own designs, pictures of heads and hands, patterns to stamp on gold for the haloes, patterns for trees and tile floors, animals, and angels' wings.

Looking up to the magnificent *Pantocrator* hanging on the wall, Emilia feared the task was beyond her. Though she knew how to draw well enough, she felt she was treading on sacred ground when it came to writing an icon.

"I'm afraid I'll make too many mistakes," she confessed to her master.

"Nothing we make with our human hands is perfect, Emilia. What matters is approaching your subject with love and humility," he reassured her, thumbing through the book until he came to an image of Mary. "The *Theotokos*. Start with her."

She believed Makarios was indulging her. It was strange to go from the real, paying work of fresco to the impractical, yet nonetheless rewarding task of creating a sacred image no one would buy. No one painted this way any more, Makarios said, yet he wanted her to continue the art he loved so well.

Emilia was laying on the imperial purple of Mary's robe when the invitation arrived. Her name appeared in a bold, ornate script on the heavy, white parchment bearing Franco Villani's distinctive seal, which was set in wax the color of burnished gold.

"*Grazie*," she told the porter, clutching the paper to her chest.

Setting his own invitation aside, Makarios continued working at his desk while Emilia raced to break the wax seal.

"*Signor Franco Villani cordially invites you to a banquet in honor of the visiting Donna Margherita di Rossetti, cousin of the Grand Duke of Tuscany, on September 8, 1460,*" she read.

She glanced over to her master, realizing he might not share her enthusiasm for the event. Makarios merely nodded as he continued to draw with his charcoal, prompting Emilia to read on silently.

Her excitement, impossible to contain, bubbled up in breathless words. "A banquet," she said, waving the invitation in the air. "A banquet with the *Duchessa.*"

"A cousin of the *Duca.*"

Unable to sit still, she paced the room. "I wonder if Cosimo de Medici will be there."

"One never knows, but I would not expect him."

"I have nothing suitable to wear," she thought aloud.

"I can't help you with that," Makarios said drolly, "but whatever you wear, I'm sure Signor Villani will be happy to see you again."

Perhaps he would be happy to see her, Emilia thought. Or perhaps he would barely notice her. Two weeks seemed an impossibly long time to wait.

Emilia begged her mother for a new dress and so Violante enlisted the *sarta*, the dressmaker, to fit Emilia's best velvet gown with new, formal sleeves fashioned from rich gold and purple brocade. The purchase of the costly alteration was hidden from Francesco, who only knew that Emilia had been invited to dinner at the home of a wealthy merchant who was a patron of Makarios.

"I'm afraid it lacks modesty, Emilia," Violante warned, looking at her daughter in the beautiful dress. "You look too much like a lady. It was a mistake to allow the brocade."

While it was true that the wives and daughters of merchants and tavern owners were not supposed to compete with the ladies when it came to dress, Emilia thought she could not very well appear like a countrywoman at the banquet. "There will be important people there, Mama. I don't want to stand out."

Violante shook her head. "Look in the mirror, Emilia. Of course you'll stand out."

On the day of the banquet Emilia awoke early to attend Mass. Finding it difficult to concentrate, she heard barely a word Father Bartolo said. When she returned home, she could not sit still, even as Violante worked on her hair, braiding and twisting, and arranging pearl ornaments and gold ribbons in it. Violante finished the elaborate hairstyle and kissed her daughter, sending her off with a cautioning word.

"Don't allow Signor Villani to whisk you off to some private corner of the house. You have to be on guard with men like him."

Dismissing her mother's concern, Emilia climbed into the horse-drawn carriage, which had been thoughtfully provided by her host. Taken away from the tedium of everyday routine, she found herself wishing her life might become an endless chain of carriage rides to countryside villas and banquets and other occasions for fine clothes. The luxurious ride to Fiesole was shared with two other young women—one a niece of the *podestà* and another Franco's second cousin. There was an older gentleman, a charming and learned physician, with them as well. Emilia remained vague regarding the nature of her own relationship with Signor Villani, yet also managed to give the impression that she was a personal friend of their host.

When she arrived at Primavera, Emilia lagged behind the other arrivals who filed up the stairs to the great hall and the sound of a string quintet. Peering into the room, Emilia was met with a riot of color—opulent dresses of exquisite silk, satin, and taffeta in numerous patterns and shades of scarlet, green, gold, blue, and crimson. The women were like flowers plucked from the garden and arranged about the room by an artist's deliberate hand. The men were quite unlike the guests at her father's tavern, there was not a drab, brown tunic in sight. These men were dashing in their colorful long stockings, embroidered doublets, mantles lined with luxurious fabrics, and pointed shoes of fine leather.

Remaining hidden at the doorway, Emilia saw that the tables were arranged in a U shape, so that the guests, when seated, would be facing the Venus. She was pleased to see that a number of the gently bred guests already stood gazing at the fresco. Others flitted about, amusing each other with clever talk or eating the carefully prepared antipasti from the lavishly arranged trays upon the credenzas. For a brief moment Emilia stepped back from the door, feeling unsure that she belonged in the great hall.

"What are you waiting for?" she heard Makarios say from behind her. "Here is your party."

Emilia smiled, seeing her master in his familiar cloak and hat, looking as he always did. Having declined Franco's generous offer of transportation, Makarios had traveled to Primavera on his faithful old mule. He held out his arm and together, they walked through the door.

"Makarios Levantes of Constantinople, painter of The Birth of Venus, and Madonna Emilia Serafini, daughter of Francesco Serafini," Tomasso announced.

Emilia's mentor was soon surrounded by a circle of well-dressed admirers, while Emilia found herself standing beside a young, curly haired man barely five feet tall. Though his appearance was almost delicate, he appeared confident and bright and had a refined demeanor.

"I am Marsilio Ficino," the man said, bowing before her. "I saw you come in—with the painter."

"I did," she replied. "Are you closely acquainted with our host, Signor Ficino?"

"I met him once previously—at the home of Andreuccio Delcica. Franco is a merchant of rare sensitivities, quite a patron of the arts," he offered.

"Yes, Signor Villani is a man of many talents," she agreed.

"And thoroughly fascinated with the ancient world," Signor Ficino said, indicating the fresco, which was boldly stunning in the light of mid afternoon. "An excellent beauty. Such exquisite hands. And delicate feet," he said, moving closer to the wall. "A soul and mind of profound love and charity. Beloved by God. She is divine wisdom. Graced with all the virtues of antiquity. She is *Humanitas*."

"I confess I was afraid the subject matter too pagan when we first began," Emilia said, delighted by the guest's sincere enthusiasm.

"You mean to say you had a hand in this painting?"

"I'm merely the apprentice of Makarios Levantes. By now, however, I am quite convinced of the virtue of our Venus."

Signor Ficino smiled in apparent amusement. "Levantes agrees, it would seem, that the ancient world has much to teach us. Secrets lie buried in the past—secrets long since forgotten."

He appeared wistful as he spoke, his eyes like those of a poet. "What secrets do you speak of?" she asked, wondering what surprising thing the young man might say next.

"There are great wonders in our world to be rediscovered," he said quietly. "Wonders not yet imagined. My patron sends his agents across the continent in search of forgotten writings."

"Your patron?"

"Cosimo de' Medici."

"Cosimo de' Medici seeks this knowledge?" Emilia asked, intrigued.

"Indeed. At his behest I have been translating the dialogues of the divine Plato. Words of the highest truth," he continued.

"Yes, Plato. How he speaks of the nature of the soul," Emilia commented, caught up in his fervor.

"Madonna," he said, eyeing her with curiosity. "Have you read Plato?"

She smiled, wondering how to explain what she had read in her *nonna's* manual. "Only a little, Messer."

"You are too modest. You must tell me more of what you have read."

"Well, when he advises to give little importance to the body and focus instead on the education of the soul, he speaks a language not unlike that of my own priest, but I would take heed to follow the words of Father Bartolo before the ancients," she said.

"Plato, as well as your good priest, might serve to guide us mortals, do you not agree?"

Franco Villani was striding towards them across the room and Emilia hoped she would be spared from responding.

"You have met the lovely Madonna Emilia. The artist's indispensable apprentice."

"I have, and I must say her words fascinate, as does her loveliness."

Franco looked at her and nodded proudly, almost as though she was one of the cameos in his collection. "What is it you have said to captivate the great philosopher?"

"Signor Ficino flatters me."

"A beautiful, young woman who is a talented painter—a rare find in Florence, is she not?" he asked, looking at Franco.

Eyebrows raised, Franco turned to Emilia. "I agree. She is a young woman possessed of rare talent. Florence must keep an eye on this one."

"I am happy that Makarios' Venus is warmly received," Emilia said, trying to change the subject.

Before she could say any more, the old physician from the carriage greeted Marsilio and struck up a conversation. At the same time, Franco moved close to Emilia, took hold of her arm and guided her out of the great hall and towards the loggia. "I want to show you something else, Emilia."

Emilia, sensing that her host wanted to show her nothing in particular at all, remembered her mother's warning. Violante had said to be cautious with men like Franco, but she was not sure she wished to be cautious as he spirited her away from the crowd.

Hermes Trismegistus

U p smooth, wide steps of polished stone, Franco guided Emilia to the balcony overlooking the pleasure garden, the rolling hills of Florence, and the city beyond.

"You can see the *Duomo* from here," he said, surveying his estate.

Although she had stolen up here during her stay at Primavera, she pretended to admire the scene as if for the first time. Standing beside her host—a wealthy and accomplished man with the great kingdom of Florence before him and a house full of worthy guests—Emilia sensed an air of loneliness about him.

"It's lovely," she said. "Does your family ever come to visit?"

"There's only my aunt in Genoa now. And a few cousins here in Florence. Perhaps some day I'll be fortunate enough to have a family of my own."

It occurred to her that Franco had been more devoted to acquiring beautiful objects than a living bride. It also occurred to her—as she thought of Tomasso's unscrupulous behavior during her stay at the villa—that even Franco's choice of servants suggested his attention was focused on matters outside the home.

Though it was hardly the place to discuss her experience with Tomasso, she was bold enough to say, "But you are, first of all, a man of business, Signor Villani."

Frowning, he said, "Surely men of business have families."

"I only mean your efforts have been focused elsewhere—perhaps you haven't had time to think about a family yet." Treading softly, she added, "Even when you are home, I imagine your responsibilities must weigh heavily. It is the same with my father."

"I assure you, my interests extend well beyond the spice trade."

Despite her best intentions to keep quiet, Emilia said, "Of course. Your talents are numerous, as your friend Signor Ficino has just reminded me. And your nature is good and trusting, as I have seen during my stay here. I only fear that the behavior of your servants has not done you honor."

"The behavior of my servants?" he demanded. "Whatever do you mean, Emilia?"

Continuing carefully, she explained, "When Makarios and I were staying with you, there was an incident—an incident involving your manservant."

"Tomasso?"

"I believe he mistreated the maid, Filippa." Unable to stop herself, she related all that she had seen, including the attempted theft, Filippa's obvious fear of Tomasso, and the argument overheard during the night.

"I didn't mean—I was reluctant to tell you this," she stammered, as he stood looking at her in stony silence. "I should not have brought this up at your party. I only thought you should know the truth."

She supposed he was appalled by her outspokenness, but he took hold of her hand as though to comfort her. "Don't be sorry, Emilia. I'm deeply disappointed to know you were disturbed in this way. But I believe you misunderstood: It was my decision to dismiss Filippa—not Tomasso's. Despite what you think, she was quite difficult.

"The argument you overheard happened when Tomasso discovered that Filippa broke a priceless ivory—an ancient piece of carved ivory from Egypt. I must say I am shocked to hear that she tried to steal from you. All the more reason it's best she's gone."

Emilia listened, wondering if it could be true. Had she been mislead by the scared young girl? Perhaps Tomasso, despite his pompous behavior, was more loyal to his master than she had perceived. Yet Filippa seemed so fragile and innocent. As she looked at Franco, who held her hand very gently now, she simply did not know what or whom to believe.

"I was quite sure," she murmured. "I didn't want to see anyone disrespect you."

"Your exceptional goodness, Monna Emilia, is one of the many qualities I find so utterly attractive about you."

Her patron's eyes bored into her, as though he was trying to tap into this well of goodness he saw within her. Much to her astonishment, Franco drew her towards him. He kissed her with a certainty that might have knocked her to the floor had he not been holding onto her so tightly. Having completely forgotten her mother's warning, Emilia made little effort to pull away.

"I should like to know you better," he said, smiling again. "Much better, Emilia."

Taking her hand, he guided her down the stone steps. She was too astonished to say a word. Her head was swimming with visions of her romance with the spice merchant and other flights of fancy that no longer seemed impossible.

The banquet table was set with white and gold linen, vases of late summer roses and shiny silver bowls heaped with oranges and plump figs. A distracted Emilia was seated between Marsilio Ficino and a merchant whose thick, hairy fingers were adorned with heavy, jeweled rings and who spoke at length about the fine religious vestments that he sold at his store.

Emilia listened politely as she rinsed her hands in the bowl of scented water, feigning interest in the things he was telling her even though she could think only of Franco Villani's kiss. To her left, Marsilio Ficino smiled at her in a strange, knowing way, but he said little until the merchant turned his attention to the first platter, which was now being presented by the servants just as the singers began performing a humorous love song.

As she tasted the delicately fried fritters plump with cheese and pine nuts, Signor Ficino leaned close and whispered into her ear. "I believe your patron has a particular fondness for you."

Looking down at her plate in embarrassment, Emilia found this difficult to deny. "Perhaps this is true, Signor Ficino. Although I confess I am entirely unsure what to make of it."

Reaching for a stuffed egg, he laughed softly. "Then this must remain a mystery for the time, as does your interpretation of the divine Plato."

"Believe me—I'm not withholding from you. I know so little."

This was true, for there were only brief passages attributed to

Plato in *Nonna's* book. Though she sensed Marsilio was a trust-worthy man, her mother had pressed upon her not to share the secrets contained in the pages of the alchemy manual, which could easily be misconstrued as witchcraft. Yet Marsilio Ficino was not just anyone—he was Cosimo de' Medici's own scholar, a man of exceptional sensitivity who would surely not condemn what was written in the book.

Relaxing with more of the good food and wine, Emilia felt inclined to make conversation, sharing a little of what she had read without revealing that the manual was in her possession. "I did have the opportunity to study a particular book once," she began. Leaning close and speaking softly into his ear, she added, "The subject was alchemy, I confess. I hope you will not think me a heretic, Signor Ficino."

When he motioned for her to continue, Emilia added, "There were passages attributed to your philosopher. Passages written about the journey of the soul after death."

"Monna Emilia," he urged her. "Do tell me what you recall of the text."

Glancing to her right to be sure the merchant seated next to her was paying them no heed, Emilia said quietly, "If the soul has nothing in common with the body and lived a good and pure life, then it has prepared for an easy death. Such a soul will reside in heaven with our Lord for all time. But if the soul was preoccupied with the body and the needs and wants of the body during its life and nothing appeared real to it but the material, than this soul cannot separate—it will be drawn back again and again to the world of the visible. These souls fear the invisible, Signor Ficino, and for this reason they may be seen roaming near the monuments and graves."

With this said, Emilia tasted the roast of pork with green sauce. Her dinner companion set down his fritter and declared, "How is it possible that a painter's apprentice has discovered *Phaedo*? There are so few copies! To think you found it in a book of alchemy. "

When she merely nodded, he pushed further, saying, "Do tell me what more you remember from the text."

"It has been some time," she lied, realizing she had already revealed more than was prudent. "I only remember the passage because it seemed so remarkable and yet so sensible at the same time."

"Yes," he agreed. "The truth of where the soul lies is perhaps quite simple, after all. But few understand."

"*The excellence of the soul is understanding,*" she quoted from her text.

Marsilio appeared lost in thought. "Could you repeat that?"

"Oh, it was just something from the book."

"This is quite improbable," Ficino began. "There couldn't be. Was there, by any chance, mention of Hermes in this text? Hermes Trismegistus?"

She readily recalled the unusual name, though she had no inkling of its significance. "Yes, the Egyptian. *The excellence of the soul*—I believe those were his words, Signor Ficino."

He was flummoxed, no doubt, as to how she—a mere painter's apprentice—might have come across such obscure writing. Despite her plan to remain discrete, Emilia just succeeded in drawing a great deal of attention to her *nonna's* book. She sat regretting her mistake and suddenly the merchant chimed in.

"What is this talk of the soul?" he demanded. "Why think so much today, when all the delights of this world are with us? Come, Marsilio, enjoy yourself and think no more of your philosophies," he enjoined.

A juggler came before the tables and began to entertain the guests with acrobatic feats and circling multiple fruits in the air. Emilia looked at the young philosopher knowingly.

"He speaks the sentiments of many," Marsilio said.

"Perhaps so," she agreed and looked over at Franco. He was seated in the middle of the center table between the beautiful and stately guest of honor, Donna Margherita, and Signor Petrini, a banker of incalculable wealth. Emilia could not help but feel envious of the beautiful woman, slightly older than Franco, seated to his right. Looking at the lady of noble bearing, she felt keenly aware of her own, more inferior social position. She thought of the kiss and feared once again that Franco was toying with her.

After the last of the candied nuts, *biscotti, tortas,* and spiced wine were enjoyed, the merchant excused himself to thank the host, giving Marsilio the opportunity to question Emilia once again.

"I still cannot help but wonder about your book," he said. When she did not respond immediately, he confessed, "You see, it is a strange coincidence—a manuscript was recently discovered in a monastery. The writing has been attributed to an Egyptian sage by the name of Hermes Trismegistus."

"Oh!" Emilia exclaimed, seeing why her comments had given Marsilio pause.

"After Leonardo of Pistoia found it and brought it back to Cosimo, I was asked to cease work on the translations of Plato at once and undertake the translation of *The Corpus Hermeticum* instead. You see, Cosimo feels the work is of great significance."

"I had no idea," she said, shocked by what he had revealed to her.

"If the text in your possession contains passages from the Egyptian author as well, then I suspect it is a most important work, Emilia—a very precious book."

She whispered back, "I should not have told you anything about it, Signor Ficino. I fear I have broken a promise in speaking of the text."

He nodded, knowingly. "Your discretion is admirable, Monna Emilia. It is true that not everyone in Florence professes admiration for the ancients. Cosimo himself suffers such criticism," he said. "Your secret is quite safe with me. Quite safe."

"I am most grateful to you for that, Signor Ficino, though I am not at liberty to share more with you at the moment."

"If it ever pleases you to change your mind, you need only send word."

While Emilia absorbed what Ficino had said, guests began to spill out of the great hall and into the gardens before returning to the city. Wishing the day would never end, Emilia saw Makarios approaching her.

"Your work was well received," she said to him.

Looking tired but contented, the old man nodded. "It is gratifying to share one's work."

"Your name will be more widely known in Florence now."

Makarios shrugged. "We have a request for a fresco from one of the guests."

She sensed her master's unspoken sentiments. Although he was grateful for another commission, he missed the work he truly loved. What Makarios longed to do was paint his beloved icons in the quiet of his workshop, but he would paint what Florence wanted him to paint. She smiled in understanding as he started away from her.

"*A domani*," she called after him.

He turned to reply, "The day after. Spend tomorrow at home. You have things to tell your mama, no?"

Her riding party was preparing to leave so Emilia did not remain at the table much longer either. She would have liked to say goodbye to Franco, but he seemed occupied with his more important guests. Once she was outside, she turned to look at the villa, gleaming in the late afternoon sun. Maybe it was impossible, but for a moment she dared to wish this was her future and not Benozzo.

She was about to walk away when Franco emerged through the front door and strode past the other guests in order to see her off.

"It was perfect. Thank you," she said, hopes and uncertainties swirling in her mind like butterflies.

He reached for her hand and kissed it softly. "You deserve many days like this. Beautiful days with the best of everything."

He kept staring at her even as his cousin and the physician approached him to say their goodbyes. Emilia stepped into the carriage wanting to believe it was possible that Franco Villani might truly care for her.

"Did you enjoy yourself?" the white haired physician asked as they began the short journey back to the city.

"Oh, yes. It was a lovely party," she replied, distracted by thoughts of Franco.

"Such extravagance," his cousin said. "His father was an ambitious man as well."

"It's a shame Franco's mother died when he was so young," Emilia commented.

The cousin shrugged. "He wasn't all that young, I think. I can't remember exactly how old he was. He sure was a bit of a devil back then."

She wondered that the cousin could not recall Franco losing his mother at a tender young age and being shipped off to Genoa. Emilia would have pushed the woman further, but she and the *podestà's* daughter started discussing the food they had eaten at the party. Emilia was just as happy to be left alone with her private thoughts of the spice merchant and the inquiring Medici philosopher.

Osiris

The morning after the banquet, Emilia awoke to the sound of a steady rain falling on the tile rooftop overhead. The first thing she thought of was Franco and the party, and it was as if her memories of the event came from the place of her dreams. She had stood on the balcony with Franco and he had kissed her, promised her something—hadn't he?

And then there was the unexpected encounter with the philosopher, Marsilio Ficino; they had spoken of Plato, Hermes Trismegistus, and her grandmother's book. Deep within the warmth of her covers, Emilia wondered if she had said too much to Ficino. His fascination with the manual led her to wonder about the true value of the text.

Leaning over the side of her bed, Emilia retrieved the alchemy manual from the basket that she carried back and forth from the workshop and leafed through the vividly colored illustrations, pausing when she came to the Egyptian god Osiris; he lay flat on his back, dead, wheat sprouting from his mummified corpse.

Emilia wondered what it was about the ancient world that so

captivated the alchemists. It was a world that compelled Cosimo de' Medici to order the monasteries of Europe to search for the lost writings of that long ago time. Settling back into her pillows, Emilia read the myth of Osiris, the ancient Egyptian mystery of the human soul.

Osiris, chopped into pieces by his brother and thrown into the River Nile, was collected and bound together with mummy bandages by Isis, who then used the corpse to impregnate herself.

> *...Out of this union the divine Horus, or the new Osiris, was born. There can be no rebirth until there is death. And so until one has experienced the blackness of the funeral coffin, one cannot begin the Great Work nor experience the resurrection.*

Thunder rolled in the distance. With a shudder Emilia closed the manual and dove beneath her quilt. It was almost as though the fate of Osiris foreshadowed her future suffering, her marriage to a man she could never love, a lifetime sentence that was like the blackness of the funeral coffin. Could this be the suffering required of her in order to begin the Great Work?

If so, it was an aspect of alchemy she could do without. Emilia wanted to fashion the world to her liking, cast spells, and call forth merchant princes to her domain. She wanted nothing to do with the dark, foreboding tale of Osiris.

"It was like a dream, mother. A marvelous dream," she said before tasting the sweet *marzapan*, a candy of almonds and sugar that her mother placed before her. She was thinking only of the party, having put aside the eerie images of funeral coffins and mummy shrines stimulated by her reading of the alchemy manual.

Emilia went on to tell Violante about the banquet and the courteous attention shown to her by her host, though she kept the kiss on
the balcony to herself.

"Emilia, your patron has been more than courteous to you,"
Violante said at length, reading into the scene described by her
daughter. "You need to keep your distance from him."

"I don't see why," Emilia argued, angry that her mother
thought to put a stop to something that had hardly begun. "He is a
wealthy and generous man."

"I'm afraid nothing good can come of it."

"You mean Benozzo might forget me if Franco Villani takes
notice of me? Would that be so terrible? Or do you want me to
suffer, just like father?"

Violante sighed. "Emilia, you must understand that a man like
that thinks nothing of flirtation. It was a party—sometimes people
say things. His intentions are not serious."

"How do you know?" Emilia demanded, even though she
knew her mother might be right. "How can you be so sure he
doesn't truly care for me?"

Chopping turnips for the midday meal, Violante shook her
head. "I think it best not to let your imagination run away with
you."

"You think I am far too common for Signor Villani."

"Oh, Emilia! You know that's not true."

"You think it's true. He could choose anyone at all, so why
would he choose me?"

Violante shook her head. "Emilia, you don't know Signor
Villani all that well. I know how you feel about Benozzo, but your
father trusts him. He is a good and honest man. Your affection for
him is sure to grow in time."

"He hates that I paint! He thinks it unseemly when my fingers

are stained! He doesn't even know about my apprenticeship!"
Emilia cried. "At least Franco appreciates my skill."

Unwilling to quietly accept a future with her father's assistant,
Emilia stormed off to her room. Her mother had read *A Manual
to the Science of Alchemy* as well. It was Violante who told her
that anything seen within the imagination was possible. Now that
Emilia had conjured up a man like Franco Villani, Violante had
grown practical. Emilia was allowed to dream, so long as her
dreams were not too big. She would not heed her mother's warning or her father's plans for her betrothal. If she could find a way to
be with Franco instead of Benozzo, she would do it. She had best
do it as quickly as possible.

After the banquet, work resumed as usual at the *bottega*.
Makarios began some preliminary sketches for the prospective patron who had admired the Venus, and Emilia returned to her icon.
Although she was careful as she added delicate lines of dark crimson
mixed with burnt sienna—creases in the Madonna's robe—she felt
her attention wandering again and again to the memory of Franco
Villani on the balcony at Primavera. Though three long days had
passed since the banquet, there had been no word from him.

As she wondered about the whereabouts of Franco Villani and
tried to hold onto each day till October, the end of her freedom,
Emilia was not unaware that she lacked the prayerful attitude required of the iconographer. Recalling how Makarios had prayed and
fasted before writing the *Pantocrator*, she was not sure if she was
truly worthy to create this image of the Holy Mother after all.

For several more days she persevered at her task. Not wanting
to fail Makarios, she struggled to achieve just the right hue for the

flesh, the proper countenance for a human but Divine Child, and to render the perfect expression for the Mother of God.

"You're getting there, Emilia," she heard Makarios say.

She looked up at him in disbelief. "I confess I do not feel all that worthy of creating what you have called a window to heaven, Makarios. My thoughts are not entirely pure and my desires are selfish at times," she admitted.

Laughing, the master from Constantinople patted her shoulder. "Don't worry. If God would allow only perfect saints to write icons, then there would be very few icons. We do our best, Emilia. We admit we are mere humans, full of imperfections." He stepped back from her *Theotokos* and said, "She will be lovely. A very fine first piece."

Looking at her Madonna with less criticism now, Emilia resumed her work. The following day, as she began to add fine lines to the head covering and flesh, she thought that despite her inadequacies, the *Theotokos* would come to life after all. It would not reach the grandness of the *Pantocrator* or her master's level of artistry, but she could feel proud of her work nonetheless.

The two of them shared a simple midday meal of bread, *salame* or sausage, and cheese, then Makarios rolled up his drawings and announced he was off to see the new patron, an elderly silk merchant. Emilia, left alone at the *bottega*, painted until she found it impossible to concentrate on her task a minute longer. Franco Villani clung to her thoughts like paint to canvas and Emilia was beginning to think he had forgotten her and that her mother was right about him.

After wiping down the table and storing away the brushes and pigments, Emilia set her icon on one of the shelves, propping the panel up against the wall. It brought her comfort to see the holy image of the Virgin, serene and knowing, offering blessings to those who stopped to speak with her. *Ave Maria, piena di grazia.* Hail Mary, full of grace, she spoke quietly just before she heard a rapping at the workshop door.

She turned and was caught completely off guard to see Giacomo Massarino standing at the entry.

"You're back!" she exclaimed, hurrying to embrace him. He had left Florence as little more than Emilia's acquaintance but he had returned to her a dear friend, admitted to the world of her private thoughts shared in her letters to him.

"I couldn't wait to see the workshop of the foreign master who has created such a stir," Giacomo said with good humor. Though he had occasionally complained of the enormity of the task assigned to him, Giacomo had clearly not languished in Pisa. He was bounding with energy, fit and lean in appearance, his thin white tunic revealing shoulders and arms made strong by the physical work of painting in plaster.

"You will only find his apprentice here at the moment," she laughed, noting his renewed vitality.

"His soon-to-be-famous apprentice," he corrected, following her into the room and taking in the assortment of panels and drawings lying about.

"So tell me, were your frescoes well received at Santa Caterina?"

"I think the friars were pleased with our homage to their beloved Thomas Aquinas." Giacomo stopped speaking when his gaze fell upon the *Pantocrator,* which was prominently displayed in the center of the room.

"Your master's work?" he presumed.

"It's important for him to have something that reminds him of his country," she said, thinking Giacomo would find the icon outdated.

"A powerful piece," he said, moving closer. "His gaze is impossible to avoid."

Glad that he did not judge the work harshly, she said, "It's nothing like what we did for Signor Villani, of course." She became aware that Giacomo was taking note of her own uncompleted panel.

"This is charming, in a way," he observed.

"It's not quite finished," Emilia said. She did not mean to discuss her interest in the Byzantine art form but added, "The work is mine."

"Yours?" he asked. "Why are you painting something like this?"

Wincing at his question, she faced her *Theotokos*, wondering how she could answer him. It made little sense to paint something no one in Florence would care for. "It is not a mere painting, Giacomo. It is more—like a form of prayer," she tried.

Staring at the icon, he said, "There is no perspective. No realism."

"The icon is a window. A window to heaven. It's not meant to be a pretty picture to look at."

Giacomo studied her Virgin, clearly trying to grasp her meaning. He sat down on the bench and looked from the *Pantocrator* to the *Theotokos*. After a few moments, he said, "What you say may be true, Emilia. The images are engaging in an unexpected way, I confess. They evoke a sort of mysticism that is not easily explained."

She smiled, feeling delighted that he did not merely dismiss her views as naïve, glad that she could share Makarios' iconography with him. "He paints what will buy bread, Giacomo. But he needs to have something that connects him to his past. He's so far from home."

Casually, Giacomo draped his arm over her shoulder and at the same moment, Emilia heard the front door of the workshop fly open. Startled by the sound, she turned to see none other than Franco Villani, dressed in an emerald green cloak and plumed hat. The sight commanded her undivided attention.

Surprised by his unannounced visit, Emilia hastened towards him. "Signor Villani. How good to see you."

He brought her hand to his lips. "I have been away from you too long." Striding inside, he appraised Giacomo and asked coolly, "Am I interrupting?"

"I am Giacomo Massarino," replied the painter, exuding the confidence of his latest success. He spoke with an easy manner to the visitor, who was unknown to him though clearly possessed of obvious wealth. "Emilia and I were both employed at the workshop of Lorenzo Jacovelli. I was in Pisa for most of a year, I've just now returned."

"And you have immediately sought out the company of Madonna Emilia," Franco Villani said dryly.

Giacomo paused, as though wondering if he should take offense to this remark. "Stopping in to see a friend after a lengthy absence is hardly unusual," he said, staring Franco squarely in the eye.

"Of course not. Especially a friend as fine as Emilia Serafini," Franco said, taking hold of Emilia's hand again.

Watching this display of familiarity, Giacomo stiffened. He looked questioningly at Emilia, as though seeking an explanation.

"Franco Villani is our patron," she said quickly. "The generous patron who commissioned the Venus."

Giacomo stared at her, obviously dumbfounded. She was not sure what more to tell him at the moment, though Franco's behavior served to make the nature of his interest in her clear. Emilia struggled to absorb the fact that Franco was apparently declaring himself for her while at the same time she perceived that Giacomo was unsettled by it all. In the many letters she had sent to Pisa, Emilia had given no hint of a romance with her patron.

Before she could even try to explain the situation, Giacomo, whose countenance had turned gloomy, was making his way towards the door.

"We will speak again soon, Emilia," he assured her, ignoring Franco's searing gaze. "You have come far from where you started at Jacovelli's," he said pointedly.

"I'm glad you're home, Giacomo," Emilia said, even though it was Franco Villani who now captivated her attention.

Before the door closed, Franco extended his long arms to pull her close. "Fetch your cloak and come with me."

Looking up into his large, dark eyes, she was amazed that he had sought her out at the *bottega* that day. Never mind that it was precisely what she had wished for. Emilia could only wonder what Franco Villani would do next.

Santa Croce

"Come with you? Now?" Emilia asked.

Franco, waiting expectantly in his green velvet mantle, merely nodded. Her mother's warning voice spoke inside her head, *You ought not to walk unescorted with him.* Of course Violante would never know, Emilia reasoned. Quickly throwing on her satin-trimmed cloak and puffed cloth cap, Emilia accepted Franco's arm and walked boldly out into the cool September day.

"I thought you'd forgotten me," she said as they reached the open piazza of Santo Spirito under cloudy skies.

"I think of you day and night."

Although she did not really believe him, Franco's words were enough to dissolve her fear that the kiss on the balcony meant nothing to him. Reassured of his affection, she traveled alongside the spice merchant, past the church towards the River Arno. Knowing very well she was doing something her father would have forbidden, Emilia stole sideways glances at her tall companion. Franco, his black hair swept back behind his feathered cap, held his head high, unaffected by the strong wind.

"Did you enjoy yourself at your banquet?" she thought to ask him.

"Why wouldn't I?"

"I only ask because you looked so serious all the time."

"You think I don't know how to enjoy myself, Emilia?" He chuckled, as if to prove her otherwise.

"I wouldn't say that. But then no one would call you light-hearted," she said in a teasing way.

"There are things you don't know about me," he said, taking hold of her around the waist and lifting her off her feet. "I happen to be a man full of surprises."

She smiled, suspended above ground, till he set her down. The sun peeked out from behind the clouds as they walked along the *lungarno*, the embankment by the river. Coming to the bridge, *Ponte alla Carraia*, they crossed over to the other side, into the district of Santa Maria Novella, Giacomo's neighborhood. Emilia wished her friend and Franco had been more amiable with one another back at the *bottega*, though Franco's show of jealousy was flattering in a way.

She was thinking what a fair couple the two of them made when she became aware of the sound of a clattering wagon. Franco's long arm stretched out in front of Emilia, pushing her behind him until well after the mule-drawn wagon sped past.

"Swine!" Franco shouted after the driver, leading her onward again.

She saw his annoyance as a sign of chivalry, a reassurance of protection when she was with him. Together, they crossed the piazza. Emilia had to walk quickly to keep pace with Franco's long strides. She gave a passing thought to Makarios, who might be wondering where she had gone. The matter of her employment did not seem to occur to Franco, who paused to observe the Dominican's church.

"Have you brought me to see Uccello's frescoes?" she asked, though she did not really suppose that Franco had thought to view the fine scenes from the Old Testament in the cloisters.

"Do you think of nothing else, Emilia?" he laughed.

"I think of you," she admitted.

Appearing pleased with her response, the man who traveled amongst the fairest of Florence reached into his purse and withdrew a small package wrapped in rose-colored silk.

"For you," he said.

Wide-eyed, Emilia carefully untied the ribbon and unfolded the cloth to find an exquisite gold and pearl pin. It bore a delicately crafted image of Leda kissing her swan.

"It's lovely," she said, stunned that he would give her something so precious. She held up the pin, admiring it, and she saw a man delighted to have pleased her.

"I'm glad you like it." He stroked Emilia's cheek lightly. Taking the expensive token from her hand, he pinned it to her hat. "It suits you," he said, and they began walking again.

"Am I the only one you think of, Franco?" she asked, trying to ascertain the significance of such a costly gift.

Laughing at her doubt, he asked, "Is that what you ask a man who has bared his heart and soul to you?"

She regarded him with seriousness, wondering if it could be true. She wanted to believe she had captured his heart, but it was easy for her to imagine many gracious ladies vying for his affection.

Before she could reply, he added, "Perhaps I should be the one asking that question."

"What do you mean?"

"The young man at the workshop. He did not seem at all pleased to see us together."

"You mean Giacomo?" she asked in surprise. It was of course Benozzo who stood between them, but she was not about to mention the inconvenient marriage her father had arranged. "He's a very fine painter. A friend of mine, that's all."

"A close friend?"

Guessing he did not wish to know the extent of her lengthy correspondence with Giacomo, Emilia replied, "We share painting, nothing more."

Walking close to Franco, Emilia began to think that matters were working out according to the plan she had envisioned. She had no idea how she would convince her father that she should marry Franco Villani instead of Benozzo or how she would elicit a speedy proposal from Franco, but as the bells of Santa Maria Novella rang through the city at *nones*, she imagined herself standing on the steps of Santa Croce in a silk wedding gown.

When she finally returned to the workshop more than an hour later, Makarios was back at his desk. Franco stood beside Emilia as she faced her master, feeling unsure of what to say.

"I beg your pardon for Emilia's absence this afternoon," he said in little way of apology.

Makarios, who sat reading in the late afternoon light, replied, "You must ask her father to pardon you for that, Signor Villani. I am merely her employer."

Franco Villani bowed his head in acknowledgement of this fact before bidding Emilia farewell and striding out the front door of the *bottega*.

At Mass on the following Sunday, Emilia was taken by surprise when she spied Giacomo Massarino.

"What could he be doing here?" she whispered to Violante, knowing very well that her friend would normally attend Mass at Santa Maria Novella.

As the processional hymn began and Father Bartolo walked down the aisle, Emilia had the strangest feeling that her friend had something he wished to say about the man who was now much more than her patron. Franco had, after all, displayed unwarranted jealousy when she had introduced Giacomo at the *bottega*. Still, it seemed strange that Giacomo would seek her out while she was at church with her family.

Emilia tried to put her thoughts to prayer, though she mostly stared at the fine, carved pulpit that depicted scenes from the life of Saint Francis. Moving her gaze to the gilded altar, she studied the Coronation of the Virgin, a work from Giotto's studio. A multitude of saints and angels looked on somberly as the Virgin received her crown. Emilia had admired the polyptych ever since she was a little girl sitting on her mother's lap. The stunning frescoes, sculptures, and panels surrounding Emilia at Santa Croce were the very images that had inspired her to beg her mother for paper and charcoal in the first place.

As Father Bartolo began to speak, Emilia glanced at Giacomo. Catching his eyes upon her, she supposed he could guess where her attention had just been. She acknowledged him with a subtle smile, sensing the shared understanding of their work between them. Emilia knew that Giacomo's devotion to his art and the subjects he depicted ran deep. Perhaps they both painted not merely for the security that the profession afforded but for the service rendered to God through their work.

She believed that Franco would understand this as well. After all, he was a patron of the arts and he had witnessed and admired her skill. Benozzo, on the other hand, cared only for numbers and could never appreciate her passion; he wanted her for his wife only because she was Francesco's daughter.

She tried to return her attention to prayer. "*Credo in Deum, Patrem omnipotentem.* I believe in God, the Father almighty." Despite her efforts, she could not stop wondering what Giacomo was doing at her church. When Mass finally ended she found him outside, waiting for her on the steps. Greeting the young painter warmly, she introduced him to her family.

"I've heard all about you," Violante said matter-of-factly.

"It's Jacovelli's name that Florence knows," he replied with good humor. "But I'm glad if Emilia thought to mention her old friend from the *bottega.*"

"You've just returned from Pisa," Violante observed.

"Is there not enough work to be had in Florence?" demanded Emilia's father, who liked to opine that the city's talent ought to serve Florence rather than its neighboring cities. He looked at the young painter with the coppery head of hair, sizing him up.

"One would think so, but it is my duty to do the master's biding, Messer," Giacomo replied politely.

Franceso Serafini allowed himself a smile after Giacomo's show of humility. "Of course."

Emilia's brother, as if to impress the new acquaintance, chimed in. "I've been to Pisa—with my father to sell saddles."

"Have dinner with us," Violante said, as though he were an old friend. "Unless you're expected elsewhere."

Both Emilia and her father looked to Violante in surprise. Emilia was about to say that Giacomo could not possibly be troubled to join them when he said, "How kind of you, Madonna. I do not wish to impose."

Violante was already holding Giacomo's arm and starting across the piazza. "You look as though you need a good meal. Didn't the friars feed you anything?"

Emilia, walking between her father and brother, could not help but remember how Franco had questioned the nature of her relationship with Giacomo. She had the distinct feeling that Franco would not like the idea of Giacomo coming to her house for dinner, though in truth she welcomed the painter's company.

When they arrived home, the house was scented with the fragrance of cloves and roasting meat. Emilia went with her mother to help Maddalena in the kitchen while Giacomo joined her brother and father in the main room. As she worked, Emilia overheard Giacomo asking her father about the shop where he sold saddles and armor. Francesco, encouraged by his admiring audience, offered his expertise on matters of commerce and the best routes to Pisa and other neighboring cities. Peering in from the doorway, Emilia saw the two men seated comfortably before the fireplace while Andrea stoked the fire. If she didn't know better, Emilia would have thought Giacomo Massarino was a frequent guest in their home.

Returning to her work of chopping apples while her mother prepared a dish of mushrooms, pouring a generous portion of olive oil over them, and Maddalena put more wood in the oven, Emilia whispered, "Why did you invite him?"

Violante seemed to think nothing of it. "He is your friend, is he not?"

"Yes, but what would Benozzo think?"

Violante looked at her in surprise. "Since when do you care what Benozzo Balducci thinks?"

Ignoring her mother's reply, Emilia set the bowl of sugared nuts on the table. When the meal was at length prepared and everyone was seated, Giacomo glanced across the table at her from time to time. After complimenting Violante for her pork and rosy apples, the young painter spoke of the wonders of Pisan architecture, the palaces, and lavish decorations of colored marble.

"I wish I could see it," Emilia said.

"You might have come with me and father—but you were a boy at Jacovelli's then," Andrea chided her as Emilia threw him a biting look.

"Well, perhaps Franco Villani will take your sister there one day," Giacomo said, much to Emilia's utter surprise.

Knowing nothing of his daughter's personal relationship with her patron, Francesco appeared perplexed. "Franco Villani? Who is Franco Villani?"

"The rich patron with the villa," Andrea reminded him.

Pushing aside his empty plate, Francesco asked, "Why on earth would Franco Villani take Emilia to Pisa?"

Avoiding Emilia's glare, Giacomo said cheerfully, "He is quite fond of her, of course."

Emilia was aghast at the mention of Franco's feelings for her. Francesco, of course, would be furious to discover her involvement with another man. He had to learn about Franco at some point, but not now, certainly not like this. "We became acquainted when I was painting in Fiesole," she began.

"Why haven't I met him? What do you know of this, Violante?" he demanded of his wife.

"It's not as if they've run off together, Francesco."

"Forgive me. I was given to think—" Giacomo began before Emilia could get in a word. "I only brought this up because I ran into Signor Villani the other day. Or perhaps I should say he sought me out at Jacovelli's."

"He did?" Emilia asked, nearly choking on her wine.

"Yes." Giacomo added slowly, "He had a few unpleasant words for me."

"What on earth for?" Violante asked.

"He took offense to the visit I made to Makarios' workshop last week. He seems to think I'm guilty of some impropriety."

"Impropriety! *Dio!*" Francesco bellowed. "He should speak of impropriety when Emilia is already spoken for. I don't even know the man! Who does this scoundrel think he is?"

Emilia shook her head in dismay. She didn't know how to begin to explain matters to her father. "It's all a misunderstanding. I'm sure it's not what it seems."

"I want to see this Franco Villani who hides in Fiesole and thinks he can dishonor my daughter. You and I will pay him a visit, Andrea."

"No! Please don't, Papa," Emilia begged.

Now that Francesco was completely worked up, Giacomo tried to reassure Emilia that this had not been his intention. "I'm sorry, Emilia. I only mentioned this because I was concerned for you. I'm not afraid for myself, though I think he was threatening me. He came under the pretense of talking to Jacovelli about a commission, but he made it clear he doesn't want me near you."

Finding it hard to believe this account, she told herself that Franco must have misinterpreted her friendship with Giacomo. "I'll speak to him," Emilia said, knowing she had already explained the way things stood once before.

Francesco rose from the table, having heard enough apparently. "Obviously events have taken place which I know nothing about! To think you have been cavorting about Florence behind Benozzo's back. With a man I have never met!"

"Makarios knows him," Andrea added as he munched on his mother's candied nuts.

"She was painting there in August, Francesco. You knew that," Violante reminded him. "He *is* quite wealthy."

"So does this entitle him to treat us as though we are mere peasants? And to dishonor my family?" Francesco fumed. "Where is he now? Is he at this villa of his?"

"I'm very sorry," Giacomo said as he stood from the table. "I didn't mean to cause a disturbance."

Emilia was not at all sure he was sorry. She suspected, in fact, that Giacomo had come to dinner with the very intention of stirring up trouble.

"I said where is he, Emilia?" Francesco repeated.

"At his house here in Florence, I suppose," she answered reluctantly.

"Where is it?" he demanded as Emilia rose to see Giacomo to the door.

"Thank you for an excellent dinner," Giacomo said, moving away.

"Where is Villani's house?" Francesco bellowed, rising from his seat.

Emilia turned to say, "It's on the Via de' Bardi. But I've never been there."

"The *Via de' Bardi*?" echoed Andrea.

"Because he is rich he thinks he can ignore propriety!" Francesco raged.

When she and Giacomo were alone at the front door, he said, "I wonder if you really know what kind of man he is."

"You could have told me all this privately," she said angrily.

"Your father has a right to know," Giacomo said without apology.

"My father expects me to marry someone else, Giacomo," she confessed at last.

"Well, then you had best decide between them, Emilia."

"You don't understand!"

As he departed with barely a goodbye, she cursed him for bringing this disaster upon her. Her mother should never have invited him to dinner. Never mind that she too disliked the idea of Franco trying to dictate Giacomo's behavior. She and Giacomo were two artists who had come to share a certain understanding. Emilia valued his friendship even while she felt he had no appreciation of her predicament; she needed Franco to save her from a loveless life of boredom with Benozzo. Giacomo enjoyed freedoms that she simply did not have. Emilia only wished she had been born a man.

Francesco

Emilia watched Giacomo vanish into the distance. He was walking serenely as though he had done nothing wrong at all that quiet Sunday afternoon, yet she was convinced he had betrayed her for a second time. She was about to slam the door closed when she spotted her father and brother leading their horses around from the stable at the back of the house.

"Please don't be angry with Franco," she pleaded, rushing out into the cold without her cloak as Franceso and Andrea prepared to leave.

Keeping his eyes fixed on the road, Francesco replied, "This is none of your concern, Emilia."

Helplessly, Emilia watched her father mount his horse and proceed down the street as though he had been elected *gonfaloniere*. Her brother, positioned behind their father, looked back at her as if to say the situation could not be helped. When Francesco's pace quickened to a canter, Andrea took off after him.

In a vain attempt to stop what was sure to occur, Emilia chased after them. "Franco has done nothing wrong!" she shouted. She did not care that the cold wind cut through her thin dress or that her neighbor, wrinkled old Monna Gemma, was outside watching her, obviously thinking that Emilia was possessed of the devil. Her only thought was of losing whatever it was she had with Franco Villani. Her father and Andrea sped off towards Santa Croce and Emilia ran back to the house in despair.

Violante was at the door. "Come inside, Emilia. Your father won't be stopped."

"He's going to ruin everything." Tears trickled down Emilia's cold cheeks as she fell into her mother's arms. "He'll tell him about Benozzo and I'll never see Franco again!"

"Maybe. But if Franco's feelings for you are sincere, as you say, he will try to appeal to your father. It is up to him now."

She had to admit there was truth to her mother's words. While it was quite likely that Francesco would accuse Franco of numerous improprieties, Franco would do what he could to appease her father if he truly cared for her. It would be a test of his affection for her. Conceding that this would be the case, Emilia wiped her eyes.

"There, there, *cara*. I know you're afraid. You must trust that everything works out according to God's plan."

"You always say what happens in life is up to me. That's what it says in *Nonna's* manual. Maybe it's nothing but lies."

"No, it's not lies, my love. We work our magic all right. Of course we do," Violante said quietly. "This doesn't mean we can alter that which God has ordained. Even alchemists have to know their place, Emilia."

Emilia was ushered back to the kitchen, where Violante filled a silver cup with Chianti and Maddalena cut three slices of fig *torta*. Gazing into the cup of dark, garnet-colored liquid, Emilia envisioned her father pounding angrily on Franco Villani's front door.

"Eat your *torta*," Maddalena said, putting an end to Emilia's daydream.

The cake, rich and dense with plump figs and pine nuts, could only distract her so much. Sitting at the table next to her mother, eating the *torta*, Emilia gloomily supposed Franco would tell her father that nothing had happened, that there was no romance between them. She hoped, being occasionally prone to vivid imagining, that she had not exaggerated the scope of his affection for her. It was possible, she conceded, that Franco might have been toying with her after all. Emilia remembered the precious gift he had given to her. Did Franco consider the gold pin a trinket, something that meant nothing to him?

She began to envision how Franco would tell her father she had misinterpreted everything. *I am very sorry, Francesco. Your daughter is a lovely young lady, but she is still quite young—and a painter's apprentice. She must have misunderstood the gratitude I showed to her and Makarios. Matters are hardly the way you suggest.*

Once again Emilia found herself in the midst of the unknown, much as she had felt when she lost her apprenticeship with Jacovelli. She was back in the *nigredo,* the first phase of the alchemical experiment, when all was confusion. Though she had supposed she was well beyond the starting point, Emilia admitted to herself that she had not followed the sequence of steps as they were laid out in the manual. She had been too eager to focus on the last step, the third phase of the experiment, when the alchemist was free to create the desired outcome. It was the *rubedo* which held her attention—the phase when the alchemist exercised mastery over the physical world.

According to the book, if one proceeded to the *rubedo* before the completion of the *albedo,* the experiment was bound to fail.

Otherwise, the outcome would be fatally tainted. She recalled this as she disappeared upstairs and curled up with her manual.

> *Caution to he who would proceed prematurely, for the alchemist must emerge from the fiery hot furnace completely whitened and pure. When the albedo is achieved, he submits himself entirely to the will of God and creates great works that serve humanity. Manifesting with a clean heart, the alchemist exercises the ultimate power of freedom and creates miracles that effect change upon the Earth.*

Emilia was dozing off when she heard the front door open and the low, rumbling voice of her father downstairs. She sat bolt upright in bed—Francesco was back. Her heart jumped at the thought of what he would tell her. She threw open her bedroom door, ran to find him.

"What did he say?" she asked breathlessly. Her father and brother looked at her strangely, as though she were some rare oddity rather than the girl they had always known.

Francesco said nothing as Violante took his cloak. Settling himself into his chair before the warm fire, her father appeared markedly subdued, utterly different from the temper he had shown at his hasty departure hours earlier. He was no longer angry, neither did he appear particularly happy. Emilia could not tell if he would give her good news or bad.

Violante stood behind Francesco, rubbing his shoulders as though trying to coax the story out of him.

"Should I assume he was not the monster you feared?" she asked.

"I suppose not," he said, reaching up to hold his wife's hand. "He was rather civil to us when we arrived at his house."

"His palace, you mean," Andrea remarked, regarding Emilia with newfound respect. "Paintings and enamels everywhere. I've never seen so many books. He showed us his collection. I counted three servants, too."

"I wouldn't know," Emilia said as her father and brother regarded her skeptically. "I've never been there," she insisted.

"He was surprised by your unannounced visit, no doubt," Violante interjected.

"I suppose he was. But Villani understood my grievance well enough," Francesco said, raising himself from his chair to stand before the fire. As though preparing to speak words of grand import, he turned to face his family. "He had planned to introduce himself, but urgent matters of business diverted his attention. He admitted what he'd done, anyway."

"He did nothing!" Emilia retorted.

Her mother gave her a look that silenced Emilia.

"I believe it is true that Villani knew nothing at all about Benozzo, because my daughter no doubt failed to mention him," Francesco said gravely, looking at Emilia. "He had no prior knowledge of Emilia's upcoming betrothal and it appears to be the case that Signor Villani did intend to arrange a meeting with me."

Emilia remained frozen, afraid to say a word.

"One thing or another happened," her father continued. "He was called away to Prato. He is, understandably, quite preoccupied. Men like him don't always know where they will be from one week to the next. He knows the situation looked quite bad."

Mouth agape, Emilia listened. She found it difficult to comprehend that Franco had managed to pacify her outraged father. Still, she did not know the meaning of the excuses offered by Franco.

"We were able to reach an agreement peacefully enough."

"What agreement?" Emilia asked, hardly daring to believe that her future had been planned according to her wishes.

"Your betrothal. The particulars of your dowry."

"What about Benozzo?" Violante asked, looking as stunned as Emilia.

"Yes, it will be a difficult blow to him. He will have to understand that an alliance with a man like Villani will be of immeasurable benefit to him as well. Villani is quite established in Prato as well as Genoa, Violante. It will change things for all of us. Change things considerably."

Alliance? Betrothal? Emilia could not absorb what was happening. "He hasn't even asked me!" she exclaimed.

Her father looked at her as though she were mad.

"What do you mean, he hasn't asked you? His affection for you is obvious. This is what you wanted, of course!"

"It's just—I thought he would ask me how I felt about it first," she replied, feeling breathless at the news of her engagement.

"Franco Villani is a fairly reasonable man, it turns out," Francesco mused as he stared into the fire's orange and blue flames. "I think I remember his father, actually. He died some years ago. He had a store here in Florence."

"Aren't you angry with him, father?" Emilia asked, overwhelmed by the news and not fully comprehending that her father had been won over so easily.

"I am not a man to hold a grudge, Emilia. Villani will make amends. You could do much worse for yourself," he said, turning to face her. "You understand he is a man of significant means."

Emilia looked to Violante, who stared blankly at her husband. She could see her mother was in a state of shock as well.

"When is the wedding?" Emilia thought to ask.

"Not for a while, *cara*," Violante replied before Francesco could speak. "We'll need some time, of course. There's much to be done. Your trousseau, your dress, the banquet. You know we cannot begin to plan until after Christmas. Your father needs my help at the tavern right now."

As the reality of the situation sank in, Emilia began to grasp that she was truly free from Benozzo. By some miracle, her father was releasing her from him. It was too good to be true. She could be free to paint. But what of her work at the *bottega*? Her contract with Makarios was soon ending.

"What about my apprenticeship?" she asked, knowing her father would not want to hear of it.

"Oh, for heaven's sake! What's the point of continuing on with that?" Francesco hissed. "It's time to put that nonsense behind you once and for all."

"But I don't want to give it up!" Emilia said, horrified at the thought of living without her pigments and brushes and of leaving Makarios. "Franco doesn't mind that I paint."

"Don't be ridiculous, Emilia. You're going to marry a rich man. It's time to give up this childish dream of yours."

Dismayed, Emilia looked to her mother, who might have said, "*I told you so.*" Violante simply stroked her daughter's hair, whispering softly, "Things have a way of working out, Emilia." To Francesco, Violante said, "Perhaps she might continue on with Makarios just until the wedding. Do you think it might keep her calm, Francesco? This has all been such a shock to her."

Francesco threw up his arms.

"She is to be the wife of a *mercatante*, a great merchant, not a painter. The little money she earns from Levantes is paltry, Violante."

Nevertheless, Francesco had not explicitly forbidden her return to the *bottega*. There was a chance that Violante might prevail upon him to allow her to continue a while longer. The matter of her career ought to be discussed with Franco as well. He would permit her to paint after they were married, wouldn't he?

She recalled Franco's warning to Giacomo: the painter was to stay clear of her. Emilia did not want to believe Franco would confine her actions just as Benozzo had seemed inclined to do. She wanted to believe that her sublimely rich and handsome fiancé was better than this, yet the truth was that Emilia's future with Franco Villani held elements yet unknown.

Via de' Bardi

That heavy burden that had been her betrothal to Benozzo Balducci weighed no longer upon Emilia. As she made her way to the *bottega*, she suffered little guilt over the loss. Her father's assistant, who had failed to embrace her talent, was now replaced by the far worldlier spice merchant who surely understood her in ways Benozzo could not. Walking past the *contadini* with their carts stocked full of meat, cheese, poultry, and produce and the crowds of ambitious, early morning shoppers who wanted the plumpest pigeon or juiciest suckling pig for dinner that day, she held her head high as she considered her future position. The citizens of Florence would come to recognize her as the young wife of the *mercatante*, and she would be obliged to act in a manner befitting her title.

Then, recalling the unpleasant encounter between her husband-to-be and Giacomo Massarino, she told herself that Franco's jealous impulses would abate in time. Surely Franco would eventually see that her relationship with Giacomo posed no threat. It was true that she and Giacomo had formed a bond through their love of painting. Emilia had to admit that this could be difficult for Franco, but she would reassure him of her loyalty. As time progressed, they would both grow more confident in their mutual affection for one another and such misunderstandings would be a thing of the past.

Gliding through the front door of the *bottego*, she called, "*Buon giorno*" to her master.

Makarios, who sat darning his sock by the fire, lifted his eyes from his work to smile at Emilia. "You are happy today."

She unfastened her cloak and tossed it on the bench before hurrying over to kneel on the floor beside him. As she looked into his kindly, old face, her heart ached slightly at the thought of ever leaving him.

"Let me do that," she said, taking the sock from his hands.

Though she feared the news of her engagement would disappoint him, she had to tell Makarios what had happened. "I didn't mean for it to happen so quickly," she blurted out, "but my father has drawn up the contract—I am betrothed to Signor Villani and my father says he will not allow me to continue on with you here, though my mother thinks I ought to keep my position until the wedding."

He looked at her not with the disapproval or disappointment she had feared, but with a quiet understanding which made her eyes tear. The old man reached down and gently touched her shoulder with his wrinkled brown hand. "This is a surprise indeed, Emilia. But why do you look so sad when you tell me this? Do you not wish to marry Signor Villani?"

"It's not that," Emilia said, wiping away a tear in the corner of her eye. "It's just the thought of ever leaving you—"

He nodded in understanding. "It was bound to happen some day."

"Not for a while," she said, recovering her composure. "If you will allow me to remain here, that is. No matter what anyone says, I have no intention of giving up painting, even after I'm married."

Standing up, Makarios chuckled softly at this notion. "Well, Emilia, you must get to work. There is still much for you to learn."

"Are you ready to start the fresco for Signor Christofano?"

"Next week," he replied. Indicating her panel that sat forgotten on the shelf, he added, "After you finish your icon."

Grateful that Makarios was indulging her with the opportunity to complete her own work that morning, Emilia gathered her supplies and sat at the worktable, finding immediate solace in the emerging image of the Holy Mother that she was creating. She felt such affection for this icon—it gave her a sense of satisfaction she could explain to no one, much like a precious gem or a cameo kept hidden in a box.

As Emilia mixed powdered pigment with egg yolk, Makarios worked on his cartoons for the Procession of the Magi. "There is a sister at the Hospital of Santa Maria Nuova—Sister Sophia," he mentioned casually. "She is from Constantinople like me."

Emilia looked up from her work.

"A friend of yours?"

"I met her through Friar Giuseppe. She is a tireless worker for the sick."

Emilia nodded her head, not sure what her master was getting at.

"I thought you might show her your *Theotokos*."

"Oh, I don't know," Emilia was quick to say, thinking her work was not ready for the eyes of a discerning nun.

"It would give her pleasure—it would remind her of home," he insisted. "And remember: God bestows talent so that it can be shared among us—not so that it can sit on a shelf next to the paintbrushes."

Grasping the compliment, she grinned at her master's remonstration. He was challenging her, trying to bring her work out into the open for others to see, forcing her to see herself as an artist.

"Very well, Makarios. I will see your friend, the sister."

There would be no harm in showing the nun the panel, Emilia decided. Resuming her mixing, she was soon interrupted by the appearance of a young porter at the door.

"I have a letter for Madonna Emilia Serafini," he said.

"*Grazie,*" she mumbled, accepting the ivory envelope and hastily breaking the wax seal imprinted with Franco's arms.

> *Cara Emilia,*
>
> *Your lord father took me quite by surprise yesterday, though it was an egregious fault of mine for having failed to make myself known to him sooner. His concern for his precious daughter's well being is wholly understandable, and I only hope you can find it in your heart to forgive my lack of propriety, as your father has perhaps done. I confess I am overwhelmed with joy over my good fortune. I could not ask for a bride lovelier or more possessed of infinite charms than Emilia Serafini. Have dinner with me tomorrow. I will come for you.*
>
> > *Eternally yours,*
> > *Franco.*

Pleased that she no longer need doubt Franco's intentions, Emilia was surprised that he had asked her to go alone, unescorted, with him to his house when they were not yet married. She supposed that great men like Franco had little patience for social convention.

It still seemed unreal to her that Franco had chosen her to be his wife. She hoped it was not the case that Franco felt coerced into the contract by her father, though she realized it was unlikely that a man like Franco could be coerced into anything. In the end, Emilia preferred to believe that she had brought her wish to life through the power of alchemy. She reminded herself of the way Franco had kissed her at the banquet. And the way he looked at her when he gave her the gold pin. She wanted to think it was, more than anything, love that brought them together.

Throughout the morning, her thoughts flew back and forth between Franco and her painting as she added delicate highlights to the Madonna's rich, purple robe. Painting one tiny line at a time with a brush three hairs in width, she settled into her task for that day. When the highlights were done, she would only have to add the inscription and varnish the panel. She wanted the icon to be beautiful. The last thing she wanted was for Makarios to think he had spent an entire year teaching her for nothing.

The following day Emilia mumbled some excuse to Makarios about going to see the dressmaker before slipping out the door at midday to await Franco. Though she was well aware that she was committing an act of indiscretion before her wedding, Emilia could not find the will to resist Franco's invitation.

"I've missed you dreadfully," her fiancé said.

Emilia, who was riding sidesaddle behind Franco on his massive black stallion en route to his townhouse on the Via de' Bardi, hoped she would not be recognized by anyone she knew. It was unlikely here in the southern *sestiere* of the city, she told herself, and so, although she was somewhat worried, at the same time she felt quite regal when strangers took note of them. She and Franco—who was tall and resplendent in his tunic with hanging sleeves lined with deep purple silk—truly did make a striking couple.

Franco's town home, as she expected, was impressive, if somewhat austere and modest in size. Lifting Emilia off his mount and handing the reins of his horse to the stable boy, Franco led her through the gate and into a wide courtyard surrounded by porticoes. She could see Franco was quite proud of the place, and Emilia held her head higher thinking this fine house would soon be hers as well.

Soundlessly, Tomasso appeared, as though from nowhere, to take her cloak.

"It is a pleasure to see you again, Monna Emilia."

She was surprised to see him, though she should not have been. In deliberately slow acknowledgment of Tomasso's greeting, she nodded silently before strolling into the adjacent parlor. Emilia had not forgotten his haughty behavior at Primavera, even though Franco insisted that Tomasso had been upright in his dealings with the unfortunate maid.

Putting the servant out of her mind, she took note of Franco's many fine objects—a bronze relief, a marble bust, many enamels and ivories, and a mosque lamp. She started to ask him about the lamp, but Franco took firm hold of her hand and said, "I have something to show you."

He guided her to the third floor. Here, a magnificent, central salon glittered with the light of a dozen or more horn lanterns and wax torches on poles. Emilia watched him as he strode over to his tall, handsomely carved bookshelves that held as many leather-bound texts as a learned scholar could hope to own. Franco reminded her of her father just then; she had seen the same look on Francesco Serafini's face when he was inspecting the fine leather saddles he sold at his store.

"Aristotle," Franco said, pulling a purple leather volume from a shelf and thumbing through the pages. He picked up another volume. "Homer. Aristophanes," he said, selecting several more. "Pliny. Have you read Pliny, Emilia?"

"I'm afraid not," she confessed.

Replacing the books on the shelf, he said, "You are fond of the ancients, are you not, Emilia?"

"I suppose," she replied, fingering an intricately carved, pale green gem on his desk. "The truth is, I know too little to comment."

"Come now. A young woman with your curiosity and intelligence? You're being modest," he laughed.

Thinking it best to make light of Franco's question, Emilia smiled. Even though he waited expectantly for her answer, she was not inclined to tell Franco anything about the collection of ancient writing found within her grandmother's manual.

She recalled the first day she met Franco: she had been sitting at the table in the workshop, reading from the manual. When Franco entered the shop, he'd spied the book immediately. He'd tried to take a closer look, but she had resisted and mumbled some sort of excuse.

"Have you read Plato?" Franco pushed her.

"One can hardly ignore Plato here in Florence. My father owns a few books, which I have read from time to time."

"I confess I'm rather surprised. Your father didn't strike me as a particularly scholarly man."

She frowned at this, thinking it rude of him to assume her father was not well educated. "As a matter of fact, he studied Greek and Latin."

"A tavern owner who reads Greek? How unusual."

Exhaling at the affront, she turned to face his bookshelves as she replied, "My father believes in the value of books and reading." She ran her fingers across the leather bindings, noting a copy of Vergil, as well as the works of Petrarch and Boccaccio, and Dante's *Commedia*. "We have Petrarch and Dante at home as well," she added. "My father says my mother indulged my curiosity too much. My mother insisted on the tutor. She is the avid reader in the family, I suppose."

Franco selected another book from the shelves—a very fine, leather-bound text embossed with gold. "Plato's *Republic*," he said like a proud father. "A most worthy purchase, don't you think?" He passed the book to Emilia.

Emilia, knowing nothing of the contents of this text, merely nodded her head and leafed through the pages, many of which were written in the form of a dialogue. "The knowledge of the ancients is surely vast, Franco. Perhaps you'd be better off discussing your book with your friend, Signor Ficino."

"He's quite busy running to and from Cosimo's palace. Still, I suspect he might welcome a lively discussion of the *Republic*. He keeps a candle burning before the bust of Plato at his house," he told her. "I do think I remember something that might be of particular interest him."

"What might that be?"

"That book I saw you reading once. What was it now?" he asked, as though trying to remember. "It was an old text, from your father's library I believe."

She tried to appear nonchalant, to give nothing away, but Emilia was taken off guard by his mention of the alchemical manual. She found it incredible that Franco still recalled the book he had seen in her possession many months ago, when she met him for the first time at the workshop. Focusing her gaze on his neatly arranged volumes, she decided it was quite possible that her grandmother's text had captured Franco's interest in a lasting way.

"What book was that?" she asked.

"I seem to recall you were reading the book the day I met you."

"My father owns a number of books, Franco. You can't expect me to remember what I was reading a year ago," she lied.

"I only remember because it was quite unusual. There was a passage written by Plato. And a drawing—of an Egyptian god I believe."

"What makes you think Marcilio Ficino would care about a book because of a picture of an Egyptian god, Franco?"

"Oh, it struck me as a rare text," he said. "You do remember it then?"

Feeling he had trapped her, she wished he would leave the matter of her book of alchemy well enough alone. "You have an entire library of books, Franco. My father should be as fortunate. I see no reason why you should care so much about some old book from his meager collection."

"I only thought you might like to share what you've read with me."

His annoyance with her was apparent now, though she could see no reason for it. Franco had plenty of books and he certainly did not need to add her grandmother's alchemical manual to his collection. Was this the only reason he was sharing the contents of his library with her? Or perhaps he was trying in his own way to feel closer to her.

"I am sorry if I have vexed you," she said quietly.

Now Franco's face was sullen. "I merely thought, my dear Emilia, that you and I might strive towards an intimacy that exists between the happiest of husbands and wives."

If they were to be married, maybe it was best that they kept no secrets between them. Even if Franco was justified in feeling the way he did, she did not feel prepared to speak with him about her *nonna's* book—not just yet. *Maybe I should,* Emilia thought as she looked into his sad, brown eyes.

"I vaguely remember the book, Franco. I haven't seen it for a long while," she said evenly. "Truly, I can't say what became of it."

"Surely it must still be in your father's library." His voice was sharp.

"Perhaps. As I said, I haven't seen it for some time."

Ignoring her answer, he said, "I'm sure your father wouldn't mind if I had a look at it."

Her father, Emilia knew, was barely aware of the worn old text that had been passed down through his wife's family. As far as Emilia knew, Francesco had never even read the book Violante had bequeathed to her on her fourteenth birthday. Her father was not drawn to the subject of alchemy, he much preferred to spend his time poring over his ledgers. Emilia only wished she could move Franco on to another subject.

"Show me the other rooms," she said, taking him by the hand and leading him away from his precious books.

He guided her to the large kitchen, where two servants were busily preparing the meal. "My future wife, Emilia Serafini," he said to the wide, pink-faced cook Emilia had come to know at Primavera.

Wooden spoon in hand, Bettina gave Emilia a knowing wink and smile before thinking to make a respectful curtsey.

"It's lovely to see you again, Monna Emilia."

Warmed by the familiar face and kind greeting, Emilia allowed Franco to lead her away to the finely appointed bedrooms and lastly to the master's chamber. In Franco's room there was a bed such as she had never seen before. A four-poster, it sat high off the floor, lavishly curtained in heavy brocade that featured purple grapes and green vines on a background of silver and gold. The mattress was covered with luxurious furs.

"It's lovely," she said, running her hand over the bed to feel the softness.

Franco lunged at her, taking her by surprise, pressing his lips against hers and lifting her off the floor and onto the bed. He held her wrists as she struggled to push him away.

"We are expected at dinner," she said, put off by his forcefulness, afraid to suggest that she found him disagreeable in any way.

A look of irritation flitted across his face. Or had she only imagined it? He released her and stepped back, smoothing his hair, his face calm.

"Of course, *amore.*"

She straightened her skirt before following him out to the dining room where the table was set with crystal glasses, silver plates, knives and spoons. Franco helped her into her chair and as she sat down, she considered that many women would give anything to be in her place. Rinsing her hands in the finger bowl of warm, scented water, Emilia Serafini thought that she and Franco would come to understand one another in time. She told herself any difficulties she might experience now with her fiancé were preferable to a life with Benozzo.

Sister Sophia

In November, after All Saint's Day, Emilia met Sister Sophia at the Hospital of Santa Maria Nuova. The tiny old woman took one look at Emilia's *Theotokos* and cracked a wide, yellow-toothed smile.

"Makarios has taught you something wonderful," she said, her voice richly accented. "Every night my mother used to light the candle under our Holy Mother. Your panel reminds me of home."

Emilia nodded in recognition of the life Sister Sophia, like Makarios, had left behind. While Florence had also known bloodshed through the years, Emilia had lived under the firm and artful guidance of Cosimo de' Medici, who managed to keep peace between his allies. A discerning patron of the arts, he had encouraged his favored talent such as architects Brunelleschi and Alberti, sculptors Donatello and Ghiberti, and painters Uccello and Fra Angelico. There was, perhaps, no better place than Florence to be an artist, better so if she had been born a man.

"Thank God for artists," Sister Sophia said. "The artists are the ones who give us hope. Who tell the truth. They speak the language of eternity." Edging closer to Emilia, lowering her voice, the tiny nun added, "Sometimes their language speaks to me even more than that of the priests."

Sister Sophia gazed wistfully at the *Theotokos* and Emilia felt inspired to make a gift of the panel. "I have much to learn before I can paint like Makarios," Emilia began. "But if you like, the icon is yours."

The nun shook her head. "You are very kind. But I couldn't take it without paying. You have to eat, after all," she said, putting a finger to her cheek. Looking slyly at Emilia, she changed her mind, saying, "All right, I will accept your gift, but I must try to arrange something for our mutual benefit."

"Oh?"

"I believe Father Ferondo might be persuaded to part with a few florins in return for a panel for the ward. If you would agree to such an arrangement, that is."

"You have to ask my master for that. I'm only his apprentice," Emilia said.

"And your master is much more costly! We cannot afford Makarios—he's become too well known in Florence," the nun said with a laugh. "His success has surprised quite a few, no doubt."

Emilia knew Sister Sophia was speaking in jest, yet it was not hard to imagine that the Doctors and Apothecaries Guild might accuse Makarios—a suspect foreigner—of conducting business illegitimately. "It's true he always manages to find work," she thought aloud.

"So you will do something for the hospital?"

"If Makarios doesn't object."

The nun dismissed Emilia's concern with a wave of her hand. "He will be pleased that you have found work. I'll speak to Father this week."

Wondering at the charity of the old nun, Emilia murmured a farewell. Delighted to have acquired her first commission, she thought to tell Giacomo all about it until she remembered their last argument. He had crossed her by exposing her relationship with Franco to her father, even so, everything had turned out for the best. Giacomo still knew nothing of her engagement, she suspected he would be disproving when he did find out.

Giacomo had been put off, for good reason, by Franco's warning to stay away from her. However, she realized Giacomo's recounting of Franco's visit to Jacovelli's workshop might differ from Franco's version of the story. Walking back to the *bottega*, she considered the fact that it was quite possible that her friend had exaggerated Franco's remarks.

"*Bene,* Emilia," Makarios said when she related all that had happened during her visit with Sister Sophia. Ceremoniously, he handed her the well-worn manual from the shelf behind his desk. "You'll need to come up with several good sketches to present to them."

Warily, Emilia accepted the weighty book, wondering if she was truly ready to begin a painting of her own. "Sister Sophia said your work is too costly—she wants to encourage me, I suppose."

"She no doubt recognizes talent and knows a bargain when she sees one."

"She has to talk to the priest first."

"Sister Sophia will have her way. She as much as runs the hospital, Brother Giuseppe tells me."

Emilia wondered how the kind little woman she met that day managed to wield such power. Mostly, she was glad that Makarios was not upset with her, though she was also overwhelmed by the task before her. "Do you think I'm capable, Makarios?"

"Of course. What God has called you to do, you can do, Emilia."

As she began to sketch the Virgin in charcoal, Emilia reminded herself that she had been drawing for years—since she was a young girl of eight or nine when she was supposed to be studying Latin, and then with Jacovelli, and then for another year with Makarios. *This is what you wanted*, she reminded herself, pushing the pencil across the page, pretending confidence she did not feel.

She found that by imagining herself capable, she became more so. In this way the drapery began to hang more convincingly from her figures and the lines began to flow more easily. She kept drawing different postures and poses, copying from memory as much as from the book as she moved the charcoal rapidly across the page. Her figures were sure of themselves, with none of the stiffness of her first attempts.

After a time she sensed her master's presence. Turning to look at him, she wondered how long he had been watching her.

"Don't stop!" he insisted. "Keep going. Whatever you're doing, it's wonderful, Emilia. Truly wonderful. You will draw like Masaccio before you're done!"

Looking up from her sketch, she thought aloud, "I'll have to go to Tedaldo for a panel."

"Yes, and be sure to tell him it's for a very special commission—for a personal friend of ours."

As the afternoon drew to a close, Emilia stacked her drawings in a neat pile and went about the room lighting the table lamps for Makarios before it was time for her to return home. In the warm glow of the studio, she felt satisfied, feeling her life was arranged like a carefully composed bowl of fruit. She was traveling in a direction where few women in Florence had ever gone before. Many had told her she would never be a painter. Neither Benozzo nor her father had succeeded in stopping her. Emilia Serafini was setting out to disprove those who did not believe in her.

Back in her bedroom at home that night, reading from her manual, an illustration of an alchemist's flask caught her attention. An image of the moon queen, wearing a jeweled crown and carrying an orb and scepter, was etched into the glass. She read:

> *Let thy creations be imbued with light. Let them be made with the intention of bettering humanity. Let them be made with the intention of bringing blessings to those who suffer on earth. Always create with the purest of heart, so as to ensure outcomes that will be true, clear, and radiant.*

Emilia fell asleep to thoughts and hopes of everything heavenly yet to be created with her paintbrush. In her dreams she was carrying her *nonna's* manual of alchemy outside the studio near the well when someone bumped into her. The book was knocked from her arms. *No!* she cried, and she watched helplessly as it fell into the pit of darkness. She heard the abysmal sound of the text hitting the water. *How will I ever get it back? What will I do?* She was crying, distraught, wondering what she would tell her mother and *Nonna Santina.*

With a start, Emilia awoke. Sitting straight up in bed, she felt around frantically for her book but could not find it. Had she really lost it? Glancing down at the floor, she saw that the manual had fallen beside the bed during her sleep.

On Christmas morning Emilia awoke to a clear, bright winter sky, her heart filled high with expectation. After she and her family attended Mass at Santa Croce, Franco joined them for dinner in their central salon, which was decorated with boughs of pine and festoons of dried berries and flowers. Beside her fiancé at the long trestle table, she wondered at the turn of events that brought Franco into her house and her heart.

The meal was sumptuous, with endless dishes of roasted meat, fowl, pasta, cabbage, and garlic *torta*, an abundance of sweets, nuts, and her father's best wines liberally shared among cousins, aunts, and uncles. Glancing at Franco, Emilia hoped he did not find the celebration with her large, extended family too common. His clothes and his height made him conspicuous; he appeared more like visiting royalty than another family member. Still, he was cordial enough to everyone, with hardly a trace of the distant, aloof manner he sometimes displayed.

Listening to Franco speak to her cousin, Leonardo, about his early childhood in Florence—before his mother died—she wondered if he had ever really recovered from the loss of his family and being shipped off to live with his aunt and uncle. *I was just a boy, ten years old when I went to Genoa. The saddest day of my life.* Ten years old? She thought he had been eight. Well, it made no difference.

On this day of celebration, Emilia did not dwell upon Franco's losses. Like everyone else, she tasted the sweet cakes and candied nuts and enjoyed the lively dancing and songs. Now that she did not have the threat of Benozzo hanging over her head and she had been allowed to continue on with Makarios for a time, there was little to worry about.

She felt especially glad for the surprising commission she had been given by Father Ferondo and Sister Sophia. She had yet to tell Franco about the panel because every time she tried to bring up the subject, he started telling her about the difficulties he was having in Prato or Genoa, or a lost shipment of spices, or the costly roof repairs needed at Primavera. Her fiancé, she understood, was a worldly man, always coming and going, and her modest employment seemed trivial in comparison.

Emilia's mother began to play another lively song on her lute and one of Emilia's cousins grabbed her by the hand and twirled her about the floor. From the corner of her eye, she saw Franco disappear from the room.

Seeking him out a little later, Emilia discovered Franco downstairs in her father's study, inspecting the modest collection of books. She realized at once that he was looking for her alchemy manual, but of course he would not find it there.

"Have you grown bored with the party?" she asked.

"No! It's only that I'm drawn to books, as you know," he replied, reaching into the purse fastened to his belt. "Now that I have you to myself, I want to give you something." He opened his palm to reveal a gleaming pearl-drop necklace set in gold.

"How beautiful!"

Franco fastened it around her neck. "Something to remember me by when I'm away."

"Where are you going this time?"

"Prato again. I leave next week," he said without a hint of sadness.

"Oh," she said, wondering if he looked forward to spending time in distant places without her. She supposed that as the wife of a successful merchant, she would have to accept frequent and lengthy separations from her husband. "How long will you be gone?"

"A month. Maybe two. I'm afraid my trusted Stagio has been stealing from me. The accounts leave little room for doubt."

"I'm sorry," she said. "Perhaps it was only an honest mistake."

Franco shook his head. "You know little of the ways of this world, my dearest."

She did not dream of challenging him on this, but said, "I've been meaning to tell you something too. We have so little time to talk—I received my first commission."

"A commission?" he asked, showing neither pleasure nor disapproval.

"It's just a small panel. I won't be paid much. Still, it is a commission—for the Hospital of Santa Maria Nuova."

"How charming," he said in a way that did not sound entirely congratulatory.

"It is an honor, Franco," she said, wanting him to recognize her accomplishment, however small.

"Of course," he agreed. "I'm glad you have something to occupy yourself with during my absence. Enjoy it while you can. After all, you'll be busy enough after we are married."

His words shook her, brought to mind her father's warning that she would have to give up her profession after she was married. Emilia opened her mouth to speak, thinking she must clear up the matter at once. Then she stopped herself. It was Christmas, she thought, as she fingered the lovely fat pearl. Franco would be leaving Florence again soon. She did not want them to part with bitterness between them.

"Yes, I'm sure the duties of our household will be many, Franco," she murmured. "I only hope I am equal to the task."

"You are quite capable, Emilia," he said. "I believe there is nothing you cannot accomplish if you set your mind to it."

"What have I done to give you such confidence in me?" she asked, wondering if he knew her at all.

"Do you forget? I've seen you at work on a scaffold. Surely a woman who can do this can see that my house is well managed."

So Franco did admire her talent, she told herself, and he recognized her worth as a painter. Plans for the wedding would soon be underway, no doubt there would be plenty of time for her and Franco to sort out their differences. In the meantime she wanted to learn all she could from Makarios, her master, for her days with him were numbered. She would spend the rest of that winter focusing on her work—the fresco of the Procession of the Magi and the panel for Sister Sophia—instead of thinking how she would manage to paint after she was married.

Lavender Bread

Emilia and Makarios were assigned to the *sala* on the second floor of the home of Signor Christofano. It was a cold, wet January, but the servants kept the fire well stoked in the central salon as the painters worked steadily on the fresco of the Procession of the Magi descending from the hills of Fiesole. They were obliged to paint only till midday, when their aging patron returned home from his store of precious silks, because his delicate health and nervous disposition made it impossible for him to tolerate the activities of painters in his home.

Makarios did not seem to mind that he could paint only half a *giornata*, though Emilia thought their patron's request absurd. They would be working on the fresco all winter long at this rate, she thought, gathering the buckets and brushes after another morning's work. She wondered whether Signor Christofano had discovered the *bottega* of Makarios Levantes only after every other workshop in Florence had refused the commission.

"If it takes all winter to finish, then it takes all winter," Makarios said calmly as he examined his latest addition to the wall—the dark face of the wise man wearing a Persian-style hat.

Emilia imagined that Giacomo would find the arrangement laughable, but she could not tell him about it because he was nowhere to be seen since the day Violante invited him to dinner. Matters between the two of them needed to be settled, and she felt compelled to tell him that she was now engaged to Franco. Emilia realized there was little chance of running into Giacomo by chance on the street, so after another abbreviated day of work, she composed a short note.

> *Dear Giacomo,*
>
> *I fear the harsh words of Franco Villani, who is now my fiancé, have caused you to absent yourself from me. I pray you will trouble yourself no longer about this matter. I have exciting news to share with you: I have received a small commission from the Hospital of Santa Maria Nuovo—a Madonna and Child. It is quite modest, of course, but I would value your opinion of my first panel. By the way, Franco has gone away to Prato. For the time being, I am fully occupied with painting.*
>
> *Emilia Serafini.*

After she had completed her letter, Emilia sat in the kitchen while Violante made bread, adding dried lavender flowers to the fresh dough.

"There will be a full moon tonight," Violante said, looking out the window.

"Perhaps a moon queen as well," said Emilia, thinking of her manual.

"You have been reading Nonna's book," Violante observed.

"Then you know of the *coniunctio*–the marriage of the male and female soul?"

"There is a picture—a merging of the moon queen and the sun king. Is that what you mean?"

"*Si*, Emilia. The sun must have the moon to illuminate, or else it would shine all alone in the sky. And so a man needs a woman. Thus, when the moon is full, her power is complete."

"Is this why strange things happen when the moon is full?"

"I have no idea, Emilia. But it wouldn't hurt to wish very hard for what you want right now."

Violante winked at her daughter before pouring olive oil into the ceramic bowl that would contain the rising dough. Up in her room, Emilia read of the marriage of the male and female soul, the *coniunctio* of which Violante had spoken.

The moon is the female soul, as the sun is the masculine body. It is the goal of the alchemical process to unite the moon queen with the sun king.

The union must be done with great care within the vessel, after the rubedo has been completed and the red stone achieved. The proper balance of the elements must then be obtained so that there is the correct amount of warmth and cold, dry and moist; one element must not overpower the other. The process must be done slowly, in due time, so that the king and queen are not burned with too much fire. Done correctly, the mixture will not turn to steam.

When these steps are completed within the alchemist himself, body and soul unite, and he is free to accomplish great deeds as God in heaven smiles upon his holy endeavors.

Emilia began to imagine what great deeds she might accomplish as an alchemist in her own little room in Florence. Perhaps, if she worked carefully, she might keep Giacomo as her friend as well as have Franco as her husband.

Darkness was falling upon the city and the moon was rising as the perfume of lavender bread floated up to her room. Emilia thought about how the mysterious power of the moon was descending from the sky, filling her with luminosity, granting her the ability to receive every miracle that God intended for her.

As a consequence of the letter Emilia wrote or perhaps the power of the full moon—Emilia was not sure which—Giacomo Massarino soon appeared at the *bottega*. Dressed in plum-colored stockings and a well-cut surcoat with cape sleeves and a belt with a silver buckle, he hardly resembled the humble painter wearing paint-splattered clothing that she remembered. He might have passed for a successful merchant, though his stained fingers gave away his true profession.

"I have come to see the work of the painter Emilia Serafini," he said with a mock air of importance.

"Giacomo!" she laughed, rushing to greet him.

He bowed to Makarios and Emilia introduced them. "Giacomo is Lorenzo Jacovelli's best painter. We used to work together when…when I was there as well," she said, hesitating to call attention to her failed apprenticeship at Jacovelli's.

"Yes, of course. The painter who sent letters from Pisa last winter, as I recall," her master said. "You are a busy young man, no doubt. Lorenzo is never without a commission."

"He turns down nothing," Giacomo replied gloomily.

"I understand he has a large family to feed," Makarios said, pulling his long, heavy cloak over his shoulders.

"You're leaving?" Emilia asked, wondering where Makarios was going this time.

"I have been invited to dinner—a friend of Friar Giuseppe's," he explained. "Give my best to Lorenzo," he said to Giacomo before slipping out the front door.

Suddenly alone in the workshop with Giacomo, Emilia was no longer sure what to say. Giacomo, however, appeared at ease as he strode towards her, merriment dancing across his face, his green eyes sparkling like the sea.

"*Come va?* How goes it?" he asked, grasping her hands.

"*Non c'è male.* Not too bad," she replied. "I'm glad you decided to come, Giacomo. I've wanted to tell you I don't blame you at all for what you said to my father. It was all for the best, I suppose."

Ignoring her mention of the incident and making no comment about her engagement, Giacomo said, "Show me what you've done. That is why you asked me here, isn't it?"

Guiding him over to her panel, she said, "Tell me the truth. Makarios has come to treat me too much like a daughter, I fear. I don't think he can easily find fault with my work."

As Giacomo stood before the Madonna adoring her child, Emilia dared not look at his face. She stared instead at her own work, at Mary down on her knees, looking tenderly at the Christ Child, who lay happily upon a carpet of wild flowers in a meadow. Behind these figures, little St. John protected them while a forest of burned and fallen trees and stumps filled the background.

Before she began the panel, she had thought of *Nonna's* alchemy and the *nigredo*. The Great Work, after all, was not irrelevant to her faith but was another way of explaining the works of

God. Emilia had painted a story of everything dead having been burned and uprooted, and new life, the garden of the soul, growing in its place. From the heavens she painted fire—the fire of the Holy Spirit. St. John would use this one day to baptize those who would be reborn.

Giacomo stood silently. Emilia was not sure if he was admiring the piece or else wondering how he might criticize her for placing Christ in a bed of flowers.

"The baby Jesus in a garden plot," Giacomo said, still looking. Then, turning to her, he said simply, "It is highly original. And well done."

"Do you mean it?" she asked.

"An image conceived by a true artist."

"Are you only flattering me? What of the child? I struggled with him so. And the Virgin's mantle. Have I succeeded at all?"

He reached for her hand, saying, "Emilia, you must know you have. It is an admirable first piece."

She smiled at the compliment and he added, "But is it only my opinion that you seek today?"

"What do you mean?"

Softly, teasingly, he said, "I thought you might have missed me a little."

Emilia was not sure what he meant by it. Was he testing her commitment to Franco? Was he trying to see if she was still beholden to Franco's decrees?

"Of course I have missed you, Giacomo," she began. "I'm sorry if you felt as though I put you out of my life."

"You mean as though *Franco Villani* put me out of your life," he said pointedly.

She could not argue that their relationship had been unaffected by her fiancé. But Giacomo had to understand that she would marry some day. Now that she was engaged, Franco had a right to expect her loyalty.

"I am to be his wife," she said quietly. "I cannot completely disregard his wishes."

If she did not imagine it, Giacomo winced. "Yes," he said wryly. "He has purchased you, Emilia. Now you must do his bidding."

Her stomach tightened in a hard knot.

"Perhaps that is your view of the matter, Giacomo," she spat. "I prefer not to look at it that way."

"All right. Say it whatever way you like. But he has changed you. You are not the same as you were when you began as an apprentice,"

"Naturally I'm not the same. I was barely fourteen when I began at Jacovelli's," she exclaimed, wondering how their meeting had veered so far off course.

"When you were fourteen you had courage—courage to dress like a boy because you wanted so much to be a painter."

"You can see I still do," she said, gesturing to her panel. "Do you think I paint just to pass the time?"

Coming closer, he grasped her firmly by the shoulders.

"No, I think you still want to paint. That's why it's a travesty that you should give it up!"

Emilia leaned away from him, afraid of what she was feeling. Giacomo was still holding her, looking at her with something other than the concern of a trusted friend. Something between them had shifted, though she couldn't say how or when this had happened. As much as she wanted to deny it, she could feel that he wanted more from her now.

She loved Franco. Of course she loved him. But Giacomo was moving closer and she knew, as her heart raced, that he would kiss her. She was no longer thinking of Franco. She was only aware of the heat of Giacomo's touch as he took her hand, threading his stained fingers with hers, the colors of their flesh forming an artist's palette.

His eyes held hers as he drew her close. She could feel his breath on her skin, smell the sweetness of him. She was scared, trying to fight the power of longing as he pulled her towards him, kissing her gently at first. She took in the warm taste of him. Then he said her name, kissed her again less patiently. Her eyes were closed as she drank in the sensation, potent and delicious.

It was completely wrong. Reminding herself that she was a betrothed woman, Emilia struggled to take hold of her senses. Finally, she pulled away.

"I cannot," she cried. "I cannot. You have no right."

Giacomo kept his eyes locked on her.

"Would you really marry him, Emilia?"

Bracing herself against the worktable, she replied slowly, "He will make a good husband. I only wonder if I am worthy of him."

"It's not too late to walk away."

"Walk away? It's all been arranged. How can you suggest such a thing?" she said, scrambling to make sense of her own feelings.

He nodded, laid a finger lightly on the edge of her panel. "Then you are quitting before you have even started, Emilia. I cannot help you."

He walked toward the front door and Emilia wondered how everything had suddenly changed between the two of them. "You do matter to me, Giacomo. I don't want to lose you!" she blurted as he opened the door to leave.

Turning, he looked at her and replied, "We all have to make choices, Emilia. We cannot choose to be everything at once."

When the door closed behind him she began to sob. Had she been fooling herself all this time? Was it impossible for her and

Giacomo to care for one another as friends and nothing more? She had imagined she would find some way to fit him and painting into her life after she married Franco—she would meet Giacomo at his studio, or he would join her and Franco at their home as a dinner guest.

But Giacomo had kissed her and nothing would ever be the same between them again. She could not act as though none of this had happened. Nor was it easy to deny what she felt when she was in Giacomo's arms.

Persephone

Emilia's thoughts were of Giacomo, of the strange and unexpected kiss. Though she told herself she ought to have been outraged by his impropriety, she found herself reliving the kiss over and over again. It was, she admitted, a form of disloyalty to Franco that would require a painful confession to the priest. Giacomo was a friend who had touched her in a way he ought not to have. Besides that, he had accused her of sacrificing her ambition for Franco.

She was trying to sort out her feelings for Giacomo as she returned home from the *bottega* that afternoon. Crossing the river at the Ponte Vecchio, she noticed a short, thick figure in a dark cape and brimmed hat standing like a sentinel on the far side of the bridge. As she neared him, the figure moved abruptly off to the west. Emilia proceeded down the *lungarno*, along the river, towards Santa Croce, but sensing something, she turned to look behind her and the same man was again watching her. Even from a distance, she could sense his eyes—the eyes of Tomasso if she was not mistaken—fixed upon her.

The sight of Tomasso, if it was indeed Tomasso, made her shudder. Emilia had to wonder why he was standing at the bridge and why he had started to go off in one direction then turned to look at her once more. Perhaps Tomasso had as little desire to see her as she to see him, for Emilia had made no secret of her dislike for him.

The near encounter with Tomasso was unsettling. Emilia felt as though her privacy had been invaded and her infidelity to Franco was somehow visible. At home, Emilia barely touched her soup of beef and pasta at supper.

"Tell me what's wrong, *mia figlia*, my daughter," Violante asked.

"She's lovesick for *Franco Villani*," her brother croaked sarcastically before following his father to the salon for a game of cards.

Emilia threw Andrea a cutting glance but did not answer her mother, afraid to tell Violante the truth. All that Emilia could do now was bury her indiscretion with Giacomo. When Franco returned from Prato, everything would be the same as it was before his departure. The wedding would move forward, her *cassone*—her wedding chest—would be packed, she would prepare for a new life with her husband and spend her summers painting in Fiesole.

"Nothing is wrong, Mama," Emilia insisted as Violante tried to tempt her with a plate of sugared dates. "I am just tired from too much work on the scaffold today. Makarios is so slow. He needs me to do everything. Working in fresco is too hard for him," she lied.

Sitting down next to her daughter, Violante chewed a date as she appeared to consider Emilia's explanation.

"Working all day usually makes you hungry, Emilia. I have to wonder if it is something more than fatigue that takes away your appetite."

Emilia did not answer at first. Violante knew her too well and was not persuaded by her tale of overwork. How could Emilia confess that Giacomo had kissed her, then accused her of sacrificing her profession and caused her to question her feelings for Franco? She would not tell her mother these things because then she would have to admit that trading Benozzo for Franco had solved nothing. Emilia was determined to appreciate the many advantages marriage to Franco would provide her and her family. She would live in the beautiful *palazzo* with Franco and honor her commitment.

"Really, I'm fine," Emilia said. "It's only the thought of leaving you and Father when I marry, I suppose. I will be happy to live with Franco, of course. But I'll be all alone with him."

Violante kissed her daughter's head.

"I won't be far away, *cara*. We will see each other all the time, you know. Franco will just have to get used to having his mother-in-law underfoot."

Emilia tried to look lighthearted for her mother. "Yes, he will. There are things we will both have to get used to, I daresay."

She was beginning to accept that life with Franco would not be quite as simple as she had imagined in the days before her engagement. The certainty she once felt about the wealthy spice merchant was now shaded by doubt. Surrounded by her family that night, she sat embroidering a pillow cover and mulling over Giacomo's assertion that it was impossible to have everything at once. *We all have to make choices*, he had said. It seemed as though *Nonna's* alchemy was failing her. Or perhaps God was punishing her for thinking she might control her own destiny. At the very least, the Great Work was not as easy as she had hoped.

During the days ahead, Emilia worked hard on the fresco for Signor Christofano, as though to atone for what had happened with Giacomo. As though the mixing and the plastering would make up for her infidelity. As though scurrying up and down the scaffold would help her to know what it was she desired most.

At about that time, Emilia began reading a chapter in the manual, "The Mysteries." In it, the author spoke of the secret rituals of the ancients, the Greater and Lesser Mysteries, though Emilia was not sure what any of this had to do with the creation of gold, metallic or otherwise. It was said that the Lesser Mysteries, celebrated in the Temple of Demeter near Athens, were attended by the thousands who came seeking the true reality of life and death.

Curled up in bed one dark winter night, the orange light of her lamp illuminating the yellowed parchment, Emilia read of the ceremonies. The secret ritual of the Greater Mysteries, Emilia read, was held every five years at Eleusis, where Persephone had first disappeared, swept below the ground to the underworld by Hades, and where Demeter had wept for the loss of her beloved daughter.

Transported to the world of the ancients, Emilia read on, learning the hidden secrets of the Greater Mysteries.

> *On the thirteenth of September, young men and women gather at Eleusis to begin the solemn, twelve-mile procession to Athens in preparation for the Greater Mysteries....*

> *Dressed in deer skins, to symbolize the animal nature, the mystics are led to the labyrinth of hell. Cut off from all knowledge and light from the external world, they are met with horrifying sounds of moaning and frightening screams. Great thunderbolts shake the passageways of the labyrinth and flashes of light reveal glimpses of gruesome creatures and ghouls.*

> *In complete darkness once again, they are seized,*

beaten, and thrown to the ground. At this point, there are those who choose to retreat, to turn back and seek the exit. In so doing, they forever lose the opportunity for initiation.

It is a form of cruelty that allows the mystics to witness the lifting of the curtain separating the visible from the invisible world. The lower depths of the spirit world—the demonic—are fully known....

The description of the elaborate ceremony continued, leading to the domain of Hades and eventually Persephone's reunion with her mother, her collapse and death when Hades again caught her, and finally her rebirth as a goddess.

At the conclusion of the ceremonies, Emilia read, the initiates were said to be filled with unspeakable happiness. The fear of death was overcome, the bright light within was revealed. The choice set forth by the drama was made clear to Emilia: to become a mystic, already immortal, before death or else to experience the true torments of hell after dying.

The temple of Eleusis, Emilia read, was closed in the year 385 by Emperor Theodosius the Great upon the decree of the Holy Roman Catholic Church. Emilia was a young girl living in the year 1461. The mysteries had long since disappeared. Or perhaps somewhere, unknown to her and the other good citizens of Florence, there were mystics wandering a labyrinth and experiencing the horrors of hell so that they would not face the same plight after death.

If she could not walk through the frightening enactment of the sacred myth, perhaps at least her own suffering counted for something. As she considered the self-inflicted misery of the ancients, Emilia wondered if it was truly necessary to experience utter darkness before finding happiness. She had known pain before and accepted this as part of life. But the horrors of hell? She was not sure she was up to the task of a mystic.

She did know one thing after reading these passages: Franco coveted her text for good reason. She did not have to be a scholar like Marsilio Ficino to recognize the rarity of the ancient writings, these strange mysteries. To protect the precious book, Emilia stored it away in her *cassone*, beneath an embroidered tablecloth, where it would be safe.

When she arrived at the workshop the next morning, Emilia went to her little nook behind the kitchen to take off her cloak and put on her apron, as she always did. It was then that she noticed her blanket was slightly rumpled, as though someone might have rested on her bed. She thought it strange, because Makarios was not known to have company.

When her master took his seat at his desk, she asked, "Was someone in my room last night?"

"Who would be in your room, Emilia?"

"It looks as though someone was in there," she said. "I think the bedding is not as I left it."

Makarios disappeared to examine the back room. He returned momentarily to report, "It looks the same to me, Emilia. No one was here that I know of, but I was out for a while last night."

She studied the room again, wondering if it was the work of ghosts. There was no reason to think anyone would enter her room uninvited. Still, she went to work with the unsettling feeling that someone had been in the *bottega* who ought not to have been.

Palazzo Vecchio

When her fiancé returned from Prato, Emilia told herself, she would forget her inconvenient preoccupation with Giacomo Massarino. She tried to remember the evening of her sweet enchantment with Franco, the way she felt when he kissed her on the balcony at Primavera. Emilia pictured the beautiful women in their brightly colored silks, the sparkling silver trays heaped with antipasti, and the look of Franco—tall, commanding, and resplendent—looking like a knight at the center of the table.

As much as she tried to dismiss him, the image of copper-haired Giacomo kept rising to the surface of her mind. She reminded herself that no painter would be able to offer her the type of life promised by Franco. Besides, Giacomo was consumed with his art and made no pretense of wanting a wife.

Determined to put Giacomo Massarino out of her thoughts, Emilia made preparations for her upcoming marriage, sometimes excusing herself early from the workshop to spend the afternoon hours selecting cloth—rose and saffron silks, purple taffeta, and blue dam-ask—for new gowns. If she was going to look the part of Franco's wife, she could not very well go about Florence in last year's styles.

Returning home with Violante after a visit to the *sarta*, the dressmaker, Emilia retired to her room for an afternoon nap. She was about to lie down on her bed when she noticed a bit of blue fabric—from her new, blue headdress it appeared—sticking out of her *cassone*.

On closer inspection, it definitely looked as though some-one had been rummaging through her possessions. Carefully, she started to refold her clothing, wondering if it was Veronica who had been rifling through her chest. Just as she had almost finished restoring order to the *cassone*, she realized with a start that her precious manual was missing. Frantically, she began tossing out linens, shifts, head coverings, and stockings. To her horror, the alchemy manual was no longer there.

Surrounded by a heap of clothing, Emilia panicked. She searched her room, looked beneath the bed, under the pillows, or any place she might have left the manual in a fit of absentmind-edness. When she still could not find the book, she thought her mother might have borrowed it. Rushing to Violante's room, she pushed open the door.

"What is it, *amore*?" Violante murmured sleepily, stirring from her *riposa*. Seeing the panic-stricken look on Emilia's face, she sat up.

Kneeling at her mother's bedside, Emilia asked, "Do you have *Nonna's* book, by any chance?"

"The manual? You haven't misplaced it?"

"I stored it in my *cassone* after I last read it. I'm sure I did. It looks like someone was rummaging through my things. Someone must have taken it."

Violante, now fully awake, declared, "We must search the house. It has to be here somewhere. Who would think to steal it?"

They proceeded to conduct a thorough search of every room and all the while Emilia considered her mother's question. She knew of one person who coveted the old manuscript: Franco Villani, her fiancé. He had as much as demanded that she share the book with him the day he invited her to dinner at his townhouse. But Franco was away in Prato now. He could hardly be blamed.

Emilia and Violante searched under the beds, through the drawers and chests, even in the pantry. Still they could not find any sign of the text. Emilia knew, with a sinking feeling, that it was gone. She recalled the other day when she had noticed the rumpled blanket on her bed at the workshop, and she wondered if the thief might have been looking for the book there as well.

She began stringing together the strange happenings of late: she recalled the glimpse of Tomasso by the bridge; she remembered Filippa looking through her belongings when Emilia was working at the villa as well as the argument she overheard between Tomasso and the maidservant. With a growing sense of certainty, Emilia began to believe this was all Tomasso's doing. Perhaps Tomasso, imagining her relationship with Franco was a threat to his position, was trying to torment Emilia. Yet how would he have known anything about the old book?

It was not hard to imagine that the manservant had eavesdropped on any number of his master's conversations. Tomasso could have easily overheard her and Franco discussing the text. There was ample opportunity the day Franco brought her to his library. Emilia could prove nothing at this point, though she had never trusted Tomasso. The idea that Franco might be involved as well was a thought she was not yet prepared to entertain.

"I hate to say this, but I'm afraid this has something to do with

Franco's manservant," Emilia confessed to Violante as the two ex-hausted women sat on Andrea's bed, having given up on finding the manual in the house.

"How would he know anything about it?"

"From Franco—he saw the manual a long time ago, when I was reading it at the *bottego*. I tried to hide it from him, but he fixed on it at once. He knows it's quite rare—he is a collector," Emilia began. "Tomasso might have overheard Franco talking about the book to someone."

She told Violante of Franco's repeated requests to see the text, his questioning of the contents, and of the strange episode when Filippa had been caught pilfering through her bag while Franco was away. Emilia also told her mother of Marsilio Ficino's inter-est in the book. When the philosopher had pushed her to reveal the whereabouts of the text that contained writings of the ancient Egyptian sage, Emilia had been vague. Cosimo's scholar might covet the book, yet he was surely above stealing. Somehow she could not say this with any sense of confidence about Franco—her own fiancé.

As Emilia spoke, Violante's countenance grew somber. "You must see then, *cara*, it is possible that Franco is the one who is behind Tomasso's actions."

"No, he wouldn't," Emilia protested.

Even as she tried to believe the blame lay all with Tomasso, she could not deny her deepest suspicion that Tomasso might have acted on Franco's behalf.

Beside herself with grief over the loss of the manual, she broke into tears. "I have to get it back. What should I do, mother?"

"I don't know, Emilia. We'll figure something out. One way or another. The book belongs to you and no one else."

Emilia could only hope her mother was right. If the book was lost forever, she would never be able to forgive herself. If her fiancé was the thief, she had made more mistakes than she could ever admit. Her heart sank, for Emilia was no longer entirely sure she wanted to be the bride of Franco Villani.

The loss of *Nonna's* manual weighed heavily on Emilia's mind the following week. She held imaginary conversations with Franco, asking him over and over again if he had put Tomasso up to the deed of stealing her book. Franco, far away in Prato, remained silent, imperious, beyond reproach. When she sat down to write her fiancé, her words spilled out as angry accusations. If Franco was innocent, he would judge her as untrue, unworthy of being his bride. She discarded the letter to the embers in the smoldering hearth fire, although part of her still feared Franco was guilty.

She could forget her worries when she was painting at Signor Christofano's, but when she was back at the *bottega,* her suspicions grew louder. Her cooking for Makarios suffered, often she made basic errors such as over-salting the soup. One afternoon she tried to make apple fritters, following a recipe from Violante's cookbook.

Boil some apples or cook them under ashes, then remove the skins and hard cores and mash them well. Mix a little leavening with meal and sugar and add this to the cooked apples, then add some egg whites. Bring a pan of fat to boil and fry the fritters. When they are done, sprinkle them with sugar and cinnamon and keep them hot.

Though she nearly burned the fritters, Makarios praised her efforts. After restoring order to the little kitchen, Emilia decided to see if the cobbler had finished her new, red leather shoes. Makarios, no doubt seeing her attention lay elsewhere, nodded in assent.

When she crossed the Piazza della Signoria, she realized she was not far from Jacovelli's. After her last encounter with Giacomo, she felt reluctant to see him, let alone tell him about the disappearance of her precious book. He would probably be quick to blame Franco and once again assail her plans to marry.

While she could not forget his accusatory words, she knew, deep down, that Giacomo cared for her. She was not naïve enough to believe that one kiss meant that he loved her; she was not sure if Giacomo could love anything other than painting. Besides, she was still betrothed to Franco and had no business thinking of Giacomo in these terms. Of course there was a chance Franco was the one behind the theft. For the hundredth time, she asked herself who else might have stolen the manual. Some random thief? Marsilio Ficino? Another of Makarios' patrons, someone who had happened to notice the text? The suspicion that the crime was her fiancé's would not leave her. Guided by these dark thoughts, she moved closer to Jacovelli's.

Soon she found herself standing at the entrance of her previous employer's *bottega*. Reluctant to enter, she waited at the door until Giacomo spotted her and rose to greet her. He showed no sign of remembering their previous disagreement, though he was quick to sense Emilia's unhappiness.

"Why so sad? You haven't come to tell me you can never see me again?" he asked, keeping his voice below the din of the workshop.

Emilia shook her head. "My present difficulty has nothing at all to do with you, Giacomo. Though perhaps you are not the person I should turn to."

"I am precisely the person you should turn to. For anything."

She was not sure what to make of his show of concern. In the background, Jacovelli's apprentices had become suspiciously quiet, obviously straining to hear the private conversation.

"Shall we walk?" she suggested.

"As you wish," he said, already turning to grab his cloak.

As she and Giacomo prepared to leave, Jacovelli's voice boomed out merrily from his desk on the raised platform, "It is our own Alessandro, is it not!"

Emilia turned to face him. "It is Emilia Serafini, apprentice of Makarios Levantes," she replied.

"The foreigner from across the river? Well, well," he said, thoroughly amused with his discovery. "You have determination, I'll give you that. Give my regards to Levantes."

"I will. *Grazie, Maestro,*" she said, warmed by his words.

It was a cold day with long shadows and blue sky as they passed Orsanmichele, the home of Donatello's statue of St. Mark, known for its penetrating stare. Emilia still wondered how much she ought to tell Giacomo. Despite the reservations she had felt about coming, she felt comfortable beside him. The familiarity between the two of them was accounted for in more ways than the mere circumstance of their shared profession.

"I'm afraid I may have erred rather grievously, Giacomo."

There was a pause in his step before he asked, "In what way?"

Without thought or plan, she confessed her deepest fear. "You might be right about my engagement."

"So what finally made you come to your senses?" he said, as though relieved.

"Something has happened," she said. "I have reason to believe that my fiancé's servant may have done something…something unforgivable."

"Tell me."

"There is a book, a very old book that belonged to my great-great-great grandmother. My mother gave it to me on my fourteenth birthday," Emilia began, choosing her words carefully, still hesitant to reveal too much. "It's a translation of a very unusual text—it contains writings from the ancients. Franco discovered it and he seemed to be of the opinion that it's quite rare."

Emilia stopped, thinking that Giacomo might suppose her quite foolish for worrying so much about a lost book. But he encouraged her to continue.

After she related all that had happened at Primavera and the recent, unexplained occurrences, she said, "The book is gone, Giacomo. Nowhere to be found. I hope Franco is not behind it. Anyway, he is away in Prato now."

"Of course it was Franco! But if you accuse him, he would deny it," Giacomo exclaimed.

"I cannot accuse him—I have no proof."

"You must find a way to prove him guilty."

"He might not be."

"For heaven's sake, Emilia. Who else knew of it? Who else could it have been?"

She shrugged. "It could be anyone who stumbled upon it, I suppose."

Emilia looked out across the expansive square. What she saw made her hope her eyes were deceiving her. There before the Palazzo Vecchio, the Old Palace, was a short, squat man walking with a familiar air of self-importance. Before she could get a good look at his face, the man turned the other way.

"It can't be him," she said.

"Who?"

"Over there," she said, "in front of the Palazzo. It looks like Tomasso. He's the one—Franco's manservant. Why would he be following me?"

"There's only one way to find out," Giacomo said, and he moved ahead of her with long, quick strides towards the massive palace with the enormous stone tower looming overhead.

"No, Giacomo," she called after him. "I don't think it's wise."

Giacomo, already halfway to Tomasso, was not listening. She watched uneasily as Giacomo loomed menacingly over Franco's manservant, who puffed out his chest in an appearance of being thoroughly affronted.

When she caught up with them, Tomasso pretended he was surprised to see her. He doffed his cap and bowed.

"She knows you've been following her," Giacomo said.

Tomasso was willing to admit nothing. "I am on an errand for Signor Villani," he said, indicating the leather bag at his side. "If Monna Emilia sees fit to go cavorting through the streets of Florence with the likes of you, it is surely none of my concern." He eyed Giacomo's paint-splattered hands and worn cloak with contempt.

This was all the provocation Giacomo needed to lunge at the man. Emilia stared in horror at the scene. Tomasso, quick and agile, managed to dart away into the open piazza. Half a dozen bystanders turned to gawk at the commotion as Giacomo chased Tomasso, managing to stick on his tail.

Emilia, seeing what she had put in motion, cried out after him, "Don't, Giacomo. It's no use." Watching the scene in dismay, she wondered what had become of the even-tempered man she had known.

"Both of you. There's no need," but her words were to no avail.

At the far end of the piazza, Giacomo finally caught up with Tomasso and overpowered him, knocking him over so that he landed on the ground with a heavy thud. The manservant lay sprawled, the breath knocked out of him, his hat tossed to the side, and Emilia was aghast to see a mean gash across his forehead. Giacomo, clenching his hand in a fist, ready to strike again, surveyed the damage without apology.

Tomasso was not down for long. Sitting up, his only visible emotion was a sinister smile. Emilia shivered. Somehow the man still perceived himself as victorious.

"I must confess I find myself at a loss."

Tomasso pulled himself up off the ground and reached for his hat. Blood trickled down his forehead. Staring at Emilia with cold, dark eyes, he carefully replaced his hat on his head.

"Your friend has accosted me, unprovoked."

Before Emilia could reply, Giacomo retorted, "You know very well what you were doing! She saw you by the bridge and then again over here. What's the meaning of it? Why are you following us?"

Dabbing his brow with a handkerchief, Tomasso replied, "As I said, I was merely on an errand of my master's bidding."

Filled with revulsion, Emilia repeated, "Your master's bidding?" Wondering if all his nefarious deeds were carried out on Franco's behalf, she envisioned Tomasso sneaking into her house, opening drawers, running his hands through her stockings, her slips and gowns. He was a man without scruples, one who would not think twice about stealing her manual.

"I had not the slightest inclination to follow you nor to inquire what you are doing, unescorted, with a man who is neither your brother nor your father. It is surely none of my concern," the man-servant maintained, smoothly, like a practiced liar.

His deceit infuriated her. At the same time, she was afraid that all would be reported to Franco. She should never have sought out Giacomo. It was a mistake, she thought. Tomasso observed her with barely concealed derision.

"We are merely on our way to the Duomo to study the frescoes," Emilia said, struggling for an excuse.

"You owe him no explanation," Giacomo interrupted. "You are entitled to come and go through the streets of Florence as you see fit. You most certainly are entitled to walk without being followed by some inconsequential house servant."

Unperturbed, Tomasso retorted, "If I happened to see Monna Emilia, who is of course betrothed to Franco Villani, it was no fault of mine. I am not the one who will have to provide Signor Villani with an explanation."

Tomasso slithered along on his way and Emilia knew he was right. Franco would not easily dismiss his fiancé's appearance of infidelity, whatever his feelings for her at this point. Deny impropriety as she might, Franco would insist that she had flouted his will. Walking with Giacomo along the Via Calzaiuoli, Emilia asked herself why Franco would employ such a despicable little man. But she already knew that Tomasso spared Franco the trouble of dirtying his own hands.

Giacomo, she realized, had put himself in harm's way to defend her. Seeing the fury in his eyes, she was not sure what to make of the swift action he had taken on her behalf. Back in the days when they worked together at Jacovelli's *bottega*, she had faulted Giacomo for his disinterest in anything other than frescoes and panels. Yet here he was, risking his painting hand, acting more like one of the guards who frequented her father's tavern than a preoccupied artist. He truly did care for her, perhaps more than she had dared to think.

Turning to face Giacomo, she said, "I don't see how I can marry Franco Villani."

"Of course not. He is a demon," he said.

"Whether he stole my book or not, I'm sure he's asked Tomasso to watch my every move. I cannot live like this, Giacomo."

"You must tell your father," he agreed. "It has to be put to an end at once."

"But everything is arranged," she said, wishing Giacomo

would say something more. Were Franco and Tomasso the only reasons she should end the engagement? Did it have nothing at all to do with the way Giacomo felt about her?

"You have no need of Franco, Emilia. You are a painter," he said, revealing nothing more. "It's what we both are."

She nodded, wanting this to be true, but knowing it was not as easy for her to declare herself a painter, impervious to the conventions of society, as it was for Giacomo. Besides, maybe there was something else she wanted in addition to the freedom to paint. But Giacomo Massarino offered not even the hint of a promise.

She parted from him reluctantly, feeling as though there were unspoken words left between them. Had Giacomo acted merely to protect her from Franco? Or did Giacomo want her for himself? If he did, she wished he would say so. Giacomo kissed her goodbye on the cheek and left her to return to the routine tasks of her day. When she walked through the door of the workshop feeling little inclined to work, Makarios eyed her with a curious smile.

"Didn't the cobbler have your shoes, Emilia?"

"Shoes? Oh, the shoes. No, they weren't ready. I'm sorry I was so long in returning."

Makarios nodded then dipped his pen into the ink. She had not fooled her master one bit, but he would forgive her absentminded state. Emilia could think only of Giacomo, the strange closeness between them that she could not put into words. The feeling gave her no lightness of heart; her precious book was still missing and she was engaged to one man but thinking about a painter who promised her nothing.

Alchemy

Two weeks after Giacomo's brawl with Tomasso, Franco sent word that he was returning to Florence.

My Dearest Emilia,

I am nearly finished with my obligations here in Prato. Several trusted workers have been acquired. Next week I will be able to return home with some degree of confidence that I will not be robbed blind once again.

I am eager to see you, my beloved darling, and to share springtime with you in Fiesole. Please forgive my extended absence. It is my deepest wish that there should never be any distance between us. With great anticipation I look forward to the blessed state of holy matrimony and to giving you everything you should ever desire, just as you, in your generosity, have always given me.

Send my kindest regards to you father, mother, and Andrea.

Faithfully yours,
Franco

So he was going on with this farce as though nothing at all was the matter, Emilia thought, tossing the letter aside. His words left her cold and uneasy. *Just as you have always given me.* Was he referring to what she had, in fact, withheld from him—the manual? Or was he referring to something else she had failed to reveal—the truth of her ongoing relationship with Giacomo?

She was not at all sure what she would do when Franco did return to Florence. Would he wait for her to tell him about the missing book while maintaining his façade of innocence? Guilty or not, he would pretend to be deeply hurt if she dared to ask what he knew of the matter.

She imagined the vicious lies Tomasso would tell Franco. The manservant would spin an ugly tale, embellished with scenes of her supposed infidelity. The accusation would serve as an excuse for Franco to be rid of her, if, in fact, he wanted to be rid of her.

Surely Franco did not believe they would follow through with the marriage? The deceit between the two of them was too serious. The matter should be brought before her father. Francesco ought to know that Franco enlisted Tomasso to watch her every move and probably to steal *Nonna's* book. But if her father learned that Tomasso had been trailing her, he might also discover that she had been seen with Giacomo Massarino. There would be difficult questions she would be forced to answer.

If only there was proof that Franco had indeed stolen the book. The servants had all been questioned and the only fragment of evidence was that Veronica heard footsteps upstairs when she was bringing in the wash one morning. Veronica had supposed it was Maddalena upstairs, but when Maddalena came up from the cellar, Veronica decided it had to be the ghost who visited from time to time.

It did not matter to Emilia that no one had seen Tomasso in the house. More and more she was convinced that he and Franco were responsible for the wrongdoing. This conviction made Franco's words of kindness all the more disturbing. It was as though he had taken his stance and was waiting for her to make a move so that he could pounce. She was not sure what she could do to save herself from him.

If there was such a thing as alchemy, it had clearly gone wrong. Emilia recalled something she had read in the manual of the preparatory steps and of the *albedo*—the whitening. The period of washing could take days or weeks or even years. If the alchemist proceeded to the next step before the washing was complete, his creations would be tainted, imperfect despite the best of intentions.

Emilia felt as though she was at the very beginning again, when all was darkness. And the darkness was the darkness in her own soul, her own thoughts. She could admit readily enough that she had wanted to marry Franco for all the wrong reasons. She had coveted the finery he could provide and she had sought an escape from Benozzo, who had seemed a much lesser man. Her so-called love for Franco was rooted in earthly desire, her own greed.

The white queen referred to in the *albedo* eluded her, so she could not possibly have achieved the fiery hot red king, the *rubedo*, which granted the alchemist the power to live beyond her imagination and bring her creations to life. It was pure foolishness to have supposed the red lapis of the third phase was within her possession. With a heavy sigh, Emilia admitted that she had set about the business of making gold before it was time.

One must empty himself of all that is not God, often through great trials, those were the words she had read. It was not possible to learn the secrets of alchemy while lusting after earthly pleasures. She had learned her lesson, but Emilia had not yet paid the entire price, for Franco would be returning home to see her. Repulsed by the thought of his touch, she thought she might flee from Florence for a time. She could pretend sudden, grave illness; her mother could say she had been sent to the doctors in Bologna for a cure.

After several anguished nights, Emilia finally confessed her plight to her parents. Although Violante was sympathetic, her father would not hear her pleas to be free of her marriage contract. Franco remained, in Francesco's opinion, a most suitable choice for his daughter, and the question of the lost book seemed like an insignificant detail in light of all that Franco could provide.

"It is a trivial matter, Emilia. Surely, you can see your way to put this all behind you," he said, unconcerned, as he sat before the fire in his favorite chair.

"Yes, perhaps she might," Violante replied for her daughter. "Though I only wonder how she could come to trust him again. Who knows where his spy has been, Francesco. It turns my stomach to think he sent his servant sneaking through our house. What if Franco really is a criminal? Who knows what else he is capable of?"

"You're making too much of this, Violante," her father said irritably. "To think you would have our daughter throw away her entire future."

"I don't want her to do that. Of course not, Francesco," she said. Emilia saw her mother was straining to control her true feelings about Franco. Under her breath she added, "We can always hope he is not a very bad man at the core."

Rising from his chair in impatience, Franceso headed to the cellar, grumbling, "He is a rich man. A very rich man! What is the point in worrying about a useless old book? There is no reasoning with this daughter of mine."

Looking at Emilia's distraught face, Violante said, "I'm sorry to say such things about him, *cara*. But I think you know I never liked Franco. He has darkness in his eyes."

Too ashamed of the trouble she had caused for her family, Emilia did not protest. "I couldn't see it. I wanted to believe he was everything I dreamed of."

"No one can blame you, Emilia. Some things we have to learn the hard way."

"What will I do when he comes home?" Emilia asked her mother. "Can I tell him the wedding is off?"

Violante stared into the flames of the fire, considering her daughter's question.

"I'm not so sure you want to do that, Emilia. Perhaps for the time being, it might be best to play along with Franco's game."

"Play along? How do you mean?"

"If Franco did arrange for Tomasso to steal the text, then he is waiting for you to react—to tell him the book is lost, to accuse him of stealing it. I'm afraid if you break off the engagement, he would have everyone in Florence question your honor. He might say cruel things about you that could tarnish your reputation. He would play the victim and he would still have your book."

Emilia wondered if her mother was correct in these assumptions. She was afraid that if she waited and did nothing, she would find herself standing next to Franco on the steps of Santa Croce, reciting her vows.

"I have to be free of him, Mother. I can't let it go on too long."

"It won't. Franco won't be able to stand your silence. If he is truly guilty, he will know you are withholding what you know from him and he will crack."

"How can you be so sure?"

"If he was a patient and honest man, he would not set spies after you. He would not try to force you to give him *Nonna's* book. He would have waited until you were ready to share it with him.

But Franco Villani is a pig—a selfish, greedy, but very insecure pig. If you remain composed, he is sure to grow uneasy."

As she went up to bed, Emilia thought over her mother's advice. She was not convinced that Franco would eventually reveal his true colors, but she could think of no better plan than to wait him out. If her fiancé learned from Tomasso that she had been spending time with Giacomo Massarino, then he would indeed be hard pressed to pretend that nothing was the matter. Perhaps this news would be enough to make him call off the wedding and return her freedom. Even so, she still did not know how to solve the problem of her missing book.

Signor Christofano was so delighted with the Procession of the Maji that he paid Makarios an additional five florins upon its completion. Happy to have finished the fresco, Emilia's master announced that he would now begin a small nativity requested by Friar Giuseppe, a wedding gift to his nephew.

As Makarios began the drawings for his latest commission, Emilia kept the studio clean and cooked for her master, wishing she had something more substantial to occupy her time. There was only so much cleaning to be done, which meant there was plenty of time to think about the mistake she had made in falling for Franco Villani.

When Makarios noticed her sulking, he commented, "You have preparations for the wedding, no doubt? Franco should be returning home soon, yes?"

"The wedding—the wedding is not that important," she said, hardly knowing what to tell him about her recent troubles with her fiancé and his manservant.

"Not that important?" Makarios said, looking at her incredulously. "Last week you could talk of nothing else. What has happened?"

There was no point in keeping secrets from him, so Emilia confessed that all was lost with Franco and that his manservant may have stolen into the workshop as well as her house in order to take a book of alchemy that had been in her family for years.

"After all this I feel no love for Franco, I'm afraid. My mother would have me remain silent for the time being. I am to pretend all is well when I see him," she explained. "My mother thinks it best that I accuse him of nothing."

Makarios appeared to consider her mother's advice before announcing, "You must paint another icon. The Archangel Michael perhaps—the protector of God's people. He will keep you safe."

"Michael. I would like that," Emilia smiled at the thought. "Will you help me?"

"I think you can manage well enough on your own now, Emilia."

That afternoon she studied the pattern book and began her sketches for the panel of Michael. She did not want to think of Franco, nor even of Giacomo. She wanted to lose herself in the rapid movement of charcoal on paper, to forget her earthly concerns. Emilia did not sit down planning to capture the divine essence of Michael, for she believed she was far too imperfect for such a task. Perhaps, if she silenced herself for a time, the Holy Spirit would work through her and there would be something sacred in the work created by her human hands. For a time, she was free from everything that threatened to trap her and keep her caged.

Street of the Painters

O nce she had completed the gilding for the archangel's halo, Emilia began laying down the rich brown color for Michael's robe over the layer of white gesso. She worked deftly with the brush, staying within the outline of the image she had incised with the stylus. As Makarios taught her, she would move to progressively lighter shades, finishing one section of the panel at a time. The work made her forget—at least for a short time—her predicament with Franco and this freed her to contemplate the icon, Makarios' window to heaven.

She was lost in her thoughts about the archangel when the front door swung open without warning, startling her from her reverie.

"I am home, my darling!" announced Franco Villani, striding towards her.

He was dressed in his usual finery, his long cape swept over one shoulder, the ornate embroidery of his doublet glittering in the sun like gold. It was a sight that might have impressed Emilia just a year earlier, now his appearance struck her as a gaudy show of self-importance and vanity.

"You are a lovely sight for a homesick man." His dark eyes fixed upon her, making her feel like hunted prey.

Her hand, still holding the brush, remained suspended in mid-air. Although she was expecting him, she had also hoped he would somehow disappear or send her a note saying he had decided to remain in Prato indefinitely.

"Franco," she managed to get out as she stood up. Doing her best to appear moved by the sight of him, she held her hands together as if in prayer and bowed her head.

"You are home safe, *grazie a Dio.*" Looking up at him with a smile pinned to her face, she murmured, "How wonderful to see you at last."

As he swooped over to kiss her, she fought feelings of repulsion. It was all she could do not to recoil from his touch. Emilia feared he could sense her feelings, because when he released her, there was a dark, brooding look on his face.

"You are charming when you paint," he said, holding her hand too firmly as he glanced casually at her panel. "Whose likeness might this be?"

"The archangel Michael," she replied as steadily as she could, wishing Makarios would come out of his room where he was resting so she would not be all alone with Franco.

He began moving about the *bottega*, taking in the various panels, drawings, and sculptures until his eyes moved up to the *Pantocrator* on the wall. Christ's eyes were watching Franco, Emilia thought. Franco turned abruptly from the image and he looked at Emilia as though he had suffered some insult.

"A strange painting," he remarked.

"I believe that panel in particular has a power I can scarcely describe. It seems that everyone who walks through the door is transfixed by the image, by its very holiness."

Franco scoffed at the notion. "Clearly it is lacking in the sophistication expected by Florentines."

Emilia felt the heat rise in her face. Franco was taunting her and worse, he was insulting the sacred art she had been taught by Makarios. It took everything within her not to lash out at him, but she forced herself to choose her words carefully.

"You, of all people, know that Makarios is able to paint what is pleasing to his patrons. It is also true that the painting of his country has mysteries that are quite unknown to you," she said, her fists clenched at her side.

Now, when Franco stared at her, Emilia could tell he had seen through her veneer of civility. Despite his greed, Franco was not a stupid man, he could tell that something had changed in her. He said nothing but he gave her an icy stare.

Emilia wished he would leave, but he stood there until much to her relief, Makarios emerged from his room. "Ah, Signor Villani," he said, shuffling slowly towards them. "I would like to think you have come to ask me for another fresco, but I suspect you are here to see Monna Emilia."

"Indeed," Franco drawled.

"I must interrupt your visit," Makarios said apologetically. "Emilia, I need you to prepare some more pigment—I'm afraid I spilled all the ochre you ground this morning, and I must get back to work on the panel for Friar Giuseppe's nephew at once."

"Of course, Makarios," she replied obediently, hurrying over to the shelves to find the ochre clay, feeling very glad for the old man's sharp hearing. Well aware that her master had no immediate need for the paint, she thanked him silently for saving her.

"I suppose I must bid you good day then, *amore*," Franco said with thickly feigned warmth. He started towards the door but turned to say, nonchalantly, "I understand you ran into Tomasso a while ago."

She held her breath, wondering how to respond. "Oh, yes. At the piazza." She spoke casually, knowing well enough that Franco was telling her he knew she had been with Giacomo. Tomasso would have given his version of the story, of course, making it sound as though Giacomo provoked the fight. "Tomasso is every-where, it would seem."

"Yes, perhaps Florence is smaller that we think," he said, a thin smile forming on his lips.

Her uneasiness grew as Franco stood before her. He was angry with her, but it was a dark, brooding anger arising from more than simple disappointment. It was clear he now perceived Emilia had chosen Giacomo over him. This was a betrayal that a man like Franco was not likely to forget. He may have stolen her book, but she doubted whether her so-called fiancé considered the score even. The man who once sought to charm her would surely have her pay. In his view she had kept secrets from him, withheld her grandmother's book, flaunted her relationship with Giacomo and therefore been untrue.

Emilia was more convinced than ever that Franco had stolen the manual to retaliate against her as well as to satisfy his greed for rare objects. Though she wished this was the end of it, she could not shake the feeling that the two of them would not part ways peacefully. When Franco finally left the workshop, Emilia shuddered.

"I think he has come to hate me," she whispered to Makarios.

Her master sighed. "Perhaps because he loves you so much."

"You think he loves me?"

"The opposite of love is indifference, Emilia. Franco cannot make you abide by his will and he no doubt knows this," Makarios told her. "I imagine there are few who have dared to defy him."

How could this be true? Emilia wondered as she returned to her work. If Franco truly loved her, why would he have lied and stolen something precious from her? Why would he have asked Tomasso to spy on her? Was it because, as Makarios suggested, he could not control her will? Franco had been, in the end, unable to capture her heart—perhaps this was something he could not accept or even tolerate. Perhaps he saw that Emilia had come to despise him.

Now that Franco had returned to Florence, Emilia sent word to Giacomo that he should stay away from her for the time being.

Giacomo,

It is not safe for us to be together, lest we provoke Franco's wrath. We must wait for this pretense of a betrothal to be over. I pray it will not be much longer that I am compelled to pose as his fiancé. I pray as well for your forgiveness for having involved you in matters of such an unpleasant nature. It pains me greatly that you have endured Franco's vengeance for my sake.

Please do not attempt to see me until I send word again.

Affectionately,
Emilia.

After she had written the letter to Giacomo, Emilia did her best to concentrate on painting rather than think about Giacomo or try to guess Franco's next move. It was difficult not to worry, but she continued on with her Michael, building up the flesh tones so that his countenance, through some form of magic, began to glow as though alive.

During the following days, Emilia imagined that Michael was protecting her, keeping her from the bitterness that surrounded Franco. She felt she was safe inside the workshop with Makarios, yet she sensed dark thunderclouds overhead, a storm brewing. She tried to console herself with thoughts of Giacomo and held onto hope that they would find some way to spend time together in the not too distant future.

Meanwhile she would have to travel along on her own, Emilia realized, making her way across the river towards home after another day at the *bottega*. Crossing the Piazza della Signoria, where she and Giacomo had encountered Tomasso, she wondered why Giacomo had not replied to her note. Perhaps he agreed it best to remain invisible until she could free herself. Still, she was disappointed that he had not responded.

At home, Emilia found her mother sitting alone in her room, embroidering a pillow.

"Hello, *madre mia*," Emilia said, kissing Violante on the cheek.

Violante smiled weakly at her daughter and motioned for her to sit down beside her.

"Is something the matter?"

Violante set aside her sewing and reached for Emilia's hand. "I have something I must tell you, Emilia."

"What is it?" Emilia said, sitting beside her mother. "You're scaring me."

"One of the boys from Lorenzo Jacovelli's studio sent word—there's been an accident," she said slowly. "It's Giacomo."

Emilia felt her heart stop. She stared, open-mouthed, at her mother.

"Giacomo?" she echoed.

"He was on his way to work a few days ago—early in the morning. It was just after daybreak, on the Street of the Painters. He was run over."

"He's not dead?" Emilia exclaimed.

"No, he's not dead. But very badly injured. He's broken several bones. His leg was crushed."

"He won't lose his leg? Will he be able to walk again?" she cried.

"Giacomo is in good hands. Lorenzo is seeing to it that he gets the best of care. The doctor is doing everything he can."

Emilia began to sob, quietly at first and then uncontrollably. "It can't be! It can't be." She collapsed into Violante's arms. "Why Giacomo? Of all people, why Giacomo?" she cried.

"I don't know, *cara*. I don't know."

"Who did this to him? Does he know?"

Violante did not respond immediately. She looked out the window, as though trying to find an answer to Emilia's question. "The driver just continued on," she said slowly. "Apparently, there were no witnesses."

Something in her mother's voice made Emilia pause. Was there something Violante was not saying?

"Didn't Giacomo see anything?"

Violante shook her head. "I only know what the boy from Jacovelli's told me, Emilia. It must have happened very fast."

Gradually, the strangeness of the early morning accident dawned on Emilia. "Why was someone racing down the street at that hour, Mother?" she asked. "And why wouldn't he have stopped after he saw what he'd done?"

Averting her face from Emilia's stare, Violante replied, "It's hard to know, Emilia."

Emilia began to see that her mother suspected foul play as well. "You think someone did this to him, don't you?"

"It's not easy to say—one could never be sure."

Emilia closed her eyes, trying to figure out what had really happened to Giacomo. "You think you know who did this, don't you, Mother?"

Violante put her hand to her mouth.

"I don't want to believe it. I don't want to think he's capable of this. But even Jacovelli thinks it might have been intentional."

Emilia gasped, thinking at once of the only man in Florence who held a grudge against Giacomo. It was Franco. Assuredly it was Franco. She said with bitterness, "I hope he burns in hell."

"We can't be sure, Emilia. We must leave judgment to God."

Franco had not been satisfied with merely stealing her book. Apparently, he felt compelled to extract his revenge in another, more violent manner. Emilia shook with rage, feeling certain that it was indeed Franco who was responsible for the harm done to Giacomo. What Franco had done was unforgivable. He was a man who was unafraid of God, his soul as lost to him as Emilia.

26

Archangel Michael

At the sight of Giacomo lying in bed, the side of his face raw and swollen, his arm bandaged from wrist to elbow, his crushed left leg immobilized in a wooden splint, his toes purple and puffy as grapes, Emilia wept.

"I am so sorry, Giacomo," she whispered, kneeling beside him, heavy with the weight of her guilt. "I am so sorry this happened to you."

He mumbled some inaudible response, barely opening his eyes. In a deep haze from the strong draught he had been given, Giacomo was hardly aware of Emilia's presence.

"Will he recover?" she asked Lisetta, his mother, who sat sewing in a chair by the window. She had not left her son's side since the day of the accident.

"I think Master Donati did a good job setting the leg. We won't know for some time how it will heal. If I know my son, he'll come through it," she said, as though trying to convince herself. "He's got plenty to live for."

"He surely does. He has you and his family. And his painting."

Lisetta looked up from the tunic she was sewing. "He was always drawing, ever since he was a little boy. It was the only thing he cared to do. He wouldn't take to carpentry, no matter how his father tried to teach him."

Emilia remembered the first time she set eyes on Giacomo. It was the first day of her apprenticeship with Jacovelli. Absorbed in his craft, he took little notice of her or anyone else, for that matter. It was only recently that she began to understand his resentment of Jacovelli and his frustration with the master's way of running the *bottega*. While Giacomo wanted each piece to reach a state of perfection, Jacovelli was always trying to hurry him along to the next commission. Giacomo's refusal to compromise when it came to his craft was something Emilia had admired about him since the beginning.

He simply had to get well, if only to return to his painting. She would gladly accept the blame for the trouble she had caused him, so long as he could paint. If he did walk again, if he did paint again, she realized he might want nothing more to do with her. It was an understanding that cut deeply, for the thought of life without Giacomo seemed impossibly lonely.

Emilia wondered if Lisetta had heard rumors about the accident or a possible culprit. Giacomo's mother was entitled to know the truth, but Emilia could not bring herself to discuss Franco Villani's loathing of Giacomo. Besides, the admission would change nothing. Burdened with sorrow for the tragedy she brought to him, Emilia touched her fingers to Giacomo's bruised cheek then held his hand, praying silently for his recovery. If he discovered the accident was

Franco's doing, how could he ever forgive her? *I have done you no favors, Giacomo,* she said to herself. Emilia could not help but think he would have been far better off if she had never set foot in Jacovelli's studio.

Seeing Giacomo's damaged body, Emilia knew one thing: she could never look Franco in the face and pretend she did not despise him. Witnesses or not, his guilt was crystal clear. The crime against Giacomo made it obvious that Emilia's happiness meant nothing to Franco. Clearly, there would be no more chivalrous attempts to win her heart.

"I'll pray for him every day," Emilia said, standing to leave. She would pray, as well, for forgiveness for the suffering she had caused. Too late, she was beginning to understand what Giacomo meant to her. Emilia only wished it had not taken a catastrophe to make her see how blind she had been.

She felt the familiar impulse to turn to her manual for solace, but there was no book to turn to. There was nothing to look at but her own guilt, her poor judgment for trusting a man like Franco, her stupidity for flaunting her relationship with Giacomo while she was engaged. She had been slow to admit that the painter was more than a friend, though Franco had seen this coming all along. Through all her regrets, Emilia continued working on her Michael and was soon adding the finishing touches—the fine, white highlights—to his clothing and his face.

It began to feel as though the archangel was staring back at her, judging her actions, telling her everything she had done wrong, all she had failed to do. She could not hide from him, for Michael knew all the weak places in her soul. Makarios, sensing

Emilia's state of mind and need for silence, tried to leave her alone for the most part. When she had gone the entire morning without a word, he consoled her.

"You must not blame yourself, Emilia," he said tenderly.

She looked up at his gentle, bearded face, wondering how he could be so kind to her after all the foolish ways in which she had conducted herself. "I wish that were true, but I'm afraid I did everything wrong. My mother warned me about Franco, but I wouldn't listen."

"Ah," Makarios sighed, sitting beside her and studying his worn, stained hands. "It is easy to say that in hindsight. But this is how we learn. You were not wrong to trust Signor Villani—it is your nature to believe the best in people, Emilia." Turning his attention to her nearly completed work, Makarios added, "You have been protected through it all. You still have your painting, your life ahead of you."

Regarding her Michael, Emilia was not so sure what manner of divine protection had been provided. "Where were the saints when Giacomo was run over? Why did it have to happen?"

"Giacomo might have died, Emilia, but he is very much alive. Badly hurt, but alive. Give thanks for Saint Michael's protection. He was spared."

She had not considered that Giacomo was spared; she had imagined the opposite, that the saints were nowhere to be seen the day he was trampled by a horse and wagon. It was possible that Makarios was right, that divine intervention had kept Giacomo in the land of the living. If Giacomo was spared, perhaps he was spared for a reason. She dared, briefly, to wish she might be part of the reason.

Though Francesco had refused to discuss the possibility that Franco stole *Nonna's* book, Emilia thought he could not easily overlook the fate of Jacovelli's gifted painter. News of the accident seemed to unsettle her father, but he still insisted on giving the wealthy spice merchant the benefit of the doubt. It was impossible to prove Franco's crime, Francesco said. Emilia sat in her room with the door open, listening to her parents debating what to do about Franco Villani.

"Besides, Emilia should not have been out walking in the piazza alone with Giacomo. Why did my daughter not tell me about this incident with the manservant before, Violante? She provoked Franco by her impropriety," Francesco was saying.

"That gives him the right to run over a man?"

"We have no proof. It might have been nothing more than an accident. Even if Franco did tell Giacomo to stay away from our daughter, that doesn't mean he wanted to kill him. Why would a man like Franco be threatened by a mere painter anyway?"

"I suppose there is no point in going to the *podestà*—what can he do?" Violante said, ignoring Francesco's comment. "He would never take our side over Franco's."

Emilia could hear her father pacing back and forth across the brick floor.

"Perhaps I should talk to him. He will prove his innocence and we can put the matter behind us."

"Francesco, he wouldn't have dirtied his hands himself. Surely one of his men would have done the deed."

Emilia could sense her mother's impatience with Francesco, she felt like screaming herself. Why couldn't her father see through Franco's polished exterior to the cold, calculating thief that he was? With disgust, she realized Francesco was loath to lose a son-in-law possessed of a small fortune. It was too much for Emilia to bear.

Barreling down the hall, she barged in on her parents.

"It was Franco who did this to Giacomo! I know it was him. I will not marry him. I'd rather die!"

Francesco eyed her without sympathy.

"First Benozzo, and now Franco. I think you will find fault with any man who would have you, Emilia."

"He is a violent man! A snake!"

"This is no longer in your hands, Emilia," Francesco rebuked her.

Violante threw Emilia a cautioning look.

"Indeed, your father would never allow anyone to intimidate his family. That is why he has decided to speak with Franco and hear him out."

Francesco nodded in agreement as Violante continued. "Franco must understand that Francesco Serafini will not tolerate anyone who would try to harm his family. But Franco must have an opportunity to speak."

"Exactly," Francesco agreed, already standing to leave.

Emilia was certain nothing good could come of a conversation between her father and Franco. Neither one of them had the courage to speak the truth.

After her father and brother departed, Violante held Emilia close. "Have faith. Guilt cannot be concealed forever."

Emilia doubted that her father would be the one to shed light on Franco's crime. In Francesco's eyes, Franco was beyond reproach for the simple reason of his wealth. Giacomo, on the other hand, was practically beneath her father's notice. She doubted that her father would ever understand what the *mere painter* had come to mean to her.

Emilia could never know exactly what happened during her father and brother's visit to Franco's overpriced spice and specialty shop that day. Andrea told her later that Franco had been entirely convincing in his portrayal of one wrongly accused when questioned about Giacomo's accident.

"He said nothing at first—he looked completely shocked. Then he sat down and held his head," her brother told her.

"How easily he lies," Emilia muttered.

After trying to kill Giacomo, Franco was able to carry on his charade of innocence, feign emotions he did not feel in the slightest. There was something wrong with him that went beyond weakness of character; the man could feel no remorse.

"He sent one of his clerks to fetch him a cup of wine. He said, *'What did I ever do to make your daughter mistrust me? She dishonors you and your family, Francesco. After all I have given to her.'*"

"What did Father say?" Emilia asked, fearing the worst as her brother continued on with his story.

"He apologized. Said he and Mother allowed you too many freedoms. That it was a mistake to let you paint. *'You deserve more than a wife who cares for nothing more than paints and brushes. I brought her to the priest, but even Father Bartolo could not dissuade her. Ah, my wayward daughter. Whatever will I do with her? She is impossible. Simply impossible,'* that's what Father said," Andrea recounted. "You have disappointed him, Emilia."

"So nothing has changed then," she sighed. "Franco admits nothing."

"He won't marry you now."

"*Dio mio!*" Emilia exclaimed. "Is it true?"

"Franco said that as much as he cared for you, he could no longer abide your strange ways. He said you would always love painting more than him and there was nothing he could do about it. Father tried to tell him you were finished with Makarios. Said he was putting a stop to it once and for all. Even when he tried to talk about a bigger dowry, Franco wouldn't change his mind! He said it was no use."

Emilia tried to absorb the fact that Franco had so easily released her. She should have felt relieved, but something was not right. It had been too easy.

"He won't admit the real reason he's done with me. It's not because of my painting, Andrea—it's because of Giacomo, even though he won't say so. Franco doesn't want anyone to think he had reason to run him over."

"Does it matter? You won't have to marry him now."

"He wanted *Nonna's* book. He wanted Giacomo dead," she thought aloud. "I wonder if he's made me suffer enough."

"You think he'll try something else?"

"I wouldn't be surprised. Maybe I'm wrong. Maybe he'll find another way to occupy his time."

Andrea looked uneasy but tried to sound fearless. "If he tries to hurt you, he'll have to answer to me."

Emilia hoped it was true that she and her family were done with the likes of Franco Villani. He had caused her and Giacomo more than enough suffering. While she was relieved that the ill-fated wedding was called off, she feared her father would forbid her to work in Makarios' *bottega* ever again. If Franco was glad to finally dispose of her, then her most immediate problem was solved anyway. They were both free to go their separate ways.

It should have been simple, except Franco was not just anyone. He was moved by the motives of men who lived to rule over others. Such men did not rest until those who dared to keep them from their desires were destroyed.

The Winged Bird

S pring came to Florence; the hills were dotted with wildflowers, but Emilia Serafini felt the chill of winter. Although her engagement to Franco Villani was broken, she could not free herself from thoughts of the man. Because of him, she was reduced to scrubbing tables at her father's tavern. If she wanted to see Makarios or paint at the *bottega*, she had to sneak away for a mere hour or two at a time. And she could go nowhere without fear of running into her former fiancé. Most painful of all, Franco had succeeded in separating her from Giacomo.

She was tormented by thoughts of all that Giacomo was suffering on her account. Emilia learned through word passed along from old Leonardo at Jacovelli's workshop that Giacomo was improving. She wanted to see him but she did not want to face the questions he would eventually ask about his accident. When he became clear-headed enough to realize it was Emilia's fiancé who nearly killed him, he would have good reason to be done with her.

Violante, trying her best to assuage Emilia's fears, encouraged her to go to Giacomo.

"It's the devil that would keep you from him," Violante said, sitting next to her on the bed. "He needs your support, Emilia."

"I'm not so sure. I've done him no favors, after all."

Violante worked a comb carved from bone through Emilia's blond curls. "He won't blame you. There's no need to worry."

"I can't help but worry!" she cried as her mother tugged through the knots in Emilia's neglected hair. "Besides, if Franco thinks he failed to keep Giacomo away from me, who knows what he'll try next. How can I live with myself if anything else happens to him?"

"You cannot allow Franco to rule your life any more, Emilia. If you give in to the fear, he wins. You owe it to Giacomo to stand by him through this. You know he cares deeply for you."

Emilia wondered if her mother was able to see the way things were or if her optimism was nothing more than wishful thinking. While she wanted to believe Violante, she could not forget the tragedy she brought to Giacomo.

"I cannot see him," Emilia said, though it broke her heart to stay away. "Maybe someday we can be friends again. Years from now, when I'm sure Franco has forgotten all about me."

Her mother chose her words carefully. "Emilia," she said, "you can't stop living and breathing while Franco decides what to destroy next."

Emilia turned in alarm to face her mother. "So you agree? You don't think Franco is finished with me either!"

Violante stroked Emilia's cheek. "Don't be afraid, *cara*. The thing that Franco wants, he cannot touch. He is a man who lives in darkness. You were his only light. Now that you are gone, he's like a blind man. He strikes out at anything in his way. Men like that only destroy themselves in the end."

That might be true, Emilia thought. In the meantime, what twisted plan was he scheming up next? Despite Violante's attempt to reassure her, Emilia felt as though Franco was watching, waiting for her to fall into his trap. She shuddered, trying to force the image of him from her mind.

When Emilia slept that night, she dreamt of Giacomo. He was in the chapel at the Carmine, making a magnificent fresco of the Assumption of the Virgin.

Looking up from his luminous work, she was shocked to see her own face reflected back at her.

"You didn't say I was to be the model, Giacomo."

Brush in hand, he eyed her from the scaffold. "You are too headstrong for the likeness."

"Then why did you choose me?"

"It was already started when I arrived. Masaccio didn't have a chance to finish."

She nodded, having no thought of questioning the dead master. On an adjacent panel she noticed another image: a winged bird standing over an upside-down wingless bird, each facing the other and trying to eat the other's tail.

"What are the birds doing here, Giacomo?"

The painter shrugged. "They are trying to kill one other, I imagine. Like you and Franco."

The wingless bird, she saw, was Franco Villani. She struggled to free herself from him. Franco smiled and kept her pinned to the ground. She could not get up. She could not breathe.

"Help me! Somebody please help me."

She awoke with a start, her heart pounding, gasping for breath. Emilia tore off the quilted blanket that covered her face, the image of Franco, the two birds, still vivid in her memory. *I'm awake now*. It was only a dream. Sitting up in bed, she realized that the image—the birds on the wall of Santa Maria del Carmine—was the illustration from *Nonna's* manual. The winged bird wanted to fly to the realm of spirit, while the wingless bird wanted to remain on the solid ground below.

Emilia likened herself to that wingless bird while she had been with Franco. At the time, she believed it possible to find happiness with the fleeting luxuries he could provide: a country villa, gardens, splendid clothing, precious artifacts and fine dishes. Her own winged bird, it turned out, would not give in so easily. Wanting to fly away to places never experienced before, it would not be content to remain in a world of mere material possessions, however gilded and encrusted with jewels.

When Emilia sat down to breakfast, she told herself that she could live simply, without finery, perhaps even without painting if this was asked of her. All that mattered was that Franco was gone and Giacomo was safe.

The inscription on the orb held by the Archangel Michael read, "Jesus Christ, the Last Judge." God's vicegerent stood in his resplendent, formal robes of gold and deep brown, the knowing of the ages in his eyes. The transformation of the plain poplar panel had been a slow process, carried out during the days and weeks of her torment following Giacomo's accident. The final stages had been completed during stolen hours, when she managed to hide her whereabouts from her father. By the power of determination, paint was layered upon paint within the adytum—the quiet, inner sanctum of the workshop—until the strong, protective presence of Michael rose from the wood.

Staring at the image, Emilia wanted to believe the angel was watching over her, keeping her from the grips of a man who had come to despise her. Some days she dared to believe Franco was gone for good, but when thoughts of him terrorized her again, working on the panel steadied her.

The final touch to her nearly finished icon was the coat of varnish, composed of resin heated with two parts of filtered linseed. Emilia sat at her familiar worktable and carefully applied the warm liquid to the surface of the paint. As far as her father knew, she was at the market, buying soup ingredients for Violante. The varnish deepened the colors slightly, bringing a warm glow to Michael's skin, making the image gleam in the bright light of day.

"So you have finished at last, Emilia." Makarios said, coming beside her to inspect the completed product. She set down the brush and waited in silence as her master examined her work. At last he reached over and squeezed her hand.

"You have done well, Emilia. I am proud of you."

"*Grazie*," she said, breathing a sigh of relief.

Having traveled far from where she started, she felt grateful to Makarios for his patience, for his belief in her, and especially for entrusting her with the knowledge of iconography, something he valued and held closely to his heart.

"You have taught me well, *Maestro*," she said. "I'm glad you took me on."

"You have ability, I have always known that. Who would have thought a young Florentine girl would write icons? I confess, I never expected to teach you such things."

"We were both surprised."

"Yes, God works in ways one never anticipates," he said. "When I fled from home, I did not know where I would go, how I would live. But at every turn, I was provided for. God has been good to me. More than once I thought everything was lost. Then there was grace. Again and again. Finally, I learned to trust."

She took his words to heart. Makarios wanted more than happiness for her, he wanted her to believe in the power of her own future as an artist. He had not taken Emilia on as his apprentice so she could dabble with her paints, only to give up art a few years later. She only hoped that some miracle would allow her to continue with the craft.

Looking at her icon with tenderness, feeling renewed certainty in her path as a painter, she mused, "I know where Michael belongs."

"Oh?"

"With Giacomo Massarino."

Makarios nodded in agreement. "It would be a fitting gift after all he has been through. Yes, you must take it to him, Emilia."

"I wish I could," she said. "I don't dare."

Makarios nodded. "This is for you to decide."

She could leave the icon at his door. It would be a small gesture, though it might mean something to Giacomo. Perhaps the gift would convey what she could not explain in words. She wanted Giacomo to know how sorry she was, that she regretted her foolishness. Perhaps someday he might be able to forgive her for having entangled the both of them with Franco Villani.

When would she ever be truly free of the man? Even as she sat within the glow of the archangel, she feared Franco had not forgotten her. She had the uneasy feeling that Franco could not forgive her for loving Giacomo Massarino instead of him.

The Horseman

Making her way to the home of Giacomo Massarino, who still lay recovering from Franco's crime, Emilia carried her Archangel Michael with great care, as though it was a holy relic. The panel, wrapped in a protective linen sack, held Emilia's prayers for Giacomo's recovery, and for his forgiveness, and she went with a heavy sadness to bid him farewell. She could not risk provoking Franco, who might still be watching her, lurking in dark, hidden places, wishing her ill. Until she could be certain that Franco was gone from her life forever, those she loved were still in danger.

As she walked towards the Piazza San Giovanni en route to the western part of the city, Emilia wanted to believe Makarios was right, that it was indeed the archangel winging down from the heavens who had protected Giacomo from death. Maybe it was true that Michael had intervened on her behalf, prodding her when she veered dangerously away from the path God had chosen for her. *Think of this*, she told herself, *and not of Franco or Tomasso waiting to prey on me somewhere in the open piazza.*

With disgust she recalled the one and only time she had been to Franco's townhouse. He had shown her his vast library and tried, unsuccessfully, to extract information from her about *A Manual to the Science of Alchemy*. Put off by her reticence, he later tried to have his way with her on his opulent bed of furs. Emilia had once considered Franco to be a man of fiery passions. Now she perceived that it was deep, hidden rage rather than desire inciting his appetites. He was a man who in his quest to acquire the riches of the world had forgotten to fear God.

Nearing the Duomo, Emilia could not help but regret the day she ever laid eyes on Franco. A band of purplish, gray clouds moved across the sun, casting shadows where she walked. It was Franco who was the darkness, who tried to rob her of light, of all that mattered most to her.

Yet she could no longer blame Franco for everything that had happened; she played a part in the story as well. She had put her belief in his considerable fortune, thinking that such wealth meant they would be happy, and she had paid a heavy price. At least she had stopped before selling her soul. Emilia prayed that God would not punish her for wanting a rich husband more than the glory of the heavens. She prayed that God would not punish her for what happened to Giacomo.

More than a month had passed since the accident. Emilia continued to petition Mary and the saints daily, asking for protection from Franco's mal-intentions. Lifting her eyes to Giotto's tall, slender campanile, Emilia told herself to focus her attention on what was yet to be rather than past mistakes. She tried to banish Franco from her mind. The truth was she could focus on nothing else.

Then, amid the din of people and horses making their way along the crowded, cobbled streets, there came the rapid clip-clop of a cantering horse. The animal was drawing closer, moving swiftly ahead of slow travelers on the road. A sudden snort of fear was followed by the thunderous pounding of hooves on brick pavement. Emilia became aware someone was shouting, calling out to her.

"*Madonna, watch out! Move away, quickly!*"

Turning her head, Emilia faced the sight of a stallion, clearly out of control and racing directly towards her. The horse was enormous, an unstoppable force that would crush whatever stood in its path. A fruit cart collapsed, wood splintering like straw, apples tumbling, as the beast broke through it without pause. Screaming bystanders scattered, fleeing the animal's furious path. Its ears were flattened as he raced, pushing hard against the reins. The rider, apparently unable—unwilling?—to draw in the spooked beast, crouched low over the horse's neck. Emilia knew she had to get away but the crazed animal was gaining ground. There was no time, she could not move fast enough.

She ran, craning to look behind her. In terror she saw she was about to be trampled. For what seemed like minutes but could not have been even a second, Emilia froze, clutching the icon close to her chest. In that moment hung the strange and terrible inevitability of being run over. She would not see her mother again. Or Giacomo. *Dio mi salvi, God help me.*

The horseman, a mere arm's length away, tipped forward over the horse, one arm outstretched like a jouster as though to drive Emilia from his path. In the same instant, she felt the jolt of impact as the icon jammed like a hard, merciless fist into her abdomen, she had not moved away fast enough. She tried to catch her breath but could not breathe.

It felt as if she was in a dream when someone grabbed hold of her waist and yanked her forcefully to the side of the road. Flying to the ground, she landed with a thud, scant inches from the flying hooves as the rider sped past. The horseman, apparently regaining control of the mad beast, veered abruptly away from her, back towards the center of the road.

Her right shoulder and hip had hit the pavement hard but Emilia still held fast to the icon. Struggling to take a breath, wincing in pain, she looked up to see the profile of the tall horseman looming high overhead against the cerulean sky. He was no longer bent low to his horse but the rider's dark hood had fallen forward, concealing his face.

The unknown horseman did not want to be seen. Instantly, she knew why. She could tell who it was by the man's stature, by the magnificent, black horse she had ridden on herself. The wayward animal belonged to none other than Franco Villani.

"_Madre de Dio_, he tried to kill me," she said with stunned certainty. _He tried to kill me, just as he tried to kill Giacomo. He is mad._

"Something spooked the horse!" It was the young tradesman who had pushed her out of harm's way. He knelt at her side, ready to help her up.

"He is possessed," Emilia stammered, lying on the ground, shaking as she watched rider and horse speeding off into the distance.

"An unfortunate accident, Madonna," he replied.

"You think so?"

The Good Samaritan shrugged off her remark. "Are you hurt?"

"I don't know." Her shoulder and hip throbbed with pain. Slowly, her breathing became regular again. She could move her arms and legs, nothing was broken, but she could not stop the flow of tears. It was overwhelming to feel the full extent of Franco's wrath. He was still fighting her and would not stop till he won the battle he had waged against her in his heart.

She became aware of a dozen or more bystanders grouped around her. Wanting to get away, she struggled to stand, but the young man stopped her.

"Don't try to get up yet."

"I'll be all right," she insisted through her tears.

"Saint Giovanni was watching," a shriveled old woman carrying a basket full of peas commented as she peered down at the two of them. "The horse barely missed you."

Though Emilia should have expressed gratitude to the stranger who saved her, she was more concerned about her Michael. The icon lay next to her on the road, its protective linen covering loose. Aghast to see that something had torn through the linen, she opened the sack and saw that the golden robes of the archangel had also been pierced.

"The panel," she said in dismay.

Michael stared out at her, his serene wisdom unaffected by the open wound in his chest. Dismayed that her painstaking work had been damaged, Emilia examined Giacomo's gift and saw that the gash appeared to have been caused by something sharp. It looked as if a knife had penetrated the heart of the archangel and entered deep into the fiber of the wood. The thin layer of clay lying beneath the gilding of gold leaf seeped like dark red blood through the wounded panel of the icon, oozing through the gold and brown robes.

Emilia clutched the image of Michael in her arms and watched as the man who had saved her picked something off the ground, near where she had fallen. Kneeling beside Emilia, he showed her a finely wrought, silver dagger, now dusted with dirt. In silence she studied the blade, which might have been intended to pierce her own heart.

The tradesman studied the slash in the wood. "It might have been you if you hadn't been holding onto that."

"Yes," she said, unable to take her eyes from the dagger. "I was protected. Much to his disappointment."

The man was puzzled. "To whose disappointment?"

"The man who tried to run me down," she said, not meaning to discuss the matter of Franco Villani.

"You think he was aiming for you?" the old woman asked, moving closer.

Blankly, Emilia looked at the woman, hardly aware why she was speaking to her. "He is a man who wants me dead."

"You know the rider?" the young man asked.

"His name—his name is not important," she said, taking hold of herself. There was no point in sharing her trouble with curious by-standers. "May I see the knife?" she asked, reaching for the dagger.

The tradesman looked at the fine weapon longingly before handing it to Emilia. She studied the wood handle with the rope-twist design and the elegant, triangular blade; surely it belonged to Franco.

"Keep it," she said, handing the weapon back to the young man. "Thank you for your help. You've been very kind." Her shoulder and hip ached when she stood, but she wanted to escape the questions and stares.

"*Madonna,* the man should be found. He must be questioned. You must go to the *Signoria* and tell them what happened," the tradesman insisted as she limped away, icon in hand.

She pressed on, half aware that she was making her way to Giacomo's house. She was in pain, but her anger with Franco and her determination to see Giacomo outweighed her discomfort. The man caught up to her, urging her to wait.

"I will send for *il bargello*."

Emilia waved him away. "Please, you've done enough. Just leave me be."

Tears filled her eyes. She knew without doubt that she had to say her final goodbye to Giacomo. He would understand why she could never see him again. It was too dangerous. It was clear enough that Franco would never leave the two of them in peace.

Giacomo

"This is the last you will see of me," Emilia told Giacomo.

She was afraid to look him in the eye and see the reproach she believed would be there. Dazed, sore, splattered with mud from her near fatal collision, she held the icon of the wounded Michael at her side.

"Franco tried to run me down as well," she told him.

Giacomo, who had been half asleep when Emilia first arrived, stared at her, eyes wide open.

"*Dio mio,* my God! Franco did what?"

"He won't be happy until he has destroyed us both, Giacomo. I was on my way to see you. He nearly ran me down at the Duomo—maybe he was following me. I suppose he thinks I've betrayed him—it's as though he's possessed," she said. Pointing to the leg, still splinted and propped on a pillow, she added, "Who do you think did this to you, Giacomo?"

Running a hand through his head of coppery hair, grown long during his recovery, he exhaled deeply. "I know of only one person in Florence who has reason to want me dead."

So Giacomo had come to the same conclusion on his own. Emilia proceeded to tell Giacomo how Franco had cunningly appeared to lose control of his enormous stallion, which was aimed directly at her. "The icon saved me," she explained, showing him the mark where the silver dagger had pierced the layers of paint and penetrated the wood. "If I hadn't been holding it, I might not be standing here."

"Are you all right?" he asked, his face flooded with concern as he finally took in her unkempt hair, muddied face, and disheveled clothing. "You should sit down."

"I'm fine. Just a bit bruised," she replied, glad to rest on the chest next to the bed.

Giacomo's eyes darted back and forth from the icon to Emilia. He picked up the image and traced the gash in the wood with his finger, exclaiming, "It's extraordinary."

She assumed he was referring to the injury sustained by the panel rather than to her talent for writing icons.

"Yes, I have a feeling Michael has been there for both of us. On more than one occasion," she said. "Giacomo, I came to tell you how sorry I am—for everything. Nothing I can say will make up for all you've been through. Still, I wanted you to have the panel. Now Franco has spoiled that too."

Giacomo hardly noticed her words. He kept staring at the icon as though transfixed. "It's a miracle," he proclaimed. "He might have killed you but for this. Your panel is somehow alive. Surely you have painted a holy image, Emilia."

"A holy image?" she echoed. "Yes, as Makarios taught me. He says an icon is a window to heaven."

Still studying the wounded Michael, Giacomo replied, "Makarios is right. It's as though your Michael is beckoning me."

She smiled at the compliment. "I wasn't sure you would care for the piece. But it's my farewell gift to you."

"Your farewell gift?"

"I cannot see you again, Giacomo. It wouldn't be fair to you."

Setting the panel down, Giacomo was adamant, fire in his voice. "We have not endured all this to have Franco Villani keep us apart now, Emilia!"

"I won't put you in danger again. You could have died. You might not have walked again," she countered, indicating his injured leg, glad to see that the swelling in his foot had receded and the color of his toes looked almost normal.

"I did not die. I did not lose my leg. You're the one I'm worried about!" He moved as if to get up. Gently, Emilia held him back. Slamming his fist into the bed, he ranted, "Villani's madness knows no bounds. What sort of man would do this to a defenseless woman?" He gestured wildly to the panel. "He must be stopped, Emilia!"

"We can do nothing," she said, feeling utterly hopeless. "I curse the day I met him."

"He is obsessed with you. Beauty can do that to a man. Beauty and talent, the more so," he said, studying her face. "I am useless to stop him now. I cannot protect you, and he knows this."

"I'm not sure that my trouble with Franco has anything to do with my talent or my appearance, Giacomo," Emilia replied. "The truth may be that Franco wanted my grandmother's book as much as he wanted me. He had an idea that it held significant value."

She recalled the first time Franco came to Makarios' studio, when he had spied *A Manual to the Science of Alchemy*. Giacomo knew little of her grandmother's book, for she had been reluctant to speak of its contents to anyone. After all that had happened, she was no longer inclined to withhold anything from him.

"The book—you came to see me after it was stolen," he recalled. "It's strange how he fixed upon it. A man who has so much already."

"It's not an ordinary book. Even Marsilio Ficino was intrigued by it."

"Ficino? Who is he?"

"He was a guest at Franco's villa—a learned scholar. One of Cosimo de' Medici's inner circle, a hunter of lost manuscripts," she said, remembering the small, curly-haired man fondly. "He began to speak with me about the ancients, and I told him a little about my *nonna's* text," she explained, not knowing how Giacomo would react to her uncommon fascination with alchemy and the writings of an Egyptian sage.

Giacomo nodded, encouraging her to go on.

"Tell me about this book, Emilia. Why has it captivated the attention of Villani and Medici's scholar?"

"The manual is a translation of an ancient alchemical text," she answered. "One containing rare passages written by Plato and Senior and Hermes Trismegistus."

"Hermes Trismegistus?" he repeated.

"He is said to be older than Plato. Older than Moses. He is the father of all philosophy and religion, Ficino says."

"So Franco did not steal the book merely to spite you," Giacomo said thoughtfully.

"No, I believe he had good reason to covet the book. He wanted it for his collection."

"Perhaps," Giacomo said, putting his finger to his lips. "A man like Franco—he wouldn't keep a thing like that to himself, would he? He would want to show it off, impress everyone with his acquisition."

"What are you getting at, Giacomo?"

"It's a matter of what he'll do with the book next," he mused, pulling himself up in bed. "He won't be able to keep it a secret—he is much too full of himself for that."

Emilia considered Giacomo's assumption. "It is true there is nothing the least bit modest about Franco Villani. Even if he shows off the book, no one will ever know it belongs to me. He'll put the book in his library and make up some story about how he acquired it during his travels. He is an adept of lies."

"Yes, but then you are not the only one who knows Franco's lie. I know. Your family knows. Most importantly, Marsilio Ficino knows that you are the owner of this text—isn't that true?"

"How can Ficino be of any help to me?" she asked, recalling the scholar's fascination with the subject of Hermes.

"You said you spoke to him about your book. So he is aware of the contents, isn't he?"

"To a degree. I was hesitant to tell him too much. My mother always warned me not to speak about the manual. Not everyone would approve of the subject matter, Giacomo—some would think it heresy."

"What is poorly understood is often called heresy," he said, dismissing her concern. "If you go to him and tell him your book has been stolen, he would believe you, wouldn't he?"

"I suppose he might—he would have no reason not to believe me. He is an honest man, a good judge of character I would say. But what if Franco tells Signor Ficino a different story and convinces him the book isn't mine? He could say I happened upon the manual when I was working at his villa and that I'm lying."

Emilia could not help but remember how Franco had managed to convince her of Filippa's guilt and Tomasso's innocence regarding the incident at Primavera. Franco Villani could lie without flinching, as a man in league with the devil could do.

"You must get to Ficino first. Tell him what Franco has done. He can help you recover your book, Emilia," Giacomo said, his eyes alight with interest, a healthy color returned to his skin.

Emilia could not help but smile at his enthusiasm, yet she was not convinced that Ficino would be able to help her. "Even if he is willing to help me, what can he say to Franco?"

"I'll tell you what you must do," Giacomo began, taking hold of her hand as he began spinning the web. "You and your mother must meet with Ficino and tell him everything. Describe the book to him in great detail so that when he sees the text, he will recognize it without doubt. Then Ficino must call on Villani. Ficino was a guest in his house, after all, and there would be nothing strange about such a visit—Franco will think nothing of it."

"Do you think that Franco will be able to keep quiet about the manual when Ficino begins to talk about this famous Egyptian sage? Do you think for one second that Franco will be able to keep the book to himself?"

Emilia nodded, following his logic. "You might be right. If Signor Ficino agrees to help us, Franco just might do himself in."

"Of course he will! He will not be able to contain himself. That's why he wanted your book in the first place, Emilia—to impress the likes of the Medici. He is a vain and greedy man."

She looked at Giacomo, wondering at the quick study he made of the situation and the plan he devised. She only hoped he was correct in his prediction of Franco's behavior. Whether or not the scheme would succeed, she was grateful that the painter stood wholly on her side.

Giacomo had suffered a great deal, but he was on the mend, the pulse of life was returning to him. More than that, the mild-mannered painter she knew from Jacovelli's studio had become her fiercest protector.

Giacomo touched his hand to her face and tenderly kissed her goodbye. When her lips left his, it was clear that her feelings for the painter were no longer in doubt.

"You have changed, Giacomo. You used to care about nothing but painting."

"Painting was all that was required of me before," he replied, caressing her hand. Before she could ask his meaning, he continued. "One more thing. Make sure Ficino sees your painting—The Adoration of the Christ Child—when he comes to your house."

"But the painting is with the Sisters of Santa Maria Nuova."

"Tell them you need to borrow it. Just for the day."

"Why?"

"Think of it, Emilia. Ficino is a man who dines with Cosimo. Imagine if he takes a liking to your work."

She thought Giacomo's idea a farfetched possibility. She could only hope his feelings for her ran as deep as his convictions about her art. Did he intend for them to be together as two artists, joined by the common bond of their craft, or was he prepared to make her his wife one day?

Whatever Giacomo's intention, he was no longer the same man he was back when she was an apprentice at Jacovelli's. He would always be a man in love with his brushes and pigments, but Emilia dared to hope he was also becoming a man who could envision life with a family—a life with her. Giacomo had surprised her before. He had knocked Tomasso to the ground to defend her. He had defied Franco's attempt on his life and now he was trying to help her recover her book. She could not take all the credit for the change in Giacomo, yet she did wonder if the practice of alchemy was not entirely lost to her after all.

Although Emilia had failed miserably in many ways over the past year, perhaps even her failures were fruitful in their own way. If she had not endured the humiliation of her disguise at Jacovelli's, she would not know Giacomo. If she had not been tossed out of Jacovelli's studio, she would not know Makarios Levantes. For the first time, she even dared to think that perhaps her relationship with Franco Villani had led her to some knowledge she might not have otherwise acquired.

It was Franco who had revealed to her the darkness in her soul. Because of him she had learned the cost of ransoming her soul for riches. Franco was, she believed, moving deeper into the darkness of the devil, but she would not join him there. But could she forgive a man who had tried to kill her?

"I will do as you suggest, Giacomo," she said, taking leave of him. "I will go to Marsilio. But it is only my book that I seek. Vengeance is not up to me."

"Franco must pay, Emilia!" he insisted. "He must be made to suffer as he has made us suffer."

She shrugged, moving to the door. Giacomo was the man she loved, but he did not yet understand her world of alchemy.

Ficino

Inspired by Giacomo's bold plan to recover her stolen manual, Emilia sought the assistance of the Medici scholar.

Honored Signor Ficino,

I recall with pleasure how you favored me with your company at the home of Franco Villani in Fiesole last November. I remember, as well, your invitation to discuss in further detail the text that I mentioned to you that day. Perhaps you would honor me and my mother, Violante, with a visit to our home on Via Ghibellina. I would like to tell you how it happened that the book fell into the possession of my family. At your convenience, of course.

Most humbly,
Emilia Serafini

Within a matter of days, a reply from Marsilio Ficino was forthcoming. It was agreed that he should visit the afternoon of the second Monday of Lent. Violante, having readily supported Emilia and Giacomo's scheme, spent hours in the kitchen the morning of the meeting helping Maddalena prepare for Cosimo de' Medici's young scholar.

Gazing out the open window of the second floor of her home, Emilia awaited Signor Ficino's arrival. The sky was overcast, the air scented with rain that would spill from the heavy purple clouds at any moment. Though it was midday, the wall torches and lamps were lit, casting flickering light as the breeze danced through the central salon.

"Where *is* he?" Emilia asked her mother, who was setting a pitcher of spiced wine on a low table already bountiful with a variety of fruit and nut *tortas,* fritters, *marzapan* and *nucatto,* or candied nuts.

"*Pazienza,* patience. He'll be here," Violante replied, unconcerned.

Emilia and her mother were alone in the house that afternoon. Violante had persuaded Francesco and Andrea to deliver a supply of flour, olive oil, and wine to her widowed sister in neighboring Siena. Francesco, still under the impression that Emilia was paying penance for her broken engagement by working at the tavern, deemed the matter of the lost manual insignificant. No doubt he would have put a stop to the afternoon gathering if he'd had any inkling about it. Emilia had never convinced her father that Franco was the thief who stole *Nonna's* book, nor had she convinced him that Franco tried to run her over. Given her father's pig-headedness, it seemed prudent to keep him well away from Marsilio Ficino.

Emilia was glad the meeting had finally been arranged but she was still unsure of Giacomo's suggestion to display her painting, the Adoration of the Christ Child. The panel had been borrowed from Sister Sophia and was propped on a table opposite the chair where Ficino would sit. Though she had gone along with Giacomo's suggestion, Emilia was determined to say nothing of the painting unless Marsilio happened to make a comment about it.

"It's starting to drizzle," Emilia observed, looking out the window again. Finally, she spotted a man wearing a blue cloak hurrying down the road. As he came closer and his short stature became apparent, she knew it was Marsilio. "It's him. He's here!" she called to her mother.

"*Calma*, be calm," Violante said. "Greet him at the door."

Doing as she was told, Emilia tried to appear composed as the esteemed scholar kissed her on the cheek and smiled at her as though she were an old friend.

"Monna Emilia, I was sure we would meet again. I have much to tell you," he said, following her into the house and up the stairs to the second floor.

"I have much to tell you as well," she said before introducing him to her mother.

"It's easy to see where Emilia gets her beauty," Marsilio said as Violante took his cloak.

"Emilia and I are honored that you've come to see us, Messer. We are not scholars, of course, but we do hold great respect for books and learning. Please, sit down," Violante said, offering him Francesco's upholstered chair near the hearth.

After Marsilio had settled himself comfortably and accepted a cup of Francesco's best wine, Emilia could contain the story of her lost manuscript no longer.

"When we met at Signor Villani's banquet, I told you about a book of alchemy—a book that contained passages written by the Egyptian sage."

"Yes, I have been quite curious to hear more about it," nodded Marsilio, somewhat preoccupied with the spiced raisin and almond cake Violante had baked to perfection. Taking another healthy bite of *torta*, he looked around the room almost as if to ascertain they were alone. "The matter of the Egyptians is a fascination the three of us share, I believe."

"Signor Ficino, I confess that the subject of alchemy and the mysteries of Egypt have been of interest to my family for several generations," Violante replied. "The book Emilia discussed with you on the occasion of Franco's banquet belonged to my great-great-grandmother."

"Truly?" Rain unleashed from the sky pounded on the tile rooftop. "I can only wonder how such a text was happened upon."

"My great-great grandmother, Santina, was something of an alchemist, though there are many details we will never know," Violante said, getting up to close the shutters, leaving Emilia and Marsilio in semidarkness scented with rain. Setting a small oil lamp on the table, Violante continued. "She was a midwife, according to my grandmother, and some thought her something of a witch. It was said that she was able to care for victims of the plague and never fall ill—*Nonna's* remedies must have been quite powerful. It was also said that she knew how to make gold."

Ficino chuckled appreciatively as Violante went on to tell the story of how the friar named Calandrino had sent a copy of the translated manuscript to Santina for safekeeping. The text traveled from Italy to Spain and back again, remaining within the family through five generations.

Lightening flashed and thunder rolled across the sky.

"Do you believe the tale?" Ficini asked, looking from Violante to Emilia.

"I believe *Nonna* Santina must have been an extraordinary woman," Violante answered. "She must have felt the manual was quite important—important enough that she made every effort to keep it in our family indefinitely. When my mother gave the book to me, she was adamant that it was something never to be parted with—not until I had my own son or daughter. I told Emilia the same thing when I passed the book to her a few years ago."

"A remarkable story," Ficino concluded, accepting a rich, buttery cheese fritter from Emilia. "I fully appreciate your discretion concerning the matter, Madonna Violante. There are those in Florence who disapprove of the dissemination of ancient wisdom. I imagine I shall be excommunicated one day for speaking too freely," he laughed, more concerned with the delicious food than with heresy, totally enjoying the fritter he brought to his tiny, open mouth.

"You may trust me completely, Madonna, for I will share with you my own secret: one of Cosimo's agents recently returned to Florence with a Greek manuscript—a codex containing fourteen treatises attributed to none other than Hermes Trismegistus."

"The Egyptian sage of *Nonna's* book," Violante said. "Cosimo de' Medici has discovered him."

"It would appear that your discovery of Hermes preceded Cosimo's, Madonna. You will no doubt appreciate knowing that Cosimo has instructed me to suspend work on the dialogues of Plato so that I might undertake the translation of the codex."

"He holds Hermes to be of greater significance?"

"So you understand why your book caught my attention," he said, smiling broadly. "If I may be blunt, Madonna Violante—I am most eager to see your text. It could prove useful to the work I am doing for Cosimo, you see. And it might further authenticate your *nonna's* book."

Violante and Emilia exchanged glances. "If only it were possible, Signor Ficino."

"I assure you, I would take great care of the book—or I could study it here, if you like. It need never leave your house."

"It's not that we don't trust you, Signor Ficino—it's much worse than that," Violante sighed, refilling his cup.

"The book has been stolen," Emilia blurted. "To be truthful, this is why we have asked you here today—we need your help finding it."

Ficino looked as if he had just heard that Donatello's pulpit was stolen from San Lorenzo.

"Who would have done such a thing? Did anyone outside your family know it was in your possession? Of course, such a rare book would fetch a good price—we must check with every bookseller in Florence," he said, words tumbling out. "Still, we can't be sure the book is still within the walls—"

Emilia held up her hand to interrupt. "I'm afraid we have an idea who stole the book, Signor Ficino. Only one person outside our family knew anything about it—someone who appreciated the rarity of the text."

"Who might that be?"

"I'm afraid it is your friend, Franco Villani," Emilia said quietly, hoping Ficino would not deny her accusation outright and storm out of the house. "Your friend, to whom I was betrothed until recently. It ended rather badly, I should say."

Ficino did not seem particularly alarmed by any of this. He merely asked, "Are you sure?"

"Upon my honor, Messer. I believe it was Signor Villani by way of his manservant, Tomasso, who does his master's bidding."

"Villani's reputation precedes him in this case," Ficino said, reaching for his cup. "He hardly left Florence on good terms, after all."

"Whatever do you mean?" Violante asked, as stunned as Emilia by Ficino's appraisal of Villani.

"The reason he moved to Genoa. It's a little known secret, it would appear."

"He told me he was sent to Genoa to live with his uncle after his mother died," Emilia told him.

"A scandal sent Franco from Florence. At least that's what the cousin of the Duke told me at the banquet," Marsilio confided.

"Donna Margherita—the one seated next to Franco?" Emilia asked, recalling the regal-looking guest of honor.

"Yes, the daughter of one of the men Franco apparently swindled. I was surprised to hear her speak of it—the party was for her, after all. She had been drinking too much wine and seemed upset that night. I believe she told me far more than she intended to."

"You said he swindled the lady's father?" Violante asked.

"So she implied," Ficino said. "It turns out that Franco was passing off several reproductions as ancient sculptures. Took in more than a few collectors at his father's store—one being Cardinal Perugino of Siena, according to Margherita."

"He sold a forgery to a cardinal?" Emilia exclaimed in disbelief.

"That's what Margherita said. Franco was a bit heartless with a certain young lady as well. Franco's father was unforgiving when he found out what his son was about—though I have to wonder if the old man was as innocent of the forgeries as he pretended. Anyway, he packed off Franco to Genoa in order to salvage what he could of his own reputation."

"To think of the lies that man has told me!" Emilia exclaimed.

"To be fair, he was quite young at the time. One would hope he had learned his lesson. Clearly he's as ambitious as ever. You *are* quite sure he's the one who got his hands on your text?"

"He's the only one outside the family who even knew of its existence—besides you, Signor Ficino."

Emilia explained how Franco came to learn of her book, and she recounted his attempts to wield it from her possession. She related the peculiar events that had taken place at Primavera, her subsequent engagement to Franco, his preoccupation with the text, and the strange encounters with Tomasso. She told the scholar how

Giacomo had been run down on the Street of the Painters and how she had been nearly trampled to death.

So that Marsilio would recognize the manual if he saw it, Emilia and Violante discussed the contents of various chapters, the illustrations, the passages from *De Chemia* and *Phaedo*, the mysteries of Eleusis, and the recipes for the precipitation of gold so far as their memories would allow.

"A most intriguing tale," Ficino concluded when he had heard the story in its entirety. "Now you must tell me, Monna Emilia, how it is I am to help retrieve your precious manual. I do want to help you, though I confess my motives are partially selfish."

Emilia looked to her mother, who nodded reassuringly, "My friend, Giacomo Massarino, thought you might be persuaded to visit Franco. If you were to spend a pleasant afternoon with him, such as you have enjoyed with us, perhaps a discussion of the ancients might arise."

"And then?" he said, prodding her to continue.

"Perhaps you would mention your current interest in the works of Hermes Trismegistus," Emilia suggested.

"I see where this might be leading."

"Don't you suppose that Signor Villani will want to show you his latest treasure? The one called, *A Manual to the Science of Alchemy*?"

Marsilio and Violante chuckled softly.

"If the book is truly in his possession, I believe Franco can be persuaded to share it with me," the philosopher said.

Emilia prayed they were correct in their assumption. Even if Franco did show Marsilio the book, she wasn't sure what would happen next. It wasn't as if Franco would confess the theft and hand over the text without a fight.

"Signor Ficino," she said. "I am convinced you will find my

grandmother's book in Franco's home. How to persuade him to return our property is another matter."

Ficino hesitated before replying, "Monna Emilia, you must leave that small detail to me. If I discover your text, then rest assured I shall find a way to return it safely to you."

Marsilio stood to leave and Emilia felt grateful for his promise of assistance. Her only disappointment, though minor, was that he had failed to notice her painting. Perhaps the panel was unobtrusive against the wall in the dimly lit room.

She was thinking her work lacked sufficient merit when Marsilio moved closer to the painting. "Curious," he said, standing before the panel. "What a delightful image. Entirely unique," he proclaimed.

Violante swept to his side and wasted no time in saying, "Yes, Emilia is truly gifted, is she not?"

Turning to face Emilia and her mother, Marsilio Ficino declared with certainty, "Remember you heard it from me: Emilia Serafini will be Florence's first great *pittoressa*."

Giacomo was right, Emilia said to herself as the scholar took leave. She had doubted his advice just as she had doubted her own talent, but her vision of herself had proven too small. Once again the possibilities for her life were expanding, moving beyond the bounds of the workshop of Makarios Levantes.

Bettina

The night after Marsilio Ficino's visit, Emilia lay awake wondering if *Nonna's* manual would ever be returned to her possession. Franco was not about to hand over the precious text to the scholar simply because a painter's apprentice claimed it belonged to her.

She felt certain Franco would call her a liar. *Emilia Serafini? She is an ambitious young girl who is bent on tarnishing my reputation for the mere sport of it. A semi-talented coquette who saw fit to toy with my heart. Now she is playing with you, Marsilio, trying to engage you in a battle on her behalf.*

Emilia could think of any number of stories Franco might fabricate to convince Marsilio that Emilia was not the true owner of the manual. But Marsilio believed her, didn't he? Rising from bed, Emilia opened the shutters. The sky had cleared, revealing a perfect half moon in the dark night.

The moon queen Emilia thought, recalling the image from the manual. She could almost see a woman's profile etched into the silvery white light. In the final stage of the alchemical transformation, the moon queen would merge with the sun king. It was a joining of the body with the spirit, called the *coniunctio* by the alchemists. It was a union that would fulfill the deepest desires of the heart.

Gazing up at the starry sky, she wondered if she would ever find the perfection promised by the author of her grandmother's text. *It would be a futile endeavor to seek the secrets of heaven while one foot remains firmly fixed upon the Earth. To learn to fly, the alchemist must set his sights upon that which is not of this Earth.*

Recalling this passage from the manual, Emilia thought of Makarios, his disregard for worldly matters, and his commitment to his faith and his art. Perhaps her mentor knew the alchemists' secrets of heaven. Though he was not a rich man, he had found success in Florence that few would have believed possible. Shivering in her white nightdress at the evening's cool breeze, Emilia closed the shutters and returned to bed. When she finally fell asleep, she dreamt of the red stone, the *rubedo*.

Nonna's manual said that the red stone was essential if one was to precipitate pure gold and live the life God intended. Only after the *rubedo* was achieved could the gold be realized. In her dream, Emilia could see the stone shining near the window in the darkness of her room. Clear, brilliant, glowing like a flame. She reached for it, picked it up, held it in the palm of her hand to stare at it in wonder. Feeling the precious weight of it, Emilia knew there was something in the stone that would allow her to create miracles.

More than two weeks had passed since Marsilio's visit, yet there was no word from him. Emilia was afraid the scholar was too busy with his important duties to Cosimo to bother with her trivial concerns. Even though she worried whether or not Marsilio would follow through with his promise to help, she tried to steal away to the *bottega* as often as she could. Makarios had begun another commission—a St. John the Baptist in the Desert—acquired through a new friend at San Marco. Preparing the pigments for the panel was a welcome diversion.

There was also consolation in the news that Giacomo could finally walk again, though just a few limping steps. When Emilia stopped by his house one morning with a basket of warm rolls, she was delighted to find him sitting at the window, pencil in hand, sketching the street scene below.

"You are becoming yourself again."

"Any word from Ficino?" Giacomo asked, looking up from his drawing.

"Not yet. Do you think he's forgotten me?"

"From what you've told me, he is too much of an idealist not to be a man of his word. You will hear from him," he replied as though it were a fact. "Emilia, you never told me—did he notice your painting?"

She had forgotten, in her preoccupation with the manual, to tell him. "You were right in this regard as well, Giacomo. He seemed to admire the panel, though I'm not sure much will come of it."

"His notice counts for something. At least one of us will find fame."

Sympathetic to Giacomo's ongoing frustration with his position at Jacovelli's, Emilia replied, "Your talent eclipses mine, you know this."

"Talent or not, I am invisible behind Jacovelli. It's his name, not mine, that people know."

Emilia knew Giacomo longed for a workshop of his own. He had grown tired of toiling away while Jacovelli reaped most of the pay and all the glory. She wished she could offer words of encouragement but she understood the politics of the *bottega* well enough.

"You'll have your own workshop one day," she said, believing this to be true. She had been impressed with Giacomo's ability from the first day she stepped foot in Jacovelli's *bottega*. His remarkable skill sparkled like magic on every panel and wall touched by his brush. Although she had often lamented his singular focus, she had come to respect his ambition, driven as it was by passion rather than greed and lust for power. "You must be patient," she told him.

"Yes, what else can I do?"

"Pray."

Emilia kissed him goodbye and silently petitioned St. Mary that Giacomo would some day receive the recognition he deserved.

Later that day, Emilia was mixing egg yolk with the ground shoots of grapevines to make a black pigment for Makarios when the front door opened to admit Franco Villani's cook, basket in hand.

"Bettina!" Makarios called out in greeting from his desk at the far side of the room. "What a nice surprise."

The tiny, round woman who had cooked enthusiastically for Emilia and Makarios during their stay at Primavera smiled broadly and proudly brought forth the contents of her basket. "I have brought you a tiered *torta*, Makarios. I know how much you like my cakes."

As Makarios accepted the cake of layered almonds, raisins,

dates, and spices, Emilia wondered if the woman could tell her any news of recent events at Franco's house. If Marsilio had come to visit, Bettina would surely know.

"You are very kind, Bettina," Makarios said, showing the rich cinnamon and sugar-crusted cake to Emilia. "How is Signor Villani? I hope he is treating you well."

"He travels so much. There's no one to cook for," she complained. "Only Tomasso and the servants. He rarely has company any more." She gave Emilia a knowing look before saying to Makarios, "If I may say something to Emilia."

"Of course."

"I wanted to tell her how sorry I am about the news."

"The news?" she said.

"That the wedding is off, of course. I suppose I'm mostly sorry for myself, since I was looking forward to having a lady in the house."

"I will let the two of you speak," Makarios said, turning away.

Emilia was quick to say, "I keep no secrets from you, Makarios. You know enough of what has happened."

"Just the same, I think I will have a small slice of the *torta*," he said and disappeared into the kitchen.

Bettina sat across from Emilia at her worktable and leaning in close, whispered. "The truth is I don't blame you one bit for leaving the scoundrel."

"Bettina," Emilia said, stunned by her words. "I'm surprised to hear you speak of Franco that way."

"I found out what he was up to and I think you ought to know the truth. I had a feeling something wasn't right when Filippa was sacked. I couldn't believe Filippa would try to steal from anyone, the way Tomasso tried to make us think. I should have told you what I knew a long time ago, but I didn't want to go and spoil things for you—tell you what a rat you were going to marry. Now that it's over, I thought it best to come and share with you what I know."

"What is it you know, Bettina?"

"It was Tomasso and Franco who made Filippa do what she did. I overheard the master and Tomasso talking about it after the banquet last year. The master wasn't pleased after you told him you'd found the girl in your room. Tomasso said he should have done the thieving himself. 'Can't trust a servant girl to do anything right,' he said. The master said the girl didn't matter any and could be gotten rid of easily enough."

Bettina shook her head. "It's a sorry lot that would bother with the little bit of money or trinkets a young girl like you would carry in her bags. It's despicable he would do something like that. Just despicable."

"I knew Filippa didn't really want to steal from me."

"What else were you to think when you found her going through your things?"

"At first I was angry with her. But she was terrified, poor thing. When I started to question her, I had the feeling someone put her up to it. I saw her at the market a few months ago and I think she wanted to tell me what really happened, but she's afraid of Franco."

"Well I'll be…" murmured Bettina. "So you already knew he was a thief."

"He tried to convince me otherwise, but eventually I found him out. It wasn't money he was trying to steal from me though—it was a book. A very old book."

"A book?" the older woman said in surprise. "Why would he want to steal a book from you?"

"It was a very special book—a book of philosophy," Emilia answered.

Bettina still appeared as if she was trying to make sense of what she'd been told.

"I know Signor Villani is peculiar when it comes to his fancy carvings and those books of his. Only the other day he was showing his books to some visitor. A braggart, just like Signor Villani. The two of them went on and on about all the fine things they own."

Emilia could barely contain herself at the mention of the visitor. "Do you know the name of the man—the man who came to look at Franco's books?"

"No, can't say I do."

"What did he look like?" Emilia asked, trying to keep her voice even.

"He was a little man—not more than twenty-five I'd say—with dark, curly hair."

"Marsilio Ficino!"

Bettina considered this, then shrugged. "Might have been his name. I served him a very fine lunch—stuffed sole, roasted capon."

Emilia struggled to remain patient as Bettina went on about the numerous dishes she had served Franco's guest. When the cook paused at last, Emilia asked, "What did they talk about, Bettina? Could you hear what they said?"

"It's not as though I tried to listen, of course. But I couldn't help but hear some of what they were saying. The little man was talking about Cosimo de' Medici—Cosimo this, Cosimo that. A bit of a name dropper, he was."

Emilia smiled to herself, thinking Marsilio had quite intentionally mentioned his intimate relationship with Cosimo in order to bring up the subject of the Hermetic text he was translating. She could only hope that Marsilio had succeeded in luring the manual from Franco.

"A couple of peacocks, they were, trying to outdo one

another. After dinner, the master brought his guest to the library. I didn't mean to overhear, mind you, but I was helping to clear off the table, so I couldn't help it really. The master, he wanted to show off his collection. Brought out his ivories, his gems. Walked around the house talking about his sculptures."

"Did he talk to his guest about his books—about any book in particular, Bettina?" Emilia interrupted, too impatient to allow the cook to ramble on. "Can you remember?"

Bettina nodded slowly. "He might have. I know they were excited about something when they were in the library, but I can't say I know what it was about," she replied. "Do you think it might have been your book?"

"I believe it was, Bettina."

"A mean thing to do, taking your book," Bettina said consolingly. "At least it was only a book. Could have been worse, I suppose."

"Do you know if the guest left the house with a book, by chance?"

Bettina shrugged. "I can't say, I didn't see him leave."

After Bettina departed, Emilia wondered what, if anything, Marsilio had accomplished during his visit to Franco's home. It would not be like Franco to permit a guest to walk out of his house with one of his prized possessions. Recovering the manual from Franco was like trying to wrest prey from the clutches of a poisonous snake.

The Holy Trinity

O ne week before San Giovanni's Day, the June holiday of the city's patron saint, Emilia received a letter bearing an elegant seal of red wax. Tearing open the seal, she began to read, her eyes darting across the page. Her mother stood waiting.

"It's from Signor Ficino," she said, still reading.

"Has he found the manual?"

"He doesn't say," Emilia answered, trying to make sense of his words. "He writes of his visit here. *It was a pleasure to visit with you and your most charming mother.* He seems to be suggesting that I present a painting as a gift to Cosimo de' Medici."

"A painting for Cosimo!" Violante exclaimed.

"He can't be serious!" Emilia said, looking up from the letter.

"He was impressed by your painting of the Christ child."

"I have to tell Giacomo. I have to tell him right away."

"But what about your lunch?"

"Later, *Madre.* This can't wait."

She stuffed the letter into her embroidered purse and took off at a quick pace down Via Ghibellina, barely noticing the neighbor children or Monna Gemma calling *buon giorno* to her as she hurried across town, taking the Via del Corso west towards the district of Santa Maria Novella.

Winded from her brisk walk, she arrived at Giacomo's now familiar home. He hobbled forward to greet her, but she was only half aware he was finally up and about, even if he was using a cane.

"Marsilio says nothing about the manual. He writes only of my painting," Emilia blurted out as she extracted the letter from her purse and began to read. "*It was a pleasure to visit with you and your most charming mother. My sincere thanks for a delightful afternoon. I have not forgotten your exceptional Adoration of the Christ Child. I took the liberty of mentioning to Cosimo that I have surely discovered Florence's most gifted feminine hand and he was intrigued. It is only a thought, naturally, but perhaps you might be persuaded to present an example of your work to him. I believe he would be most receptive.*"

Emilia waved the letter at Giacomo, who was carefully lowering himself to a bench. "Why on earth would Cosimo de' Medici care to see the work of Emilia Serafini?"

At first Giacomo seemed puzzled by the invitation as well. Emilia handed him the letter and he began to read it for himself. "*Florence's most gifted feminine hand.* Well, he is right about that," he said. "You should be happy, Emilia. Cosimo is a generous patron. If someone he knows and trusts bothered to mention you, then he would want to see what you're about. I suppose you might be something of a novelty to him."

Emilia's excitement dimmed at the thought of being nothing more than a novelty. She sat beside Giacomo, slightly deflated. "So it is only because I am a woman that he is curious to meet me."

"It matters little. The point is, you will use the situation to your advantage. Perhaps he only seeks to satisfy his curiosity, but you will do more than that—you will dazzle him."

"I will?"

"You will make another painting, Emilia. An exceptional piece. Then you will send it to Cosimo as a gift."

"How am I to make an exceptional piece?"

"The same way you did the last one."

Emilia was not in the least assured. None of this had anything to do with the recovery of her grandmother's text, besides which, she was not at all sure she was up to the task of painting to please the eye of Cosimo de' Medici. "I should be happy, I suppose. But I thought Ficino wanted to help me get back my *nonna's* book."

Giacomo shrugged. "I doubt he's forgotten your book, Emilia. If Ficino thinks enough of you to try to arrange an audience with Cosimo, I suspect he will honor his promise to help you."

"Do you really think so?"

Giacomo gave her shoulder a reassuring squeeze. "Don't worry. Just paint."

Though he looked happy for her, it dawned on Emilia that Giacomo would surely welcome such an invitation himself. For years he had remained the faithful and silent talent behind the enormous presence of Lorenzo Jacovelli. He had dutifully served his master, reaping no recognition of his own. Yet here he was congratulating her on the enormous opportunity that she, a mere novice, was being given.

"Have you never thought of sending something to Cosimo yourself?" Emilia asked.

Giacomo shook his head. "My name will mean nothing to him."

"He knows Jacovelli."

"It is better to wait until I am noticed."

"This is how he might come to notice you. He would be pleased to meet the talent behind Jacovelli, I should think."

Giacomo seemed unconvinced and Emilia knew better than to push him, his pride would not allow him to beg for recognition. For now, she would begin her panel, and she would present Cosimo with the best she could achieve. Giacomo's success would come in time, Emilia told herself. Perhaps she would eventually find a way to help him.

She knew she ought to be grateful for the chance to paint for Cosimo de' Medici, yet she could not stop worrying about her lost book. Marsilio Ficino was a busy man, a frequent guest at the palace, and he was in the midst of completing the translations commanded by Cosimo. Had Ficino concluded that nothing could be done about Franco but thought instead to help her succeed as an artist? Why else had he failed to mention his visit to Franco's home?

In a moment of panic, she feared the scholar coveted the text for himself. She envisioned Franco in his library, offering her book to Marsilio or Cosimo for a hefty sum. Would Marsilio accept such an offer? She reminded herself that Marsilio was a man of principle who would honor his word. Her experience with Franco was causing her to mistrust good and honest men.

"You will not see me for a while," Emilia said as she prepared to leave Giacomo.

"Of course—you will be too busy painting."

She set off for the workshop with the intention of dazzling Cosimo de' Medici and the determination to be more than a novelty. Her future or lack of future with Giacomo Massarino was put aside, at least for the time being.

Feigning a mysterious fever and displaying a red rash made visible by cinnabar applied with a fine brush, Emilia avoided work at her father's tavern so that she might sneak away to Makarios' *bottega*. It was a ruse that gave her time to complete the gift for Cosimo de' Medici. For several days Emilia struggled to come up with the ideal subject to paint. She leafed through all the usual books, visited the city's great churches, and drew dozens of sketches but could find no way to distinguish herself and the gift for Cosimo.

One day, after sitting at the Carmine for a while, thinking herself entirely unworthy, she wandered back to the workshop. "It's no use. I can't do it," she announced to Makarios. "What can I possibly paint that will be good enough?"

Makarios, who was creating a background of luminous rocks for his St. John the Baptist, hesitated before replying. "There are no new subjects, Emilia. It has all been done before. The difference is that it has not been done by *you* before. You are a young Florentine with a skilled hand. Paint as you have—with your own authenticity. Paint something you love, something close to your heart. If you pretend to do something else, if you try to be who you are not, it will be obvious in the paint."

Taking in her master's words, Emilia felt comforted. Perhaps she did not have to strive to create a masterpiece after all; she only had to paint what was most truly Emilia Serafini. She would paint a subject she loved. Something that spoke to the deepest place in her heart.

Thoughtfully, Emilia looked around the studio at the various panels on the walls, the St. John in progress, and the *Pantocrator* on the wall. Her gaze came to rest upon the Holy Trinity now hanging behind Makarios' desk. This icon, carried with him from home, had inspired Emilia to learn the sacred art in the first place.

Father, Son, and Holy Spirit were seated serenely at a table, each one identical to the other. It was the icon that spoke to her above all others, yet it would hardly impress the likes of the Medici. The art of iconography, which she had been lovingly taught by her master, was something she would keep for herself. If she was to make an impression at the palace, she would have to look to the work of Fra Angelico or Uccello, whom Cosimo favored.

Nevertheless, she could not forget Makarios' Holy Trinity. Studying her master's panel, she felt moved to paint this very subject despite knowing that no one in Florence would look twice at a Byzantine icon. She returned home, feeling no closer to a solution than when she started. Lying in bed, gazing at the doorframe in her dimly lit room, she visualized the Trinity before her, floating in darkness overhead. The robes of the Father, Son, and Holy Ghost were transparent, their luminous colors forming a thin veil over the wall behind them.

She was falling asleep when she saw with brilliant clarity what she would paint for Cosimo de' Medici.

"I need your help," she implored Giacomo. She stood at his front door once again, declining his offer to come inside.

"Come now, Emilia. You are capable enough. We both know that."

"Not for what I have in mind." She brought out the sketch she had hastily drawn that morning and revealed her plan to him. There was no time to waste, and every day she feared her father would discover her on the streets of Florence when she was supposed to be at home, sick in bed.

"It is ambitious, Emilia. The architecture will require exactitude."

"Which is not my talent, Giacomo. It is yours," she said, knowing he could not deny his mastery of Albertian perspective. "Are you well enough to draw?"

"As far as Jacovelli knows, I am not. For you, yes."

She sensed that Giacomo's unspoken resentment towards Jacovelli had kept him home longer than necessary. It would be good for him to get out of the house, Emilia decided, and to stop dwelling on his injury. "You'll come tomorrow then? Your father will help you get to the *bottega*?

"Very well, Emilia."

She hurried off before Giacomo could change his mind.

The setting of her Holy Trinity was a magnificent chapel in the manner of Florence's master architect, Brunelleschi, with two tall, marble Corinthian pilasters flanking a coffered barrel vault. The illusion of the architecture was rendered so expertly—with the generous assistance of Giacomo, who was able to work from a chair—that the surface of the panel disappeared and the chapel became real.

Before this chapel she set her Trinity. The three figures were arranged in the form of a pyramid, the center one highest, ascending to the arch. The composition below the figures formed a descending pyramid, which converged at the base of the table where the three figures sat in silent, serene harmony.

On the second Friday of July, after more than three weeks of diligent work, she stood staring at the panel. It was nearly finished and Emilia believed she truly might succeed. The image of her faith, the heart and soul of her religion—the Holy Trinity—stood before her. The details of the arms, hands, and feet were given a sculptural reality, yet they were rendered with such lightness and transparency, very much in keeping with the icon, so as to evoke the mystery of the Three who were yet One in the kingdom of heaven.

Makarios, for his part, said little as the work progressed. He continued working on his St. John, as though disinclined to influence the young painters in any way. When Emilia had added the last of the highlights and was ready to lay down the varnish, he finally gave his opinion.

"When you began, I feared it was too ambitious. Yet it succeeds."

"It lacks the purity of the icon," Emilia said, wondering if he was at all disappointed in her interpretation of the Trinity.

Makarios pulled up a stool to sit before the panel. "You will have plenty of time to write icons if you so desire, Emilia. While we remember the old ways, we should not be afraid to create new works. Look how beautifully you have expressed your love of God," her master said. "History, life, art continue on and on. We must not be afraid of what is new."

Emilia lowered her head in acknowledgement of the compliment. At these words of praise, the image of more paintings flashed before her eyes. They were modern in design yet inspired by the quiet, meditative quality of the icon. She wondered if she would ever have the chance to paint them. Her father had other plans for her, and she was far from convincing him to allow her to return to her craft.

The Palace

"You mean to say your girl did this?" asked Tedaldo.

Though Emilia had been working with Makarios for almost two years, the old woodworker had managed to hold onto his well-worn skepticism. He had been summoned to help deliver her completed Holy Trinity to the palace of Cosimo de' Medici and now stood staring at her panel.

"She is a painter, like me, Tedaldo," Makarios reminded him.

"Who ever heard of such a thing." Shrugging off another inexplicable work from the *bottega* of Makarios Levantes, Tedaldo proceeded to wrap the Holy Trinity carefully in long lengths of soft wool for the journey by cart. On the way out the door he nodded to Emilia, saying, "*Non c'è male.* Not bad."

After the gift was delivered, Emilia did not have to wait long for a response from the palace. Only a week later she received an invitation from Cosimo de' Medici himself. Violante stood reading the elegant script on fine, cream-colored paper over Emilia's shoulder.

"You'll need a new dress. There's little time," her mother said. "What will I tell Father?"

Violante paused before replying, "I think we may be able to tell him the truth about this, Emilia. Invitations to the palace don't come every day. Your father's pride is such that he will want to boast of it. But we will have to let him think the piece given to Cosimo is something you did last winter. He cannot know that you've been painting again."

With the matter of the invitation settled, Violante marched Emilia to the *sarta*, the dressmaker, who fitted her for a splendid gown with sleeves of the sheerest silk, like gossamer wings of pale pink. After the dress was ordered, Emilia began to fret over what to say to the illustrious Cosimo de' Medici when she met him. Her preoccupation with the upcoming event was such that she had little time to dwell on the missing manual and Marsilio's vague promise of help.

"Hold your curtsey," Violante advised, "and for heaven's sake, don't let your eyes wander. Be yourself, of course. You will charm him."

When the day arrived and Palazzo Medici on Via Larga loomed three stories tall in front of her, Emilia was not at all sure she was capable of speaking any words at all. She was already running late, for Violante had spent too much time braiding and twisting her hair with ornaments and ribbons, but she stood for several minutes gazing up at the massive, seventy-foot-tall home built of rough-cut stones in the manner of an ancient Roman monument. Besides its immense size and air of antique fortitude, the building did not draw attention to itself; the home might have belonged to any rich merchant in Florence had the windows not been decorated with the telltale Medici arms—red balls on a gold shield.

Emilia took a deep breath, reminding herself that she was an invited guest, and made her way to the impenetrable wood door. She gave her name to the porter, who carefully checked a list before ushering her into an enormous room filled with antique sculptures, priceless tapestries, and paintings. Walking by an inlaid cabinet, she marveled at the collection of colorful Murano glass, exquisite cameos, and intricately designed enamels.

When she realized that she was lagging behind the porter, Emilia quickened her pace. She was shown through a wide, marble doorway leading to a spacious central courtyard where an arcade of Corinthian columns surrounded a rectangular table. Before a lavish display of rare fruits and nuts at the center of the table, she saw the unmistakable figure of Cosimo de' Medici himself.

She did not allow her eyes to wander to the faces of the other guests, though she was curious to see if Marsilio was present. As her mother had instructed, she kept her eyes focused on Cosimo. When her name was announced, she curtseyed low.

"Ah! Here she is!" the patrician, white-haired man wearing a simple but elegant robe of red silk called out in welcome. "The fair young woman who would be our next Fra Angelico."

Heartened by his welcoming words, Emilia was nonetheless afraid her voice would tremble if she spoke.

"I am deeply honored, *Magnifico*," she answered, staring at the polished stone floor.

"It is I who am honored by your beautiful gift. A rare combination, I must say, of geometric perfection—carried out with such conviction—and grace and charm. And by one so very young."

The compliment warmed her, encouraging her to look into Cosimo's kind, smiling face.

"I shall find a special place for your Trinity, Madonna Emilia. I shall also see to it that you are paid."

"Then I am even more deeply honored." Still looking at

Cosimo, Emilia noticed out of the corner of her eye that Marsilio was seated to his right. She felt comforted to know he was there, though she dared not speak to him.

It was then that Cosimo turned to Marsilio. "I believe you told me that Madonna Emilia has painted for Franco Villani, is that not true?"

"Indeed," Marsilio replied.

Emilia turned towards Marsilio; she nearly fell over, for she saw that Franco was seated near the far end of the table, half concealed behind a huge vase of lilies. If she appeared shocked to see him there, it was nothing compared to the livid look on Franco's face.

It was obvious that Franco was not expecting to see her. Though it could be no accident that the two of them had been invited to the palace at the same time, she was not sure why Franco was being subjected to the glory of her success. The sight of the man who had wooed her, then tried to trample her to death, rendered Emilia speechless, but she had no choice but to maintain a sense of decorum and show fitting gratitude to her host.

"So you have discovered Madonna Emilia before the rest of us, is that true?" Cosimo inquired of Franco.

Franco, dressed in a heavily ornamented tunic, shifted uncomfortably in his seat, and Emilia could sense his outrage. He remained mute as Emilia was offered a seat on the other side of Marsilio, next to Donna Margherita, the stately guest of honor from Franco's banquet. Emilia supposed it could hardly be coincidental that Margherita was present that day as well. She guessed the lady's knowledge of Franco's tainted past might somehow fit into whatever scheme Marsilio had devised.

Finally, Franco responded, "Yes, she was apprenticed to the foreigner—Levantes is his name. He gets by on charity, not being a member of the guild." Emilia's blood boiled as Franco added casually, "She has apparently risen beyond his small studio south of the river. The commissions were surely too small for such an ambitious young woman."

Marsilio laughed heartily. "Come now, Franco, you are being too modest. I have been to your home in Fiesole, as you recall. Levantes painted your Birth of Venus."

"I saw the fresco," put in a venerable looking old man, who sat peeling an orange. "Quite good."

"Brilliant, I should say, Ridolfi," Marsilio replied.

"Levantes did succeed, it would appear. The work kept him from starving during the winter," Franco said smoothly. "But what do I know of art? I am a man of business, after all."

"Oh, you are a man possessed of exquisite taste," Marsilio insisted. "Your gems and ivories—such rare quality! And your books." Turning to Cosimo, he said, "Several volumes that rival your own collection, I must say.

"One book from Signor Villani's library will interest you in particular, Cosimo. I suggested he bring it along today." Addressing Franco, he said, "Do show your discovery to Cosimo, Franco. Your *Manual to the Science of Alchemy*."

The others at the table watched as Franco scanned the room, desperately seeking a route of escape. His eyes moved to the end of the table, where a green velvet pouch concealed a flat, rectangular object. Emilia knew at once what lay hidden within.

Franco, it would appear, had been summoned so that Cosimo might view his rare alchemical text. Emilia observed the silent machinations of Franco's mind as he weighed his choices. He could run away, feign illness. Or he could carry on with the charade and insist that the text belonged to him. He could tell the truth—the least likely scenario, she thought. Emilia waited with the others, wondering what he would do.

Franco regained his composure, wiped his brow, and glanced ever so briefly with his hollow, dark eyes at Emilia.

"It is a strange coincidence to see the young woman I was to marry here today," Franco said, as though trying to control his anguish. Emilia cringed, thinking he would use their failed engagement to discredit her in some way.

Cosimo, clearly surprised, asked, "You mean Madonna Emilia?"

"Yes," Franco said, looking wounded. "We were to be married."

Feeling all eyes upon her, Emilia did not know how to reply. "I think this is of small interest to our host and his guests," she said quietly, wishing she could disappear.

"You must forgive me for supposing you would be happy to see one another. I had no idea, of course. After the delightful time we all had together in Fiesole," Marsilio said, with well-feigned remorse.

"An innocent mistake," Franco said. "Emilia Serafini is an ambitious, young painter—one who esteems painting above all else, I have come to accept."

Emilia saw Donna Margherita and an older woman, apparently the wife of Ridofi, exchange looks of unconcealed surprise.

"I'm sorry, but it is not easy to be here," Franco stammered, eyes downcast. Emilia burned inwardly. He would do his best to turn Cosimo against her, suggest that her show of talent was unnatural and unseemly in a woman.

"Oh dear, obviously I have erred, erred most grievously," Marsilio said sadly over the uneasy silence that hung in the room. Then, in a determined voice, he exclaimed, "But I will not allow us to be deterred from enjoying your discovery, Franco. Not after you were kind enough to come today."

Franco looked to Cosimo and said, with strained civility, "Perhaps it would be best if we wait until a more suitable time, if it pleases you."

Cosimo nodded, as though to agree, but Marsilio was already out of his chair and reaching for the green velvet bag. It appeared he was not willing to allow Franco to slip away from the scene quite so easily. Emilia, wide-eyed and disbelieving, looked from Franco to Marsilio to Cosimo.

"I will not allow my blunder to ruin your afternoon, dear Franco. You will have the opportunity to show Cosimo your treasure, just as I promised." He slipped the book from the jacket and with a flourish, set it before their host before Franco could stop him. "It is a most rare text you stumbled upon, Franco. You must take a look, Cosimo."

"Yes, it is a curiosity," Franco muttered, clearly vexed that his strategy to escape had been thwarted.

"Who is the author?" the old man inquired.

"A large portion was written by a man who identified himself as Isaac the Jew, though there are also passages from Plato, among others," Franco said with little enthusiasm.

"Including Hermes Trismegistus," Marsilio added.

"The Egyptian sage? The author of the codex?" Cosimo asked, his heightened interest having the effect of turning everyone's attention from Franco to the manual.

"Yes, the same one it would appear. Marsilio mentioned your recent discovery of the ancient manuscript," Franco replied, apparently resigned to staying in his seat and discussing the manual. "It is an odd coincidence that we should have discovered Hermes concurrently."

Unsure of what to say or do, Emilia sat quietly, taking in the dialogue between the men while the other guests at the table stared at her *nonna's* book. Did Marsilio expect her to stand up and claim the book as her own? If she did, a battle was likely to ensue. She saw no way of proving the manual belonged to her; all she could give was her word.

"Fascinating," Cosimo murmured, studying a colored drawing of Thoth, the Egyptian God. "A most remarkable text. One must wonder where you happened upon it."

Keeping his eyes fixed upon the manual, Franco replied without hesitation, "I suppose I was in the right place at the right time."

"So it would seem."

Marsilio scratched his head. "Emilia, do I recall correctly that you happen to own a text on the subject of alchemy as well? I seem to remember you mentioned something to me." He stopped himself, as though embarrassed. "I'm sorry—it was at Franco's banquet when we spoke."

Franco's face was tense as he turned to the scholar. Emilia could sense his fear that his lie might be discovered at any moment. He seemed to be straining against some invisible force, as though he wanted to reach out and strike her, remove her from his great moment of success with Cosimo de' Medici. However, his every move was being observed, and he could not afford to show the slightest anger toward her. Emilia knew he would offer no confession, and it might be impossible to drag the truth from him. She wanted to cry out, *The text is mine! You know it is mine!* But she knew it was best to wait and see what Marsilio would say next.

"Yes," Emilia replied, playing along. "I might have mentioned it to you."

"It has been in your family for many years, didn't you say?"

"For generations," Emilia replied, her heart pounding.

"Yes, yes. It is a very old book, I think you said," Marsilio said, as though trying to reach back into the recesses of his brain.

"More than one hundred years old, according to my mother."

"I vaguely remember," said Marsilio, as Cosimo's attention was still focused on the alchemical manual. "And what is the title?"

"As it turns out, the book I mentioned to you is also entitled *A Manual to the Science of Alchemy,*" she said.

Franco's face flushed with fury.

Cosimo lifted his gaze from the book, his brows arched in wonder. "You mean to say you are also in possession of a text entitled *A Manual to the Science of Alchemy?*"

"I was—well, it was a book that belonged to my grandmother," she said, unsure if Marsilio expected her to come right out and accuse Franco of stealing her book.

"Surely, only the titles are the same," Marsilio laughed. "There could hardly be two copies of such a rare book floating about Florence."

Cosimo ignored Marsilio's comment. "Does your text resemble this book in any way?" He closed the manual and passed it down the table to her.

Emilia caressed the book she had held in her hands so many times. She thumbed through the pages—the pictures, special passages, and notes in *Nonna's* own hand leaping out at her like old friends. Almost inaudibly, she murmured, "I should say this looks exactly like the book that belonged to my grandmother."

"This is an afternoon of strange coincidences, is it not, Marsilio?" Cosimo said.

Marsilio, appearing thoroughly confused, looked from Emilia to Franco as though waiting for an explanation. "It is a very strange coincidence. So you mean to say you have an exact copy of this book at home, Monna Emilia?"

"No," she said quickly. "It was stolen—only a few months ago."

Franco erupted, unable to contain himself any longer. "The girl is a cunning little witch. She only seeks to make me suffer more than I have. What crime did I commit? Only to ask for her hand in marriage! She has sought to take everything from me, ever since the day I met her! It was not enough to break my heart—she thinks nothing of claiming my possessions as well!"

Cosimo and his guests froze, stunned by the outburst. Emilia, horrified that Franco was painting her as a lying thief, had no idea what to say to defend herself. Who would believe her if she said that Franco had put his servants to the task of stealing her book and that he had tried to kill Giacomo and run her over in broad daylight?

She struggled for words when the elderly Ridolfi offered, "I don't believe Madonna Emilia accused *you* of stealing her book, Franco. I believe she merely indicated that her book was stolen. Perhaps you unwittingly stumbled upon a stolen text."

"Yes, who sold you the text, Franco? Someone here in Florence, I presume," Cosimo inquired.

Franco was now clearly struggling under the scrutiny of everyone at the table. His face was contorted with anger and sweat trickled down the side of his face to the stiff collar of his tunic. There was nothing handsome or desirable about him now, Emilia observed.

"I came here today so that I might share something I thought would be of interest to you, not to be interrogated," Franco said in a voice that could not conceal his hostility. "If I had known this wretched woman was to be here, then I certainly would not have come."

Cosimo, clearly unwilling to tolerate Franco's behavior, rebuked him. "You surely would not have been invited had I known your proclivity for rudeness."

"Then I shall ease your burden and take my leave." Franco rose from his seat. In his rage he seemed not to care that he was falling out of grace with Cosimo and his friends as quickly as he had fallen into it. Franco reached to pick up the book as departed, but Marsilio grabbed his arm to stop him.

"Please, just a moment," Marsilio said, pushing Emilia's manual out of reach. "I believe the matter of the text has not been settled. Surely, you would not wish to keep stolen property, Franco."

"You don't mean to say you believe that lying little tart? If you insist on the truth, then ask her father!" Franco blurted. "It was Francesco Serafini who gave me the book, if you must know. He had enough sense to know it belongs with someone who appreciates its worth. Emilia Serafini has no claim to the text."

Horrified, Emilia stared at Franco. She did not want to believe him. Could it be true that her father had handed over her precious family heirloom? Had her *nonna's* text served as an addition to the dowry Francesco offered Franco? If so, it was a betrayal that cut to the bone.

Her eyes welling with tears, Emilia said, "The book was not my father's to give, Franco. It belonged to my mother. She gave the book to me."

Donna Margherita, looking up casually from the bunch of grapes she was daintily plucking, said, "Cosimo, perhaps it is for you to decide the rightful owner of the text: a young artist of apparent talent and virtue, or one of your city's most successful merchants. A merchant, I might add, who was once exiled from Florence after making a small fortune selling forgeries of antique statues at exorbitant prices."

The room fell into another stunned silence. All eyes turned to Franco, who said nothing.

"What are you implying, Donna Margherita?" Cosimo asked.

"Franco Villani is a known thief," she said, looking over to the culprit. "I'm sorry, Franco, but it is well known. My dear father, I'm afraid, is one of the unfortunate owners of your fake cupids."

Emilia watched, open-mouthed, as her former fiancé received this very public blow. She would never have believed that Margherita, after the lavish banquet Franco had given her, would speak ill of him.

"How could you, Margherita?" Franco demanded, as though greatly wronged.

"It is one thing to swindle stupid rich men, Franco. It is quite another to rob an innocent young woman of something that is clearly irreplaceable. You and the girl's father should be ashamed of yourselves."

Cosimo, appraising Franco, asserted, "I imagine you would be loath to keep a book that you have acquired in this unfortunate manner, Signor Villani."

"Everything else has been taken from me," Franco said hoarsely, looking directly at Emilia with accusing eyes. "What does the book matter? I must say I deeply regret that it ever fell into my hands."

In disgrace Franco Villani slunk out of the room and the genteel, cultured society that forever eluded him. Emilia pitied him, but then she had known for a long while he was a sad snake. It was her father's misdeed that shook her to the core.

Donna
Margherita

Speechless, Emilia watched Franco Villani, the vainglorious spice merchant, leave Cosimo de' Medici's table, fallen from grace. It gave her no particular pleasure to see Franco suffer this ignominy, yet she could not help but feel that justice had been served. She was appalled by the part her father had played in the theft of the manual, but she had to put aside thoughts of retribution for his deed while she was still a guest at the palace.

Marsilio Ficino, sharing silently in her victory, smiled at her in complicity. Cosimo, appearing not the least perturbed by the strange turn of events in his loggia, thumbed slowly through the pages of *A Manual to the Science of Alchemy*. Studying the image of the god Thoth, it was as if he had already put the matter of Franco Villani behind him.

"You must tell me," Cosimo said, turning to Emilia, "how a book such as this came to be in your family."

"It happened long ago, during the time of the deadly pestilence. A Franciscan Friar by the name of Calandrino was said to be an adept of the Great Work," Emilia began. She tried to clear her head and forget about the wicked thing her father had done. All eyes rested on her, waiting for her to relate the story of the manual and how it came to be passed from Calandrino to Santina, her great-great-great-grandmother, for safekeeping. She continued and the small audience listened attentively. Emilia forgot her shyness, as well as her father and Franco. Soon she was spinning a colorful tale, embellishing what little she knew of Santina's journey to escape Pisa at the time of the plague.

"The journey to Spain was difficult, the roads very bad. She had to travel alone with her little boy, my great-great-grandfather, Pietro. She crossed the mountains and there was little to eat—she gathered wild plants along the way. Her husband was dead, we suppose, and Santina very nearly didn't make it either. She was so tired and weak, but she kept hold of the book, no matter what.

"When she finally arrived in Toledo, she settled there and made a home for her son. She was a midwife and quite skilled. People sought her out, my mother said, though some said she was a sorceress and that she knew the way to make gold," Emilia said, studying Cosimo's response. When he smiled and waited expectantly, she added, "The precious metal is not the greatest aim of alchemy."

"What *is* the greatest aim then, Emilia?" asked Marsilio, eager as always to begin a debate.

"The philosopher's stone. The stone is the key to the transformation of the soul, Messer," she replied with the ease of one who had given the subject careful thought.

"The subject of the codex," Cosimo nodded in assent. He paged thoughtfully through Emilia's manual, pausing at the image of Hermes Trismegistus holding up a tablet.

"*I entered a tomb and found a statue with a tablet,*" Cosimo recited before reading silently for a time. Then he raised the book so that his guests could see the image of Hermes and the tablet of the two birds flying away from each other.

"It was Hermes who authored the Emerald Tablet as well," Emilia said. "On that tablet, he recorded the process for the transformation."

"A recipe for transforming the soul," Cosimo mused.

"It is, essentially, the art of gnosis," Marsilio commented before saying to the benefit of everyone else at the table, "that which gives one the ability to see the face of God. It is the subject of a certain *Corpus Hermeticum*—the codex to which Cosimo referred. The writing is attributed to the man in the picture. A text only just discovered by Leonardo of Pistoia."

Ridolfi chimed in from the end of the table, "It is an odd coincidence, is it not, that the two books should be discovered at once?"

Cosimo shook his head. "It seems *A Manual to the Science of Alchemy* has been in Madonna Emilia's family for over one hundred years, Ridolfi. How it came to be discovered by Friar Calandrino remains a mystery. But yes, it is a curiosity that the two books should find their way to this house at the same time."

Marsilio replied quickly, "Of course the text must now be returned to Emilia, the rightful owner."

She felt grateful for this, but she did not hesitate to say, "Please, keep the book for a time. Perhaps it may prove useful as you complete the translation of the codex."

"A most gracious young woman," Cosimo observed. "One deserving kind favor."

Emilia smiled warmly at the elegant ruler of Florence, wondering where his favor might lead. She tasted the refreshing cold wine in her square crystal glass that was trimmed with gold, thinking that everything in her life was changing. Filled with a sense of possibilities, she wished her day with Cosimo de' Medici would never end. In a corner niche of the loggia, the palace quintet—a harpsichord, two violas, a lute, and a harp—entertained them with beautiful music for a time. All too soon, Donna Margherita and several others were standing to leave.

Before returning to her ordinary life, Emilia thought to say one more thing to her host. "I cannot take all the credit for the panel, *Eccellenza*. You should know that Giacomo Massarino—from the studio of Lorenzo Jacovelli—is responsible for the fineness of the geometry. Giacomo is the gifted hand who has stood behind Jacovelli for several years now. You will have seen much of his work throughout the city."

"You are gracious again, Madonna Emilia," he replied. "Few wish to share credit where credit is due. Be sure I have made note of the name."

"*Grazie mille,*" she said, feeling truly thankful for the generosity of the great Cosimo de' Medici.

With Cosimo's gift—a red silk sack weighty with gold florins—jingling in her purse, Emilia Serafini walked home in the sun from the Medici Palace. She was so grateful for the turn of events brought about by the efforts of Marsilio Ficino and the grace of God. She dared to hope that she might find fame as a painter after all, now that she had received the blessing of the city's great patriarch. But she could do nothing before she settled matters with her father.

Emilia was waiting for Francesco when he returned home from the saddle shop that evening and followed him into his study.

"Cosimo de' Medici paid me for my painting today, Father," she said, struggling to contain her anger as she poured the contents of the red silk sack onto Francesco's desk.

Francesco looked at the small pile of gold before him and listened as Emilia told a partially true story of how the lord of the city had acquired one of her panels. Clearly surprised, her father refrained from congratulating her on her success.

"So at last you have something to show for the trouble your painting has caused, Emilia. It will not make up for the losses you have cost this family. Nonetheless, it is a contribution."

"Franco Villani was invited to the palace today as well," Emilia said boldly.

"Franco Villani was there?"

"Yes, as it turns out, he is the one who had *Nonna's* book."

"Oh?" Francesco said, fingering the coins.

"He brought the book to the palace. It seems Cosimo shared an interest in the text as well," she said slowly. "Franco mentioned that you were the one who gave him the book, Father."

Emilia watched Francesco closely, holding her breath, awaiting his response. She was not sure if he would deny Franco's claim or else confess his misdeed. Part of her hoped that Franco was lying and that her father had never even touched the book. Francesco remained silent and did nothing to deny the accusation, and Emilia grew stronger in her conviction that Franco had been telling the truth.

Finally, Francesco pulled out the chair from behind his wide desk, sat down heavily, and sighed. "Emilia, there are many things you do not understand. It is not an easy thing to survive in this world. I am your father, it is my duty to provide for your future." His voice was weary. "The book was a mere trifling in comparison to what a man like Villani could have done for our family," he said. "You and your mother—you think it is easy to put bread on the table. You live in a world of childish dreams."

Emilia was incensed by this logic.

"What does that have to do with stealing from your own daughter?" she demanded. "How could you have done such a thing? It was *Nonna's* book. It was never yours to give!"

Francesco, resolute, would show no remorse. Fists planted firmly on his desk, he declared once more, "I am your father, Emilia. *Everything* in this house belongs to me! You forget your place."

Her father stared at her in fury but Emilia did not look away. She saw a man, tired and worn, one who had ceased to think beyond the daily struggles of life or to look outside the tiny world of Florence. *A Manual to the Science of Alchemy* and the art of transformation were meaningless to him. As far as he was concerned, nothing of value could be created within the realm of the spirit. To Francesco Serafini, the world of physical matter was the only world that existed. Emilia finally grasped the central fact that her father had not acted to rob her of something she cherished but to provide her with a future he deemed safe and secure.

As Francesco Serafini, secure in the truth of his pronouncements, sat before her, Emilia saw there was no point in trying to convince him of the value of the text; her father would never understand. Arguing would only antagonize him further and quite possibly cause him to drag out her penance at the tavern. At last, Emilia was learning to stop and look where her actions would lead.

Still simmering inside, Emilia lowered her head, murmuring, "Forgive me, Father. I was wrong to question you."

Francesco appeared somewhat appeased. "What am I to do with a daughter such as you, Emilia?"

Emilia had little choice but to continue working at her father's tavern, though she slipped out to the *bottega* every chance she could. Francesco tended to turn a blind eye to his daughter's frequent disappearances. Perhaps he had given up trying to control her behavior and was learning to accept her unconventional ways. Perhaps he felt guilty for taking *Nonna's* book. Or maybe Cosimo's payment had cast doubt on Francesco's belief that his daughter could never be a painter. Emilia was just grateful that she was not expected to marry Benozzo Balducci or Franco Villani and that she was able to steal precious time with Makarios.

Several weeks after her visit to the palace, Emilia arrived at the workshop to see that her master had finally completed his painting of St. John the Baptist in the desert. St. John was depicted as a graceful youth who had cheerfully exchanged his clothes for camel's skin. It was an exquisite work, Emilia thought, though the commission had not been easy for Makarios. His back and legs were causing him more pain lately, preventing him from working more than a few hours at a time. Emilia regretted that she had not been able to provide her master with more assistance. Now that Francesco was easing up on her a bit, she hoped to do better for Makarios.

A light breeze swept through the open door and windows of the workshop as Emilia began to mix the varnish of heated resin and linseed oil for Makarios' panel. In the distance were occasional sounds of commerce, voices of children, and the footsteps of the weavers overhead, but Emilia and Makarios worked in the silent rhythm they had developed over time. The stillness was broken by rapping at the front door. Emilia looked up to see the proud, elegant figure of Donna Margherita stepping across the threshold.

"Donna Margherita!" Emilia exclaimed in surprise. "What brings you to our quarter?"

"I have business with both of you," she proclaimed, her pale green satin dress swishing across the floor as she walked. Approaching Makarios' desk she said, "We met in Fiesole, at the home of Franco Villani."

"So beautiful a lady I could never forget," said Makarios in his usual, congenial tone. "How may I help you today?"

"I admire your work, Makarios. I want you to paint something for me."

"What do you have in mind?"

"Judith slaying Holofernes," she replied with alacrity.

A smile escaped Makarios before he calmly replied, "A violent scene, is it not? The slaying of the general in his drunken sleep."

"A satisfying subject matter for an artist, I should think," she said, a mischievous gleam in her eye as she looked to Emilia. "It was Judith's brave act that prevented defeat by the attacking army."

"Please, sit down," Makarios said, offering Margherita his own chair. He pulled up a stool for himself and motioned Emilia to come join them. "You must speak to Emilia as well," he said to Margherita. "I am getting old and she will help me with the work."

"How your studio executes the painting is your concern," she said. "So long as the painting is remarkable. And the head of Holofernes bears the likeness of Franco Villani."

Makarios and Emilia exchanged glances. It was Emilia who spoke first.

"I confess I am as surprised by your request as I was surprised by the kind alliance you offered me at the palace, Donna Margherita. I had been given to think you and Signor Villani were on amicable terms."

The refined woman scoffed at the notion. "Who could be on

amicable terms with such a man? Did you not know he disposed of me after you arrived at his banquet looking impossibly lovely? He practically ignored me the entire day. I was furious with the both of you, of course. I have since come to appreciate my great fortune in avoiding the fate of marriage to that swine."

Recalling the comments Margherita made at the palace regarding Franco's forged sculptures, Emilia wondered why the lady would have considered marriage to him in the first place. "You knew from the beginning that his dealings were dishonest," she said. "Why did you ever wish to marry him?"

"When a woman comes to a certain age, Emilia, she begins to expect less of her life," Magherita said. "Compromises are made. But as I sat at Cosimo's table, I finally saw how far Franco had fallen. He was reduced to nothing before the greatest man in Florence. I saw that he would have destroyed my honor had you not arrived to save me from such a fate."

Emilia considered Margherita a fine and beautiful woman, one worthy of great respect, though she did not relish the idea of painting Franco's likeness. "I will be happy to help you," she said with sincerity. "Without a model, it will be difficult to capture the subject's likeness. Are you sure you don't wish to put your memory of the man behind you?"

"It is not that I wish to nurse a grudge against Franco Villani forever," Margherita explained. "It's that the painting will remind me never to forget to live with dignity before God."

Emilia and Makarios both nodded in understanding. When the lady sashayed towards the front door, her head held high, Emilia could not help but think that Margherita must surely count among Franco's significant losses.

Emilia was not the only one to receive a new commission. It was early September when Giacomo Massarino, limping slightly, returned to the studio of Lorenzo Jacovelli. That was when he received a letter from none other than Cosimo de' Medici himself. Emilia discovered the news when Giacomo tracked her down at the steps of Santa Croce after Sunday Mass.

"Apparently, he took note of the frescoes at the Convent of the Carmine. I suspect you mentioned my name to him as well. My pride should suffer for this, but I'm too happy to care, Emilia," he said.

"The pay will allow me to leave Jacovelli and start my own studio. It's what I've wished for, but it seems strange now that it's happened so suddenly." Giacomo sounded somewhat unsure of his own success.

"Suddenly?" she replied. "You've been working for Jacovelli since you were a boy. People are not blind, Giacomo. They know you have been standing behind the name for some time."

"Cosimo has requested some frescoes for the palace—a guest-room to start."

"*Stupendo*! Marvelous," Emilia exclaimed, glad that Giacomo chose not to be resentful of her. He had no reason to be, for Cosimo would never bother to commission an artist he did not truly admire. "You must believe me when I say that Cosimo's interest in you has almost nothing to do with me. I put in very little word on your behalf. I only mentioned your name in regards to the execution of the geometry, Giacomo."

"I believe you, *cara*." Giacomo stroked her cheek gently. "However it happened, I am grateful. If Cosimo is pleased, there is the promise of plenty of work. I'll be able to afford my own workshop when I am done, I should think."

"It's what you always wanted."

Emilia looked at Giacomo, wanting him to say something more. She was happy for him but could not help wondering how she fit into the plans he was making for the future.

"I will need to find a suitable space," Giacomo said, thinking aloud. He laughed, adding, "I suppose I'm rushing ahead."

"Not at all," she said, thinking that he might need an extra pair of hands in this new *bottega*. After all, she knew one or two things about the art of fresco.

Emilia might have said more, but right then, her mother and father joined her.

"It's so good to see you up and about, Giacomo," Violante said.

"Cosimo de' Medici has just commissioned Giacomo for the palace," Emilia blurted, unable to keep the good news to herself.

"*Magnifico,*" Violante said at once.

Even Francesco looked mildly impressed. "What will Jacovelli have to say about that?"

"I would like to think he will wish me well, Messer. I have been with him so long and I am grateful for all he has taught me, but a man must start off on his own at some point."

Violante spoke up again before Francesco could reply. "Come to dinner, Giacomo. You must tell us all about your plans for the Medici."

Giacomo accepted the invitation readily enough. He walked with her father and brother towards Via Ghibellina while Emilia and her mother strolled behind, arm in arm. How Emilia wished he would speak about more than just his plans for the Medici, but she knew well enough that Giacomo would not rush to promise her anything.

Botticelli

fter Giacomo began working on his fresco for the palace guestroom, Emilia thought he had all but forgotten her. The painter had time for nothing but Cosimo de' Medici's Annunciation. He had envisioned Mary's chamber with a loggia outside an arched door. She regretted that she was not the one assisting Giacomo with this important commission but counted herself lucky enough to be spending several hours each day with Makarios. As long as she swept the tavern floor, cleaned the tables, and delivered Violante's freshly baked meat pies and *tortas* every morning, Francesco complained little of her extended midday absences. At Makarios' workshop, the Judith and Holofernes was coming along nicely, although Emilia avoided looking directly into the face of Holofernes, which vaguely resembled Franco Villani.

The days grew shorter and bright red berries, rose hips, and burnt-orange leaves appeared, and Emilia wondered how two years with Makarios had passed so quickly. She wished that autumn could last forever, but her time at the *bottega* felt fleeting, like a flaming sunset descending into the hills. The large panel for Donna Margherita would be completed soon and after that, she had no idea what they would paint next. She tried to emulate Makarios, to breathe with the ebb and flow moving through their quiet space in the southern quarter of the city.

When Emilia returned home from her duties at the tavern and another quarter *giornata* of work at the *bottega*, she was surprised to learn from Violante that Giacomo had come looking for her. He was still waiting for her, in fact, in the back courtyard. Emilia found him sitting alone on the bench beneath the lemon tree, deep in thought.

"What brings you here, Giacomo?" she asked, sitting beside him. Realizing he would normally still be working at this hour, she hoped he did not come with bad news.

"Cosimo's guestroom is finished," he announced. His expression gave away nothing, although the nervous, repetitive tapping of his foot made Emilia wonder if something had gone wrong.

"Was he pleased?"

Looking down at his hands, Giacomo answered, "He has paid me generously, Emilia. And now the dining hall is to be done in fresco."

"You will be busy," Emilia said, thinking she would not see much of him for the rest of autumn and into winter. He was venturing out on his own, making a name for himself as he had always wanted to do.

"There is ample work. I will need another pair of hands," he said, shifting uncomfortably on the bench.

Emilia studied him carefully, wondering where this was leading.

"I was wondering…" he began. "I was wondering if I might persuade you to work with me, Emilia."

"You mean you want me to help you with the fresco?"

"Cosimo was convinced of your skill before mine. It seems, well, natural that you and I might join our talents. I understand you are committed to Makarios. It's just that the opportunity has arisen."

"I'm flattered, Giacomo. I would like nothing better," she said, pleased to be asked but puzzled by his apparent uneasiness. She wondered if he might be asking for her assistance because he felt obligated to her. "Are you quite sure you want my help?"

He looked at her as though annoyed by the question. "Why wouldn't I?"

"I only thought you might feel obliged to me for having mentioned your name at the palace. That's not at all the case, of course. You owe me nothing."

Her response did not appear to put Giacomo at ease. He stood, plucking a leaf from the lemon tree. "I did not ask for your help because I felt indebted to you, Emilia. I was of the opinion that we work rather well together," he said. "Perhaps you feel differently."

"No, not at all. I would love to help you," she replied quickly. She only wished it could be simple for her to say, *Yes*, but the freedom to paint had never come without a fight for her. "In a few more days Makarios and I will be finished with Donna Margherita's Judith and Holofernes, but I still have responsibilities at the tavern. I can only paint a few hours at a time; my father has not forgiven me for another failed betrothal. He thinks he will never be rid of me now."

"I have anticipated that small complication," he said.

"Then you must see it's no use," she said, deflated.

"I have spoken with your father, Emilia. I asked him if he might spare you from the tavern because Cosimo de' Medici requested your gifted feminine hand once again."

"You didn't!" Emilia said, surprised by his boldness. "What did he say?"

"He asked what the pay would be," Giacomo replied, his demeanor still serious. "And he agreed."

Her wildest dream, to be painting at the palace with Giacomo, was held before her like a miracle. She wanted to throw her arms around him and kiss him but he seemed preoccupied, almost distant. Unsure of what might be troubling him, she said simply, "Then I will be most happy to paint with you, Giacomo."

"I came to ask for more than that."

"Oh?" Did he want her to run his errands, purchase the pigments at the apothecary, or pack their lunches so they could work through the day?

"I came to ask if you would paint with me. And also to speak of the future. I cannot give you the life you might have hoped for, Emilia. But I am sure that I can give you a decent home—if you would be my wife," he said, getting down on one knee. "Would it please you to marry me, Emilia?"

The birds in the trees replied in song while Emilia stared at Giacomo in silence. She had held hope that he might ask her eventually, but she thought the day Giacomo would settle down was far off in the distance. She thought also of her father, who had done his best to marry her off twice already. Francesco, she feared, thought of her as an embarrassment and would be little inclined to consider a third betrothal at this point.

At last she said, "Have you spoken with my father?"

"His only comment was that he was not sure you could ever be persuaded to marry. I confess I am not entirely sure either." Relieved of the burden of proposing, a smile finally lightened Giacomo's nervous face.

Emilia saw everything good and honest within him.

"Yes, of course," she said, and she leaned forward, meeting his lips and the future of her life with the painter. His arms encircled her, his warm skin touching hers, igniting the promise of their life yet to be. Softly he kissed her neck, then again her parted lips. He held her head gently in his hands, stroked her hair.

"*Ti amo,* I love you."

There beneath the lemon tree, Emilia kissed Giacomo and ran her hands along his shoulders, muscles made firm by a painter's work. She would spend years and years exploring the wonders of him. *Ti amo, Giacomo, you were always the one.*

She was learning to precipitate gold after all and, as it was written in the manual, God was smiling upon her endeavors. The pain of the previous year faded away into the brightness of the future—she could not quite believe her good fortune.

A notary came to Emilia's house for the *matrimonium*, ring day, in May of 1462. The extended families of the bride and groom were present as the official asked the appropriate questions and read the marriage contract. As the particulars of the dowry, including Emilia's extensive trousseau, were reviewed, the men nodded solemnly while the women looked at each other knowingly and the younger children squirmed impatiently in their best clothes, waiting for dinner.

The following Sunday, after the banns were read once again to ensure there was no legal impediment to the marriage, Father Bartolo presided over the ritual on the steps of Santa Croce before a large crowd of family members and ever-growing number of well-wishing Florentines standing in the piazza. When Emilia recited her vows, Giacomo gazed at her in adoration. Beneath her crown of flowers and rosemary, she looked back at him lovingly. Afterwards, the couple moved inside the church along with the wedding guests to attend the nuptial Mass.

The *nozze,* the banquet, was held at the tavern. Violante had transformed it with lavish bouquets of lilies and irises, garlands of greenery, and a carpet of red rose petals on the floor. Emilia's gown was of pale yellow brocade, embroidered at the bodice, slashed sleeves and a hem with copper thread in a pattern of intertwining vines and birds. Around her neck she wore a gift from Violante—an ascending phoenix, the liberated soul. The necklace was an heirloom, given to Violante on her wedding day by *Nonna* Elena, Santina's granddaughter. *Today you marry, Emilia, but you must remember that the alchemist walks her own path to God,* Violante had said.

Seated beside her bridegroom at the table, Emilia fingered the pendant, thinking of the remarkable women who had worn it before her. Grateful for the accomplishments of her grandmothers, she tasted the roasted peacock that had been brought to the table with its tail feathers in full display. Francesco's best wines accompanied the succulent meats, delicate fish dishes, pasta, assorted cakes and *marzapan.* Her father, no doubt relieved that a wedding was finally taking place, had allowed Violante and Emilia every extravagance.

Addressing those gathered, Francesco spoke freely of his daughter's talent (noting that he had encouraged her since she was a child), of her work that now hung in a place of great prominence in the palace, and the couple's favored position among the Medici. Listening to Francesco, seated there among her family and friends, it seemed to Emilia that it was a scene conjured by magic. Emilia knew her dream had in fact been wrought of her own efforts, abetted by the grace of God. As a quartet played lively songs, visions of the years stretching out before her took hold in her imagination—long days of painting beside Giacomo, raising a family, sharing meals and holy days with loved ones.

Her brief reverie was interrupted when Makarios, who was seated between Bettina and Tedaldo, stood to speak from his end of the U-shaped table.

"I must say, Francesco, that I feel I am losing a daughter today, too," he said in his slow, rich, accented voice. "She came to work with me only a few years ago, but during these years I have watched Emilia become a fine painter as well as a young woman of virtue.

"Since the first day I met her at the Carmine, where she was sketching away with the fury of a hailstorm, I knew she would be a painter. Thanks to God, she has found a husband—also possessed of abundant talent and virtue—who has the good sense to celebrate these gifts." Raising his glass to the couple, he said, "Bless you both on this day."

Listening to the words of her mentor, Emilia felt tears come to her eyes. Makarios Levantes had given her the opportunity that almost everyone else told her was impossible, nonexistent, and for this she owed him everything.

Before the dancing began, Emilia embraced Makarios.

"You believed in me when no one else in Florence would give me a chance. Without you, I would be nothing," she said, holding his hand.

"You were the one who did it, Emilia. When there were difficulties, you did not give up, you persevered. God rewards hard work. Dreams that come from the deepest place of the soul are always possible. You know this now. It is your *nonna*'s alchemy, is it not?"

"What do you know of alchemy, Makarios?" she asked, amused by his allusion to her book.

"The practice of alchemy is nothing new, after all. It is not so different from the way you made your Michael. The iconographer takes wood and pigments and uses them to make a bridge—a bridge between the picture and the saint. The alchemist works with metals and tries to touch heaven. They are both paths to God," Makarios explained. "We all seek to find him."

Emilia and Makarios stood suspended in this moment of quiet understanding, then Marsilio Ficino, dressed in blue hose and a tasteful velvet tunic, approached the two of them.

"The painter and his protégé," he said grandly. "It is a fine thing to celebrate a joyous occasion among such rich talent. I only wonder how you will manage the workshop, Makarios, now that Giacomo has taken Emilia from you."

"You need not concern yourself about Makarios—I could never leave him," Emilia told Marsilio before Makarios could reply. "Giacomo has found a studio for the three of us—it's on the Street of the Painters."

"You would leave the quiet of Santo Spirito for this?" Marsilio asked Makarios.

The old man smiled. "One thing I have learned, Marsilio, is to hold fast to nothing. Even at the age of seventy-six, I must be willing to follow where God would lead me. I consider myself fortunate to work with two remarkable young talents. At some point, if the teacher has done his job, the student exceeds the master."

"Or perhaps the approaches simply come to differ, as with Plato and Aristotle," Marsilio said, seizing upon this comment. He began a discourse of his revered philosopher at which point, Giacomo invited Emilia to dance.

"It was good of Ficino to come," Giacomo said to Emilia as they joined the dancers moving in a sequence of graceful steps.

"He has been very kind to me. I owe him a great debt."

"If he was any other man, perhaps. Being Ficino, I suppose his great reward was reading that book of yours."

"Perhaps you are right, Giacomo. It is a wonder about *Nonna's* manual. It contains many passages that are also in the codex he is translating for Cosimo."

Giacomo raised his palm to hers and walked around her in circle. "So now that we are married, will you share the text with me as well?"

It had not occurred to her that Giacomo would care to read *A Manual to the Science of Alchemy*. When her mother gave her the text for safekeeping, Emilia was told that it was for her eyes only and then for her daughter or son after that. It was the way it had always been in her family. Now that the book had been seen by Marsilio Ficino, Cosimo de' Medici, and to a brief extent his guests, it was not the great secret it once had been. Besides, she trusted Giacomo completely.

"There are not now nor will there ever be any secrets between us, Giacomo," she whispered in his ear. "Whatever is mine is yours as well."

"You are my virtuous wife and for this I am grateful. But I think one alchemist among us will suffice. Keep your alchemical manual for yourself, Emilia."

She accepted this, feeling no particular desire for Giacomo to take on the mystical pages of the text. Emilia dared to believe that husband and wife, joined in love, were not required to share identical thoughts. Giacomo was prepared to allow her uncommon freedoms for a wife and for this she counted herself most fortunate. In turn, she vowed that she would respect the decisions Giacomo made for himself.

The feasting continued on until the dancing spilled out into the street, where enthusiastic strangers joined the festivities. Near the end, a little child was thrust into Emilia's arms and a gold florin tucked into her shoe—ceremonial acts to ensure fertility and riches. After darkness had fallen, Emilia was escorted in a triumphal procession by torchlight through the streets of Florence to her new home with Giacomo.

Emilia, Giacomo, and Makarios settled into a comfortable routine in their snug, light-filled studio on the Street of the Painters. Emilia, aided by the invisible hand of Cosimo, was permitted to sign the Doctors and Apothecaries Guild agreement. This granted her the full benefits and privileges afforded to all Florentine artists. Makarios, who never did concern himself with matters like contracts and the way things were supposed to be done, offered his sagacious guidance to the two young artists when asked. He continued to receive a slow but steady stream of commissions on his own. When the pain in his joints made it difficult for him to work extended hours, he was content to retire to his small room in the back of the workshop or allow Bettina to comfort him with her gifts of soups, pies, and *tortas*.

During her first year of marriage, Emilia could afford just one servant to help her in the home they rented—the third story of a stone building with rust-colored shutters and a quiet courtyard with a flourishing apple tree. With the help of her mother's cook, Maddalena, she was able to locate Filippa, the maid Franco had so wrongly dismissed. The young girl required little convincing to come to work for Emilia, only too pleased to leave the employ of a wretched woman who worked her mercilessly for low wages.

Filippa grew less timid as the months went by and even began to confide in her new mistress. Working beside Emilia in the kitchen one day, Filippa finally admitted that it was Tomasso who had asked her to search Emilia's belongings for the manual.

"Tomasso said he only wanted to have a look at it. He was going to have me put it back again," she said. "I am sorry, Madonna. I had to do as Tomasso said."

Maybe it was true that Franco had only sought to satisfy his curiosity, Emilia thought. Perhaps he wanted Tomasso to help him ascertain if the book was worth the trouble of stealing. Or maybe he wanted to know if the book was worth the cost of marrying Emilia. Regardless, Franco Villani was a part of the past and she did not bother herself with thoughts of the man.

Commissions came in slowly but steadily to their *bottega* on the Street of the Painters. Near the end of their first year together, the couple received a commission to fresco the cloisters at Santa Maria Novella and also to make an altarpiece for the Church of Santissima Annunziata.

It then became apparent that an apprentice was needed. To fill the position Giacomo's young sister, Felice, was hired, much to her father's dismay. An apt learner, she was eager to run errands, grind pigments, and keep the studio neat and tidy. The four of them managed to keep apace of the work until the following spring, when Emilia was nearly due to deliver her first child. It was at this time that a commission for a large fresco for the *Mercanzia*, the cloth merchants' confraternity, was acquired and Giacomo became overwhelmed by the prospect of so much work before him.

Emilia shook her head as her husband complained of the mounting commitments. For years she had listened to him lament his lowly position at Jacovelli's. He had often been heard to say that the old man took on more than he should yet never hired any new apprentices or increased his overworked apprentices' pay.

Giacomo could little see his resemblance to his old master, which amused Emilia, nonetheless she wished to ease her husband's burden. It so happened that when she and Giacomo were working at the Carmine, she had befriended Alessandro di Mariano Filipepi, a young man known to his friends as Sandro Botticelli, *the little barrel,* for the roundness of his chest.

It occurred to Emilia that young Sandro, who had been in the employ of Fra Filippo Lippi, might be persuaded to assist Giacomo, whose reputation in Florence was steadily growing. When Emilia presented the idea to Giacomo, he complained bitterly of the cost, but she railed against him.

"You know I will be indisposed for some time, Giacomo. I have a strong feeling about Sandro. He is devout, he is at Mass every day. And he has learned a great deal from Fra Filippo—he will be useful to you. I'm quite sure you won't regret it."

Giacomo consented to this assistance only reluctantly, but he immediately found Sandro likeable enough. The fresco, as agreed upon by the merchants, was to be of St. George slaying the dragon. The scene conceived by Giacomo would depict the brave knight leaning dangerously from his beautifully stylized horse the very instant before the lance pierced the heart of the mythological creature. The entire scene was to be set before the undulating Tuscan countryside, with the skyline of Florence in the background.

As it turned out, Sandro was particularly gifted when it came to drawing heads, and he was able to convey a sense of great determination and valor in the face of St. George. Sandro brought an expressive quality to the figures that Giacomo could not have achieved on his own, her husband confessed to Emilia. The work for the *Mercanzia* proceeded without difficulty throughout the autumn, during which time Sandro often spoke to Giacomo of his interest in mythological subjects.

"He is captivated by the ancients," Giacomo told Emilia. "I told him he should see the fresco you did for Villani."

"Yes, I imagine Marsilio would be glad to show it to him,"

she replied, still amused by the fact that Ficino had been the one to purchase the estate after Franco quietly removed himself once again to Genoa.

Years later, Emilia and Giacomo were invited to the Medici villa of Castello, to view the mature Sandro's *Birth of Venus*.

Otherworldly as the image was, it could not help but remind Emilia of the summer of her folly with Franco Villani. It was hard for her to believe she had once thought to marry the man. Silently, she thanked God for protecting her from her mistakes, imagining she had been protected in countless ways since.

As much as Emilia had studied the art of alchemy, the creations of her life were not yet perfect. She sometimes lacked patience with her four small children and with Giacomo, and she had to admit that she sometimes lacked discipline with her painting and prayer. Too many of her moments were spent in idle chatter, and she surely concerned herself too much about what she should wear or what her family should eat. She had not given up the material things of this world.

The whitening, the purification, went on and on. With each passing year, Emilia hoped to gain another tree-ring of wisdom. She still read her manual from time to time to remind herself that her work was not yet complete.

Be certain, therefore, that the purest whitening is obtained. Be patient and steadfast in your endeavors, knowing the saints and angels applaud your earnest efforts. When days and years pass and still the gold eludes you, remember this and know reward will come to those who persevere in the Great Work.

Alchemy was, like her art, a process of continual refinement. The perfection that was sought often slipped through her hands, though at times it seemed close enough to touch. Perhaps on rare occasions and certain God-given moments, her soul soared high above the deep blue sky of Tuscany and merged with the light of the heavens.

To Emilia, a beautiful painting was an expression of the soul's aching wish for the alchemist's *coniunctio,* the merging of the body and spirit. Looking again at Botticelli's *Birth of Venus,* she saw the Virgin Mary, immaculate, lovely, virtuous, filled with light and love. She was stunned by the scene before her and could not help but admire the subtle fusion of Christian and pagan themes.

Turning to Giacomo, she said, "I must confess it surpasses the fresco Makarios and I did at Primavera."

"We all stand on the shoulders of those who came before us," Giacomo replied. "Where would any painter be without Masaccio?"

Emilia nodded at the veracity of his statement. She could have accomplished nothing in her life without the painters and alchemists who had practiced long before her birth.

Glossary

ost of the Italian words used in this book are translated when they first appear in the text. Some of the words are particular to the period and have no modern usage.

Time of day is indicated by canonical hours, the time when prescribed prayers were recited by religious orders. These times changed depending on the season and the time of sunrise and sunset. *Sext* was noon or the hour of the midday meal. *Nones* was around three in the afternoon. *Vespers* was the time of evening prayer.

In the fifteenth century, Florence was organized into four quarters, or *sestiere*. These were named for whatever major church was located in that quarter. The north or central part of the city—where the Cathedral of Santa Maria del Fiore (the Duomo) and the Baptistry with the famous bronze doors are located—was called San Giovanni. The eastern part, where Emilia lived, was Santa Croce. The western part, Giacomo's *sestiere*, was Santa Maria Novella. The southern part, the location of the *bottega*, the workshop where Emilia was apprenticed to master painter Makarios, was named Santo Spirito.

A list of Italian words used in the book include:

A domaini – Until tomorrow

Amico – Friend

Amore – Love

Arrivederci – Goodbye

Aspetto – Wait

Ave Maria, piena di grazia – Hail Mary, full of grace

Bargello – *Captain of Police*

Biscotti – Cookies

Bottega – An artist's workshop

Buon giorno – Good day

Buona sera – Good evening

Calma – Be calm

Cara (fem.) & *Caro* (masc.) – Terms of endearment

Cassone – A large chest, often used to store a bride's belongings

Come va? – How goes it?

Contadini – Peasant farmers

Dio mi salvi – God help me

Dio mio – My God

Donna – An honorific title for noble ladies

Duca – Duke

Eccellenza – Excellency

Fantastico – Fantastic

Grazie – Thank you

Grazie a Dio – Thank God

Grazie mille – Thanks a million

Gonfaloniere – Governor

Idiota – Idiot, fool

Lungarno – A path beside the River Arno

Madre – Mother

Madre de Dio – Mother of God

Madre mia – Mother mine

Madonna – How a married or unmarried woman was addressed

Maestro – Master

Magnifico – Magnificent, magnificent one

Marzapan – Marzipan, a candy made with almond paste

Mercatante – A great merchant

Messer – Mister or Sir

Monna – A familiar address to a woman

Nones – Around three in the afternoon

Non c' e mal – Not bad

Nonna – Grandmother

Nozze – Wedding banquet

Nuccato – Candied nuts

Padre – Father

Palazzo – A mansion

Palma – A measure of length, about the length of an adult palm with
    fingers spread wide

Pazienza – Have patience

Piazza – A public square

Pittoresso – Paintress

Podestà – Mayor or chief magistrate

Primavera – Springtime

Riposa – An afternoon nap

Sala – A room

Salame – Sausage

Sarta – Dressmaker

Scusa – Sorry

Sestiere – City area, or quarter

Sext – Noon

Signore – Mister or Sir

Signoria – Governing authority

Spiacente – Sorry

Straniero – Foreigner

Stupendo – Marvellous

Stupido – Fool, idiot

Ti amo – I love you

Torta – Cake

Vespers – The time of evening prayer

Bibliography

As I wrote this book—and learned about Renaissance and Medieval history, Italian art, and alchemy—I drew from numerous sources. For those who wish to read more on these subjects, I offer the following brief bibliography, which includes fiction as well as nonfiction:

Goddard, David. *The Tower of Alchemy: An Advanced Guide to the Great Work.* New York: Weiser Books, 1999.

Hartt, Frederick. *History of Italian Renaissance Art: Painting, Sculpture, Architecture.* 2nd ed. New York: H.N. Abrams, 1979.

Helmond, Johannes. *Alchemy Unveiled.* Salt Lake City: Merker Publishing, 1997.

Jung, CG. *Psychology and Alchemy.* Trans. R.F.C Hull. 2nd ed. Princeton: Princeton/Bollingen, 1968.

Manchester, William. *A World Lit Only By Fire: The Medieval Mind and the Renaissance Portrait of an Age*. New York: Little Brown and Company, 1993.

Martin, Linette. *Sacred Doorways: A Beginner's Guide to Icons*. Brewster: Paraclete Press, 2002.

Stone, Irving. *The Agony and the Ecstasy: A Biographical Novel of Michelangelo*. New York: Signet, 1987

Tuchman, Barbara W. *A Distant Mirror: The Calamitous 14th Century*. New York: Ballantine Books, 1987.

Von Franz, Marie-Louise. *Alchemy: An Introduction to the Symbolism and the Psychology*. Toronto: Inner City Books, 1980.

Vreeland, Susan. *The Passion of Artemisia*. New York: Viking, 2002.

The Ways of Hermes: New Translations of The Corpus Hermeticum and The Definitions of Hermes Trismegistus to Asclepius. Trans. Clement Salaman, Dorine Van Oyen, William D. Wharton, Jean-Pierre Mahé. Rochester: Inner Traditions, 2000.

A GLIMPSE OF THE PREQUEL:

Alchemy's Daughter

MARY OSBORNE

Madonna
Adalieta

"God help me!" came Mama's muffled cry through the closed bedroom door.

Madonna Adalieta, Santina's mother, had gone into labor at daybreak and Trotula, the midwife who lived in a hilltop cottage outside the wall of the village, had just arrived with her basket of herbs and fragrant ointments. As she was ushered to Mama's room, Santina tried to follow her.

"You can't go in there," said Lauretta, her plump older sister, blocking the door.

"Why not?" twelve-year-old Santina Pietra wanted to know. The groans from the bedroom were frightening her, and she wanted to make sure Mama was all right.

Trotula, who carried herself like a great lady even though she was a woman of modest means, paused to look kindly at Santina.

She was the niece of old Ninetta, who had delivered babies in San Gimignano for as long as anyone could remember. "I'll take good care of your mama. I'll let you know how she's coming along."

The heavy bedroom door banged shut, separating Santina from Mama and the mystery of whatever Trotula would do to bring the new baby into the world. Santina slid to the floor and might have stayed there all day if Margherita, Mama's maid servant, had not led her away.

She sat at the kitchen table with Isabella, her little sister, and the two watched as the cook went to work making the day's bread. Santina listened to the voices and footsteps coming from Mama's room and watched Margherita, who was alternately wringing her hands, praying, and wandering back and forth from the kitchen to the bedroom.

"Your poor Mama. She's in terrible pain this time. I don't know how much longer she can go on like this."

"She's done it three times already, Margherita. She'll be fine with the fourth," said the cook, brushing the flour from her hands. She set some soft cheese and figs on the table, but Santina was not tempted.

Again she heard the cry, "*Dio me salvi*—God help me."

Santina rose from the table and darted toward the bedroom before Margherita could catch her. When she burst through the door, Trotula looked up at her but said nothing. There was Mama, drenched in sweat, her long, disheveled hair strewn across the pillow. Santina threw her thin, little arms around Mama's shoulders.

"Please be all right, Mama," she murmured before Margherita pried her away and the door closed behind her once again.

Tears streamed down Santina's cheeks, and she ran out the back door and away from Margherita, Lauretta, Isabella, and Papa—wherever he was. She wanted to find Calandrino, the kind friar who knew all about plants, remedies, and the science of alchemy. She would tell him about Mama's trouble. Maybe Papa's young friend had discovered the magic stone that could grant wishes and reverse their misfortune.

She ran until she reached the city square, the Piazza della Cisterna, and the slender, soaring, brick towers that were built by Tuscan nobility long ago. Continuing north toward the church of Saint Augustine, Santina passed beneath the Roman arch of the city gate. Beyond the walled Italian village, she traveled a dirt road into the hills of rolling Tuscan countryside and moved up along rocky terraces planted with vineyards and olive orchards.

When she came at last to a wide expanse of grassy meadow, the impressive tall bell tower of the friary, San Clemente, came into view. Santina did not approach the elaborate cast-iron gate because she had already spotted a slim, gray-robed figure. Surely it was Calandrino? She had discovered him foraging for wild plants before—for only cultivated plants were grown in the friary garden. Perhaps he was gathering the flowering crocus to make into a powder for use in a remedy or to flavor a dish in the friary kitchen. Though he was not yet twenty, he knew a great deal about herbs, and many other subjects as well.

"*Buon Giorno*, Santina!" the friar with the fringe of curly, dark hair called out as she raced across the field.

"Thank goodness you're here," she said, out of breath, when she finally reached him.

"What's the matter?" he asked, his lighthearted expression turning sober when he saw the look on Santina's face.

"Mama's having the baby, but I think something's terribly wrong. It wasn't like this when she had Isabella."

"Surely the midwife has been summoned?"

"Trotula can't seem to help her. But I thought—I thought you might be able to," Santina began, "if you let her have the magic stone."

"The magic stone?"

"You told Papa that if the alchemist has the stone, he can transform the metal. And he can change himself into whatever he wants."

"Ah, the philosopher's stone," the friar said, nodding. "You have been eavesdropping, Santina."

Too worried about Mama to feel embarrassed by his accusation, Santina merely shrugged. "I know about the experiments, Calandrino. I know Papa reads everything he can about making gold."

"The subject is endlessly fascinating," the friar mused. "The matter of Egypt—that's what alchemy means in Arabic."

"What does Egypt have to do with it?"

Santina almost forgot about Mama as Calandrino spoke of the ancient Egyptians. She walked beside him along the bank of the meandering stream as he told her the story of Osiris, a beloved pharaoh of Egypt, who was killed by his evil brother, chopped into fourteen parts and thrown into the Nile River. Beautiful Isis, his wife, came to search the water and collect the fragments of the corpse and then magically unite them.

Santina did not see what the Egyptian legend had to do with turning lead into gold, but the friar's story further convinced her that alchemy could help Madonna Adalieta.

"Those who died and went through the ritual of the resurrection could move freely between life and death. They could appear in any shape, any day," Calandrino said, still speaking of the Egyptians. "The dead could leave their coffins and walk out of the tombs of the pyramids in broad daylight. They could appear as crocodiles and swim in the Nile or turn into sacred birds like the ibis and fly through the sky."

As Calandrino spoke of what was written in the papyri of the Egyptian prayers for the dead, Santina imagined the ability to transform, to change shape, to be able to walk through closed doors, ghostlike. If what Calandrino said were true, then he held the keys to a magic kingdom where she could come and go from San Gimignano in the year 1331 at will. It was a world where Mama would always be safe.

"Do you have the stone then, Calandrino?" she asked, when he had finished. "Can you help my mother?"

Suddenly remembering her mother's plight, Calandrino looked downcast. "Not yet, Santina. I'm afraid I have not found it yet," he said. "But I will pray to the One who gives life to all things. You must also."

Then he picked up a red stone flecked with bits of gold and black. Handing the stone to Santina, he said, "There are many things in this world we might not understand, but the truth of God's love is pure and simple, just like this stone."

Santina clutched Calandrino's stone in her hand all the way back on her return to the city. She wanted to believe that because God loved her, Mama would be all right. She no longer felt so afraid when she prayed the way Calandrino had advised.

When Santina walked through the front door of her house, the first person she saw was Master Traverseri. He was dressed in his scarlet robe that was lavishly trimmed with fur. Her fear rose again when she heard the family physician speaking to Papa in hushed tones outside Mama's room. Margherita, who stood a little way down the hall in the shadows, was listening, wringing her hands.

"It's the baby's position, Jacopo," Master Traverseri was explaining. "The shoulder is caught."

"Can't you help her?" Papa asked, his voice desperate, running one hand nervously through his silver hair. "Why is it so difficult?"

"Trotula has been trying to turn the baby."

"She can't go on like this. Surely there must be something you can do."

"Trotula has her own ways, Jacopo. But I won't give her much more time."

Santina panicked, knowing something was terribly wrong with Mama and the baby. Barging in on Papa and Master Traverseri, she cried, "Why is Mama having so much trouble? Why doesn't anyone know what to do?"

"It's in God's hands," Papa told Santina. He stroked her head, trying to comfort her, but Santina could see the torment on his face.

The moans from the bedroom, more sad and quiet now, continued through the afternoon. Still there was no news. The time of vespers approached, heralded by the darkening sky, and once again Santina sat at the table. Unable to eat, she stared at her soup and bread.

"It will be over soon," Lauretta said, though Santina could hear the doubt in her voice.

"The soup doesn't taste good," eight-year-old Isabella complained, squirming in her seat.

"Just eat," said Lauretta, who never seemed to lose her appetite.

Her two sisters continued to chatter, perhaps so they would not hear Margherita's fervent Hail Marys, but Santina could do nothing but think about Mama and the exhaustion in the sounds from the bedroom.

"Enough sitting around," the cook finally told them as she cleared away the uneaten food. "Go on."

Santina followed behind her two sisters as they tiptoed as

quietly as they could to their room. Lauretta tried to smile as she took Isabella's hand, but Santina could tell that she was afraid now, too. Isabella crawled into bed quickly and curled beneath the soft wool blankets while Santina undressed, trying to hide her tears.

"Did Papa tell you anything?" Lauretta whispered to Santina.

"I heard him talking to Master Traverseri," she admitted. "The baby is trapped and can't get free."

Isabella poked her head out from beneath the covers. "Is the baby never coming out?"

Lauretta scooped up her little sister in her arms. "It's just taking a very long time."

Santina jumped into bed and huddled close with her sisters. The house was quiet, except for an occasional whimpering, like the sound of a trapped, wounded animal, coming through the thin walls.

"She's going to be all right," Lauretta said, trying to comfort the little one. "It is not an easy thing to have a baby. It was very hard when you were born as well, Isabella. It took nearly two days before you finally came."

"It wasn't like this," Santina said.

"You're too young to remember," Lauretta replied.

"It's the baby's shoulder. It's caught. That's what Master Traverseri said."

"Don't scare Isabella," Lauretta told Santina. "We should try to sleep now. In the morning we'll wake up and the baby will be here."

Lauretta put out the candles, but Santina did not feel like sleeping. The stillness of the night was pierced here and there by the sound of voices and footsteps. Outside, the branches of the apricot tree brushed against the shutters. Mama's bedroom door opened and closed. Then there was nothing; just a long, uninterrupted silence.

The silence stretched on and on and Santina sensed that something had happened. Had the baby brother or sister finally arrived? Yet she could not hear the cries of a newborn infant, or relieved, happy voices. Santina bolted upright in bed and felt the eerie stillness of the house. She did not want to know what she already sensed in her heart. She looked at the shadowy shapes of her sisters in the dim light and her eyes brimmed with tears. Still, she prayed that she was wrong. *Don't let her be dead. Don't let Mama be dead.*

She felt something—was it a soft breeze?—waft through the room. She turned to the window, but the shutters were closed to the cold night air. Then she saw a misty, silver film, almost like smoke, suspended at the foot of the bed.

"It's Mama," Santina whispered. "Mama's gone," she said to her sisters, who were barely awake and uncomprehending. "Do you see it?"

"See what, Santina?"

"It's not there any more," she said, for the spirit had already faded away. "It was Mama. I'm sure it was Mama."

"Did Mama have the baby?" Isabella asked sleepily.

Lauretta, then Isabella, jumped out of bed and ran toward Mama's room, but Santina knew what they would discover. Following slowly behind, Santina saw her two sisters standing before Papa, whose eyes revealed everything.

He stretched out his arms, encircling his three daughters. "Mama died," he said. "Your brother too. They're with our Father in heaven now."

Santina stood sobbing with Papa and her sisters until the priest walked out of Mama's room, followed by Master Traverseri. The doctor nodded solemnly as he departed, and eventually Trotula emerged.

"I am deeply sorry." Through her tears, the midwife looked at each of them in silent, sincere apology before proceeding soundlessly down the hall.

Papa seemed to take no notice of the doctor or Trotula. Wordlessly, he left his daughters and continued down the stairs. Santina followed him.

"Why did she die, Papa?" she called after him, though he did not answer. "Why?" She hurried across the ground floor hall, trying to catch up, but Lauretta chased after her and held her back.

"He needs to be alone now," Lauretta said, wiping her cheeks. "Come with me, Santina." Her older sister guided her back upstairs and the young girls started nervously at the noise when the back door banged shut.

When she reached her bedroom, Santina could hear Papa crying out in the night. She tore open the wooden shutters and looked out to the garden. Papa stood there, clearly visible in the pale light of the moon. Jacopo Pietra, who had always appeared as strong and immovable as the hills of their homeland, trembled and shook as though the ground beneath him was giving way.

"This cannot be! *Dio mio*! How can this be?" Papa wailed into the darkness. Then he was crying out for Mama. "Adalieta! Adalieta! Adalieta!" Santina watched and listened as Papa went on and on, cursing the loss of Mama and the baby.

Frozen at the window, Santina was unable to move, unable to call out to him. She was petrified at what she saw. It was as though Papa stood on the cliff from where Mama had fallen; Santina was afraid he might leap after her beloved Mama to his own death.

She thought again of Calandrino's alchemy. She recalled what he said about the alchemist's ability to transform, to change shape, to be able to walk through closed doors. She wondered if Mama could do this now and if she would be able to come and go from heaven. If what Calandrino said was true, then Mama might find a way to return to them. She might be right here, at this very moment, standing beside Papa, telling him she would be home soon.

Yet Santina could not see Mama. She longed for someone, anyone, to come hold her. It hurt so badly. It felt as if her heart was being ripped from her bleeding chest. Mama was dead, but this did not seem possible. Mama was dead. Who would take care of them?

Her mother was dead, and yet Santina could somehow feel her. Before drifting off to a fitful sleep, she told herself she had to find the philosopher's stone. She had to discover the Egyptian secret of coming and going between heaven and earth. She would ask Calandrino to help her. Somehow, she had to find her way to Mama.

About the Author

Mary Osborne, author of *Nonna's Book of Mysteries* and *Alchemy's Daughter*, is a writer, artist, and registered nurse living in Chicago. An honors graduate of Rush University and Knox College, where she was mentored in the Creative Writing Program, Osborne has degrees in chemistry and nursing.

Nonna was conceived during a springtime trip to Tuscany. Set during the days of Cosimo de' Medici the Elder's lordship, the story sprang from the cobbled streets of Florence and into the author's ear. Carrying her notes from Italy, Osborne attended the International Women's Writing Guild's Summer Conference at Skidmore College in New York. Here, her historical novel began to take shape. *Nonna's Book of Mysteries* and *Alchemy's Daughter* are part of a four-book series.

Learn more about alchemy and Osborne's books at www.MysticFiction.com.